HELL A FURY

D BYRON

ISBN: 979-8-9926110-0-7

Printed and bound by IngramSpark

For more about the author, upcoming books, and exclusive content, visit d-byron.com

Chapter 1

Maddie lifted her mimosa with practiced ease, the sunlight catching the crystal and setting the golden bubbles aglow. At Le Petit Jardin, the September breeze lifted the edge of her Hermès scarf, but her styled hair remained undisturbed.

"And then I told him, 'Not a chance. There's no place for that shade of marble in my guest bathroom,'" Charlotte declared with a flourish, her tennis bracelet catching the light.

"I mean, travertine is so passé."

"Nouveau riche," Barbara quipped with a smirk.

Maddie gave herself a small, composed smile, taking a sip as she surveyed the vast expanse of the restaurant.

Her command over this table—this view—had been cultivated through years of careful maneuvering. The maître d' acknowledged her with a subtle nod, a gesture of respect earned over two decades of patronage. They knew her preferences—the table, the mimosa chilled to an exact 41 degrees, and her demand for a comfortable distance from others.

"Speaking of renovations," Susan leaned in conspiratorially. "I heard Bethany Wilson is redoing her house yet again—for the third time in five years."

"Poor thing," Maddie said, setting her glass down with precision. "Thinking drapes can save a marriage?" Her comment, effortlessly delivered, drew appreciative laughter. "Some women never learn—true happiness isn't built on the latest trend in home decor."

Maddie barely needed to speak. The slight tilt of her glass, a well-timed glance—small cues dictated the flow of conversation. She observed them as a gardener might tend to roses, shaping their opinions with subtlety and precision.

Pastries appeared, freshly baked and impeccably flaky. Maddie selected a croissant, breaking it open with her manicured fingers to release tendrils of steam. All aspects—weather, company, and service—aligned with her crafted world, operating under her serene command.

She took another sip, savoring the champagne's coolness as a manifestation of her control. In her world, power lay not in overt displays, but in quiet assurance.

Everything adjusted to her preference, just as expected.

With a well-timed pause, she dabbed her lips with her linen napkin. Her mastery lay in making others anticipate her words. "Remember, a woman who frequently remodels must question what she cannot find within her walls—or within herself."

Charlotte's eyes widened with understanding. "Do you think—"

"I couldn't possibly comment," Maddie demurred, adjusting her Cartier watch—a gift from Jackson on their fifteenth anniversary. "Though, I did see Tom's car outside the country club just past midnight last Thursday."

Gasps and whispers erupted around the table. Allowing speculation to fester, Maddie redirected her gaze, noting the thinning lunch crowd. She paused, her focus catching on a solitary blonde checking her phone— a detail unaligned with her ordered world.

"Maddie, how do you think she should proceed?" Barbara's inquiry pulled her focus back.

"With dignity," Maddie asserted, straightening with an elegant poise. "There is no power greater than a woman who knows her worth."

The others silently absorbed her counsel, each committing it as gospel. Over time, under her guidance, they had come to understand the gravity of her silence, the weight of her approval, and the sting of her disapproval.

"Shall we have more mimosas?" The server's question interrupted with impeccable timing.

Maddie signaled her glass. "Jean-Marc, darling, these were superb. Perhaps Veuve Clicquot instead? The 2008 if available."

"Yes, Mrs. Callahan."

As their eyes regarded her with admiration—her casual expertise in selection, the staff's trained deference—her domain was affirmed. Her crafted persona was enduring, untouched even by Jackson's midlife turbulence.

Maddie's gaze flicked to Sandra's floral dress—a gaudy relic from last season's Nordstrom collection, hanging on her like a desperate memory. The polyester fabric didn't flatter Sandra, accentuating her recent weight gain since her divorce.

"That print is quite... bold, Sandra," Maddie complimented, her fingers brushing her own silk.

"Admire how you ignore fleeting trends."

Sandra's fork hesitated mid-air. "I... thank you?"

The uncomfortable silence was telling; Charlotte and Barbara exchanged glances, pretending distraction. Maddie savored the pause—necessary, she thought, as Sandra had become too familiar, too assertive. A gentle but clear reminder of social order.

"Truly refreshing," Maddie continued, her tone benevolent. "In a world where everyone competes to conform, you embrace what pleases you."

Sandra blushed, self-consciously adjusting her dress's hem. The others remained silent, unwilling to challenge Maddie's subtle dominion. Thus was her art, cruelty cloaked in civility, leaving doubt as its aftermath.

"I picked it up at—" Sandra began.

"More champagne?" Maddie lifted her hand again, preemptively inviting the server to forestall explanation. Always assure the lingering uncertainty.

Her attention shifted abruptly as a fly intruded—its small, black body an affront against the immaculate white tablecloth. Her breath paused; it buzzed about erratically, breaching her fortress of order.

The fly landed briefly on her glass, an unwelcome blemish on her curated universe—a reminder that chaos could infiltrate even the best-laid plans.

"No." The word escaped, soft yet carrying authority, silencing the table momentarily.

She flicked her wrist with precision, dismissing the insect. Yet, in her mind, its marks were irreversible. The water glass she once cherished now seemed sullied, tainted in irretrievable ways.

Her chest tightened, but her face betrayed nothing. She had long mastered the art of maintaining her composure in the face of intimidation.

Jean-Marc promptly returned, offering aid. "Mrs. Callahan, is everything alright?"

"Remove this." Her eyes remained locked on the offending glass. "Bring another. And please, address... the fly situation."

Jean-Marc nodded with urgency, recognizing the unspoken command.

The seconds stretched before his return, the marred glass mocking her. Its presence was a tangible reflection of her slipping control—a sensation unbecoming of her station.

As he approached with a pristine replacement. Yet the lemon slices, though three, were misaligned.

"Is there anything else?" His voice carried an edge of impatience, an imprudence.

It was the aggregation—the imperfect serving, his oversight, his tone—that embodied decline, a reminder intolerable to her sensibilities. She excused herself from the table.

The click of her Louboutins resonated as she glided toward Philippe's office. She entered unannounced; her visit was expected, if unscheduled.

"Mrs. Callahan." Philippe's greeting bridged trepidation with recognition.

"Philippe," she began softly, seated confidently. "Weekly, I've entrusted you with my presence here. Yet today, standards falter."

His complexion turned ashen in acknowledgment. "I wasn't aware—"

"You are aware now. Actions trump words, don't they, Philippe?"

She returned to the table to find the former server replaced, and a glass of water awaiting her—the symmetry restored, the wrongs righted. Conversation resumed around her as if uninterrupted.

She balanced the new glass and allowed herself a flawless sip, savoring its purity.

"Jackson's coming home soon," she announced, reclaiming full command of her audience.

Charlotte brightened. "From Dubai? I thought the project..."

"Finished ahead of schedule," Maddie replied, aligning the bracelet on her wrist, ensuring its familiarity. "You know Jackson—efficiency personified."

Her friends' attentions refocused on her, confirming her reestablished authority. They hungered for news of Jackson, craving the details of his protracted absence, the separate excursions, the avoided galas.

Barbara leaned in, inquisitive. "Three months, yes?"

"Four," Maddie responded, fingertips gracing her napkin before recollecting poise. "But who's counting?"

Her joke, effortlessly delivered, was a veil over a methodical tracking of his affairs.

Breaking a croissant with elegance, she considered, "A welcome dinner is in order. Intimate, of course."

She savored the ripple of interest such a prospect inspired, each woman subtly vying for inclusion. Maddie would take her time, allowing them to wonder, to aspire for inclusion within her selected circle.

Everything had to match her vision for Jackson's return. Every detail, every facet, would be orchestrated to perfection. No unwelcome intrusions would breach her architecture of order—no flies disrupt her serene world.

◆ ◆ ◆

Maddie guided the Bentley through Belle Meade, its pristine streets a stage upon which she never missed a performance. The luncheon had been a masterclass in social manipulation—she'd left her so-called friends quivering, their positions in the hierarchy reaffirmed. And yet, a tendril of disquiet twisted through her mind, marring her satisfaction.

She paused at the intersection, checking her reflection in the rearview. Not a hair out of place, not a smudge on her crimson lipstick. (Of course not. She was Maddie Callahan.) With a practiced flourish, she reapplied her signature Chanel powder, the ritual as much about steadying her nerves as maintaining appearances. Structure. Control. That was the only way to survive in this world.

The Cartier tennis bracelet Jackson had gifted her for their twentieth anniversary danced along her wrist, sunlight refracting off the diamonds. Every last detail was exquisite, just as she demanded. Just as it must be, now that her husband would soon return from his business trip.

That little matter with Jean-Marc had been handled. Her position as society matriarch remained unshaken.

And yet, a shard of unease sliced through her confidence.

Her fingers tightened around the buttery leather steering wheel until her knuckles blanched. A jogger cut across the street, avoiding her grille. How long had she been sitting there, paralyzed? She slammed the accelerator, the Bentley surging forward with a predatory growl.

"All is well. Everything is going according to plan," she said, adjusting the rear-view for the thousandth time.

Still, she white-knuckled the wheel as she turned onto the circular drive of the Callahan estate. Their mansion loomed before her, a monument to old Southern money and prestige. Light blazed from the upper windows, welcoming her home.

She killed the engine but stayed inside, fingers tracing the wheel. Silence had a way of inviting things in—things she'd rather keep locked out.

Shifting the mirror's angle ever so, she froze. There—a subtle crease near her temple, defying the thousands lavished on treatments and procedures. Just last week her dermatologist had proclaimed her more radiant than women half her age.

Yet the damning line mocked her efforts.

She prodded at the flaw, desperate to smooth it away. Useless. The crease only deepened, taunting her.

Impossible...

Schooling her features, she slipped back into her ed expression of serene sophistication. Of course, it disappeared. A mere trick of the harsh sunlight, surely.

"My beauty endures," she stated, voice as steady and assured as her gaze in the mirror.

The words hung in the air, commanding reality to obey. She examined her reflection from every angle, daring her eyes to defy her. Clearly, the poor lighting outside had created that illusion. Once inside, bathed in her designed illumination, the truth would be revealed.

Those bulbs never lied.

Sure enough, the flaw had vanished, obliterated by sheer force of will.

She was Maddie Callahan. Ageless. Perfection personified.

Retrieving her phone, she pulled up Rosa's contact, manicured nail hovering above the call button. The house would need to be prepared for Jackson's homecoming. Every detail pristine, as always.

"Rosa," she said when the housekeeper answered promptly. "Prepare for Jackson's arrival. I want absolute perfection in every room. Not a single thing out of place."

There was the faintest pause before Rosa's reply. "Certainly, Mrs. Callahan."

Maddie's grip tightened on the phone. A fraction of a second—too long. Rosa never hesitated. This was different.

"Something troubles you?" she asked, aiming for nonchalance.

"Nothing, Mrs. Callahan. I'll see to the preparations."

Again, that slight delay. As if Rosa were...holding something back.

Maddie's free hand clenched in the folds of her silk blouse. The staff understood their place. Rosa had never once stepped out of line before.

But there had been...indicators. Tiny transgressions. Hints of a shifting dynamic that Maddie couldn't quite put her finger on.

"Pay extra attention to polishing the silverware," she instructed, keeping her tone brisk and authoritative. "And refresh the floral arrangements—no lilies. You know how Jackson despises them."

"Understood." A pause that stretched a beat too long. "Are you coming inside? I noticed you arriving a few minutes ago..."

"When I'm ready," Maddie snapped, cutting her off. "See that my instructions are followed to the letter."

She ended the call abruptly, glaring at her own reflected eyes. What had that tone in Rosa's voice suggested? Some hidden knowledge? A judgment being passed?

Her gaze raked over her appearance, searching for whatever flaw the housekeeper might have noticed. Her fingers trembled faintly as she bared her teeth in a calculated smile, the same look that had cowed even unflappable Charlotte, that had reminded hapless Sandra of her tenuous place in their circle.

Something wasn't quite right.

The smile never reached her eyes.

Those same green depths that had once captivated Jackson now seemed to interrogate her, probing for answers she didn't want to give. They looked. ..hollow, somehow.

She adjusted her expression, shifting the light just so, erasing the fine lines she refused to acknowledge.

"Everything is flawless," she said, though her hands refused to stop trembling.

The words hung crystalline in the air as she watched her mouth form them, her poise never slipping.

Yet something inside her felt...constricted. Strained.

The veneer remained, as immaculate as the upholstered seats around her. But the muscles along her jaw ached from the effort of maintaining it.

The truth continued to elude her.

Cracks slivered through her facade of perfection.

Not since that night Jackson had—

No. She wouldn't think about that. Couldn't.

She was Maddie Callahan. The architect of her world. The curator of every illusion.

But those eyes in the mirror...her own eyes...saw through the illusion she'd so constructed.

Chapter 2

Maddie adjusted the hem of her cream Chanel dress, smoothing an invisible wrinkle as she stood in the private terminal of Hartsfield-Jackson International Airport. The place was nearly empty apart from a concierge at the far desk, quietly murmuring into a phone, and a businessman sipping an espresso in the lounge.

She noted how he glanced at her—appreciative but subtle. Good. She still commanded that effect.

The silence suited her. It always had.

Her Louboutins clicked against the polished marble floor as she shifted her weight. The soft, rhythmic sound was oddly comforting, a reminder that she was here, in control, waiting—as she always did. As she had done for twenty-seven years of marriage.

Her fingers drifted to the Cartier watch encircling her wrist, an anniversary gift from three years ago. 4:47 PM.

Jackson's plane was thirteen minutes out. She'd timed this arrival with precision—early enough to be expected but not so early as to appear eager. She had calculated this moment down to the second, just as she had calculated everything else about this encounter.

She smoothed the lapel of her tailored jacket, her reflection catching in the floor-to-ceiling windows overlooking the runway. She had chosen this ensemble with precision—cream-colored silk, a high neckline, and pearl accents. Elegant but not ostentatious. A reminder of the woman he had fallen in love with, the woman who had waited through deployments and lonely nights.

Her fingers curled around the Saint Laurent clutch at her side, the cool metal clasp a familiar weight. Inside, she carried only the essentials—her Chanel Rouge lipstick, her phone, and the deliberate stillness she had ed over the years. The stillness that had kept her sane through wars and absences.

Outside, the golden remnants of sunset stretched long shadows over the tarmac. The first glint of approaching headlights flickered in the distance, and something inside her chest tightened—though her expression remained serene.

Her breath was measured, controlled. Yet, there

was something satisfying about watching Jackson emerge from the jet.

She had envisioned this moment so many times—Jackson stepping off the plane, his eyes finding hers instantly. She pictured the recognition, the shift in his posture, the way he would inhale sharply, remembering what he had left behind—what he had tried to throw away.

Surely, he had missed her. If he hadn't, he would pretend.

She imagined him quickening his steps, reaching for her, pressing a kiss to her cheek like he used to do when he came home from deployments. The scent of his cologne—warm, crisp, expensive—would wrap around her, grounding them back into place. Back where they belonged.

Back to normal. She would make sure of it.

A private jet approached, its sleek body gliding onto the runway with military precision. Just like Jackson—always precise, always controlled. Until now.

Maddie inhaled slowly, tasting victory on her tongue.

The plane door opened.

Jackson emerged.

Her posture remained impeccable, even as she took him in, cataloging every detail like ammunition for later use.

His charcoal-gray suit was cut to perfection, but the tie was loosened—a small rebellion she noted with displeasure. His jaw was sharper, leaner, more defined than before. He looked younger somehow, and that made her blood simmer beneath her maintained smile.

His ice-blue eyes scanned the terminal, landing

on her with all the warmth of a winter morning.

She smiled. A slow, practiced expression of warmth that had won her every social battle for decades.

She waited for the flicker of longing, the sharp exhale of recognition. The moment he would remember who they were together.

Instead—nothing.

Jackson's expression remained neutral, almost clinical in its assessment.

No softening. No relief. No hunger. Just emptiness where their history should have been.

He walked toward her with measured steps, each one deliberately placing distance between them.

"Maddie."

Just her name. A statement, not a greeting. As if she were a stranger he had to acknowledge at a cocktail party.

She stepped forward, tilting her chin, allowing herself the smallest display of expectation. A wife knew when to hint at vulnerability.

He accepted her embrace, but his touch was mechanical—a polite, brief press of his hand against her back. Like a colleague. Like someone he was trying to dismiss.

She inhaled. His cologne was different. Sharper. Foreign. Young. Her stomach churned at the implication.

She pulled back, letting her fingers brush his sleeve, marking her territory in the subtlest way possible.

"I thought we'd have dinner. Just us." An olive branch wrapped in silk.

His phone buzzed. He glanced at the screen before acknowledging her words, and she the ghost of a smile that wasn't meant for her.

"I ate on the plane."

Her stomach twisted, but she gave a soft nod, as if this was nothing. As if he hadn't just dismissed twenty-seven years of tradition.

wives didn't show disappointment. They planned revenge.

She followed him toward the black Mercedes idling at the curb, noting how he didn't wait for her, didn't hold the door as he always had.

Jackson's stride was longer than usual, purposeful, as if he was trying to outpace her. As if he thought he could escape what was coming.

The suit was new. Not his usual Brooks Brothers. Italian cut, younger styling. Someone else's influence.

The watch on his right wrist was a matte-black tactical piece—a far cry from the gold Rolex she had gifted him. Another deliberate erasure of their past.

She noted each shift, each unfamiliar detail, filing them away like evidence.

The Jackson she knew was in there somewhere, beneath this stranger's skin.

She just had to find him. Or destroy him trying.

The front door opened, and Rosa stood in the marble-lit entryway, her dark eyes watchful as always. Maddie registered her presence, though she noted how Rosa's hands were clasped—waiting, observing, judging.

Her focus was on Jackson.

He strode inside, his shoes clicking against the marble with military precision. His gaze skimmed over the house—not with the warmth of familiarity, but with cold detachment. Like an appraiser examining property. Like a visitor who had no intention of staying.

Then—small footsteps echoed from above.
"Daddy!"

Carrie appeared at the top of the grand staircase, her blonde curls bouncing as she sprinted downward, her face lit with pure joy that made Maddie's stomach twist.

Jackson her effortlessly, lifting her into the air as though she weighed nothing. His entire demeanor transformed instantly, like a switch being flipped.

The ice in his expression melted away.

"There's my girl," he said, his voice rich with an affection that made Maddie's teeth clench.

He kissed her forehead, his arms tightening around her, his eyes softening in a way Maddie remembered from years ago. From before. From when those looks had belonged to her.

Maddie's chest tightened until she could breathe.

That smile. That tenderness. That unguarded affection.

It had been meant for her once, back when she was young enough, enough, before time had made her disposable.

From the landing, Nate stood motionless, a silent observer like his mother.

His small hands gripped the railing, knuckles white with tension that no ten-year-old should carry.

Jackson's smile dimmed as he looked up, the warmth receding like the tide going out.

"Hey, buddy."

Nate didn't move. Didn't speak. Didn't offer the easy affection his sister gave so freely.

The distance between father and son stretched wider with each second of silence, a gulf too vast to cross with casual greetings.

Jackson didn't push. He never did anymore.

Jackson turned back to Carrie, murmuring about a trinket from Dubai, the currency of his affection always measured in gifts, never presence.

Maddie's fingernails pressed crescents into her palms, deep enough to draw blood if she wasn't careful. She had spent decades perfecting it: the wife, the mother, the hostess. Always composed, always watching.

And yet, here she stood—on the outside, looking in at her own family.

Edited out of the frame like an unwanted extra.

"Dinner's ready," she said, smoothing her silk blouse with hands that wanted to shake.

Jackson's gaze flickered toward her, as though she were speaking from another room.

"I'm exhausted. Maybe tomorrow."

He shifted Carrie against his hip and started toward the stairs, dismissing twenty years of marriage with four casual words.

Maddie swallowed hard against the acid rising in her throat.

She had chosen the menu herself, spent hours planning each course, had Rosa prepare all his favorites - the herb-crusted lamb, roasted asparagus with garlic, that chocolate soufflé he always praised. She had arranged everything down to the last detail, even placing his favorite crystal whiskey glass by his usual seat. The welcome home.

Yet he didn't care. Didn't even look. Like she was invisible, a ghost in her own house.

She her reflection in the ornate mirror across the room, the one she'd chosen years ago when they'd first bought this house. When everything still made sense.

Not a hair out of place in her chestnut waves, each strand positioned to frame her face.

Not a flaw in sight on her maintained face, preserved through thousands of dollars of treatments and creams.

And yet, something was wrong. Something fundamental had shifted while she wasn't looking, like waking up to find all the furniture moved two inches to the left.

She could feel it unraveling beneath her manicured fingers, could sense the control slipping away no matter how tightly she tried to hold on.

Bit by bit.

Thread by thread.

The fractures were there, spreading like spiderwebs across glass, impossible to ignore once you noticed them.

Jackson had stopped seeing her. Had stopped trying to see her. She'd become as meaningless as the artwork on the walls - present but unremarkable.

She wasn't his home anymore.

She was just another part of his past he had outgrown, like old uniforms gathering dust in the closet. Another relic he was ready to discard.

And Maddie Callahan was not a woman who got left behind.

Not ever.

Chapter 3

Cora navigates the ship's labyrinthine corridors, Maddie lay motionless as the soft morning light crept across the untouched expanse of Egyptian cotton sheets, illuminating the stark vacancy on Jackson's side of the bed. Her hand moved almost instinctively to his pillow—cold and pristine, still marked with the razor-sharp angles maintained by Rosa's meticulous morning routine. Not even a hint of warmth where he might have sat.

With a delicate touch, she traced the undisturbed duvet, as if each stroke could whisper away twenty-five years of shared habit somehow reduced by his choice to sleep elsewhere. The thought of him on the guest room bed, or perhaps stretched out on the leather couch in his study, turned over in her mind with disquieting clarity. Just the vision of him, shoes on, tie loosened—a carelessness echoing the image of a man adrift—made her jaw tighten.

From the gilt-framed mirror, her reflection observed her ritualistic smoothing of the sheets—one, two, three precise strokes of her palm. This routine, usually a refresher, felt hollow today, like ironing a suit destined to remain on its hanger.

Each smoothing motion made her breath shallower, more erratic. Maddie stopped herself, pressing her hands into her lap. Control. The thought settled her. If the sheets remained perfect, so did she.

Her fingers worked in a practiced, mechanical manner, adjusting the duvet until it lay like a parade display. Jackson once appreciated such things, noticed them—back when his gaze lingered on her and her precision held weight.

Yet, the never-ending expanse of mattress rebuked her efforts. She could smooth the bedding countless times—it would not change the fact that Jackson had chosen to find solace elsewhere.

In the kitchen, Maddie measured coffee grounds with meticulous exactitude—two and three-quarters tablespoons. Her ritual was as familiar as her breath. Jackson liked his coffee bold, yet never bitter, with just a whisper of cream—sweetness was not part of his palette.

Their years together had ed this dance. Italian roast, freshly drawn and brewed each sunrise. The bone china cup, a relic from their wedding collection, warmed with intent before receiving its hot, aromatic contents. A delicate splash of cream turned the brew a faultless shade of caramel, meant just for him.

The kitchen shone, its surfaces immaculate beneath Rosa's attentive care, though Maddie couldn't recall her entering. Sunlight streamed through the pristine glass, casting elongated tendrils of light across the marble surface.

She discerned his footfall before he entered—a rhythm she would know anywhere. Yet today, it faltered. His cadence was too brisk, as if he intended not to stay.

Jackson stepped in, clad in running gear, a paper cup from a franchise clasped in hand, sweat marking his back. Running was a novelty.

"I made your coffee." Her tone was light, free of burden—the voice of a dedicated spouse. Yet her grip tightened around the delicate porcelain of his cup.

"I grabbed one on my way back," he replied, his eyes locked on his phone rather than the brewed coffee resting untouched on the counter. His steps were directed towards the stairs, absorbed in the glowing screen.

Steam rose subtly from the mahogany liquid she'd crafted, its bouquet chosen for him alone. in all respects, yet utterly forsaken.

At breakfast, they sat across from each other, the table an island between them, his fingers over the device forming an almost impervious wall. His eggs benedict cooled, only notated by mechanical bites.

She noted his attire—a sharply cut charcoal gray

suit holding a blue pinstripe's whisper. Possibly Tom Ford. The tailoring was distinctly European, hanging impeccably across his frame.

"The children miss you at breakfast," she ventured.

A mere grunt was his response as he continued scrolling upward.

Her gaze lingered on his belt—rich brown leather crowned with a modest silver buckle, not the Hermès she gifted last Christmas, a piece he once wore with religious devotion. This was new, something he chose independently.

As a speck of hollandaise drifted perilously close to soiling his pristine collar, a vanished reflex urged her to reach out and clean it, yet she merely observed, pondering if he would notice any imperfection.

The morning's luminous veil highlighted the intricacies of his suit's stitching, yet amidst the familiar threads, everything about him seemed altered—the suit, the buckle, his demeanor. Even his scent had shifted to something sharper, younger than the Tom Ford she historically selected.

Her cup met its saucer with a soft clink. Jackson didn't stir.

Tracing the rim of her cup, Maddie watched the interplay of light across its fine surface. Everything was arranged with intention—the table, her appearance, the breakfast. Yet amid all this precision, an intangible wrongness hung like a discordant note.

She analyzed Jackson's composed profile, eyes unwaveringly fixed on his phone. These changes in him—subtle but unmistakable—told of new undercurrents. He was still her husband, undeniably, yet somehow not.

Dubai must have exhausted him, she assured herself. Extended periods apart could shift anyone's routines. Time would realign them. He would recall their cherished rituals—the shared breakfasts, the evening martinis, the steadfast routines that had long fortified their union.

But beneath her careful reassurances, she felt a chill spreading—a whisper at her core. Perhaps it wasn't just travel that created this space now lying between them, broader and deeper than any physical separation.

Hands steeling over her lap, she enacted her small rituals of control, aligning fabric and ceramic, denying the invasive wrongness that threatened her structured world. Yet, a persistent voice inside murmured of a deeper shift, of an absence that no routine could fill.

Her grip steadied as another message brought a soft, unfamiliar smile to his lips—a gesture whose warmth seemed reserved for someone else now.

Maddie chose her usual corner table at Café Laurent with the practiced ease of someone accustomed to having her surroundings ideally arranged. Positioned against the wall, she could discreetly observe each entrant, while effectively keeping her own counsel. The maître d' had, as usual, executed this maneuver with subtle precision, seating Charlotte across from her to allow for a complete view of both her friend's expressions and the gentle hum of activity throughout the restaurant.

"The foie gras here is divine," Maddie remarked, her voice carrying just enough to ensure those within earshot noted her presence. Her Hermès scarf lay elegantly across her shoulders, adjusted to perfection.

Charlotte scrutinized the menu with a mild knit of her brows. "You seem... different today. Everything alright?" she asked, her tone both casual and probing.

Maddie's fingers involuntarily tightened around her water glass. She'd dedicated an extra twenty minutes to her morning routine, ensuring every feature was enhanced. Her Chanel suit displayed no crease or flaw; her hair captured the light as intended. What perceptible alteration could Charlotte possibly have detected?

"Different?" Maddie queried, her brows lifting in a calculated show of nonchalance. "I am as I always am."

Charlotte put down her menu slowly, her eyes never shifting from Maddie's. "How's Jackson settling back in?"

The inquiry landed like a sudden gust, though Maddie's practiced smile did not falter. She had rehearsed her response before her bedroom mirror that morning—the precise note of warmth in her tone, the tilt of her head.

"Oh, you know him. Straight back to business as usual." Maddie waved her hand dismissively in a gesture that appeared casual, though it was, in truth, rehearsed to the last detail. "Four months away accumulates quite the backlog."

Yet, something must have slipped, indicated by the subtle change in Charlotte's expression—a slight furrow of her brow, the hesitant pause before she sipped her water. Charlotte seemed to harbor suspicions, which meant others might as well.

Maddie's fork gently tapped the delicate china while Charlotte dabbed her lips with a pristine napkin. Their conversation meandered towards the recent children's hospital fundraiser; an event Maddie had orchestrated in Jackson's absence.

"The silent auction surpassed expectations," Maddie said, repositioning her bracelet to better catch the light, each diamond refracting an array of brilliance. "We raised over two hundred thousand more than last year."

Charlotte's voice then slipped into an ironically light tone that hinted otherwise. "Oh, that reminds me. I bumped into Greg Lowry last week. He mentioned he saw Jackson at the Four Seasons bar in Dubai. But you said he was on base the entire time?"

A chill of realization coursed through Maddie's veins, her spine rigid against the chair's curvature. Only for the briefest moment did her mask waver, but she swiftly reassembled herself, drawing on years of disciplined poise.

"Oh, Greg always gets these things mixed up." Maddie laughed, the sound deliberately airy and dismissive. Her hand steadied by the motion of lifting her water glass, concealing a slight tremor. "Remember when he insisted, he saw Barbara in Aspen last Christmas? She was in Palm Beach all along."

Yet beneath her polished exterior, Maddie's mind whirred with precision. The Four Seasons? Jackson had assured her of his location—stationed at Al Dhafra Air Base, quarters restricted and Spartan at best. Their brief conversations had been peppered with complaints about the heat and sand.

Even if Greg Lowry could be a fool, his familiarity with Jackson spanned fifteen years. His mix-ups were not a matter of mistaking identities, and certainly, he had no reason to fabricate tales of seeing Jackson in such a specific setting.

Thoughts of recent developments lined up sharply in Maddie's mind: Jackson's new cologne, the crisp shirts she had never purchased, the secretive smile he bestowed upon his phone when he believed she wasn't observing.

The Four Seasons bar was known from travel magazines—a place of dark wood, supple leather seats, and intimate lighting, for meetings that were intended to stay unnoticed.

Maddie signaled for the bill, her movements measured and impeccably composed. "You know the saying about gossip, Charlotte—it's more entertaining at breakfast than at dinner." Her voice enfolded the right touch of amusement, treating Greg's report as a trifling piece of idle chatter.

Charlotte nodded, yet an indescribable glint in her eyes lingered, leaving Maddie's skin tinged with unease. That doubt, though unspoken, bore weight.

Once settled in her Mercedes, Maddie remained still, her engine humming softly in the restaurant's parking lot. Her manicured finger hovered momentarily over her phone screen before she accessed Jackson's shared work calendar—the one she had insisted remain synced to hers "in case of emergency."

The weeks labeled "Dubai" charted out in orderly colors: discussions with defense contractors, conference dialogues with the Pentagon, with base visits logged. But within this tapestry lay peculiar gaps—entire afternoons and evenings unaccounted for.

February 15th: "Meeting with Sheikh Abdullah," yet she recalled Sheikh Abdullah penned to have been in London—her knowledge sourced from recent society page articles.

March 3rd: "Base inspection" engulfing a span of twelve hours?

March 17th: A Thursday rendered bluntly blank, devoid of appointments or logged activities.

Her thumb glided through dates, each void becoming a fissure in her crafted world. The view from the Four Seasons bar at sunset would have been breathtaking—during all those empty evenings Jackson professed were consumed by meetings.

Staring at the calendar, the once distinct blocks blurred into shades. She blinked, refusing to disrupt the makeup she had painstakingly applied. There must exist a plausible explanation. Jackson was a General; some meetings bore classifications, not all of which could be recorded.

But Greg Lowry had seen him. At a hotel bar. While he was supposedly confined to base.

Chapter 4

The grandfather clock in the hallway marked the hour with a solemn chime, its sound waning softly into the quiet expanse of the house. Maddie listened closely as if the silence held untold secrets. Jackson's study door, closed, emanated a faint blue glow from beneath, cast by his laptop—the sanctuary of his solitude. Elsewhere, the children's rooms were shrouded in darkness, their peaceful slumber secured since nine. Rosa had left with her customary punctuality.

Her world remained unruffled. Almost immaculate. Everyone situated where they were meant to be.

Her heels resonated gently against the polished marble as she moved toward her sanctuary—a room crafted with the same meticulous care as her public persona. Everything in its place, every surface gleaming like a mirror reflecting her composed exterior. Reaching for a crystal wine glass, Maddie filled it with Bordeaux that poured dark and rich from the bottle. The soft glow of her desktop beckoned, and she settled into her leather chair, a queen upon her throne.

Jackson's calendar materialized on the screen, each entry an ordered disarray she had committed to memory. But now, in the stillness, she could examine the cloistered space, unobserved by Charlotte's scrutinizing eyes or the weight of societal expectations.

February 15th—a supposed meeting with Sheikh Abdullah. Browser tabs flickered open with deft keystrokes, uncovering society pages from London. The Sheikh had attended his daughter's graduation. His presence firmly rooted in England, nowhere near Jackson.

March 3rd—an inspection at the base, absurdly documented as a twelve-hour endeavor. Maddie knew better; years as a military wife had bestowed her with that insight. The inspection times felt exaggerated, suspicious.

March 17th lingered in her mind, a Thursday that floated unanswered across her thoughts. Blank and unusually devoid. In two-and-a-half decades, a tabula rasa was implausible for someone as disciplined as Jackson. Unthinkably empty.

She took a measured sip of Bordeaux, her lips leaving a mark reminiscent of a signature upon her entwined existence. On the screen, the cursor blinked with indifference, each unaccounted-for moment a fracture spreading through the facade of her life.

Her fingers moved over the keyboard, a dance of instinct leading her to the familiar landscape of their shared finances. She had traversed these records innumerable times—scrutinizing expenses, navigating the financial labyrinth with practiced accuracy. But tonight, the tremor in her hand revealed a novel intention as she entered the password.

The financial statements unfolded: February awash with mundane, yet suddenly suspicious, transactions. A café in Dubai when Jackson ought to have been twelve time zones to the east. A tailored men's suit acquired when board meetings supposedly consumed his days.

Her throat tightened. One hundred and twenty dirhams at La Serre—a name said in circles for its exclusivity. The kind of place meant for connections deeper than mere business.

Her wine trembled in midair as her eyes fixed upon another charge, stark against the pristine white of the statement: The Four Seasons Dubai, not just a meal but a room charge. March 17th—the empty slot in his agenda.

With meticulous care, she set the glass down, though it longed to be hurled. There it was, insignificant at first glance yet undeniable—a breach in the edifice of truth he'd constructed around them.

Each additional entry on the ledger felt like a needle tracing beneath her skin. Exclusive eateries. Luxurious boutiques. Places rich with intimacy, concealed under the guise of unclaimed hours. Days he had vowed were consumed by strategy and duty.

The screen lit her face, revealing nothing. Shadows gathered elsewhere. Her manicured nails traced the mousepad's edge, a relentless back-and-forth. Details blurred into a tapestry of betrayal.

An explanation simmered beneath her rationalizations. Jackson's dealings were delicate; clandestine contracts demanded discretion. The Four Seasons abounded with opportunities for covert meetings. It made sense. sense.

Yet, her chest constricted with each shallow breath. Despite the regulated ambient temperature, the room seemed to warm. A bead of perspiration threatened her flawless foundation, ready to betray her composed facade.

Business engagements, she reassured herself. Surely, those boutiques were for gifts, both diplomatic and essential. These gestures were requisite maneuvers within the realm of courtesy—a dance Maddie understood well.

Her hand descended, closing the laptop's lid with a definitive snap, shrouding her sanctuary in shadows tempered by the faint halo of her desk lamp. Solitude enveloped her, yet her thoughts clamored with discord.

Her fingers found the desk's edge, the wood grounding her amidst the tumult. She drew a breath, as she had done countless times during Jackson's lengthy deployments, when solitude attempted to fill the void.

Her lips brushed the clouded crystal, the half-filled glass gleaming under the lamp's steady gaze. Her lipstick imprinted an unspeaking token, a crescent reflecting crack yet unexamined. She reached for it, paused. She wasn't prepared—not for the wine, not for the truth, yet hidden within the lines of expense and relinquished time.

Maddie gently closed the laptop, a familiar action rendered unsettling by her trembling fingers grazing its cool finish. Her sanctuary now felt confining; the height of its ceilings unable to quell the advance of reality's press.

A soft, hollow laugh slipped from her lips—a chime of recognition. There would always be a woman, she understood, recalling countless narratives woven within their social circle. The signs of change: the renewed scent of cologne, the refreshed wardrobe, the relentless phone-checking, the silent nights of separate rooms.

She stood, smoothing her blouse with meticulous grace. Her reflection gazed back from the study window—a woman still striking, still steadfast. Yet Jackson's gaze, once warm, had long cooled.

"Everything's fine," she said to her reflected self, the reassurance sounding as if it came from a script, etched deeply into her being. Her hands clenched beneath the desk's polished surface, nails biting her palm briefly. ", even."

The clock continued its unwavering beat, a rhythmic comfort among chaotic thoughts. She needed clarity, a plan. There were countless nights to uncover each inconsistency, to follow the jagged ends of his deceits. For now, she must marshal her poise.

Her laughter arose once more, bolder and nearly

convincing. She would orchestrate another gathering—controlled, intimate, upholding the impeccable Callahans. To the world, unchanged and unbreakable.

Yet beneath the desk, her hands defied her control, unyielding in their tremor.

◆ ◆ ◆

Maddie chose Café Amelie for her lunch with Barbara—a venue that exuded just the right blend of discretion and public decorum. Through the restaurant's expansive windows, the spring sunshine painted the white tablecloths and gleaming silverware with a gentle, golden light.

Barbara was, predictably, five minutes behind schedule. Normally this would've been an annoyance, but today it allowed Maddie a precious moment to compose herself, to secure the flawless veneer of casual interest on her face. When Barbara arrived, designer bag swinging with her usual flair, Maddie stood, offering the customary air-kiss to her cheeks.

"You look radiant," Barbara exclaimed as she settled into her chair. "Is that the new Hermès scarf?"

Maddie's fingers brushed the silk at her neck lightly. "Last season, truthfully. But thank you for noticing."

Their orders were predictable—Barbara opted for her reliable Niçoise salad, while Maddie chose a simple cup of Earl Grey. Conversation drifted over familiar terrain: Charlotte's ongoing renovation debacle, Sandra's stumbling forays into post-divorce dating. Maddie allowed Barbara to dominate the dialogue, acknowledging her friend with timely nods while observing her animated gestures.

When their luncheon arrived, Maddie

purposefully waited for Barbara to take that first forkful
before she delicately picked up her sterling silver spoon,
stirring her tea in measured circles, watching the amber
liquid ripple.

"Have you ever visited the Four Seasons in
Dubai?" Maddie inquired, her tone light, almost offhand,
as if it were just another conversational morsel.

Barbara's fork halted midair; a moment of
hesitation so faint it would pass unnoticed by anyone not
attuned to her. But Maddie was attuned, and she
observed it all: the slight widening of Barbara's eyes, the
fleeting parting of her lined lips.

Maddie let Barbara linger in her thoughts over
lunch, her own mind already strategizing her next move.
She knew that Colonel Lowry enjoyed his afternoon
coffees at Maxwell's—a quaint haunt near the base where
retired military men congregated to savor memories of
valor.

As the bell above the door chimed, Maddie
entered Maxwell's. Greg sat alone at his familiar corner;
newspaper sprawled out before him. His lined face
registered surprise at her appearance, though he quickly
veiled it, standing with military composure as she
approached.

"Mrs. Callahan," he acknowledged, motioning to
the vacant chair. "What a surprise."

Maddie eased into the seat, elegantly adjusting
her Chanel skirt. The dim light couldn't obscure the
tension in Greg's shoulders, the nervous tapping of his
fingers against his coffee mug. She recognized these
signs—reminiscent of people aware they were in the
crosshairs but not yet spotting the sniper.

"I was nearby," she said, dismissing his offer of

refreshment with a wave. "And I thought, why not drop in on one of Jackson's closest confidants?" Her head tilted, her smile warming. "I heard you were in Dubai not too long ago."

Greg laughed; a quick bark devoid of genuine mirth. "Ah, Maddie, you know the drill. Gossip flies, and more often than not, it's hot air."

Maddie's smile remained steady; her eyes unwavering on his. She watched the nervous bob of his Adam's apple and noted the increased tempo of his fingers on the cup.

"Charlotte mentioned she saw you at the Four Seasons bar alongside Jackson," she said, her tone syrupy sweet.

A shadow crossed Greg's features. "I might have been mistaken. Could've been anyone."

"You've always valued honesty with me, Greg," Maddie said, adjusting a bracelet on her wrist. "And I truly do value that quality."

Her words struck home—the subtle widening of his eyes and the tension knitting his shoulders were telltale signs. Greg grasped her meaning fully: their dance was far from over.

Chapter 5

Maddie sat in her private sanctuary; the house's silence broken only by her laptop's gentle hum. She'd chosen this secluded room to breathe life into the secrets multiplying like bacteria. Greg Lowry's hesitation about Dubai, his telling stutter and tightened face revealed his guilt over Jackson's betrayal. Maddie had become adept at reading the subtleties - twitches, pauses, careful phrasing - that betrayed lies, a new skill alongside hosting soirees.

Greg's reaction was telling - his momentarily forgotten military posture, the tremor as he reached for his bourbon, his inability to meet her eyes when pressed about Jackson's suspicious business trips. Her manicured fingers hovered over the keyboard, a trail of digital breadcrumbs leading to whatever Jackson had buried in Dubai's sands.

In this sanctuary, Maddie could slip the devoted wife's mask, acknowledge the dark satisfaction of catching Greg's loyalty to Jackson, and plan her next strategic move in their chess game where she now played for keeps. Jackson had taught her that wars were won through exploiting weaknesses, and Greg had just provided ammunition.

Her fingers moved deftly, pulling up the financial records mocking her previous obedience - the Four Seasons charges, regular upscale expenditures on restaurants and boutiques despite Jackson's fiscal lectures. A pattern emerged of controlled betrayal - room service, couples' massages, a "Luxury Romance Package." The Valentine's Day charges stung deepest when he'd claimed meetings, leaving her alone while he indulged another woman.

Social media revealed her name - Lillian Hart, wearing Maddie's anniversary Trinity necklace in an Instagram post from the Four Seasons. Twenty-five years reduced to hand-me-down jewelry, the betrayal transcending the physical into the sacred. Sunlight highlighted Maddie's aging features Jackson once loved as she studied Lillian's youthful beauty, effortlessly maintaining what cost Maddie years of disciplined effort.

Let Lillian enter Maddie's world, sleep in her bed, wear her jewels, play stepmother to her children. Lillian hadn't learned that war wasn't just battlefield, that deadly weapons came disguised as smiles. Maddie would reign in hell before watching her kingdom crumble. She imagined Lillian's face realizing she'd inherited more than a general's name - she'd inherited war with a woman who'd turned scars into armor, preparing this battle longer than Lillian lived. The game had begun, and Maddie would remind all why the Callahan name commanded respect.

◆ ◆ ◆

Rosa's footsteps reverberated softly across the marble of the breakfast room; a sound almost soothing in the morning stillness. Maddie sat composed at the head of the table, surrounded by the muted elegance of Wedgwood china and sterling silver. The light filtering through the expansive windows played upon the grapefruit spoon held delicately between her fingers. Her movements were meticulous—slice, separate, lift—a practiced choreography that kept her thoughts from unraveling.

The coffee in her cup sat cold, ignored since Rosa had poured it a full twenty minutes prior. Maddie found she could not bring herself to sip it, not with the image of Lillian imprinted on her mind. That carefree smile bright in her profile picture, the way her golden hair the light—it all blared youth, freedom, a life unburdened by the weight of a quarter-century marriage.

She cut the grapefruit with perhaps more force than necessary, and a rogue droplet of juice fell to the pristine white tablecloth. Maddie's gaze lingered on the tiny blemish, her grip tightening around the silver handle, calm yet laden with an unspoken tension.

Rosa appeared beside her once more, a fresh pot

of French roast in hand, and the familiar, rich aroma permeated the air. Yet rather than her customary quiet exit, Rosa lingered, an almost tangible presence just at the periphery of Maddie's awareness.

Maddie kept her eyes trained on the fruit, allowing the steady rhythm of her actions to govern her focus: slice, separate, lift. Rosa's attentive gaze was nearly a physical weight, those astute eyes that had seen two decades of Maddie's cultivated image of flawlessness.

The silence between them grew dense, fraught with unspoken inquiries. Rosa remained, her hand poised above the coffee pot, her hesitation now unmistakable. Maddie refused to yield to it, concentrating instead on the mechanical sequence of her breakfast ritual. Each action measured; each gesture precise as if this dance of normalcy could indeed hold her disordered world at bay.

Then came Rosa's voice, unexpected in the stillness—a challenge, veiled but undeniable. "You seem... tense, Mrs. Callahan."

Maddie lifted her gaze from the grapefruit to meet Rosa's, studying the weathered planes of her face. The morning light etched deeper shadows, underscoring lines that had formed over years of unnoticed service. Two decades of silent observation, understanding unspoken truths.

She inclined her head, weighing the import of Rosa's words. Rosa always knew—she had an uncanny intuition. But what detail, exactly, had laid Maddie bare? The untouched coffee? The precision of her slicing? Or perhaps the ever-so-subtle quiver in Maddie's hands when she thought herself unobserved.

A faint smile, controlled and calculated, curled

the edges of Maddie's lips. "Do I?" Her voice emerged softer than intended, a note of vulnerability embedded within. Denial seemed superfluous with Rosa, who had witnessed every ebb and flow of her faltering marriage. The quiet nights Jackson spent away, calls unanswered, the diminishing warmth between their walls.

Rosa's words cut cleanly through Maddie's poised exterior. "Men change, you know. When they've been gone too long."

The knife felt icy in Maddie's grasp, her fingers wrapping tighter until her knuckles blanched. Her eyes stayed on the half-eaten fruit, watching its pink flesh detach with clinical detachment. Her mind whirred—what had Rosa perceived? What fragments did she piece together?

Maddie, however, would not let Rosa see her crack. Her response was a honed whisper, smooth, controlled, as unyielding as the facade she upheld. "Did your husband?"

The question was deliberate, a gentle nudge of boundaries, a reminder of the hierarchy between them. Despite Rosa's experience, she was still the help—her insights into Jackson's behavior uninvited.

Rosa stood rooted, the coffee pot still in her grasp. The light adorned her silver cross, lending it a fleeting luminescence. Her answer, when it came, was a simple word: "Yes."

There was a resonant truth embodied in that 'yes'—not merely an acknowledgment, but a personal testament to decline, a mirror to Maddie's silent turmoil. It wasn't an observation, but a caution pointed enough to distress.

Maddie noted the tremor in Rosa's hand as she

reached for the half-consumed grapefruit. The clinking of the silver spoon against fine china resonated sharply, aggravating nerves already taut. Her temples pulsed.

Rosa's careful gathering of silverware was methodical, deliberate—each piece clinking together reverberated in the quiet, a sound now oddly discordant. Normally, the coffee pot wouldn't linger, but today it stayed as though marking the gravity of morning.

Maddie's fingertips traced the delicate embroidery of the tablecloth, her gaze steadfastly avoiding Rosa's. She could sense the weight of Rosa's scrutiny, dense with unsaid truths collected over twenty years. The light flitted over Rosa's cross, casting fleeting reflections that danced across the room's still walls.

Rosa's hand hovered over Maddie's forgotten coffee cup, an unintended pause becoming an unanswered invitation. Maddie held her silence, her jaw set firm against the inquiry threatening to surface. She would not allow her doubts expression—not now, not here, and certainly not with Rosa.

The silence stretched thin, punctuated only by the clock's steady tick and the distant whisper of sprinklers commencing their morning symphony. Rosa's fingers curled around the cup's handle, lifting it with her usual careful grace.

The clatter of dishes being arranged on Rosa's serving tray prickled the quiet—each sound deliberate, bisecting their wordless exchange. Through it all, Maddie sat unchanged, her visage a mask of serene neutrality, hiding the volatile mix of dread and suspicion that roiled beneath.

◆ ◆ ◆

Maddie stood before the full-length mirror in her

walk-in closet, the afternoon light streaming through the window. Her cream silk blouse hung, each pleat falling where it should. She'd chosen it that morning - another piece of armor in her daily battle.

Her fingers traced the edge of her collar, adjusting it though it needed no adjustment. Everything was in place. Her makeup was flawless, her chestnut hair swept into an elegant twist. The diamond studs in her ears the light, throwing tiny prisms across the mirror's surface.

But there - just there. Her head tilted, examining the spot beneath her jawline where the skin had started to soften. When had that happened? She pressed her fingertips against it, pulling the skin taut. Better, but the moment she released, the softness returned.

Her eyes narrowed, scanning her reflection with surgical precision. A fine line creased the corner of her right eye, visible only when she smiled. She didn't smile now. The line remained, etched into her skin like a betrayal.

The familiar scent of her Chanel perfume suddenly felt cloying in the enclosed space. She leaned closer to the mirror, her breath fogging the glass. The imperfections multiplied under her scrutiny - microscopic flaws that she'd somehow missed before. How long had they been there? How long had others noticed them?

Her manicured nail traced the line near her eye, following its path across her skin. She'd spent thousands on creams, treatments, procedures. She'd done everything right. And yet here it was - evidence of time's steady march forward, carved into her face like graffiti on a wall.

Maddie's hand fell from her face as realization

crashed through her constructed walls. Of course. Of course he'd chosen someone younger. The signs had been there - the Dubai hotel charges at places she'd never been allowed to visit, the boutique purchases that weren't her size, the late-night phone calls he took in his study.

Lillian Hart. The name tasted bitter in her mind. She'd seen the photos - sun-kissed skin without a trace of time's markings, that effortless beauty that only youth could provide. No expensive creams needed, no angled selfies to hide imperfections. Just natural, uncomplicated perfection.

Fresh. Exciting. Everything Maddie had been twenty-five years ago, when Jackson first saw her across a crowded officer's ball. Back when her beauty had been effortless too, when she hadn't needed to wage daily war against time's steady advance.

She'd given him everything—her youth, her beauty, her devotion. She waited through deployments, preserved their social standing, raised his children. And for what? To be replaced by a younger model who hadn't earned any of it?

The mirror reflected her fury back at her. That softness under her jaw, the fine lines at her eyes - they weren't just imperfections anymore. They were weapons being used against her. Every mark of age was another reason for Jackson to stray, another victory for Lillian Hart and her, unlined face.

Her palms stung where her nails broke the skin. Red crescents welled up, stark against her pale flesh. Twenty-five years of marriage, and he'd thrown it away for someone who probably wasn't even twenty-five years old.

Maddie's hand drifted across the closet rack,

fingers trailing over silk and cashmere until they found it - the ivory Hermès blouse. Jackson had brought it back from Paris five years ago, one of the rare times he'd remembered to buy her something while traveling. She'd worn it to countless events, always drawing compliments, always feeling like it was proof of his love.

The silk opened as she pulled it from its wooden hanger. Such a delicate thing, so easy to destroy. Like marriage. Like time. Like everything she'd built over twenty-five years.

Her fingers tightened around the fabric. This blouse - he'd smiled when she first tried it on. smiled, the way he smiled now at his phone when messages from Lillian came through.

The sound of tearing silk cut through the closet's silence. Maddie stared at her hands, at the way they'd acted without her permission, ripping the ivory fabric straight down the middle. The tear was jagged, ugly - everything she tried so hard not to be.

Her chest rose and fell in sharp, quick movements. The ruined blouse hung from her grip, its edges frayed and damaged. Like her. Like everything about her that wasn't good enough anymore.

She forced her breathing to slow, her spine straightening by instinct. Even alone, even now, her body remembered its training, posture, and control. But her hands shook as she held the torn silk, and something wild clawed at the edges of her composure.

Maddie released the ruined blouse, letting it drift to the floor like a broken butterfly. Her hands trembled as she smoothed her hair, each movement precise and practiced. The face in the mirror watched her—composed, controlled. She adjusted her cream silk blouse, erasing invisible wrinkles with practiced strokes.

The torn Hermès could be replaced. Everything could be replaced.

She squared her shoulders, lifted her chin. The afternoon lights her diamond studs again, throwing those prisms across the mirror. Her lipstick hadn't smudged. Her mascara remained unsmeared. No evidence remained of her momentary lapse, that flash of weakness when the world had tilted sideways.

It hadn't happened. Like so many things in her curated life, this moment would be edited out, erased, forgotten. The torn blouse would disappear before Rosa's next cleaning. No one would know. No one would question.

Her reflection showed what she needed it to show - Maddie Callahan, put together, in control. The softness beneath her jaw vanished at this angle. The fine lines disappeared in this light. She was what she had always been - flawless, untouchable, superior.

But as she stepped out of the closet, her hands still shook. She clasped them together, willing them still, but the tremors persisted - tiny betrayals of the storm that raged beneath her surface.

Chapter 6

Maddie quietly tucked the torn Hermès blouse into a Bergdorf Goodman shopping bag, gently surrounding it with tissue paper to stifle any sound. Swiftly, she concealed the evidence in her car's trunk, setting a course for a distant donation bin. No one would suspect, least of all Rosa, who had long learned to overlook such matters.

In her secluded study, Maddie deftly reapplied her trademark red lipstick, her hand steady and sure. In the mirror above her desk, she saw only calm, control

❖ ❖ ❖

Maddie stood before her walk-in closet, scanning the organized rows of designer pieces like a general surveying her troops. Her fingers brushed past silk blouses and structured blazers - each one a battle armor she'd collected over the years - until they found what she wanted: a dove gray cashmere sweater from Brunello Cucinelli. Subtle luxury. The kind that whispered wealth rather than screamed it. (The way new money screamed, the way Lillian probably screamed.)

She slipped it on, smoothing the soft fabric over her frame with practiced precision. Pearl studs in her ears, her grandmother's pearl strand at her throat - a lineage of proper women who'd known their place and kept it. The mirror reflected what she intended: a woman of refinement, not desperation. Someone who belonged in Buckhead's elite circles. Someone who'd earned her position through years of careful curation, not stumbled into it through a man's midlife crisis.

Her Cartier watch showed 10:15 AM. timing - late enough for morning traffic to clear, early enough to catch the lunch crowd at the high-rise. She selected her oversized Celine sunglasses, dark enough to mask her eyes but not so dark as to seem suspicious. Every detail mattered. Every choice calculated. That's what Jackson never understood - the work that went into perfection.

The Mercedes purred to life beneath her, that familiar new car smell wrapping around her like an old friend. She'd insisted on updating to the latest model every two years, a habit Jackson had once indulged without question. (Before he started questioning everything about her.) Her manicured finger pressed the

GPS screen, typing in The Peninsula Residences. Unit 2801. The numbers felt like a code to a vault she needed to crack.

The route displayed: twenty-eight minutes via Peachtree Road. Maddie adjusted her rearview mirror, checking her reflection one final time. Her chestnut hair fell in waves, her lipstick was applied, her complexion flawless. No one would guess she'd been awake since 4 AM, rehearsing this moment, playing out every possibility like chess moves in her mind.

She backed out of the circular driveway, past the pristine hedges and manicured flowerbeds Rosa maintained. (Rosa, who'd seen everything but said nothing. Rosa, who probably pitied her now.) The gates opened silently, and Maddie merged onto the quiet street of their exclusive neighborhood. The morning sun her diamond wedding ring as she gripped the steering wheel. She'd debated removing it but decided against it. Let it serve as a reminder - to herself and to anyone watching - of who she was. Who she'd always be.

The building stretched skyward, all glass and steel, like a monument to everything new money could buy. Through her tinted windows, she observed the steady stream of residents. Young women in Lululemon heading to late morning pilates, their bodies still tight and responsive to exercise. Men in tailored suits rushing to business meetings. A doorman in an impeccable uniform holding the door, offering practiced smiles. This was Lillian's world now - everything handed to her on a silver platter that Maddie had spent decades polishing.

Time crept by like honey dripping from a spoon. 10:45. 11:15. She sipped water from her S'well bottle, never taking her eyes off the entrance. A couple emerged

- the woman younger than Maddie, wearing a tennis dress that probably cost more than most people's monthly rent. The man's hand rested possessively on her lower back. (Just like Jackson used to touch her, before his hands became distant, before they found younger skin to caress.)

When Lillian appeared at 11:42, the sight of her hit Maddie like a physical blow. The girl floated out of the private entrance, her sundress dancing around her knees, her blonde hair catching the sunlight like something out of a shampoo commercial. Everything about her radiated that particular kind of youth that couldn't be bought or maintained - it existed, thoughtlessly, like wildflowers growing through concrete.

The sundress was Zimmermann - Maddie recognized it from their spring collection. The fabric danced around her legs as she walked, ethereal and light. Everything about her radiated youth, from her bare shoulders to her natural makeup to the way she moved with unconscious grace. She adjusted the strap of her Bottega Veneta bag - another gift from Jackson, no doubt. The same Jackson who'd told Maddie that designer bags were "frivolous expenses" during their early years of marriage, when she'd been young too, when she'd been the one who made his breath catch.

Lillian's face lit up at something said on her phone, her smile wide and unguarded. She had the kind of beauty that required no effort, no applied serums or regular Botox appointments. No weekly appointments with stylists or hours spent maintaining the image. She existed in a state of grace that Maddie had spent decades trying to manufacture.

The rage that filled Maddie's chest was different

from anything she'd felt before. Not the hot flash of anger she'd experienced when discovering the hotel charges. Not the burning humiliation of realizing everyone knew before her. This was colder, calmer, more precise. This was clarity.

As Lillian disappeared around the corner, still lost in her little world, Maddie's thoughts crystallized like ice forming over a lake. It wasn't enough to hurt this girl, to teach her a lesson about taking what belonged to others. No, Lillian Hart needed to disappear. To be erased, as if she'd never existed. As if she'd never dared to step into Maddie's constructed world.

Because that's what Maddie did best - she constructed things. Built them piece by piece, brick by brick. And now she would construct something else: Lillian Hart's complete and total destruction.

Maddie trailed her fingers across a rack of silk dresses at Maison Belle, each piece more exquisite than the last. The boutique's soft lighting and champagne-colored walls created an intimate atmosphere - for what she had planned.

She'd memorized Lillian's schedule through her Instagram posts. Every Thursday afternoon, like clockwork, the girl visited this store. Maddie had called ahead, scheduling her appointment to overlap.

The sales associate, Claire, hovered nearby with practiced deference. "Mrs. Callahan, would you like to try the Valentino in cream?"

"In a moment." Maddie checked her watch - 2:45 PM. Right on time, the bell above the door chimed.

Lillian walked in, her designer bag swinging

carelessly from her arm. She moved with that unconscious grace that made Maddie's teeth clench behind her smile. Claire's eyes darted between them, uncertain who to attend to first.

Maddie turned, positioning herself to appear absorbed in a rack of evening wear. She could see Lillian's reflection in the mirror - the girl was heading toward the new arrivals, where Maddie had predicted she would.

"Claire, darling," Maddie called softly. "Could you help me with the sizing on this one?" She held up a gown, deliberately choosing one close to where Lillian stood.

The trap was set. Now, she just had to wait for the moment to spring it. Maddie had spent twenty-five years perfecting the art of timing - she wouldn't rush this. Let Lillian browse a bit longer, let her feel comfortable. The best predators knew when to be patient.

Through the mirror, Maddie watched Lillian select a few pieces, her movements light and carefree. She had no idea she was being hunted. No idea that every step she took brought her closer to where Maddie wanted her.

Maddie angled herself toward the mirror, watching Lillian's reflection with predatory focus. The girl paused at a rack of cocktail dresses, her fingers trailing over a red silk number that Maddie knew would look stunning on her younger frame. The thought made her jaw tighten.

Through the reflection, Maddie the exact moment Lillian noticed her. The girl's eyes flickered up, met Maddie's in the mirror, then darted away with that instinctive politeness of strangers sharing space. She didn't recognize Maddie - of course she wouldn't.

Jackson had been careful to keep his two worlds separate.

Maddie turned, allowing surprise to wash across her features. She'd practiced this moment for days in her own mirror, posing the exact arch of her eyebrows, the precise curve of her smile. "Oh!" She let her voice carry just enough to command attention without seeming deliberate.

Lillian looked up again, this time directly. Maddie watched the girl's face, searching for any flicker of recognition, any tell-tale sign of guilt. There was none.

"Oh, my dear-" Maddie glided closer, her voice honey-smooth, "you must be new to Atlanta. You have that fresh, unspoiled look about you."

A small laugh escaped Lillian's lips - uncertain, between wanting to be polite and not quite sure if she'd been insulted. the reaction Maddie had hoped for. The girl's hand tightened on the red dress, her knuckles whitening just enough to betray her discomfort.

Maddie stepped closer, drinking in every detail of Jackson's mistress. Up close, Lillian's youth was even more apparent - that dewy skin that hadn't yet learned to fear time. Her perfume was light, floral - probably Jo Malone. Orange blossom, if Maddie wasn't mistaken. How fitting - the scent of innocence.

"Let me help you settle in," Maddie purred, reaching out to brush Lillian's forearm. Her fingers lingered a heartbeat too long, just enough to make the touch feel wrong. "Atlanta can be a small town. You never know who's watching."

The words slipped out like silk, but Maddie saw it - that tiny flutter in Lillian's expression. The way her smile faltered for just a fraction of a second. The girl was smart enough to sense the threat, even if she didn't understand it yet.

"That's... kind of you," Lillian replied, taking a small step back. Her fingers tightened on the red dress she held, creating small creases in the fabric.

Maddie allowed her smile to widen, showing just a hint of teeth. "Well, I won't keep you from your shopping." She turned toward the door; each click of her heels against the marble floor precise and measured. She didn't look back - she didn't need to. She could feel Lillian's eyes following her, that seed of unease already taking root.

The first move had been made. Now it was time to let Lillian stew in the uncertainty of their encounter.

Chapter 7

Maddie parked her sleek Mercedes along the winding path of Oakland Cemetery, settling into the cocoon of climate-controlled silence. timing, as always. The late afternoon sun stretched shadows across the grounds like grasping fingers, and most of the living had retreated to their comfortable homes, leaving her alone with the dead. Just the way she preferred it.

Through her Chanel sunglasses (last seasons, but who would dare comment?), she studied the granite angels and weathered crosses rising from the earth. They were silent sentinels, these stone guardians, watching over secrets as old as Atlanta itself. Rather like her, in a way. She'd kept her share of secrets over the years, hadn't she? Some of them were even buried here, metaphorically speaking.

Spanish moss veiled the ancient oaks, swaying like forgotten mourners. How often had she driven past, recognizing herself in the cemetery's curated decay? Here, even death bowed to maintenance, to order. To control.

Her fingers drummed absently against the leather steering wheel as she gazed at the historic section, where brick paths wound between family plots enclosed by ornate wrought iron. The names etched in stone were as familiar to her as the contents of her own closet: Thornton, Ashworth, Montgomery. She'd shared champagne with their descendants at the Capital City Club just last week. Poor Elizabeth Montgomery, still trying to hide her son's gambling debts. (As if Maddie hadn't noticed the gradual disappearance of the family silver.)

Closer to her car, modern granite markers gleamed like mirrors in the fading light. Someone had left fresh peonies on the Watson plot—probably Anne, always so dutiful about appearances. The flowers were a garish splash of pink against the manicured grass, each blade trimmed with military precision. Just like her own garden, where Rosa spent hours ensuring every hedge, every bloom, every leaf met her exacting standards.

The grounds crew had done their usual impeccable work. No fallen leaves marred the pristine paths, no weeds dared breach the sanctity of these hallowed grounds. Control, always control. Wasn't that what life—and death—was about? Maintaining the facade, never letting anyone see the decay beneath the surface?

She adjusted her sunglasses again, a habit born of years spent hiding her true thoughts behind designer frames. The late afternoon lights the diamond on her left hand, and for a moment, she was lost in its cold fire. Twenty-five years of marriage captured in that stone. Jackson had chosen well back then—flawless, expensive, impressive to others. Sometimes she wondered if that's all she'd ever been to him: an accessory, selected to enhance his image.

But things were different now, weren't they? The maintained order of their lives had been disrupted, like fallen leaves scattered across these pristine paths. Jackson thought he could sweep her aside, replace her with a younger model. (That vapid little princess, with her skin and empty head.) He'd forgotten one crucial detail: Maddie had spent decades learning from these old Atlanta families. She knew where all the bodies were buried, figuratively speaking.

She allowed herself a small smile, the kind that never quite reached her eyes. The cemetery's silence wrapped around her like an old friend's embrace. There was something comforting about being surrounded by all this managed decay, these beautiful monuments to endings. After all, everything ended eventually. It was just a matter of who controlled the ending.

The sun dipped lower, casting longer shadows across the grounds. Soon it would be time to leave this peaceful sanctuary and return to the world of the living, where her plans were already in motion. But for now, she sat in her climate-controlled bubble, surrounded by the dead and their secrets, thinking about endings and beginnings, and how thin the line between them could be.

A vibrant cardinal alighted on a nearby headstone, its crimson feathers a stark contrast against the weathered marble. Maddie observed the bird as it hopped along the stone's edge, musing on how the cemetery managed to be simultaneously beautiful and unsettling—a tranquil oasis, yet laden with unspoken stories. It was not unlike the constructed facade she had maintained throughout the years, beneath which lay a multitude of buried secrets.

At this hour, the grounds were nearly deserted, as Maddie preferred. In the distance, a worker pushed a cart, their figure blurring in the late afternoon haze, while an elderly woman arranged flowers at a grave several sections away, her movements slow and purposeful. Apart from them, Maddie had this corner of Oakland Cemetery to herself—just as she had planned. She had timed her visit with the same precision she applied to every aspect of her life.

As Maddie stood before her mother's headstone, a bitter laugh escaped her lips before she could suppress it. Her hand flew instinctively to her mouth, fingers pressing against her lips to silence the harsh sound. Even here, in solitude, the deeply ingrained instinct to maintain control ran through her veins—a lesson her mother had relentlessly drilled into her from a young age. The manicured nails beneath her leather gloves dug into her skin, leaving crescent-shaped indentations of pain that she welcomed. The sensation grounded her, reminding her of her purpose here, of what needed to be done.

With gloved fingers, Maddie traced the engraved letters of her mother's name: Elizabeth Marie Kensington. The surname felt alien now, like a half-remembered dream from a distant life, its edges faded and worn like an old photograph. When she had married Jackson, she had erased every trace of Kensington from her identity, becoming Madeline Callahan, utterly, irrevocably. Her mother had cautioned her about that too—about losing herself in the shadow of a military man. About becoming nothing more than a decorative ornament on his dress uniform, a silent companion at officer's dinners, the wife who smiled and nodded and never, ever revealed the turmoil that churned beneath the surface.

Pressing her fingers harder against the cool stone, Maddie silently demanded answers from the lifeless rock, feeling the rough edges of each letter bite through her leather gloves. The pressure sent tiny jolts of pain through her fingertips, but she embraced it—needed it. A sharp gust of wind sounded through the oak trees, lifting a strand of hair from her face and carrying with it the scent of decay and autumn leaves. Maddie inhaled sharply, her breath shallow and quick, her heart stuttering in her chest. A sign? Her mother had always believed in signs, in voices or messages from beyond. Perhaps now, in her moment of greatest need for guidance, her mother was attempting to communicate with her.

A solitary leaf drifted down, coming to rest at her feet like an ominous harbinger. Maddie's pulse throbbed in her throat; each beat a reminder of time slipping away. Then—nothing. Just silence. The distant hum of traffic floated over the cemetery walls. The ordinary world continued on, oblivious to her pain, to her rage, to the way her manicured nails were digging crescent-shaped marks into her palms.

"You tried to warn me, didn't you?" Maddie said, her voice disturbing the cemetery's tranquility. Her tongue felt thick with unshed tears that she refused to let fall. "About men like Jackson. About what happens when they stop seeing you. When they start looking through you as if you're made of glass."

Her mother had recognized the signs earlier—the way Jackson's eyes had begun to wander at social functions, how his touches had become mechanical, perfunctory, like ticking items off a checklist. But Maddie had been too up in the romance of it all, in being the military wife, hosting dinner parties where other officers' wives whispered enviously about her china patterns, wearing her sacrifice like a badge of honor. Such a fool she had been.

She turned away from the grave, her body stiffening for just a moment as if waiting for a response—for her mother's voice to cut through the silence with one of her sharp warnings about men and their wandering eyes. But there was nothing, only the weight of unspoken truths pressing down on her like a physical thing, threatening to crack her constructed facade.

The stillness was suffocating—the absence of her mother's presence a tangible void that she could feel in her bones.

The pearl earrings her mother had given her felt heavy, each one a sphere of reproach, a reminder of all the lessons she had ignored. "A lady always knows her worth," her mother used to say, adjusting these earrings in the mirror. The memory was so vivid, so real, that for a moment Maddie could almost feel her mother's fingers brushing against her ear, could almost hear the gentle clink of the pearls as they settled into place.

"I gave him everything," she said, her voice harder now, edged with steel. "My youth. My best years. I waited through deployments, through wars, through the deafening silence of his absence. I shaped myself into the officer's wife, always poised, always understanding, always there with a smile and never a complaint. And for what? To be replaced by some young, vapid princess who hasn't earned the right to wear my crown? Who plays at being sophisticated but wouldn't know true breeding if it slapped her across her botoxed face?" The words tasted bitter on her tongue, the anger rising up from some deep, primal place within her, a place she had long kept hidden beneath layers of propriety and grace.

The wind picked up, tugging at strands of her styled hair like mischievous fingers. She tucked them back into place with steady hands, refusing to let even nature disrupt her maintained composure. Control was everything—her mother had taught her that, if nothing else. It was the one thing she could cling to, the one thing that kept her from shattering into a million jagged pieces.

"For him to come back and forget me?" Her jaw tightened, the pain in her chest hardening into something sharper, something that felt dangerously like purpose. "To act as if I'm nothing more than a relic of his past? Some embarrassing first draft he can file away and forget?" The indignity of it all was staggering, the realization that she had sacrificed so much, had given so freely of herself, only to be discarded like yesterday's news.

She shook her head, forcing her breathing to even out, determined to regain control over her emotions. The familiar mask slipped back into place, comfortable as an old glove. It was a mask she had worn for so long, a mask that had become almost indistinguishable from her true face. After a long moment, she leaned in close to the headstone, her voice inaudible even to her own ears, a secret between mother and daughter.

"You always told me—never let them see you lose. Never let them see you break. And I won't, Mother. I promise you that." The words were a vow, a sacred oath sworn on the grave of the one person who had truly understood her, who had seen the steel beneath the silk.

Rising smoothly to her feet, she adjusted her coat and dusted off her gloves, ensuring every detail of her appearance was in its proper place. The moment of weakness had passed, replaced by something colder, more focused. A sense of clarity washed over her, a certainty that she had not felt in years. She cast one final glance at the headstone before turning and striding purposefully toward her waiting car, her heels clicking against the stone path with each resolute step. Each click felt like a countdown, though to what, she wasn't quite sure yet. But one thing was certain—Madeline Callahan was not a woman to be trifled with, and heaven help anyone who dared.

Chapter 8

The antique desk lamp cast a warm circle of light across Maddie's mahogany desk, leaving the rest of her study in shadow. Mother's words from the cemetery echoed, sharp and clear as the day they were spoken: Never let them see you break. How many times had those words saved her? Guided her? Made her stronger when everything threatened to crumble?

The weight of that warning settled over her like a familiar cloak as she pulled out her personal stationery.

Thick cream paper with a subtle watermark—the kind reserved for formal correspondence with ambassadors' wives and thank-you notes after charity galas. (Not that there had been many of those. The invitations had slowed to a trickle since Jackson's announcement. As if divorce were contagious.)

Her fingers traced the edge of the paper, feeling its substantial weight. Quality always spoke volumes, didn't it? Even now, especially now, she wouldn't lower her standards. That's what they'd expect—for her to crumble, to become less than what she was. Like poor Sandra after her divorce, showing up to lunch in last season's Nordstrom dress, roots showing beneath badly maintained highlights.

The Mont Blanc fountain pen felt satisfyingly heavy in her hand as she uncapped it. Jackson had given it to her on their fifteenth anniversary, back when he still remembered the proper way to celebrate milestones. Back when he still remembered her. Dark ink flowed onto the pristine surface in, measured strokes, each letter formed with the precision she'd learned at finishing school. Her penmanship revealed nothing of the ice in her veins, nothing of the way her hand wanted to shake with fury.

Leave my husband alone. This is your only warning.

Nine words. Simple. Direct. The threat clear yet wrapped in civility, like poison in a crystal glass. Like the way Charlotte could destroy someone's reputation with nothing more than a raised eyebrow and a worded concern about their children's education choices. Maddie studied the message, satisfaction curling through her chest at its elegant menace. No signature needed—

Lillian would know. (Sweet, young Lillian with her skin and her yoga-toned body, who thought she could just walk in and take what belonged to someone else.)

The not-knowing would eat at her more than any signed name ever could. Let her wonder. Let her lie awake at night, questioning every shadow, every unexpected sound. Let her feel what it was like to have her world start to crack.

Maddie lifted the paper, examining it in the lamplight. No smudges, no hesitation marks. She folded it with crisp, exact corners, each crease sharp enough to cut. The precision of her movements brought a sense of calm, a momentary respite from the chaos swirling in her mind. This letter was more than words on a page—it was a declaration of war, a promise of retribution.

The envelope sat ready, equally unmarked. She could almost see Lillian's face when she opened it, that maintained expression of innocence faltering. Would she tell Jackson? (Of course she would. She was the type to run crying to him.) But what could he do? There would be no proof, no signature, nothing but Lillian's growing paranoia to suggest Maddie had anything to do with it.

She slid the letter inside, her movements deliberate and controlled. For a heartbeat, her finger rested on the unsealed flap. One second of pause—not doubt, never doubt—before she pressed it closed with firm, manicured fingers. The seal was a final commitment, a point of no return. Maddie felt a flicker of something dark and dangerous stirring within her, a hunger for the destruction to come. After all, hadn't she learned from the best? Hadn't Mother always said that sometimes you had to break things to fix them?

(And if they couldn't be fixed? Well, then they

deserved to stay broken.)

Maddie lifted the Wedgwood teacup to her lips, savoring the temperature of her morning coffee. Every detail mattered—the crisp line of her silk blouse, the way sunlight her diamond tennis bracelet, even the precise angle of her chair at the breakfast table. These small perfections were her armor, her way of maintaining control in a world that seemed determined to slip through her fingers. The envelope sat beside her plate, its cream surface unblemished, a silent harbinger of the storm brewing on the horizon.

Rosa's footsteps silent across the marble floor, bringing with them the scent of fresh croissants. The housekeeper set down a silver breakfast tray with practiced care, each movement as familiar as the morning itself. Twenty years of the same routine had trained her well. But beneath the veneer of normalcy, Maddie sensed a shift, a subtle unease that permeated the air like the faintest hint of smoke.

Maddie's fingers drifted to the envelope. The paper made a soft sound as it slid across the polished mahogany. "I need this delivered," she said, her voice light and casual as she adjusted her napkin. The words were simple, but the implications were anything but. This was not a request—it was a command, a test of loyalty in a game where the stakes grew higher with each passing day.

Rosa's hand stopped mid-reach for the coffee pot. Just a fraction of a second, but Maddie it—that slight hesitation, that perceptible shift in the morning's rhythm. In that moment, Maddie saw the truth in Rosa's eyes, the unspoken questions, the flicker of fear. The housekeeper knew, perhaps better than anyone, the depths of Maddie's obsession, the lengths to which she would go to maintain her grip on the life she had built. And as their eyes met across the breakfast table, Maddie felt a cold smile tug at the corners of her lips, a silent warning that hung in the air between them.

"Where to, Mrs. Callahan?"

Maddie looked up then, looked at Rosa for the first time that morning. Their eyes met, and Maddie let the silence stretch between them, heavy with unspoken understanding. Twenty years of service meant Rosa knew when questions weren't welcome. When certain tasks required discretion.

"It doesn't matter," Maddie said, her tone carrying the weight of an order beneath its casual surface. "Just make sure it gets to her."

Maddie watched through her car window as the young woman's morning unfolded as predicted. Lillian emerged onto her balcony in silk pajamas, green smoothie in hand, phone already glued to her manicured fingers. Like clockwork.

Maddie watched Lillian from across the street, her Mercedes providing the cover for surveillance. The leather seats cradled her like an old friend as she observed the younger woman's morning routine unfold with clockwork precision. (How many mornings had she spent studying Lillian's habits, learning her rhythms, waiting for the moment?)

The doorman appeared right on schedule, armed with Lillian's mail. Maddie's pulse quickened as she watched those manicured fingers (probably fresh from yesterday's salon appointment) sort through the stack with practiced indifference. Bills, magazines, junk mail— until they found it. The cream envelope. Maddie's little gift, delivered with surgical timing.

The transformation was exquisite. Like watching a butterfly in a spider's web, Lillian's movements became jerky, uncertain. Her green smoothie—that Instagram-worthy concoction she posted about every morning—lowered slowly to the balcony rail, forgotten. Her shoulders, usually so relaxed in that affected casual way that probably took years to, went rigid. Once, twice, three times she read the message. Each pass drained more color from that flawless complexion Jackson so adored.

A car horn shattered the moment, and Lillian startled like a spooked deer. Maddie sank deeper into her seat, satisfaction blooming warm and rich in her chest as she watched fear settle over the younger woman., it was almost too easy. The pretty ones always thought themselves untouchable until someone came along to prove otherwise.

Right on cue, Lillian's phone buzzed. Jackson, of course—he was nothing if not predictable in his morning check-ins with his precious "Princess." (How that nickname made Maddie's teeth ache. As if Jackson had invented pet names just for her.) Lillian stared at the screen, her thumb hovering indecisively. Not so confident now, was she? Not when reality was creeping in around the edges of her fairy tale.

"What will you do, little girl?" Maddie said, savoring each word like fine wine. "Run to Jackson? Or realize you're in over your head?"

Hours later, seated at her vanity, Maddie drew the silver-backed brush through her chestnut hair with methodical precision. One hundred strokes, just as her mother had taught her. Ninety-eight, ninety-nine, one hundred. The ritual soothed her, each stroke a quiet victory.

She imagined Lillian now, probably pacing her tastefully decorated apartment, jumping at every shadow. The letter would be crumpled somewhere visible—Lillian wouldn't be able to bring herself to throw it away, but wouldn't want it out of sight either. The words Maddie had chosen so would be burning themselves into the younger woman's brain, poisoning every moment of her picture- day.

The vanity's marble top was cool beneath Maddie's fingertips as she stared at her silent phone. Part of her hoped it would ring—Jackson, perhaps, his voice tight with contained rage. Or better yet, Lillian herself, trying to sound brave while terror trembled beneath each word. But the phone remained quiet, and that was fine too. Sometimes silence was the sweetest response of all.

After weeks of watching Jackson's slow withdrawal—the way his eyes slid past her at breakfast, how he angled himself away from her in every room as if she were toxic—this small act of revenge felt like coming up for air after drowning. Let Lillian feel what it was like to lose her footing, to question every shadow. Let her taste the bitter medicine of uncertainty that had been Maddie's daily bread these past months.

A smile curved Maddie's lips as she set down her brush, admiring her reflection. In the quiet of her bedroom, she could almost hear Lillian's panicked breathing, could see those fingers trembling as they dialed and redialed Jackson's number. The younger woman would learn, as everyone eventually did, that trying to replace Maddie Callahan came with consequences. Steep ones.

And this? This was only the beginning.

Had Lillian shown the letter to Jackson yet? Were they huddled together now, trying to decipher Maddie's intentions? Or was Lillian hiding it, too afraid to admit that Maddie had found a chink in her armor? The possibilities swirled in Maddie's mind, each one more tantalizing than the last.

She studied her reflection in the mirror—the face that had captivated Jackson all those years ago. Time had only sharpened her features, honing them into weapons of precision and grace. She traced the line of her jaw, her touch a poor substitute for the caress of Jackson's fingers. But those days were gone, stolen by a blonde interloper with a sweet smile and an empty head.

The clock's steady ticking filled the room, a metronome marking the passage of time. Each second brought Maddie closer to her goal, to the moment when Lillian would realize just how gravely she had miscalculated. Would the girl crumble under the weight of her fear, or would she try to maintain a facade of bravery? Either way, Maddie would savor the victory, would revel in the knowledge that she alone held the power.

Eighty strokes, then ninety, then a hundred. The brush moved through her hair in a soothing rhythm, a counterpoint to the anticipation thrumming through her veins. This was just the beginning, a mere taste of what was to come. Maddie had patience in spades, and she would use every ounce of it to ensure that Lillian paid for her sins. One way or another, the girl would learn the price of crossing Madeline Callahan.

She set the brush down on the vanity, studying her reflection with a critical eye. Not a hair out of place, her makeup flawless, the picture of a woman in control. But beneath the polished exterior, a storm was brewing, a tempest of rage and betrayal that threatened to consume everything in its path. Lillian thought she could steal what was rightfully Maddie's, thought she could waltz into their lives and tear apart a decades-long marriage without consequence. Oh, how wrong she was. Maddie would make sure of that.

Chapter 9

Maddie's fingers trailed over the pristine rows of designer shoes; each pair aligned on illuminated glass shelves. The walk-in closet had always been her sanctuary—a testament to two decades of careful curation, each piece selected with the same precision she applied to everything in her life. She paused at a pair of Louboutins, their red soles gleaming like fresh blood under the recessed lighting. Jackson had given her these on their fifteenth anniversary, back when he still remembered the importance of such occasions—back when he still saw her.

"Carrie, sweetheart?" She called out, her voice soft and inviting—the voice she used when she wanted to be loved, when she needed to be reminded that someone still looked at her with pure adoration. "Come help Mommy choose her accessories for dinner."

The dinner where she would see him again—where she would sit across from Jackson and that child he called 'Princess.' And she would need to be precise. More than precise. Devastating

Carrie appeared in the doorway; her small frame dwarfed by the vast expanse of organized luxury. Her blue eyes widened at the sight of the jewelry cabinet Maddie was opening—rows of sparkling diamonds and pearls catching the light. Such a precious thing, her daughter. So innocent. So trusting. So unlike Nate, who watched everything these days with those knowing eyes of his.

"These were from your father," Maddie said, lifting a strand of South Sea pearls. She remembered the moment he'd given them to her, how his hands had fastened them around her neck in that hotel room in Tokyo. How he'd said that no one wore them quite like her. "He bought them in Japan before you were born. Would you like to try them on?"

She watched her daughter's face light up, savoring the moment. These days, she collected such moments like the precious gems in her cabinet—storing them away, hoarding them against the darkness she could feel creeping in at the edges of her constructed world. Something inside her warned that she should be careful, that using Carrie like this wasn't right—but she silenced that voice. After all, hadn't Jackson used them all? Hadn't he discarded twenty years of marriage, of memories, of aligned shoes and chosen jewelry, for something newer, something younger?

Maddie's hand tightened—almost imperceptibly—around the pearl strand. Almost. She was always careful about such things. Control was everything. She had spent too many years training her mask to let it slip now. Besides, she thought, watching Carrie's delicate fingers reach for the pearls, sometimes the most effective weapons were the ones wrapped in beauty.

She would wear the pearls tonight. And maybe— just maybe—when Jackson saw them around her neck, he would remember. And if he didn't... well, Maddie had other plans. She always did.

"Here, angel," she said, bending down to Carrie's level. "Let Mommy show you how to wear them properly. Everything is in the details, you know. That's what makes a woman unforgettable."

And Maddie Callahan had no intention of being forgotten. Not by Jackson. Not by anyone.

Carrie stepped closer, drawn by the gentle weight of the pearls as Maddie draped them around her daughter's neck. The pearls looked over-sized against Carrie's delicate collarbones, but Maddie smiled at their reflection in the full-length mirror.

"Beautiful," Maddie said, running her fingers through Carrie's soft blonde hair. "You'll have all of these someday, angel. Everything in here will be yours."

She turned to the neatly folded Hermès scarves, each arranged with military precision. "Which color should Mommy wear tonight? The rouge or the navy?"

"The red one," Carrie said, still mesmerized by the

pearls at her throat.

"Choice." Maddie selected the scarf, letting the silk slip between her fingers. "You have excellent taste, just like your mother. We'll go shopping together soon—would you like that? Just us girls?"

Carrie nodded, leaning into Maddie's side as they stood before the mirror, two reflections merged into one image.

Maddie watched her daughter's reflection, savoring how Carrie's small fingers traced the pearls with such reverence. This was what she'd always wanted—these precious moments of connection, of passing down the careful cultivation of beauty to the next generation. Jackson might be slipping away, but Carrie was still purely hers.

"Would you like to see something special?" Maddie reached into the jewelry cabinet's bottom drawer, pulling out a velvet box she rarely opened. Inside lay a delicate gold bracelet with a single diamond charm. "This was my first piece of real jewelry. My mother gave it to me when I was just about your age."

Carrie's eyes lit up. "?"

"Here, try it on." Maddie clasped it around Carrie's thin wrist, adjusting it so the diamond the light. Her daughter's complete trust, the way she stood so still and patient, filled Maddie with a fierce pride. Unlike Nate, who'd grown distant and watchful, Carrie still believed in the perfection of their world.

"It's pretty," Carrie said, turning her wrist to make the diamond sparkle.

"You can wear it to dinner tonight." Maddie smoothed Carrie's hair, noting how her daughter leaned into the touch like a flower seeking sunlight. "We'll dress up together, just us girls. Would you like that?"

Carrie nodded eagerly, still admiring the bracelet. This was how it should be—mother and daughter, sharing the secrets of presenting oneself to the world. Maddie saw none of Jackson's growing coldness reflected in Carrie's warm response, no hint of suspicion or fear. Just pure, innocent joy at being included in her mother's sacred space.

Maddie unclasped the pearls from Carrie's neck, returning them to their velvet bed. Her fingers lingered on the cool stones for a moment before she turned back to her daughter.

"You know, sweetheart, Mommy used to wear every time your father came home from deployment." She kept her voice light, conversational. "He'd walk through that door, and his eyes would light up seeing me in them."

Carrie twisted the gold bracelet on her wrist. "Did Daddy give you lots of presents?"

"He did. Though..." Maddie paused, arranging a Hermès scarf with deliberate care. "Well, I suppose he's been quite busy since coming back from Dubai. Have you had much time with him, angel?"

"Not." Carrie's small shoulders drooped. "He's always on his phone now."

Maddie nodded, watching her daughter's reflection in the mirror. "I've noticed that too. Have you noticed anything else different about Daddy since Dubai? The way he acts, perhaps?"

"He doesn't eat breakfast with us anymore," Carrie said quietly. "And he missed my dance recital last week."

"Did he?" Maddie's voice remained neutral as she selected another scarf. "That doesn't sound like the

Daddy we used to know, does it?"

Carrie shook her head, her fingers still playing with the bracelet. The diamond the light, throwing tiny rainbows across her face.

"Daddy's just busy with work," Carrie said, her chin lifting with childish certainty. "He told me he has lots of important meetings."

Maddie kept her face neutral as she adjusted the bracelet on Carrie's wrist. Inside, a familiar anger coiled tight in her chest—Jackson using the same excuses with their daughter that he'd used with her for years. But she wouldn't let it show. Not here. Not now.

"Of course, angel." Maddie smoothed an imaginary wrinkle from her silk blouse. "Your father has always been dedicated to his work."

She let the silence stretch, watching Carrie's reflection in the mirror. The girl's fingers twisted the bracelet, around and around, the diamond catching the light with each turn. The quiet seemed to weigh on her daughter, and Maddie could see the certainty in Carrie's expression beginning to crack.

"He promised to come to my next recital," Carrie added, but her voice had lost some of its conviction. Her eyes dropped to the bracelet, no longer meeting Maddie's gaze in the mirror.

Maddie nodded, letting another careful pause fill the space between them. She could feel Carrie shifting beside her, uncomfortable with the silence, with the unspoken questions it raised. Just as she'd planned.

"The meetings must be important," Carrie said, but this time it sounded more like a question than a statement.

Maddie kept quiet, pretending to be absorbed in

organizing her scarves while she watched her daughter's reflection. The seed of doubt had been planted. She didn't need to say anything more—Carrie would do the work herself, just as Maddie had done all those years ago when she first suspected Jackson's betrayals.

Maddie adjusted the pearls back into their velvet bed, her thoughts drifting to the first time Jackson had given them to her. She'd been so young then, standing in their first apartment near the base, believing every promise he'd made.

"You know, Carrie," she said, keeping her voice soft and dreamy, "your father used to write me the most beautiful letters when he was deployed. He'd tell me how he counted the days until he could come home to me."

She traced the edge of the jewelry box, remembering the way she'd waited by the mailbox each morning, how her heart would leap at the sight of his handwriting.

"He always said family came first. That no matter where the military sent him, his heart stayed with us." Maddie smiled at Carrie's reflection, though her chest ached with the memory. "He promised me that once he made General, things would be different. We'd have more time together."

Carrie played with the bracelet, hanging on every word. "Did he keep his promise?"

"Well..." Maddie paused, letting her daughter fill the silence with her own conclusions. "Your father had choices, angel. Every officer does. Some choose to stay close to home, to make time for ballet recitals and family dinners."

She lifted another necklace, this one a delicate diamond pendant. "Remember last Christmas? When he said he'd be home for the holidays, but then decided to take that consulting job in Dubai instead?"

The word 'decided' hung in the air between them. Maddie watched Carrie process this, seeing the subtle shift in her daughter's expression as she began to understand that her father's absences weren't always unavoidable.

"But he said it was important," Carrie said, though uncertainty crept into her voice.

"Of course he did, sweetheart." Maddie stroked her daughter's hair. "Everything is always important to your father. Though sometimes I wonder what could be more important than watching his little girl dance."

Maddie watched as Carrie's small hands dropped away from the designer shoes she'd been admiring. Her daughter's shoulders tensed, and the light that had danced in her eyes moments ago dimmed. The transformation hit Maddie like a physical blow—her little girl, seeing the cracks in their maintained facade.

"Well, yeah, I guess he doesn't seem like he's here, but that's just how Dad is." Carrie's voice wavered. She glanced up at the rows of pristine shoes, but this time without the wonder she'd shown before.

Maddie's heart clenched. She recognized that tone, that slight hesitation—she'd heard it in her own voice years ago, when she'd first started questioning Jackson's absences. But she kept her face neutral, allowing only the faintest hint of sympathy to show in her eyes as she watched her daughter process this new reality.

Carrie twisted the gold bracelet on her wrist again, but the movement was different now—less playful admiration, more nervous energy. The diamond the light, but Carrie didn't seem to notice its sparkle anymore. Her brow furrowed in thought, creating tiny lines that reminded Maddie so much of herself.

Maddie could see the wheels turning in Carrie's mind, could trace the path of her daughter's thoughts as they wandered down the same dark corridors, she herself had explored. The careful construction of their world was beginning to show its seams, and Carrie was starting to notice the loose threads.

Maddie knelt before her daughter, adjusting the gold bracelet one final time. The diamond sparkled, but Carrie's eyes had lost their earlier shine. She cupped her daughter's face between her palms, drinking in those familiar features—so much like looking in a mirror from decades past.

"No matter what happens, sweetheart, we have to stick together. You and Nate and me." Maddie's voice was gentle but firm, her thumbs stroking Carrie's cheeks. "That's what family does."

She searched her daughter's expression, noting the subtle shifts—the slight downturn of her mouth, the way her gaze dropped to the floor. Carrie nodded, but remained silent. The enthusiasm from earlier had evaporated, replaced by something more contemplative, more uncertain.

Maddie stood, smoothing her silk blouse. She'd planted the seed—now she'd let it grow. No need to force it, to push too hard. Carrie would think about their conversation, about Jackson's absences, about all those missed moments. She'd draw her own conclusions.

"Why don't you go try on that new dress I bought you?" Maddie suggested, giving Carrie space to retreat.

"The blue one with the ribbon sash."

Carrie nodded again, her fingers still absently playing with the bracelet as she turned toward the door. She paused at the threshold, glancing back at the rows of pristine shoes and arranged scarves, but said nothing before disappearing into the hallway.

Maddie watched her go, noting how her daughter's shoulders had slumped ever so. The posture she'd praised just minutes ago had crumbled under the weight of new doubts. Just as planned.

Chapter 10

Maddie's heels clicked against the hardwood as she entered Jackson's office, her silk dress a splash of feminine color against the stark military precision of the room. Everything about this space screamed control—the aligned books, the arranged medals in their glass case, the desk positioned for maximum authority.

She ran her finger along the edge of his desk, noting there wasn't a speck of dust. Rosa knew better than to neglect any room, even those Jackson no longer used.

The leather chair still held his shape, though he spent more time at his "satellite office" these days. Her lip curled at the thought.

His degrees and commendations lined the walls like soldiers standing at attention. Each frame hung parallel to the floor; each achievement spaced with mathematical precision. A large map of the Middle East dominated one wall, dotted with pins marking his deployments. Twenty-five years of service mapped out in tiny red dots, each one representing a month she'd spent alone.

The room smelled of leather and that sandalwood cologne he'd started wearing after Dubai. (After that business trip where everything changed—though he probably thought she hadn't noticed.) Maddie's fingers tightened on the brass handle of his desk drawer, cool and unyielding beneath her touch. Inside, everything reflected Jackson's obsessive need for control—files labeled and color-coded, pens arranged by type like little soldiers awaiting inspection. No personal touches, no family photos. Nothing to suggest the man who worked here had children or a wife of twenty-five years waiting at home. Then again, that was like Jackson, wasn't it? Compartmentalizing his life into neat little boxes that never quite fit together.

She noticed a legal pad, half-hidden under some papers, like a secret trying not to be found. Jackson's precise handwriting filled the page with what looked like meeting notes, each letter formed with that military precision she used to find so impressive. (Back when she believed his discipline signified stability, not rigidity.) But between the lines about defense contracts and quarterly projections, she a glimpse of something else—a doodle of a lily in the margin. Just a simple flower. Amazing how such a small thing could feel like a knife between the ribs.

Her chest tightened, the careful composure she had maintained during her conversation with Carrie cracking like fine china dropped on marble. She gripped the edge of the desk, her manicured nails pressing into the polished wood until she thought they might snap. The contrast struck her—her soft pink nails contrasted against the unyielding surface, her delicate perfume mingling with his cologne, her reflection fractured in the dark window glass.

How fitting. She was becoming a ghost in her own home, wasn't she? Fading a little more each day while he drew his little lilies and dreamed of spring.

Maddie closed Jackson's office door behind her with deliberate softness, though the sound still echoed through the hallway like an accusation. Her hands trembled from discovering that lily doodle—such a small thing to break her composure. (But wasn't that how it always worked? The smallest cuts bled the longest.) She needed to focus on her next task—Nate. Her clever, observant boy who saw too much and said too little.

His bedroom door stood ajar, a slice of warm light spilling into the hallway. Through the gap, she watched him hunched over his desk, pencil moving across paper with the same precise movements as his father. Math homework, from the looks of it. The sharp angles of his shoulders reminded her too much of Jackson. (Was this what genetic memory looked like? This echo of a man who was there anymore?)

"Nathaniel?" She pushed the door open wider, letting her presence fill the space.

He didn't look up, so like his father in his studied

indifference. "I'm doing algebra."

"That can wait. We need to talk." The words came out softer than she intended, almost pleading. When had she started pleading with her own children?

"I have a test tomorrow." His pencil kept moving, scratching against the paper like a metronome counting down her patience.

Maddie crossed the room, her Chanel No. 5 cutting through the boy's space that smelled of pencil shavings and old books—such a pure, innocent smell. She perched on the edge of his bed, arranging herself. "Your father's been different since Dubai, hasn't he?" A careful probe, testing the waters.

"He's always different." Nate's jaw tightened, just like Jackson's did when he was annoyed. (God, would she never escape these little mirrors of him?) "Can I finish this problem?"

"Don't you want to know why he's changed?" She kept her voice gentle, coaxing. The voice she used to use when he was small and afraid of thunderstorms.

"Not." He looked up, his hazel eyes sharp and assessing in a way no children should be. "Mom, I know what you're doing. You did it with Carrie earlier."

The direct challenge her off guard, a slap of cold water to the face. She hadn't expected him to be so... aware. When had her little boy grown so perceptive? (And why did it feel like a betrayal?)

"I heard you in her room," he continued, wielding truth like a weapon. "Telling her about Dad missing her recital. Making her sad about him."

Maddie's fingers dug into the bedspread, twisting expensive Egyptian cotton between manicured nails. This wasn't going according to plan. Her careful choreography was falling apart. "I'm just trying to help you understand—"

"No, you're not." He turned back to his homework, dismissing her as effectively as Jackson ever had. "You're trying to make us pick sides. I don't want to play that game."

Maddie studied Nate's profile, the way his brow furrowed in concentration. Her fingers smoothed invisible wrinkles from her silk dress, a nervous habit she thought she'd broken years ago. "You look just like your father when you work."

The pencil paused for a fraction of a second. A subtle tell, but she it. (She'd spent twenty-five years learning to read these little signs, after all.) She let the silence stretch between them, watching his shoulders tense under the weight of her words. Sometimes the heaviest blows were the ones you never saw coming.

Nate's jaw tightened. His eraser skidded across the page, breaking clean in half. "What are you saying?"

"Have you noticed how much he's been traveling?" Maddie kept her voice light, casual. She traced the pattern on his bedspread with one manicured nail. "Three trips to Atlanta this month alone."

His pencil pressed harder into the paper. The lead snapped.

"I suppose it's just strange that he never used to be this busy." She tilted her head, watching his reflection in his desk mirror. "Even during active duty, he managed to call more often."

Nate reached for his pencil sharpener, his movements precise and controlled—so much like Jackson it made her chest ache. But where Jackson's control came from years of military discipline, Nate's came from something else. Something that looked almost like fear.

Maddie watched her son's reflection, noting how his shoulders hunched forward protectively. Everything about him reminded her of Jackson—the way he held himself, the sharp intelligence in his eyes. But there was something softer there too, something vulnerable that Jackson had lost long ago.

"Your father's been spending a lot of time in Atlanta," she said, keeping her voice neutral.

"He's a general now, Mom. What do you expect?" Nate's words came out sharp, defensive. He grabbed another pencil from his desk, still not turning to face her.

Maddie let the silence stretch, studying her son's reflection in the mirror. She arched one groomed eyebrow, waiting. The technique had worked countless times with Jackson in their early years—sometimes silence said more than words.

Nate's pencil stilled over his algebra homework. His eyes flickered to her reflection, then away. "He has important meetings and stuff."

"Mm." Maddie smoothed an invisible wrinkle from her silk dress. She didn't contradict him, didn't point out how Jackson's "important meetings" never required this much travel before. Instead, she let her skepticism show in the slight tilt of her head, the knowing look in her eyes.

The pencil in Nate's hand tapped against the desk—once, twice. His certainty wavered, just as she knew it would. "Right?"

"Of course, darling." Maddie's voice was honey-sweet, but her eyes in the mirror held his. "Though it is curious how he managed to call more often during actual wars than he does now."

Nate's jaw clenched. He looked down at his homework, but Maddie could tell he wasn't seeing the numbers anymore. The seed of doubt had been planted, just as she intended.

Maddie shifted on the edge of Nate's bed, letting her shoulders drop. She didn't need to maintain posture here—not when she was about to share something that pained her as a mother.

"Your sister drew a picture yesterday," she said, her voice soft. "A family portrait. She put your father so far in the corner, I almost missed him at first."

Nate's pencil stopped moving. His reflection in the mirror showed the slight furrow in his brow, the way his mouth tightened at the corners.

"She asked me why he doesn't read to her anymore." Maddie smoothed her silk dress, hiding the tremor in her hands. "Remember how he used to do all the voices in those fairy tales? She loved that."

The pencil snapped in Nate's grip. He set the broken pieces down, —just like Jackson would.

"Yesterday, she wanted to show him her new dance routine. The one she's been practicing for weeks." Maddie watched Nate's reflection. "He was too busy on his phone to watch. She practiced it three times, hoping he'd look up."

Nate's shoulders tensed. His protective instinct for Carrie had always been strong—stronger than his loyalty to Jackson, stronger even than his resistance to Maddie's influence.

"She misses him, you know." Maddie's voice dropped lower, intimate. "She asked me the other day if he's even happy to be home."

Nate turned in his chair then, meeting her eyes directly instead of through the mirror. The hurt in his expression was raw, unguarded. Carrie had always been his weak spot, the one thing that could crack his careful defenses.

"What did you tell her?" His voice came out rough.

"What could I tell her?" Maddie spread her hands helplessly. "How do you explain to an eight-year-old that her father's attention is somewhere else now?"

Maddie watched the emotions play across Nate's face—doubt, hurt, anger. His features shifted between Jackson's hard angles and something softer, more vulnerable. More manipulable.

His pencil lay forgotten on the desk now, the broken pieces a metaphor for his crumbling certainty. She could see his mind working, processing all the small details she'd planted: the missed dance recital, the constant phone checks, the Atlanta trips.

"Are you saying..." Nate's voice. He swallowed hard, tried again. "Are you saying he's cheating?"

The question hung in the air between them. Maddie kept her expression neutral, letting her eyes fill with just enough sadness to be believable. She smoothed her silk dress again, buying time, making the moment stretch.

"I don't know, sweetheart." She let her voice catch. "I just know he's been lying."

The words landed as she intended. Nate's shoulders slumped, his defenses cracking. He looked younger suddenly, more like the little boy who used to wait by the window for Jackson to come home from deployment.

Maddie watched the truth settle over him like a shadow. She didn't need to say more—the seed was planted. Sometimes silence was the sharpest weapon of all.

Maddie shifted on the bed, letting concern soften her features. "Your father told me he was confined to Al Dhafra base during his deployment." She kept her voice gentle, maternal. "But Greg Lowry saw him at the Four Seasons in Dubai."

Nate's eyes narrowed, that sharp intelligence she both loved and feared flickering across his face. She watched him process this information, seeing the same analytical mind that made Jackson such a brilliant strategist at work in their son.

"You're smart, Nate. You notice things." She smoothed her dress, a practiced gesture of composure. "Don't you think it's strange? The way his stories don't quite add up?"

His fingers found a pencil shaving on his desk, turning it over and over. "He said the base had strict protocols."

"That's what he told me too." Maddie nodded; her voice warm with understanding. "But then I saw the hotel charges. The restaurants. Places that were nowhere near the base."

Nate's hand stilled. "Maybe it was work stuff."

"Of course, darling." She paused, letting him hear the doubt in her voice. "Though I don't remember his work requiring so many visits to luxury hotels before."

The pencil shaving crumbled in his fingers. Maddie watched his reflection in the mirror, seeing the exact moment his certainty began to crack. He had

Jackson's mind for strategy—he could see the pattern forming, even if he didn't want to acknowledge it yet.

"Your father always said military life was about precision, about everything being where it should be." She kept her tone thoughtful, patient. "But things aren't adding up, are they?"

Nate's laptop closed with a sharp snap that echoed through the room. Maddie watched his hands tremble as they rested on the computer's surface. Her words had hit their mark.

"I have homework." His voice came out flat, controlled— like Jackson when he wanted to end a conversation. "I should go to the library."

Maddie smoothed her silk dress, satisfaction warming her chest. She didn't press further. The seed was planted; pushing now would only make him defensive. Sometimes victory looked like retreat.

"Of course, darling." She kept her voice gentle, maternal. "You know I'm here if you want to talk more."

Nate gathered his books and laptop, his movements precise but rushed. He didn't look at her as he stood, didn't acknowledge her words. But he didn't argue either. Didn't try to defend Jackson. The silence spoke volumes.

She watched him leave, noting how his shoulders hunched forward —a physical tell of emotional burden. The door closed behind him with a soft click.

Maddie remained perched on the edge of his bed, savoring the moment. He would think about their conversation later, when he was alone. The doubts she'd planted would grow in the quiet moments, taking root in his mind just as they had in Carrie's.

Her fingers traced the pattern on his bedspread,

remembering how he used to curl up here while waiting for Jackson's calls during deployments. Those memories would work against Jackson now, highlighting the contrast between then and now.

◆ ◆ ◆

Maddie lifted her glass of sparkling water, the cool condensation slick against her fingers, as she sat across from Charlotte at their usual table at Le Petit Jardin. The restaurant hummed with the soft clink of silverware, polite laughter, and whispered gossip—a well-orchestrated symphony of their world.

Charlotte was in full swing, recounting the latest scandal involving the Wilsons when, as if in passing, she dropped a casual grenade onto the table.

"And then," Charlotte leaned in, eyes bright, "you'll never guess who I saw at Maison Belle last Thursday. Lillian Hart."

Maddie's grip on her glass didn't falter, but in her mind, the words hit like a thunderclap. Maison Belle. Last Thursday. The same day. The note.

She let out a soft hmm, tilting her head with measured curiosity. Not too interested. Not too disinterested. "Lillian shops there?" Her voice was just surprised enough. "I wouldn't have thought that was her style."

Charlotte, unaware she had wandered into dangerous territory, twirled the stem of her Chardonnay glass between manicured fingers. "Oh yes. And here's the strangest part—a note was found in her shopping bag that same day." She leaned in conspiratorially. "Can you believe it?"

Maddie took a slow sip of water, letting the weight of the words settle without reacting. Instead, she kept her gaze trained on Charlotte, studying her. Was this a careless remark? Or was Charlotte testing her?

That was the real question.

, she set down her glass with deliberate care. "Strange," she mused, offering a knowing little smile. "People should be more careful with their personal belongings."

Charlotte chuckled, shaking her head. "I know, right? But I wonder what kind of person would leave a note like that."

A test. Maddie recognized it now. She let a beat of silence stretch, just long enough to make Charlotte notice, before tilting her head ever so.

"Perhaps someone who doesn't appreciate having their secrets exposed."

It was said lightly—so lightly it could have been a joke. Could have been anything. But the shift in Charlotte's posture was immediate. A slight freeze in her fingers. A fractional pause before her next breath. She felt it. Even if she didn't understand why, she felt the shift in the air.

Maddie's lips curled in the softest hint of amusement, watching as Charlotte quickly recovered—too quickly. A forced little laugh. Good. That meant she was thinking about it.

Before Charlotte could regain control of the conversation, Maddie leaned back, switching gears effortlessly. "Anyway, I've been meaning to ask—have you decided on a caterer for your garden party next month? I hear Bon Appétit is wonderful this time of year."

Charlotte blinked, then exhaled—grateful for the change in subject. "Oh yes, I've heard good things about them too."

Maddie nodded along as Charlotte launched into menu options, but beneath the surface, she was still assessing. Charlotte had hesitated. That hesitation meant she was questioning herself.

Which meant Maddie was still in control.

She stirred her water with her straw, expression serene, but her mind was already working ahead. She would have to watch Charlotte more closely now. The woman wasn't as easy to manipulate as Sandra or Barbara.

And that meant Maddie might need to remind her, in the most delicate way possible, why some things were better left unsaid.

Chapter 11

Maddie settled at her mahogany desk, smoothing the cream-colored Crane & Co stationery before her. The paper's weight felt substantial between her fingers—expensive, formal, the kind used for wedding invitations and diplomatic correspondence. She'd selected it specifically for this purpose, just as she selected everything in her life with meticulous attention to detail. The texture reminded her of her own wedding invitations, twenty-eight years ago. How fitting. She ran her fingertip along the edge, remembering how Jackson had smiled when she'd shown him the sample. He'd called her particular then, but he'd meant it as a compliment. Everything had been a compliment back then.

Her Mont Blanc fountain pen glided across the surface. The ink flowed in cursive strokes: "He's not yours to keep." Simple. Direct. The threat lay in its certainty rather than its specifics. The words felt delicious in her mind, like dark chocolate melting on her tongue. She could almost taste the fear they would inspire.

She examined each letter, ensuring her handwriting bore no resemblance to her usual elegant script. The message needed to feel anonymous yet purposeful. Not a random act, but a calculated warning. She'd practiced this altered handwriting for weeks, repeating every curve and angle until it felt natural yet foreign. Charlotte would have called it obsessive, if she knew. But Charlotte didn't know everything. Nobody did.

Maddie slipped on a pair of silk gloves before folding the paper with precise creases. The matching envelope bore Lillian's name in the same altered handwriting. No return address, no additional marks. Clean. Professional. Untraceable. Just like everything else in her orchestrated plan. Like the way she'd arranged for Rosa to be visiting her sister when this letter would arrive.

She drove to Maison Belle during their morning delivery window. The boutique's back entrance stood propped open as staff sorted through new arrivals. Maddie approached confidently, envelope in hand, dressed in a way that suggested she belonged there—because she did belong, far more than that little princess ever would. The staff glanced up as she added her letter to their pile of correspondence. They knew her face, trusted her presence. That's what twenty years of patronage bought you.

Lillian shopped here every Thursday afternoon—a pattern Maddie had observed over weeks of careful surveillance. The letter would find its way to her with the store's regular client communications. Just another envelope among many, yet carrying a weight all its own. Maddie had watched the girl try on dresses, preening before mirrors like she owned the place. Not anymore. She'd seen how Lillian touched each garment, the way Jackson touched her—like something new and precious. But new things tarnished. Precious things broke.

Maddie returned to her Mercedes, satisfaction settling over her like a familiar perfume. In the quiet of her leather seats, she closed her eyes and pictured Lillian's manicured hands trembling as they opened the envelope. The girl would try to maintain composure—they always did at first—but Maddie knew better. She'd seen that facade crack before. She'd made it crack before. Like Sandra, who still flinched whenever Maddie mentioned her ex-husband.

The image crystallized: Lillian alone in her sterile Buckhead apartment, that false confidence crumbling as she read those seven words. She'd check over her shoulder, perhaps double-lock her door. She'd call Jackson, but stop herself—how would she explain knowing about his wife? No, Lillian would suffer in silence, jumping at shadows, questioning every stranger's glance. The thought made Maddie's skin tingle with pleasure. This was what control felt like.

Maddie's lips curved into a smile as she imagined Lillian canceling her standing Thursday appointments at

Maison Belle, second-guessing her routine. The girl would feel watched, hunted. That delicious paranoia would seep into every corner of her curated life. It was almost too easy. These young women never understood what they were up against until it was far too late. They thought love was enough. As if love had anything to do with marriage.

A warm flutter rose in Maddie's chest. This was power—real power. Not the hollow authority of Jackson's military rank or Lillian's youth. This was the quiet dominance of knowing how to unravel someone's sense of security, one careful thread at a time. She'd learned this art over decades, ed it like a fine wine aging in darkness. While Jackson commanded soldiers, Maddie had learned to command fear itself.

She opened her eyes, catching her reflection in the rearview mirror. composure, not a hair out of place. While Lillian's world began to tilt on its axis, Maddie remained unmoved, unchanged—the eye of the storm she'd just set in motion. Let the girl learn what it meant to take what belonged to Maddie Callahan. This was just the beginning. After all, she had so many more letters to write, so many more threads to pull. By the time Jackson realized what was happening, it would be far too late for his precious princess.

❖ ❖ ❖

The morning light slanted across the imported marble counter-tops, casting shadows that seemed to dance and mock. Maddie watched her family over the rim of her coffee cup, each sip measured and deliberate, like everything else in her curated life. The kitchen's morning silence felt heavy, oppressive even, broken only by the clink of silverware against fine china—the

Wedgwood set her mother had given them as a wedding present. Twenty-five years ago, when Maddie still believed in forever. How fitting that even the dishes had outlasted their marriage's warmth.

Her gaze settled on Carrie, who pushed eggs around her plate with the same restless energy that used to drive Maddie's own mother to distraction. The girl's eyes kept darting between her parents, uncertainty written across her small features. Those features—so much like Jackson's—made something twist inside Maddie's chest. A reminder of what she'd given him, what he was so carelessly throwing away. Nate hadn't even touched his breakfast, his shoulders hunched as he stared at his orange juice, looking so small in the over-sized chair she'd specially ordered from Italy. (Eight thousand dollars, and Jackson had called it wasteful. As if anything for their children could be wasteful.)

Jackson scrolled through his phone, seemingly oblivious to the tension he'd created, the invisible fissures spreading through their family tableau. His new cologne—the one he'd started wearing after Dubai— drifted across the table, making Maddie's stomach turn. Armani Code. She'd seen the bottle in his bathroom, replacing the Clive Christian she'd chosen for him years ago. Because of course he had to change everything, didn't he? Even his scent needed to be scrubbed clean of her influence.

"The children miss having dinner together," Maddie said, setting down her cup with practiced precision, her manicured fingers steady despite the rage building beneath her skin. The same rage she'd been swallowing for months now, watching him slip away one missed dinner at a time. "We used to be quite good at maintaining family traditions. Don't you agree, Jackson?"

He glanced up, jaw tightening in that way she'd grown to hate. "Work demands what it demands, Maddie."

"Of course. We all make sacrifices for family." She emphasized the word 'sacrifices,' watching his reaction, cataloging every micro-expression like she'd learned to do over their years together. The slight twitch at the corner of his mouth, the way his shoulders tensed almost imperceptibly. "Though some sacrifices seem more... selective than others."

Jackson's phone buzzed. Maddie's teeth clenched. His eyes flicked to the screen, and there it was—the telltale flicker of warmth, the ghost of a smile he failed to bury. She knew that look. God, how well she knew it. It wasn't for her, hadn't been for years. She'd seen that same expression in their wedding photos, back when she was young enough, new enough to warrant such tenderness.

Lillian.

The knowledge crystallized in her chest, sharp and cold as diamond. Her mind spun with possibilities, each more satisfying than the last. She'd been right to send that note to the boutique, warning them about Lillian's "unfortunate habit" of writing bad checks. But it wasn't enough. Not nearly enough. The little princess needed to learn what happened to women who tried to steal what belonged to Maddie Callahan. (And oh, there were so many delicious ways to teach that lesson.)

"May I be excused?" Nate's voice cracked, pulling her from her darkening thoughts.

"Of course, darling." Maddie smiled at her son, noting how he couldn't quite meet her eyes. Another thing Jackson had stolen from her—her children's easy affection. They used to look at her with such love, such trust. Now they watched her like she was a storm about to break. "Both of you may go," and when they hesitated—when they dared to question her authority in her own kitchen—something snapped inside her. "Go! "

The coffee cup shattered in her grip, handle breaking clean off, scalding liquid spreading across the imported tablecloth like a Rorschach test of her unraveling marriage. The children fled, leaving their touched breakfast behind. Jackson remained absorbed in his phone, typing out what Maddie knew was a response to his precious Lillian. The sight of his fingers moving across the screen made her want to break more than just the coffee cup. Perhaps starting with those typing fingers. One joint at a time.

She dabbed at the spilled coffee with her napkin, watching the brown stain spread. Some stains, she knew, never came out. They just sank deeper—became part of the fabric itself. Like hatred. Like revenge.

❖ ❖ ❖

Maddie's fingers danced across her phone screen, each message a careful incision into the fabric of her social world. Her nails—fresh from her standing appointment at Le Petit Salon—tapped out the words with surgical precision. How satisfying it was, watching the responses flutter in like autumn leaves. Within minutes, her curated trio arrived at Le Petit Jardin, right on cue. Charlotte, Barbara, and Sandra descended upon the table in waves of Chanel No. 5 and desperation.

The restaurant hummed with the quiet conversation of the lunch crowd, but Maddie knew better than most that the real symphony played out in the subtle dance of power around tables just like this one.

She'd chosen their usual corner spot, where the lighting was forgiving and the acoustics carried just enough to make eavesdropping tedious. Twenty years of marriage to a military strategist hadn't been wasted.

"I had to see you all," Maddie said, adjusting her Cartier bracelet—the one Jackson had given her on their fifteenth anniversary, back when forever still meant something. She Sandra's envious glance and filed it away, like a weapon she might need later. "The house feels so... empty." The pause hung in the air like perfume, waiting to be noticed.

Charlotte, reliable as a Swiss timepiece, leaned forward. Her auburn bob swayed with the movement, freshly styled and probably still warm from the salon. "Is everything alright, darling?"

"Oh, you know how it is." Maddie let out a laugh that she'd spent years perfecting, like a vintage wine aging to the right note of casual dismissal. She thought of Lily—sweet, stupid Lily—probably wearing something inappropriate at her desk right now, batting those Disney-princess eyes at Jackson. "Men of a certain age sometimes forget what truly matters. They chase fantasies, thinking youth equals substance."

Barbara's eyes lit up like a child on Christmas morning. Maddie could see the gossip taking root behind that Botoxed forehead. "Speaking of age-inappropriate behavior, did you hear about Richard Thompson? His new assistant can't be more than twenty-five."

"Some women don't understand their place." Maddie stirred her tea, three times counterclockwise, watching the amber liquid swirl like the thoughts she kept contained. The silver spoon clinked against fine bone china—a sound that always reminded her of her mother's lessons in proper tea service. How proud Mother would be, seeing her daughter wield social warfare with such precision. "They mistake attention for affection, lust for love. It's rather pathetic." Just like Lily would be, once Maddie finished arranging all her pieces.

Charlotte and Barbara exchanged glances loaded with unspoken understanding, their minds already spinning the web Maddie had so designed. Sandra, poor Sandra, shifted in her chair like a guilty child, the movement making her last-season blazer pull awkwardly across her shoulders. The sound of synthetic fabric against the chair made Maddie's teeth ache., there was no excuse for polyester at this level of society.

"Men can be so foolish," Charlotte offered, playing her part. "Throwing away decades of history for... well."

"Indeed." Maddie savored the moment, watching speculation bloom across their faces like a cultivated garden. She didn't need to mention Lillian by name—these women would do that work for her, each believed conversation adding another brick to the wall she was building around Jackson's precious princess.

Barbara, unable to resist showing off her own intel, leaned in conspiratorially. "I heard someone new moved into The Peninsula. A young thing from Dubai, apparently."

"How interesting." Maddie lifted her cup, inhaling the delicate Earl Grey that Rosa had taught her to appreciate years ago. The warmth of satisfaction spread through her chest as she watched her laid groundwork take root. This was her domain, her battlefield, where every raised eyebrow was a signal flare and every whispered aside was a bullet. Here, she wielded more power than Lillian could comprehend with her community college education and off-the-rack sundresses.

"It must be difficult," she continued, "starting over in a new city. Especially when one doesn't understand the... social landscape." The emphasis hung in the air like smoke, acrid and impossible to ignore.

The table hummed with unspoken understanding. These women might not know every detail, but they recognized the opening moves of a social execution. And they'd chosen their side, just as Maddie knew they would. After all, she hadn't spent decades cultivating these relationships just to have them fail her now. Each of these women was a piece on her chessboard: Charlotte, her reliable bishop; Barbara, her attack dog knight; and Sandra, her sacrificial pawn.

Maddie surveyed their faces with the practiced eye of a general assessing troops. Sandra's slight frown betrayed her discomfort—she'd never had the stomach for these games, which was why Maddie kept her around. Charlotte and Barbara leaned forward like greyhounds at the track, eager for the chase. They were ready for blood, hungry for the kind of drama that only Maddie could orchestrate with such elegance.

Yes, Maddie thought, allowing herself the ghost of a smile, everything was falling into place. By evening, the whispers would begin. By tomorrow, they'd be rumors. By next week, they'd be facts that everyone "just knew." And Lily? Well, Lily was about to learn what happened to little girls who played with other women's toys.

Chapter 12

Maddie sat at her vanity, applying her signature red lipstick with practiced precision. The morning light filtered through the gauzy curtains she'd chosen years ago (back when everything felt permanent when Jackson still noticed such details). Her reflection caught the golden rays, and she allowed herself a small, private smile as her mind drifted to Maison Belle, where her latest message waited like a coiled snake in designer wrapping.

The boutique had always been one of Lillian's favorites. Of course, it was—the kind of place that catered to women like her, women who thought money could buy belonging. Maddie could picture it with clarity: Lillian's freshly manicured hand (probably that trendy milk-bath style that had been all over Instagram) reaching for what appeared to be cream-colored boutique stationery, the kind reserved for their most valued customers. The kind Maddie had been receiving for two decades before this child learned to spell Louboutin.

She traced her lips with the gold-cased applicator, savoring each stroke like a caress. The lipstick was Chanel—the same shade she'd worn the night she met Jackson. Funny how some things stayed the same while others crumbled so easily. In her mind's eye, she watched Lillian's face transform as she unfolded the note. Those annoyingly perfect features would freeze (and oh, how satisfying that would be), the blood draining from those young, unlined cheeks. Those fingers, adorned with a tennis bracelet that should have been Maddie's twentieth anniversary gift, would tremble, crinkling the expensive paper's edges.

The boutique's curated playlist—all soft French jazz and contemporary ambient music—would fade into meaningless noise as the words sank in for her. Maddie had chosen each one, wielding them like sharpened knives. Lillian would glance around the store, past the racks of designer clothing she hadn't earned the right to wear, searching for watching eyes. Every customer would become a potential threat, every sales associate a possible spy. (After all, who did she think had helped Maddie plant the note? These women had known Maddie for years. Loyalty, unlike love, could be bought.)

Setting down her lipstick with a soft click against the marble vanity top, Maddie felt satisfaction curl through her chest like warm brandy. She knew what would happen next: Lillian would stuff the note into her Hermès bag—that Kelly model Jackson had purchased last month, the one that cost more than Maddie's first car. She'd hurry out, those Christian Louboutins (red soles flashing like warning signs) clicking against the marble floors, no longer interested in whatever dress had her vapid eye.

The fear would follow her home like a faithful pet. Each passing car might hold watching eyes. Each friendly smile could mask malicious intent. The constructed fantasy of her affair would begin to crack, letting in the cold reality of consequences. The same consequences Maddie had been planning since the first time she'd seen Jackson's hand on the small of Lillian's back at that charity gala three months ago.

Maddie didn't need to witness it firsthand—though Rosa had promised to text her the moment it happened. She knew fear intimately; how it crept in like evening shadows, how it transformed the familiar into something strange and threatening. How it turned luxury into a cage, comfort into exposure. Hadn't she felt it herself, watching Jackson pull away, seeing the way his eyes slid past her at dinner parties? But fear, like everything else, could be weaponized if you were patient enough.

Running her fingers over her curls (three hours at Alexandre's yesterday, worth every penny), Maddie smiled at her reflection. The note was just the beginning, the first domino in a long, arranged line. Soon, little

Lillian would understand what Maddie had known for years: borrowed time always ran out, and the interest it collected was devastating.

Maddie adjusted her Lululemon leggings before stepping into the exclusive Pilates studio at The Windsor Club, where the morning light filtered through floor-to-ceiling windows and the scent of eucalyptus hung in the air like a promise of renewal. Everything had its proper time and place in her world—Wednesday mornings were sacred, a delicate balance of maintaining both her figure and her curated social web. These routines had kept her sane during the divorce proceedings, giving structure to days that might otherwise spiral into chaos.

She positioned her reformer mat next to Claire Bennett's, a choice that appeared casual but was, like everything else in Maddie's life, calculated. Claire was a goldmine of information, working part-time at Maison Belle less out of necessity (her husband's hedge fund saw to that) and more for the employee discount and gossip. The girl lived in that boutique, soaking up every held conversation and sideways glance like a designer-clad sponge.

"Claire, darling." Maddie stretched her arms overhead, her tennis bracelet catching the light—the one Jackson had given her for their fifteenth anniversary, back when forever still meant something. "I haven't seen you at the store. Tuesday afternoons are usually your shift, aren't they?" She kept her tone light, conversational, the way she'd ed over decades of these delicate social dances.

"Oh, Mrs. Callahan!" Claire beamed with that eager-to-please energy that reminded Maddie of a young golden retriever. "I switched to Thursdays now." She adjusted her own mat, inching closer. "Though yesterday was... interesting."

Maddie kept her face neutral as she moved into her warm-up position, though her heart quickened with anticipation. "How so?" She let the question float between them, casual as a leaf on the breeze.

"Well, you know that new client? Lillian Hart?" Claire's voice dropped to that conspiratorial whisper that Maddie had been counting on. "She's usually like clockwork, comes in around two, browses for at least an hour." A pause, timed. "But yesterday she stayed fifteen minutes. Left in such a rush she forgot her store credit receipt on the counter."

"?" Maddie arched an eyebrow, maintaining form in her plank while her mind raced ahead like a chess player seeing the next five moves. "That doesn't sound like her at all. Was she feeling unwell?" The concern in her voice was flawless—she'd practiced it in front of her bathroom mirror that morning, along with three other variations.

"She looked... rattled? Almost scared?" Claire's words sent a warm surge of satisfaction through Maddie's core. "I tried asking if everything was okay, but she ran out."

Maddie felt a flutter of victory in her chest as she transitioned into her next pose, smooth as silk. "How concerning. I do hope everything's alright." The words tasted sweet on her tongue, like the first sip of a chilled martini. Poor, Lillian Hart—so young, so naive, so unprepared for what was coming.

The instructor called the class to attention, her voice cutting through the quiet murmur of morning gossip. Maddie focused on her breathing, each controlled movement matching the steady rhythm of her triumph. Inhale. Exhale. Hold. Release. Lillian Hart's world was beginning to crack, right on schedule. Just like the anonymous notes Maddie had been leaving in her mailbox, each one a hairline fracture in the younger woman's confidence. Just like the "accidental" meetings Maddie had orchestrated at Lillian's favorite places, each appearance a reminder that Jackson's past wasn't going to disappear quietly.

Maddie moved through her routine with practiced grace, already planning her next move. After all, this was just the beginning—the first tremors before the earthquake that would shake Princess Lillian's foundation to its core. And Maddie? Well, she'd always been good at keeping her balance.

Maddie watched Jackson from across the dining table, noting how his fork pushed the couscous around his plate without ever reaching his mouth. His tie hung loose around his neck—the Windsor knot she'd ed for him that morning now askew, like their marriage. (She remembered teaching herself to tie it, back when she thought details like that mattered.) His phone lay face-down beside his water glass, but his eyes kept drifting toward it like a compass finding true north.

Something had shifted. The question was: what? Twenty years of marriage had taught her to read the microscopic changes in his demeanor, the way a sailor reads the sea before a storm.

Rosa cleared their -touched plates, her movements careful and measured. The children had already escaped to their rooms, leaving that hollow silence Maddie had grown to hate. It reminded her of all those nights alone during his deployments, except now he was physically present but mentally elsewhere. With someone else.

"I noticed someone lingering outside the gates today," Maddie said, keeping her voice light as she dabbed her lips with her napkin—light, always light. Never let them see the rage simmering beneath the surface. "It felt rather... unsettling. Like being watched." She watched his face with the precision of a sniper, waiting for the tell-tale twitch that would confirm her suspicions.

Jackson's hand twitched, but he didn't look up. Just like he hadn't looked at her properly in months. "The security system works fine."

"Of course, darling." The endearment tasted like acid on her tongue. "Still, one can't help but feel vulnerable sometimes." She studied his face for any flicker of recognition, any sign that Lillian had broken down and confessed. But Jackson's face remained as impassive as ever. (He'd ed that blank expression in war zones, but Maddie knew how to wage her own kind of warfare.)

"You're being paranoid, Maddie." He reached for his phone, thumb hovering over the screen like a lover's caress. "If you're that concerned, I'll have the company review the cameras."

His dismissal told her everything. No tension in his shoulders, no defensive edge to his voice. Lillian hadn't breathed a word about the note. The pretty little thing was suffering in silence, as planned. (Poor Princess, learning that glass slippers can cut.)

"You're right," Maddie conceded, allowing a small

smile to play across her lips. The same smile she'd practiced in mirrors for decades, perfecting the right blend of warmth and submission. "I'm sure it was nothing."

Jackson pushed back from the table, already absorbed in whatever message had captured his attention. He didn't even notice when Maddie's fingers curled around her wine stem hard enough to whiten her knuckles. (He used to notice everything about her. Every new dress, every subtle change in her perfume.)

The familiar click of his study door's lock echoed through the foyer like a gunshot. His phone had left his hand these days—probably texting his precious Lillian, assuring her everything would be fine. As if anything would ever be fine again.

She traced the rim of her wine glass, remembering how Lillian's hands had trembled in Maison Belle. The girl's facade had cracked so easily. One note, and those designer clothes couldn't hide her fear anymore. (Amateur. Did she think she could step into Maddie's life without consequences?)

Rosa moved silently around the kitchen, loading the dishwasher with practiced efficiency. The clink of plates filled the emptiness Jackson left behind. Twenty years of dinners, and this is what they'd become—the sound of dirty dishes and unspoken threats.

"Rosa," Maddie called out, her voice honey-sweet. "Leave those for tomorrow."

Rosa hesitated, dish towel frozen mid-wipe. "Sí, señora." Her eyes held knowledge she'd never voice aloud. (Good girl, Rosa. Know your place.)

"And Rosa?" Maddie's voice dropped lower, intimate as a secret. "Did you notice anything... unusual when you were running errands today?"

Rosa's eyes darted toward Jackson's study before returning to meet Maddie's gaze. "The young lady at the boutique—she seemed upset."

"Upset?" Maddie kept her expression neutral, though satisfaction bloomed in her chest like a dark flower. "How unfortunate."

Rosa nodded once and retreated upstairs, her footsteps fading into silence. Always knowing when to disappear—that's why she'd lasted so long in this house.

Maddie pulled her phone from her purse, scrolling through her contacts. Lillian might be suffering alone now, but that wouldn't be enough. The girl needed to understand that her fairy tale with Jackson would never have a happy ending. (After all, every princess needs a proper villain.)

She found the number she was looking for and pressed dial. Time to ensure that Lillian's world crumbled just a little bit more.

Chapter 13

Maddie's manicured nails tapped a delicate rhythm across her phone screen as she connected with Midnight Messenger. Such a useful little service—trust Barbara's endless social gossip to occasionally produce something worthwhile. Barbara always did have a knack for collecting other people's secrets, even if she couldn't keep them properly. The woman who answered spoke in those measured tones that screamed discretion-for-hire.

"I need a special delivery tonight." Maddie's voice

remained as smooth as the Château Margaux she was currently sampling. "A black gift box, wrapped with a silver ribbon." She recited Lillian's address at The Peninsula Residences with practiced precision, each word dropping like a polished stone into still water. "Inside, place a single lily. White. Fresh. condition only."

The symbolism made her lips curve into a smile that would have worried anyone who knew her well. That first lily—God, how long ago was it now? Twenty-eight years, four months, and sixteen days. Not that she was counting. Jackson had been so dashing in his dress uniform at the officer's ball, all sharp angles and burning intensity. He'd plucked that lily from the nearest centerpiece, dropped to one knee right there between the punch bowl and the band, and declared her the most beautiful woman he'd ever seen.

(He'd meant it then. She was certain he'd meant it then.)

Maddie settled deeper into her favorite chair by the window, the leather warm and accommodating after all these years, like an old friend who kept your secrets. The city lights winked at her through the glass, co-conspirators in tonight's little drama. She could see it all so clearly: Lillian (sweet, naive little Lillian) wrapped in whatever silk confection Jackson had bought her last week, probably that pale blue one from La Perla that Maddie had seen on his credit card statement. The princess would answer that late-night knock, confusion furrowing her brow. The black box would catch the hallway light just so, seeming innocent enough until those French-manicured fingers lifted the lid.

The antique clock in the hall (a wedding gift from Jackson's mother, who'd never quite warmed to Maddie) ticked past eleven when her phone buzzed with confirmation. Delivered.

Maddie closed her eyes, letting the scene play out behind her eyelids like a favorite film. Lillian's hands would tremble—they always did when she was nervous, Maddie had noticed that at the country club last month. There would be that sharp intake of breath, the kind that catches in your throat when fear first takes hold. Those wide doe eyes (what did Jackson call them? Innocent? Pure?) would dart to her door, checking the locks once, twice, three times. Who could have sent this? Who knew where she lived? Who was watching?

She wouldn't call Jackson. No, that wasn't Lillian's style. She'd handled the note at Maison Belle alone, after all. Maddie had watched her discover it, had savored every micro-expression that crossed that face. The pretty princess wouldn't want to appear weak—they never did, these younger women. They were all so desperate to prove they could handle anything, right up until they couldn't.

Maddie took another slow sip of wine, letting it linger on her tongue. The same way she was letting this moment linger, treasuring it like an aged vintage. Lillian would spend tonight jumping at shadows, questioning every creak in her luxury apartment. Every shift of the building, every distant siren would become something sinister. The darkness would press in around her, thick with questions she couldn't answer.

Let her wonder. Let her lie awake in that king-sized bed (Egyptian cotton sheets, no doubt) and contemplate every possibility. Let her realize that her little world wasn't as secure as she'd thought.

After all, Maddie had waited twenty-eight years

for her happily ever after. What was one sleepless night for the woman trying to steal it?

◆ ◆ ◆

Maddie glided through the Peninsula Club's mahogany-paneled hallways, her Louboutins clicking against marble floors with the precise rhythm of a metronome. The morning crowd parted before her like subjects before their queen – doctors' wives fresh from tennis in their color-coordinated Lululemon, trust fund babies pretending to work on laptops while scrolling Instagram. She fragments of their whispered conversations falling silent as she passed. Just like old times. Just as it should be.

The familiar scent of money and privilege wrapped around her like a cashmere blanket as she approached the juice bar. And there, as if the universe itself was conspiring to make her morning, sat Claire Bennett chatting with Marcus, Lillian's personal trainer. Lillian's attractive, chatty personal trainer. The same one who had mentioned, just two weeks ago, how "committed" the princess was to her fitness goals.

Maddie's red sole the light as she settled onto a leather bar stool, positioning herself just so – close enough to appear casual, far enough to suggest she hadn't noticed them at all. The movement was choreographed, practiced. Like everything else in her life.

"Marcus, darling." She gestured to the bartender with the kind of elegant wave that took years to. "Green juice, extra ginger." Her diamond tennis bracelet – the one Jackson had given her on their fifteenth anniversary – sparkled as she turned to face the trainer. The weight of it felt different now, heavier somehow. Like a reminder of promises broken. "I've been meaning to ask

– how's that sweet young woman doing? The one who just moved in? Lillian, isn't it?"

She watched Marcus shift his weight, noticed the slight tension in his shoulders. Poor boy. He had no idea he was just another piece on her chessboard. "Miss Hart? I haven't seen her this week. Or last week."

"Oh?" Maddie's shaped brow arched with calculated concern. Inside, satisfaction bloomed like a dark flower. So, the princess was hiding already. How... predictable. "That's not like her. She seemed so committed when I saw her here before. Didn't she have standing appointments?"

"Three times a week." Marcus glanced at his schedule, probably not even realizing he was giving Maddie what she wanted. "She's canceled the last four sessions. Said she wasn't feeling well."

"Poor thing." Maddie sipped her juice, letting concern color her voice while amusement danced behind her eyes. The game was almost too easy. "I heard she's been... anxious. Jumping at shadows." She leaned in, lowering her voice to that conspiratorial whisper that always made people lean closer, want to be part of her inner circle. "Between us, I've noticed her looking rather pale when I've passed her in the lobby. Almost frightened."

Claire perked up like a bird spotting a shiny object. Of course she did. Claire had always been reliable that way – desperate to be included, to feel important. "? Tommy at the front desk mentioned she's been requesting security escorts to her car."

"Has she?" Maddie's lips curved, savoring the moment like a fine wine. Inside, she was already calculating how long it would take for this tidbit to spread through their social circle, how many hours before it reached Jackson's ears. How concerning indeed that his precious princess didn't feel safe in their building. In their neighborhood. In their world. "How concerning. I do hope she's all right."

She took another sip of her juice, remembering how Jackson had once told her that vengeance was beneath her. But then again, Jackson had said a lot of things that turned out to be lies. And vengeance? Well, vengeance wasn't beneath her at all. It was where she belonged.

◆ ◆ ◆

Maddie smoothed her Hermès scarf and settled into her usual corner table at Café Laurent, a small ritual she'd ed over two decades of lunches. The familiar weight of the antique pillar at her back felt like an old friend, offering just enough cover while giving her an unobstructed view of the entrance. Barbara's loose tongue had provided this little gift—the knowledge of Lillian's standing Thursday lunch appointment with her Realtor friend., Barbara should know better by now than to gossip so freely. (Though Maddie had to admit, sometimes Barbara's inability to keep a secret worked in her favor.)

The maître d', Antoine, had fallen over himself accommodating her specific seating request. Of course he had. Twenty years of timed appearances, generous tips, and cultivated loyalty meant something in places like this. Unlike some people, Maddie understood the value of investing in relationships.

When Lillian walked in wearing that cream Valentino dress, Maddie's fingers tightened imperceptibly around her water glass. She recognized it from the photos Jackson had sent her from Dubai last spring—back when he still bothered with such pretenses, showing her his business trips through curated images. "Just keeping you in the loop, darling," he'd say, as if she were some sort of corporate shareholder rather than his wife of twenty-three years.

Taking a measured sip of sparkling water (San Pellegrino, never Perrier), Maddie watched Lillian's eyes dart around the room like a frightened deer. How amusing that the girl who'd been so bold in taking what didn't belong to her now couldn't even manage to sit still through lunch. Every few minutes, that coiffed head would snap up at the slightest sound—footsteps, silverware, even the gentle pop of a wine cork across the room. Her hands trembled as she reached for her water glass, those French-manicured fingers (probably Jackson's preferred nail salon on Fifth Avenue) betraying her nerves as she compulsively checked her phone.

Maddie dabbed her lips with her napkin, using the gesture to mask her satisfaction. Through the antique mirror—the one she'd helped select during the restaurant's renovation fifteen years ago—she Lillian's gaze. Just for a moment. Just long enough. Then Maddie turned back to her salad (butter lettuce, pear, and gorgonzola—a classic that never went out of style) as if Lillian were nothing more than another piece of the restaurant's curated ambiance.

When Lillian's first course arrived, Maddie their server's eye with the subtle gesture she'd ed over years of commanding attention without seeming to ask for it. "Send a glass of the '82 Bordeaux to that table," she instructed, her voice carrying just enough authority to be obeyed without question. She slid a folded note across the crisp white tablecloth, the paper heavy and expensive against her fingertips. "Place this under the napkin."

The show that followed was better than anything playing at the Metropolitan Opera. Maddie watched as the waiter delivered the wine, noting how Lillian's California-tanned face drained of color as she unfolded the napkin and discovered the three words Maddie had penned in her script: "You look tired." Such a simple phrase. So devastatingly effective.

The screech of Lillian's chair against the floor was like music. The girl jumped up, gathering her purse (Chanel, last season's model—Jackson was slipping in his gift-giving) with hands that shook so badly she nearly knocked over the untouched wine glass. Nearby diners turned to stare, their curious gazes following Lillian's hasty retreat.

Maddie raised her water glass in a silent toast as those designer heels clicked frantically against the marble floor. The sound echoed through the restaurant like gunshots, each step carrying Lillian further from the constructed world she thought she could step into. Poor thing. She should have known better than to play games with someone who'd invented all the rules.

After her triumph at Café Laurent, Maddie glided into her bedroom suite, her sanctuary, where even Jackson knew better than to intrude without invitation. The satisfaction of the afternoon's performance still hummed through her veins like expensive champagne. She reached into her Hermès bag (a Christmas gift from Jackson three years ago, when he still remembered such things) and withdrew the receipt from La Petite Fleur with the delicate precision of a curator handling a precious artifact.

The paper was crisp, pristine—just like the arrangements Jackson had sent to his precious Lillian in Dubai. Maddie's fingers traced the elegant script of the florist's logo before placing it on her vanity, positioning it with mathematical precision so it peeked out just enough from beneath her jewelry box. Everything in its place, as always. (Order, after all, was power, and Maddie had learned long ago that power lay in the details.)

A single white lily—twin to the ones that had made Lillian's face drain of color at lunch—stood sentinel among her collection of Chanel perfume bottles. The flower's presence felt like a secret joke between old friends. Maddie plucked one petal, watching it drift down to the polished mahogany like a feather. The sweet, funereal scent wafted up, and for a moment, she was back at Café Laurent, savoring the way Lillian's hands had trembled around her water glass. Poor princess, so young, so easily rattled. She hadn't even begun to understand the game she'd stepped into.

The familiar cadence of Jackson's footsteps in the hallway pulled her from her reverie—left foot heavier than the right, a habit from an old combat injury he thought no one noticed. Maddie rose in one fluid motion, retreating to her walk-in closet with the practiced ease of someone who had spent decades choreographing such moments. She left the door open just enough—three inches, —to observe without being seen.

Through this careful aperture, she watched Jackson appear in her doorway. Twenty-five years of marriage had taught her to read his every micro-expression. The way his eyes moved across her vanity—

methodical, analyzing, just as he'd been trained to survey potential threats. First the lily petal, stark white against dark wood. Then the receipt, its edge a paper blade waiting to draw blood.

He stepped into her domain, and oh, how telling that his military bearing grew more pronounced, shoulders squaring as if preparing for battle. Some part of him must have known he was walking into a trap, yet he couldn't help himself. Men like Jackson always needed to know everything, to control everything. It was their greatest weakness.

The moment of recognition was exquisite. She saw it in the sudden tension of his jaw, that little muscle jumping beneath his skin like a trapped thing. Had he looked this way when he'd ordered flowers for Lillian? Had his hands been steady when he'd written whatever saccharine message accompanied them?

Jackson lifted the receipt with the care of someone handling evidence at a crime scene. Studied it. Replaced it in its exact position—and wasn't that just like him, trying to pretend he hadn't disturbed her careful arrangement? But his reflection in the vanity mirror betrayed him. Uncertainty had crept into those ice-blue eyes, and Maddie savored it like fine wine. When was the last time she'd seen the great General Callahan look uncertain? Not since that night in Dubai, perhaps.

His exit was silent but heavy with unspoken questions. Maddie emerged from her hiding place, settling at her vanity like a queen ascending her throne. She took up her Mason Pearson brush (another gift, from better days) and began the ritual of one hundred strokes through her hair. In the mirror, she tracked his shadow as it paused outside her door—one beat, two beats, three—

before continuing down the hall.

Let him wonder, she thought, each brush stroke precise and purposeful. Let him lie awake tonight, turning over possibilities in that tactical mind of his. Let him feel what she had felt all those months, watching him slip away, powerless to stop it. But unlike her, Jackson wouldn't have to wonder long. Soon enough, he'd understand what was coming next. And by then, it would be far too late to stop it.

Chapter 14

Maddie watched Jackson over the rim of her coffee cup, observing how twenty years of military discipline had begun to crack. His posture—the one that had first caught her eye at that officer's ball so long ago— had betrayed him. His shoulders hunched as he stared at his untouched eggs, a plate she'd prepared the way he liked them (two over medium, toast browned, a precise sprinkle of pepper). The morning paper lay folded beside his plate, ignored, when he used to guard it like territory during breakfast.

His eyes darted to her hands as she set down her cup, the fine bone china making the softest clink against the saucer. She noticed how he tracked her movements now, studying her with the same intensity he once reserved for battlefield strategies. How amusing, she thought, that she'd become the enemy in his own home.

"More coffee, dear?" She kept her voice light, pleasant—the same tone she'd ed over decades of military wives' luncheons and charity galas. A voice that said everything was fine, just fine.

Jackson's jaw tightened, the muscle jumping beneath his skin. "No." He checked his phone, then set it face-down on the table—something he never did. In twenty-three years of marriage, his phone had always remained face-up, at attention, like a good soldier.

Maddie spread butter on her toast with precise, measured strokes, the way her mother had taught her. "A lady never rushes at breakfast, darling." She felt his gaze following the knife in her hand, watching as she cut the bread into triangles. The weight of his attention made her want to smile. He'd looked at her for months, and now he couldn't look away.

"The children miss you at dinner," she said, dabbing her lips with her napkin, careful not to smudge her lipstick. The same shade she'd worn on their honeymoon in Paris. "Perhaps tonight—"

"I have meetings." His response came too quickly, too sharply. Amateur move. He used to be better at lying.

She smiled, warm and gracious, the political wife's smile she'd practiced in mirrors since she was twenty-two. "Of course you do."

His coffee cup clinked against the saucer as he set

it down, the sound sharp and discordant in the morning quiet. His hands weren't quite steady—another crack in his usually flawless control. The great General Jackson Callahan—rattled by breakfast with his wife.

Maddie straightened the flower arrangement between them—a fresh bouquet of white lilies, Lily's favorite flower, according to the florist's receipt she'd found in his jacket pocket last week.

Jackson flinched at the movement; his eyes fixed on the blooms. Did he remember telling her, years ago, that white lilies reminded him of funerals?

"Something wrong?" she asked, genuine concern dripping from each syllable like honey-coated poison.

"No." He shoved back his chair, the scrape against the floor breaking the silence. A mistake. Jackson was always precise, always controlled, "I need to go."

Maddie noticed he left his phone on the table. She didn't touch it, didn't even look at it directly. She poured herself more coffee and waited, counting the seconds in her head. The way she used to count the days between his deployments, the hours between his calls, the minutes until he came home.

Ten seconds later, he returned, snatching the phone up without meeting her eyes. The screen lit up as he grabbed it—a message notification. From "Princess." How original.

She took another sip of coffee, savoring the bitter taste as his footsteps retreated down the hallway. wives didn't snoop through phones. wives didn't notice their husbands' hands shaking. wives didn't plot revenge while arranging white lilies. wives smiled and poured more coffee.

And Maddie was nothing if not.

◆ ◆ ◆

Maddie watched Jackson's reflection in the gleaming kitchen window, tracking his movements with the practiced patience of a woman who had spent decades learning to read all his tells. The coffee maker hummed, a mechanical counterpoint to the silence stretching between them. His shoulders—still muscular despite his fifty-seven years—were held with that familiar military rigidity that always betrayed his unease. She remembered a time when those shoulders had relaxed under her touch. Now they might as well have been carved from marble.

The eggs on his plate (organic, scrambled the way he liked) had been touched. He'd pushed them around in precise little patterns, reminding her of how Carrie would avoid eating her vegetables. The comparison almost made her smile. Almost.

She smoothed her napkin across her lap, enjoying the cool silk against her skin. The fabric was Hermès, like the scarves his little princess favored. "You seem preoccupied this morning, darling. Not sleeping well?" The endearment felt like honey laced with arsenic on her tongue.

The coffee pot met the counter with a betraying clink—just a fraction too hard, a moment too fast. There it was, that microscopic fissure in his control. Twenty-five years of marriage had taught her to spot these hairline cracks, the places where his facade threatened to splinter.

"I sleep fine." Three words, delivered with the emotional depth of a weather report. But Maddie heard the undertone, the slight strain that spoke volumes. He was lying, and they both knew it.

"Hmm." She lifted her bone china cup (their

wedding china, a detail that didn't escape her), observing him over the delicate rim. The morning light the steam rising from her coffee, creating a translucent veil between them. "It's just that you didn't even check the security cameras last night like you said you would. That's not like you." Not like the man who had built his reputation on attention to detail, on never missing a threat.

His shoulders—if possible—stiffened further. The spoon in his coffee froze mid-rotation, suspended like the moment between a gunshot and impact. "The cameras?"

"Yes, after that incident at The Peninsula." She paused, letting concern seep into her voice like water through cracks in a foundation. "That sweet young woman who looked so frightened—" Another deliberate pause, another crack widening. "Has she mentioned what's troubling her?"

The spoon clattered against the granite counter top like a dropped weapon. Coffee splashed onto the immaculate surface, dark drops marring the gray stone. Maddie watched each droplet spread with satisfaction. perfection, after all, was meant to be corrupted.

"What woman?" His voice had found its edge now, sharp as the knife lying unused beside his cold eggs.

"Oh, you know the one." Maddie dabbed her lips with her napkin, a gesture as choreographed as any ballet. She could taste her lipstick on the silk—Chanel's Rouge Allure in Pirate. A shade that had always made him think of Paris and hotel rooms and promises. "Blonde, lives in the penthouse. Always wearing those lovely Hermès scarves." She looked up at him through mascaraed lashes. "She seemed quite shaken when I saw her at Café Laurent."

Jackson turned to face her then, his military bearing on full display. A general facing down an enemy. But Maddie saw what he tried so desperately to conceal—the slight pallor beneath his maintained tan, the tightness around eyes that had once looked at her with desire instead of dread.

"I don't know what you're talking about."

Maddie smiled, warm and understanding, the way she used to smile at cocktail parties when the other officers' wives would complain about their husbands' deployments. Poor dears, they never understood that absence wasn't the real threat to a marriage. Presence was. "No? My mistake then." She took another sip of coffee, savoring the bitter taste of victory.

◆ ◆ ◆

The late afternoon sun cast long shadows across Maddie's vanity as she retreated to her bedroom, her fingers dancing over the collection of crystal bottles that the light like diamonds. little soldiers, all lined up and ready for battle. The new Chanel N°5 stood apart—a mirror image of Lillian's signature scent. (How many times had she that fragrance lingering on Jackson's collar? Too many to count, but who was counting? Certainly not Maddie.)

She lifted the bottle with the reverence of a priest handling holy water, though her intentions were far from sacred. The application was methodical, precise—just enough to haunt the air without announcing itself. Like a ghost. Like a warning. Like the memory of another woman's presence.

The study beckoned, its heavy oak doors standing sentinel as she glided inside. The cream-colored stationery waited in her desk drawer, identical to the kind she'd used for those little notes to Lillian. (Amazing what details you could learn about a person when you had their housekeeper in your pocket.) Her hand moved with practiced grace across the paper: "I know what you're doing. I won't let you—" The threat dangled, unfinished, like a knife held over a throat. Sometimes the most effective threats were the ones left to the imagination.

She crumpled the paper just so—not too much, just enough to suggest genuine distress—before letting it fall into the wastebasket. Jackson would see it during his evening ritual, when he poured himself that predictable glass of whiskey. He was nothing if not a creature of habit, her husband. Twenty-five years of marriage had taught her that much.

Jackson's footsteps echoed down the hallway, each measured step a reminder of his military precision. Even now, years into civilian life, he walked like a general inspecting his troops. Maddie arranged herself at the desk, shuffling papers with practiced nonchalance. She didn't need to look up to know the exact moment the perfume reached him—she could hear the slight catch in his breathing, sense the confusion radiating from his rigid frame.

"New perfume?" His voice was careful, controlled. Always so controlled, her Jackson. Even when his world was crumbling around him.

"Oh, this?" She touched her neck with delicate fingers, the gesture reminiscent of a younger woman—of Lillian, perhaps? The thought almost made her smile. "The lovely sales associate at Nordstrom recommended it. Do you like it?" The question hung in the air like the perfume itself, deceptively innocent.

The buzz of his phone cut through the tension. Maddie watched his reflection in the window, cataloging every micro-expression like a curator examining priceless art. The slight tightening of his jaw (she remembered kissing that jaw, once upon a time, when love felt real and permanent). His thumb hovering over the message, uncertain. She could feel Lillian's desperation seeping through the screen. Poor Princess, wondering why her knight in shining armor was suddenly so distant.

Jackson slipped the phone back into his pocket without responding—the first thread of her web holding fast. His eyes on the paper in the wastebasket, lingering just long enough to read, to wonder, to worry. He left without a word, but his silence spoke volumes.

Alone in her study, Maddie allowed herself a small smile. Not the practiced one she wore like armor at charity galas, but something darker, more genuine. The trap was set with all the precision of a spider weaving its web. Jackson was already, pulling away from his precious Lillian not because of any direct threat, but because something felt wrong. Dangerous. Like a shadow in the corner of his eye that disappeared when he turned to look at it.

That was the thing about fear—it worked best when you couldn't quite pin down its source. When it crept into the cracks of your certainty and made you question everything you thought you knew. Maddie had learned that lesson long ago, in the lonely nights while Jackson was deployed. Now it was time to teach it to others.

She traced her fingers along the edge of her mahogany desk, remembering those endless nights of waiting. Twenty-three years of marriage, and how many of those had she spent alone? Waiting for phone calls that might never come, for a husband who felt more like a ghost than a man. She'd become an expert in fear during those years—the way it wrapped around you like silk, how it revealed possibilities in your ear at three in the morning.

(Funny how things worked out, wasn't it?)

The corners of her mouth lifted in a delicate curve as she remembered her younger self, so naive, so desperate for Jackson's approval. That Maddie would have done anything to keep him. This Maddie? Well, she had different priorities now.

She picked up the crystal paperweight from her desk—a gift from Jackson on their fifteenth anniversary. He'd been in Dubai then and had sent it with a card signed by his secretary. Such a thoughtful man, her husband. Always remembering the important dates, even if he couldn't be bothered to be present for them. The crystal the late afternoon light, sending prisms dancing across the walls of her study. How beautiful fear could be when you were the one wielding it.

Jackson thought he understood strategy because he'd commanded armies. But he'd never truly grasped the art of psychological warfare, the delicate dance of making someone destroy themselves while you stood back, hands clean, expression concerned. That's what those nights alone had taught her—the true nature of power. It wasn't in the grand gestures or direct attacks. It was in the quiet moments, the subtle doubts, the slow erosion of certainty.

Poor Lily (or "Princess," as Jackson so unoriginal called her) was about to learn that lesson. Maddie set the paperweight down with precise care. She'd already planted the first seeds of doubt in Jackson's mind about his precious new beginning. Now she just had to wait, to watch them grow in the fertile soil of his paranoia. A whispered word here, a concerned glance there. The beauty of it was, she didn't even have to lie. The truth, properly arranged, could cut deeper than any fabrication.

She smoothed her silk blouse, adjusting the pearl buttons with meticulous attention. Everything had to be. That's what people never understood about revenge—it required patience, precision, and above all, the appearance of absolute control. Even now, as her mind spun with possibilities (each more delicious than the last), her exterior remained flawless. Polished. Untouchable.

Let Jackson think he was escaping. Let him believe he could walk away from twenty-three years of marriage with a younger model on his arm. She'd show him what real fear felt like—the kind that made you question not just your choices, but your reality. After all, she'd had plenty of time to practice, all those nights alone, learning to transform her own fears into weapons.

A small sound escaped her throat—not quite a laugh, not quite a sigh. Outside her window, the garden she'd cultivated with such care bloomed in riotous color. Beautiful things required attention, dedication, and sometimes, a little bit of poison in the soil. She'd learned that lesson too, hadn't she?

She reached for her own phone, checking the time. Soon, Lillian would be calling Jackson again. Soon, he wouldn't answer. And soon after that, well... Maddie had plans for soon after that.

Chapter 15

The late afternoon sun painted long shadows across The Peninsula Residences as Maddie sat motionless in her Mercedes, her manicured fingers wrapped around a cheap burner phone. The contrast between the device and her Cartier bracelet wasn't lost on her. Twenty-five years of marriage had taught her that sometimes the most effective weapons were the least expensive.

She'd chosen this parking spot —close enough to see Lillian's balcony, but far enough that the "Princess" wouldn't notice the black S-Class among the sea of luxury vehicles. Not that Lillian would recognize Maddie's car anyway. The girl noticed anything beyond Jackson's adoring gaze these days.

Lillian's number beckoned from the screen; each digit seared into Maddie's memory from hours spent studying Jackson's phone bills. (Amazing what you could still get in paper form if you knew how to ask.) The afternoon lights her wedding ring, and for a moment, Maddie was back in Paris, Jackson slipping it onto her finger, promising forever. Forever. What a quaint concept.

Her thumb ghosted over the keypad. Timing was everything. She'd learned that from countless charity galas and social maneuverings. The message needed to land just as Lillian was settling in for the evening, when the shadows grew long and the mind became susceptible to darker thoughts.

"I'm sorry for what's coming."

Five words. Simple. Elegant. Like the appetizer before a feast of anxiety.

Send.

Through the specially tinted windows (an upgrade she'd insisted on last year, though Jackson had called it paranoid), Maddie watched Lillian's balcony. One minute passed. Two. Three. Then, like a wound music box beginning its performance, Lillian appeared.

Even from this distance, Maddie could appreciate the girl's innate grace—the way she moved like someone who'd never known real fear. That was about to change. Lillian's fingers clutched her phone, her other hand white-knuckled on the balcony railing as she scanned the street below. Looking for ghosts. Finding nothing.

The show continued as Maddie had choreographed. Lillian retreated inside, only to emerge moments later with what could only be wine in her hand. (Probably that cheap Sancerre she favored—the one Jackson pretended to enjoy because he thought it made him seem sophisticated.) She paced the length of her balcony, phone pressed to her ear, her movements becoming more agitated with each unanswered ring.

Poor thing. She didn't know that Jackson was thoroughly occupied with the series of meetings Maddie had orchestrated through careful manipulation of his secretary's calendar. Nothing too obvious—just a few urgent calls from long-term clients who happened to be old friends of Maddie's family. The kind of meetings a man like Jackson couldn't ignore.

A smile played at the corners of Maddie's lined lips. The genius was in the ambiguity. Lillian would assume the message came from someone in their circle—a concerned friend, a meddling wife. She'd waste hours dissecting its origins, never realizing that the real threat sat three stories below, reapplying her signature red lipstick in a Mercedes.

Let her imagine conspiracies. Let her jump at shadows and question every sympathetic glance from their mutual acquaintances. The uncertainty would burrow into her consciousness like a splinter, too small to warrant removal, just deep enough to hurt with every touch.

Maddie had spent years being the wife, learning the art of warfare through dinner parties and charity events. She knew that true power lay not in the strike, but in the anticipation of it. Lillian would learn that lesson too, though she'd never know who her teacher was.

The burner phone made a satisfying crack as Maddie snapped it in half. She'd dispose of it in pieces across different dumpsters on her way home. After all, a woman in her position couldn't be too careful. (That's what Jackson always said, wasn't it? Right before he started sleeping with his "Princess.")

Maddie's fingers traced the edge of Jackson's spare key, the metal cool against her skin. The afternoon sun the black Mercedes in his reserved spot at Callahan Defense Solutions, making it gleam like polished obsidian. Her lips curved into a small smile. She'd orchestrated this moment down to the second—Jackson would be trapped in meetings until six, and those idiots in security never realized their shift change left a precise three-minute window. (Not that she'd mention that particular detail to anyone. Some secrets were better kept close.)

The steady click-click-click of her Louboutins against concrete echoed through the parking structure. Such a familiar sound. How many times had she walked these same steps as Mrs. Jackson Callahan, the devoted wife? Now each click felt like a countdown. The fabricated receipt between her fingers was —crisp, clean, just worn enough at the edges to seem authentic. The St. Regis Atlanta. She'd chosen it specifically because sweet, predictable Lillian drove past it every morning on her way to the Peninsula Club, probably daydreaming about the life she thought she'd have with Jackson.

Oh, Princess. If only you knew.

The car door yielded with a satisfying click. That sound—it transported her back to countless moments when she'd slipped into this same passenger seat, back when Jackson still opened doors for her, back when he still saw her. The leather still smelled the same. Maddie positioned the receipt with surgical precision, sliding it halfway under the passenger seat. Just visible enough to catch a searching eye, but not so obvious as to seem planted. Art. The small details made all the difference.

Her burner phone vibrated against her hip. Right on schedule—her hired car service had made the delivery to Lillian's building. Maddie allowed herself a moment to appreciate how beautifully everything was falling into place. The envelope she'd had delivered contained what appeared to be a printed text conversation, courtesy of one of those delightfully useful message generators she'd found online. The timestamps aligned with Jackson's "business trips" to Atlanta, and she'd crafted the messages with just the right amount of desperation. Enough to seem real, enough to plant doubt.

"I miss you," one message read. "L isn't the only one who needs me."

Maddie checked her watch—a Cartier that Jackson had given her on their fifteenth anniversary. (Before Lily. Before everything changed.) In approximately twenty minutes, Lillian would discover that envelope. And tomorrow morning, when Jackson picked her up for their routine breakfast date—because Jackson was nothing if not predictable in his new romance—she'd "happen" to find the hotel receipt.

Her phone buzzed again. Her contact at the Peninsula Club was worth every penny: "Envelope delivered to Ms. Hart's mailbox."

Walking back to her car, Maddie didn't need to

stay and watch the dominoes fall. She could already picture it: Lillian, her little face crumpling as she read about these other women—these phantoms Maddie had conjured from thin air. She'd confront Jackson, of course. And Jackson, already fraying at the edges from Maddie's earlier machinations, would react as expected. He'd get defensive. He'd snap. Because that's what Jackson did when he felt cornered—he lashed out.

Their fairy tale was about to show its first cracks, and Maddie would be nowhere in sight when it happened. That's what they never understood about her. She didn't need to wield the knife herself. She just needed to hand it to the right person at the right time.

Let them destroy each other. She'd provided the matches and the gasoline.

She slipped into her own car, adjusting the rearview mirror. Her reflection showed applied lipstick, not a hair out of place. No one looking at her would guess she'd just lit the fuse on a bomb. But then again, they never did. That was her gift—she could smile and destroy simultaneously. And wasn't that what Jackson had loved about her once? Her ability to make everything look effortless?

Well, he was about to remember how effortless she could make destruction look.

Maddie traced her manicured fingernail along the edge of her Hermès bag, feeling the supple leather beneath her touch. She'd positioned it just so on the Peninsula Club's marble counter, the logo visible but not obviously displayed. (After all, true elegance never screamed.) The young receptionist, Amy, was already leaning forward, eager as a puppy. The girl loved to gossip, especially about members who seemed troubled, and Maddie had learned long ago that the best information came from those who thought they were your friend.

"I couldn't help but notice Miss Hart earlier," Maddie said, infusing her voice with the blend of concern and curiosity. She watched Amy's face light up at the mention of Lillian. Poor, fragile Lillian, who thought she could step into Maddie's life and wear it like a borrowed dress. "She looked so pale, almost ill." Maddie pulled out her membership card with deliberate slowness, though everyone knew who she was. Twenty years of membership had earned her that much, at least. "I do hope she's not unwell."

The bait was set, and Amy, predictably, couldn't resist. The girl leaned closer, her cheap perfume wafting across the counter. "She's been acting strange. Called to cancel her tennis lesson again—third time this week."

"?" Maddie allowed her eyebrows to lift just, a practiced gesture of surprise that she'd ed over years of social manipulation. Through the glass doors, she sights of Barbara and Charlotte arriving for their regular lunch. timing. Barbara, who could never keep a secret, and Charlotte, who pretended to be above gossip while drinking in every word. They were who she needed for the next phase of her plan.

"And she keeps calling Mr. Callahan's office," Amy continued, dropping her voice to a conspiratorial whisper that carried just far enough. "The front desk there asked us to stop putting her through."

Maddie permitted a small frown to crease her forehead, careful not to disturb the Botox. "How concerning." She paused, then added the garnish to her crafted narrative. "You know, just yesterday at Café Laurent, she jumped out of her skin when someone dropped a glass." A slight smile played on Maddie's lips. Of course, Maddie had arranged for that glass to be dropped, but such details weren't important.

"Maddie, darling!" Barbara's voice carried across the lobby, right on cue. Barbara always did have impeccable timing, even if she didn't know she was being used.

Maddie turned to watch their approach, noting how their eyes darted between her and Amy, hungry for information. They'd just enough of the conversation to be intrigued— as she had planned.

But Charlotte hesitated.

A second too long.

Maddie moved, but she cataloged it instantly— the way Charlotte's gaze flickered over the receptionist's desk, to Maddie's poised expression, then away again. Like she was searching for something unseen. Like she was wondering if she'd walked into a conversation that wasn't meant to be heard.

Charlotte forced a bright smile. "What's this about Lillian Hart?" she asked as they walked toward the dining room, trying to sound casual and failing miserably.

Interesting.

Maddie shook her head, letting her concern appear genuine. "I probably shouldn't say anything, but.. ." She paused, counting the seconds in her head. One, two, three— just long enough for their curiosity to peak. "Well, people are starting to notice things. The constant cancellations, the nervous behavior." She let the implications hang in the air like smoke.

"I heard she's been calling Jackson's office

incessantly," Barbara jumped in, predictable as ever. "My friend Margaret works in the building; says she's becoming quite the nuisance."

Maddie nodded, a queen accepting tribute. By dinner, the whispers would spread through their social circle like wildfire.

But Charlotte's reaction wasn't like Barbara's.

Charlotte reached for a glass of Château Lafite Rothschild from a passing server—not for the taste, but as if she needed something to hold. Something to steady her hands.

Maddie let the moment stretch.

Charlotte's fingers tapped lightly against the stem of her glass. A tiny movement. noticeable. But Maddie noticed.

She's nervous. She knows something.

Maddie smiled, slow and knowing. "Are you all right, darling?" she asked, her tone silk-smooth.

Charlotte's fingers tightened around the glass, but her expression remained neutral. "Just thirsty," she said, taking a sip. Too quick.

Barbara, oblivious, continued prattling about Lillian's instability, but Maddie wasn't listening anymore. Her focus was on Charlotte.

This was new.

Charlotte wasn't just interested in the gossip—she was evaluating it.

A flicker of something passed over Charlotte's face—a question she hadn't quite formed yet. Or maybe one she didn't want the answer to.

Maddie's expression remained unreadable. But in her mind, she adjusted the pieces on the board.

Charlotte might need... closer attention.

For now, though, she let her stew. No need to play a card too early.

Maddie nodded, a queen accepting tribute. She didn't need to say more. By dinner, the whispers would spread through their social circle like wildfire, each retelling making Lillian sound more unstable than the last. And the best part? Maddie wouldn't have to say another word. They would do all the work for her, while she remained above it all, concerned and blameless.

Let them whisper about poor, troubled Lillian. Let them wonder why Jackson's young princess was starting to crack. And let Jackson see what happens when a man forgets what belongs to his wife.

Through the upstairs window, Maddie watched Lillian's Mercedes pull into the circular driveway, its headlights sweeping across the manicured lawn where she had spent twenty years. Her fingers tightened around the stem of her wine glass—crystal, from their wedding registry. How fitting that she should use it tonight.

The scene below unfolded like a rehearsed play, one where Maddie knew every line before it was spoken. The security lights (installed last spring, when Jackson insisted, they needed "better surveillance") illuminated Lillian's face like a spotlight. Even from this distance, Maddie could appreciate the artistry of it all—the smeared mascara (Dior, if she had to guess), the wild desperation in those young eyes that had once looked so confident. Her Hermès scarf (a gift from Jackson, no doubt) hung askew, her blonde hair tangled by the wind. Not too obvious, just disheveled enough to seem unhinged.

"Jackson, please!" Lillian's voice carried through

the glass, high-pitched and desperate. Just like Maddie knew it would be. "Something's wrong—someone's following me, sending messages—"

The front door opened, and there he was. Jackson. Her husband of twenty-five years, standing there in his pressed slacks and button-down shirt, every inch the decorated general. His posture was rigid with military precision—the same stance he'd used when addressing his troops. How many times had Maddie watched him practice that pose in their bedroom mirror?

"Lower your voice," he commanded, and Maddie could mouth the words along with him. "This is inappropriate."

She took a slow sip of her cabernet, letting its rich complexity bloom on her tongue. Beneath the window, Lillian reached for Jackson's arm—a rookie mistake. He stepped back as if her touch might contaminate him, and Maddie felt a flutter of satisfaction in her chest. The same arm that had held "Princess" so tenderly at the country club last month now recoiled from her presence.

"You need to leave," Jackson said, his tone cold and final. The same tone he'd used with Maddie countless times, but she'd learned to weather it. Poor Lillian had no such experience. "Whatever's going on with you—I can't be involved."

"But the notes, the flowers—" Lillian's voice cracked beautifully.

(The flowers had been expensive, but worth every penny. Red roses, delivered daily, each with a card that grew increasingly desperate. The notes, slipped under her windshield wipers, each one more unhinged than the last. All in Lillian's handwriting, of course. Amazing what people could do with the right motivation and a generous check.)

"You're becoming unstable." Jackson checked his watch—the Rolex Maddie had given him on their twentieth anniversary. "I have an early meeting."

Maddie watched Lillian's face crumple as the realization hit. All those orchestrated moments had done their work: the planted evidence in her desk at work, the held rumors among the country club wives, the "concerned" phone calls to her office. Jackson wasn't seeing his precious "Princess" anymore. He was seeing what Maddie needed him to see—a liability.

Lillian stumbled back toward her car, mascara-stained tears marking her cheeks. Jackson didn't wait to watch her leave. He turned and walked inside, closing the door with a decisive click that echoed through the house like a judge's gavel.

Maddie raised her wine glass in a silent toast to the empty driveway. She hadn't needed to confront Lillian directly. Hadn't needed to raise her voice or make a scene like some common divorcée. She'd shown Jackson what he needed to see—that his young mistress wasn't so after all.

She took another sip of wine, letting the satisfaction settle in her bones. The night wasn't over yet. Soon, Jackson would come upstairs, and she would pretend not to have witnessed any of it. She would be the wife, concerned but not prying, supportive but not smothering. And tomorrow? Well, tomorrow she would make sure those photos of Lillian outside his office found their way to the right people.

After all, what was that saying? If you love something, set it free. If it comes back, it's yours. If it doesn't... destroy anyone who tries to take it.

Chapter 16

Maddie descended the stairs, her heels clicking a victorious rhythm against the marble. Everything was. The house stretched around her, silent and pristine, just the way she liked it. Jackson had disappeared into his study (hiding, probably, from the mess he'd created), and the children were safely tucked away at their various activities. Even the afternoon light seemed to bend to her will, casting elegant shadows across the foyer.

The satisfaction of Lillian's breakdown still

tingled through her veins like expensive champagne. She could still see the girl (because that's all she was, —a girl playing dress-up in a woman's world) crumbling on the front lawn, mascara tracking down those young cheeks. Maddie had watched it all from behind the living room curtains, savoring each sob like the last sip of a fine wine.

She found Rosa in the kitchen, doing what Rosa always did—maintaining order. The housekeeper's hands moved across the granite counter tops, the cleaning cloth making soft, circular motions. Twenty years of the same movement, the same routine. Some things, at least, remained constant.

"Did you see her?" Maddie couldn't help the smile that curved her lips, the way satisfaction warmed her voice. "Out there on the lawn, begging like a child?" The word 'child' tasted sweet. Because that's what Lillian was—what Jackson wanted. A child to make him feel young again.

Rosa's hands stilled on the counter, and something in her silence made Maddie's smile falter. The housekeeper wouldn't meet her eyes, and for a moment, Maddie felt that familiar flicker of paranoia. Rosa knew too much. Had always known too much.

"It worked." Maddie moved to the fruit bowl, selecting an apple, needing something to do with her hands. She examined its flawless surface, remembering how flawless Lillian had once been. "You should've seen her face—she's falling apart." Just like I planned. Just like she deserves.

The tension in Rosa's shoulders spoke volumes, but Maddie pushed past her discomfort. She needed this taken care of. Now.

"The key from the messenger service." She

lowered her voice, letting steel edge into her tone. This wasn't a request. This was an order. "And burn the key. I don't want it found."

A floorboard creaked behind her, and something in the sound—its weight, its timing—made her blood run cold.

The apple slipped from her fingers as she turned, hitting the floor with a dull thud that seemed to echo through her bones. Jackson stood in the doorway, still wearing his suit from work, his tie loosened—the only sign of the long day he'd had. But it was his face that made her heart stutter. That dangerous stillness she recognized from their worst arguments, the kind that preceded explosions.

The silence stretched between them like a wire about to snap. She watched his eyes move from her to Rosa, then back again, and she could see him processing what he'd just heard. The pieces were falling into place—the notes, Lillian's paranoia, the planted evidence. All her careful work, her plan to destroy his young mistress, laid bare in a single moment of carelessness.

His jaw clenched. The muscle there twitched once, twice. (He'd done the same thing the night he told her he was leaving—how had she forgotten that tell?)

Maddie felt her constructed world begin to crack, hairline fractures spreading through everything she'd built. Her heart hammered against her ribs, but her face remained composed—years of practice keeping her features arranged just so. The apple rolled across the kitchen floor, a red blur in her peripheral vision. Behind her, Rosa's cleaning cloth scraped against the granite counter, the sound suddenly deafening in the silence.

"Burn what key, Maddie?" Jackson's voice cut

through the air like a blade.

She turned to face him fully, calling upon decades of social performance. Confusion painted her features—practiced confusion. "What are you talking about?"

"What worked?" His words came out clipped, precise—the way he spoke during military briefings. The tone that meant someone was about to be destroyed.

"Darling, you must have misheard." She stepped toward him, reaching to touch his arm, to reclaim control. "You've been under so much stress with work—"

Jackson her wrist before she could make contact. His grip wasn't tight, but it was final—like the closing of a door. "Stop. The notes to Lillian. The black box with the lily. The 'stranger' following her. The planted evidence in my car."

The blood drained from her face. For the first time in years, fear slithered cold and slow down her spine. The game was over. And she wasn't the one holding the board anymore.

Maddie stepped toward Jackson, her Louboutins clicking against the marble floor like a metronome counting down the seconds before her world imploded. "Darling, you must have misheard." The word 'darling' rolled off her tongue with practiced ease, the same way it had for twenty-eight years of marriage. (Though, it felt more like a weapon than an endearment.)

She reached for his arm, muscle memory guiding her fingers toward the familiar gesture of control. How many times had she done this? Hundreds? Thousands? Those little touches that reminded him who kept his world spinning on its axis. Her fingertips ached with the desire to smooth his collar, to adjust his tie—those intimate gestures that had always marked him as hers.

The same way she used to straighten his uniform before deployments, back when she was young enough to believe waiting would be worth it.

"You've been under so much stress —" The excuse sounded hollow even to her own ears, but Maddie had built a life on making the unbelievable sound reasonable. After all, wasn't that what being a good wife was? Helping your husband maintain the illusion of control while quietly steering the ship?

But Jackson moved with that calculated precision she'd watched him over decades of military service. Before her fingers could make contact, his hand locked around her wrist. The grip wasn't painful—Jackson never left marks, not like that—but it was final. Like the closing of a door. (She'd always hated doors in their marriage. How many had she watched him walk through? How many times had she stood on the wrong side, waiting?)

She imagined him in Afghanistan, closing doors with that same decisive finality. Clean. Professional. Strategic. Everything he did carried that weight of military precision, even now, even here in their own home where he was supposed to be just her husband, not General Callahan. The thought made her fingers twitch against her palm, a nervous habit she'd developed over twenty-five years of marriage. Twenty-five years of watching him move through spaces like they were war zones, mapping exit strategies and calculating risks.

How many times had she watched him pack his bags with that same methodical attention to detail? Shirts folded with hospital corners, boots arranged just so, everything in its designated space. (He'd tried to teach her once, early in their marriage, but she'd laughed it off. Back then, his rigidity had seemed charming, even sexy.

Now it felt like a wall between them.)

She remembered the way he used to close their bedroom door at night, back when they still shared a room. The soft click of the latch, followed by three measured steps to the bed. Always three. Always measured. As if even intimacy needed to follow protocol. These days, he closed doors differently—with purpose, with finality, with the clear message that she wasn't welcome on the other side.

The military had given him that walk, that stance, that way of assessing every situation like it might explode. She used to pride herself on being the exception to his rules, the one person who could make him lose control, forget his training. Now she wondered if she'd ever known him at all, or if she'd just been another mission to accomplish, another objective to secure.

In their early years, she'd romanticized it all—his discipline, his focus, his unwavering sense of duty. She'd imagined herself the devoted military wife, keeping the home fires burning while her brave husband served his country. What a little story she'd told herself. What a little lie.

The truth was messier. The truth was that while he'd been closing doors in war zones, she'd been here, teaching her own kind of strategy. While he'd been commanding troops, she'd been building her own army of cultivated friendships and social alliances. While he'd been planning tactical maneuvers in the desert, she'd been orchestrating her own campaigns in their manicured suburb.

Now here they were, facing each other across a battlefield he didn't even recognize. He still thought this was about doors and wrists and maintaining control. He hadn't figured out yet that she'd learned from the best— that she'd watched him for years, studying his precision, his strategy, his ability to wage war without ever raising his voice.

Poor Jackson, still fighting the last war while she prepared for the next one. He'd taught her too well, hadn't he? All those years of military precision had rubbed off on her in ways he never anticipated. He'd shown her how to identify a target, how to wait for the moment, how to strike with surgical precision.

The irony almost made her laugh. Almost.

"Stop." His voice cut through her thoughts with that sharp, commanding edge she'd secretly despised all these years. It was the voice that had made soldiers snap to attention, that had earned him stars on his collar—and God, how she hated when he used it on her. She wasn't one of his troops to be commanded. She was Madeline Callahan, and she had sacrificed her entire youth waiting for him to come home.

But then he continued, each word falling like an aimed bullet: "The notes to Lillian. The black box with the lily. The 'stranger' following her. The planted evidence in my car."

The blood in her veins turned to ice water. She felt it happening—that slow, creeping chill that started in her fingertips and worked its way toward her heart. (Funny, how the body betrays you in moments like these. How it remembers to be afraid even when your mind is still catching up.) Her curated world was cracking, and through those cracks, she could see the darkness she'd been trying so hard to keep contained.

For the first time in years, Maddie felt true fear

slither down her spine, cold and familiar, like an old friend she'd hoped never to meet again. The game was over. She had lost. But as the realization settled over her like a shroud, another emotion bubbled up beneath the fear—something darker, something that had been waiting for this moment. Because Maddie Callahan didn't lose. Not, anyway. And if Jackson thought he could close this door like all the others, well... he was about to learn that some doors, once opened, refuse to stay shut.

The blood drained from her face, and for the first time in years, she felt true fear slither down her spine. Barbara. Of course it was Barbara. That woman never could keep her champagne-loosened mouth shut. How many times had Maddie watched her prattle on at charity luncheons, spilling secrets like wine? But Maddie had never imagined Barbara would betray her. (After all, Maddie knew enough about Barbara's indiscretions to bury her socially ten times over.)

The game was over—and she had lost.

Maddie's fingers found her pearls—a nervous habit she'd developed over twenty-five years of marriage. They were the first real piece of jewelry Jackson had given her, back when he was just a promising young officer and she was a military wife. She'd worn them to every promotion ceremony, every military ball, every social gathering where she'd helped him climb higher and higher. Now they felt like a noose.

Her mind spiraled through the evidence she'd left behind. The notes—she'd been careful, hadn't she? Gloves. Different paper. Random locations. But Lillian, the stupid girl, had kept them all. (Of course she had. Lillian was the type to document everything, to build her victim narrative. Just like she'd documented every "chance" meeting with Jackson at that ridiculous coffee shop.)

The black box had been a masterpiece of subtlety. A single black lily, left on Lillian's doorstep—a warning wrapped in beauty. Maddie had watched from her car as Lillian found it, saw how her hands trembled as she lifted the lid. It had been. Too perfect, perhaps. She should have known that anything that satisfying would eventually come back to haunt her.

And the "stranger"—well, that had been Barbara's son's college roommate, paid handsomely to make Lillian feel watched. Another thread that could be pulled, another lie that could unravel. (She should have used someone untraceable, someone without connections. But she'd been so angry, so desperate to make Lillian feel the fear that had been eating at Maddie's own insides.)

The planted evidence in Jackson's car—it had been reckless. But necessary. But by then, the rage had taken over. The sight of his silver Lexus in Lillian's driveway that Sunday morning had shattered something inside her. She'd stopped thinking like a chess player and started moving like a wounded animal.

Her eyes darted to the family photo on the wall—her masterpiece of manipulation. Everyone posed, color-coordinated in cream and navy. Carrie's hair had taken an hour to curl just right. Nate's collar had needed constant adjusting. Jackson stood behind them all, his hand on Maddie's shoulder, looking every inch the decorated General. The photo said everything she wanted people to see: power, perfection, control.

But now Jackson was looking at her the way he looked at enemy combatants in those classified briefings he thought she never saw. Like she was a threat to be neutralized. A target to be eliminated.

The facade she'd maintained for twenty-five years cracked like fine china dropped on marble floors. She could almost hear it shattering, the sound echoing through their house with its furnishings and its hidden secrets.

The game was over. But Maddie had learned long ago, watching her mother navigate three divorces and countless social wars, that when one game ended, another always began. Her lips curved into a smile that didn't quite reach her eyes. She'd lost this round, but she'd be damned if she lost the war.

After all, she hadn't spent twenty-five years as a general's wife without learning a thing or two about strategy.

◆ ◆ ◆

Charlotte's fingers were still. No fluttering, no nervous energy. Just the slow, methodical turning of her wine glass between manicured fingers. That was new.

"I was thinking..." Charlotte's voice was casual—too casual. But this time, it didn't waver. "It's strange, isn't it? How quickly things have unraveled for Lillian? First the notes, then the police reports, then the... well, everything."

Maddie let a smile curve her lips, just enough. "Poor girl must be exhausted."

Charlotte lifted her glass, took a sip, held eye contact.

Maddie's fingers hesitated over her napkin. The smallest misstep, but she noticed it. (Why did she seem so calm?)

Charlotte set her glass down with quiet precision. "I heard from Barbara." The words were neutral.

Noncommittal. A trap waiting to be sprung.

Maddie gave a light chuckle, but the sound tasted thin on her tongue. "Oh, darling. You know better than to listen to Barbara."

Charlotte tilted her head, just slightly—mirroring Maddie's own gesture from minutes before. A deliberate echo.

"Yes. I suppose I do."

A pause.

Too long.

Something shifted. Maddie could feel it.

Charlotte took another sip, waiting.

And suddenly, Maddie hated the silence.

Chapter 17

Maddie adjusted her Chanel jacket, a gesture as practiced as breathing. The mirror reflected perfection back at her—every strand of chestnut hair in place, makeup precise enough to hide the shadows beneath her eyes (the ones that appeared after Jackson left, not that anyone needed to know about those). The St. Catherine's Annual Charity Luncheon sprawled before her; a battlefield disguised as a social gathering. Valets scurried like well-trained soldiers, women performed their ritualistic air-kisses on the marble steps, and photographers lurked, hungry for a shot of Madeline Callahan's first public appearance since The Incident.

Her hand remained steady as she applied the Dior Rouge—number 999, the same shade she'd worn at last year's luncheon when she'd been the one greeting others, secure in her position as General Jackson Callahan's wife. The lipstick was armor, the color of power and composure. Let them whisper behind their manicured hands. Let them dissect her appearance in their group texts, wondering why she had the audacity to show her face when her husband was probably in bed with his princess at this moment.

When the valet opened her door (Thomas, who had worked here for years and still called her Mrs. Callahan with the proper respect), Maddie emerged with the grace of a woman who had spent decades raising her public persona. Her Louboutins struck the pavement in a precise rhythm—click, click, click—each step a small victory. The sudden silence was delicious. Conversations withered and died. Heads swiveled like spectators at a tennis match. On the steps, Charlotte stood frozen, her champagne flute hovering awkwardly between earth and sky, looking for all the world like a statue of betrayal in mid-pose.

"Maddie!" Barbara's voice shattered the silence, pitched high enough to make dogs wince. Barbara, who had texted her every day for a week after Jackson left, until the messages suddenly stopped. (Maddie knew why—she'd seen Barbara having lunch with Lily last Tuesday. Noted. Filed away. Not forgotten.) "We didn't expect—I mean, it's wonderful to see you."

"Barbara, darling." Maddie leaned in for the

traditional air-kiss, catching a whiff of Barbara's new perfume. Chanel No. 5. How predictable. How safe. "I wouldn't miss supporting the children's hospital. It's such an important cause." The words rolled off her tongue, sweet as honey laced with arsenic.

They gathered like moths to a flame, these women who had been her court when she was queen. Sandra clutched her last-season Prada bag like it might shield her from Maddie's presence. Charlotte's fingers worked her pearl necklace as if counting rosary beads, probably praying she wouldn't be the next topic of Maddie's crafted verbal daggers.

"We've all been so worried," Charlotte ventured, always the brave one. Or the foolish one. Time would tell. "After everything..."

"Oh." Maddie flicked her wrist with practiced nonchalance, a gesture she'd ed over countless mornings in her master bathroom, timing it against the soft hum of her heated marble floors. The diamond tennis bracelet— Jackson's guilt offering for their twentieth anniversary, back when he still bothered with guilt— the afternoon light, scattering prisms across the tablecloth. She wore it like armor now, each diamond a reminder of the years she'd invested, the life she'd crafted, the power she wouldn't relinquish to some dewy-eyed homewrecker who thought youth was a substitute for cunning.

"It's all so tragic, but we're handling it like adults. Jackson and I both want what's best for the children." The words tasted like copper on her tongue, bitter and metallic. What Jackson wanted was to pretend twenty-three years of marriage could be neatly packed away like last season's clothes. What Maddie wanted was to remind him why he'd once feared her mind more than he'd desired her body.

She let her smile crack just enough—a calculated fissure in her facade. These women had spent years studying her like anthropologists observing a rare species. Charlotte, with her nervous hands working that strand of pearls (real, but outdated); Sandra, clutching her last-season Prada like a shield (as if designer bags could protect her from becoming another cautionary tale); Barbara, vibrating with poorly concealed glee (she'd always been the worst of them, feeding on others' misfortunes like a vulture in Valentino).

"Though I do worry about how they're adjusting to Virginia." She infused the word 'Virginia' with just enough disdain to make it clear what she thought of Jackson's new life in the suburbs with his princess. "Such a... provincial environment compared to what they're used to." The word dropped like cyanide into a champagne flute, and Maddie watched it dissolve behind their eyes. Let them connect the dots, let them wonder how she knew where Jackson had stashed his mistress-turned-fiancée. Let them realize that while Jackson was playing house in Virginia, Maddie was here, orchestrating his social execution with the precision of a surgeon.

Their glances bounced between each other like a game of social tennis. Maddie could read every micro-expression, every subtle shift. Poor, fragile Maddie transformed before their eyes into something more dangerous, more calculating. She saw the moment they began to question Jackson's judgment, saw Barbara's lined lips purse with fresh speculation.

"Shall we?" Maddie gestured toward the entrance with liquid grace. "I believe they're serving that delightful butternut squash soup today." The same soup they'd served at the charity gala where she'd first noticed Jackson's wandering attention, his eyes following Lily across the room like a heat-seeking missile. How long ago was that? Eight months? Nine? Time had become fluid since then, measured not in days but in orchestrated moves and countermoves.

She glided past them, her Louboutins clicking against marble like a metronome. Their whispers followed her, as she'd planned. By dessert, the entire room would be dissecting Jackson's character. By dinner, every country club from here to Buckhead would be questioning the judgment of General Jackson Callahan, war hero turned suburban cliché.

The bruises had been a masterpiece of timing and technique. Ice, then pressure, then the precise application of makeup to enhance rather than conceal. She'd practiced the movements in front of her vanity, timing each gesture until it looked natural, unplanned.

When her silk sleeve slipped back as she reached for her water glass, exposing the artfully crafted purple-yellow marks circling her wrist, Maddie counted silently. One (Charlotte's sharp intake of breath), two (Barbara's predatory lean forward), three—

"Maddie!" Charlotte's voice sliced through the careful chatter. "What happened to your arm?"

The table fell silent, all eyes fixed on her wrist like spotlights. Maddie tugged her sleeve down with just the right amount of self-conscious haste, but not before they'd all gotten their fill of evidence.

"Oh..." She let her spoon hover above the soup, trembling just enough to be noticeable. "It's nothing. Just. .. stress, I suppose." The lie settled like silk over steel.

Barbara couldn't help herself, leaning forward with the eagerness of a woman who'd just been handed social dynamite. "Those don't look like stress marks."

Maddie kept her eyes down, counting breaths like she'd counted the days since Jackson's betrayal. One, two, three—

"Maddie." Charlotte's voice dropped to a theatrical whisper. "Did Jackson...?"

The silence stretched like a garrote wire. Maddie maintained her focus on the soup, letting them see her hand shake. Just once. Just enough.

"I shouldn't discuss it." She dabbed her lips with her napkin, allowing them to see the slight tremor in her fingers. "The lawyers are handling everything."

Sandra's gasp could have been lifted from a daytime soap opera. Charlotte's hand flew to her throat, pearls clicking against her wedding ring.

"I'd appreciate if we could change the subject." Maddie made her voice waver with the precision of a master violinist. "The children don't need to hear any rumors." But they would. Oh, they would. And by the time Jackson realized what she'd done, it would be far too late to stop the avalanche she'd just triggered.

◆ ◆ ◆

Maddie studied her reflection in the master bathroom, the cool silk of the Hermès scarf pressed against her cheekbone like a lover's whisper. Twenty years of marriage had taught her the art of manipulation, but this—this required a surgeon's precision. The metal paperweight from Jackson's study—a gift from some general, some war she'd stopped caring about—sat on the marble counter, its weight satisfying in her palm.

She'd spent the previous night practicing the

angle, like a dancer mastering her routine, until she knew exactly how much pressure would create the storm of sympathy.

The bruise needed to be a watercolor of suggestion. Natural enough to raise eyebrows but not so dramatic it would raise questions. After all, the best lies were the ones people told themselves.

Rosa's footsteps echoed down the hallway—the steady, predictable rhythm of a woman who had seen too much and said too little. Maddie's fingers danced across the counter, sweeping the paperweight into her vanity drawer with practiced efficiency. How many secrets had that drawer swallowed over the years?

"Mrs. Callahan?" Rosa's voice carried the weight of two decades of silent judgment through the heavy oak door. "Charlotte called. She wants to know if you're still coming for bridge this afternoon."

"Tell her I'll be there at two." Maddie pressed the ice harder against her skin, watching with clinical fascination as the flesh darkened beneath it. The pain was inconsequential—merely the price of a performance.

When Rosa's footsteps faded away (like everything else in Maddie's life seemed to these days), she reached for her professional-grade makeup case. The stage makeup techniques she'd learned years ago had been an investment in her future without her even knowing it. Funny how life worked that way. She worked with delicate precision, adding touches of yellow here, deeper purple there, creating shadows that softly spoke of violence while screaming of vulnerability.

Charlotte's living room was a stage set for destruction, the afternoon light streaming through French windows like a spotlight waiting for its star. Six women, all friends (if you could call them that in this world of sharp smiles and sharper tongues), gathered around the card table like vultures circling fresh meat. Maddie had calculated her entrance down to the second, tilting her face just so, letting the golden light catch the artfully crafted bruise.

Barbara's reaction was everything Maddie had hoped for—cards scattered across the imported linen tablecloth like confetti at a funeral. "Oh my God."

"It's nothing." Maddie touched her cheek with trembling fingers (practiced in front of her mirror for an hour), wincing with just enough restraint to seem brave. "I... fell. Against the bedside table." The pause was deliberate, the slight catch in her voice timed.

Sandra's hand flew to her mouth—always the weakest link, always the first to show emotion. Charlotte set down her gin and tonic, ice cubes clinking like tiny warning bells.

"Maddie." Charlotte's voice carried that careful tone, the one reserved for wounded animals and women who married powerful men. "You don't have to protect him."

"I'm not protecting anyone." Maddie arranged her cards with steady hands, keeping her eyes downcast like a martyr at prayer. "These things happen during divorces. People get... emotional." She let the word hang in the air like smoke, knowing they would inhale it, let it poison their thoughts about Jackson.

The room fell silent except for the nervous symphony of ice cubes against crystal. She could feel their stares, their assumptions building like a castle in the air. She didn't need to say more—they would do the work for her, their imaginations far crueler than any truth could be. After all, wasn't that what friends were for?

The bruise throbbed beneath her makeup, a reminder of her own handiwork. Jackson had taught her about strategic warfare without realizing it. Every battle was won before it began, he'd always said. Well, she thought, straightening her cards with manicured precision, let's see how the great General handles this particular front.

◆ ◆ ◆

The phone felt like ice in Maddie's palm as she traced another lap around her study. Three days. Three orchestrated days since she'd unveiled her masterpiece at bridge club, and still nothing. The antique grandfather clock in the corner ticked away the seconds, each movement of its hands another reminder of Jackson's silence. No angry calls. No threats. Not even a text message telling her she'd gone too far this time.

She pressed Barbara's number again, muscle memory taking over. Barbara always answered on the second ring—reliable in her desperation to be needed, just like clockwork.

"Did you mention the bruise to Susan?" Maddie kept her voice as smooth as aged bourbon, practiced and. She'd learned long ago that desperation was an ugly perfume, and she refused to wear it. "You know she plays tennis with Jackson's lawyer's wife." Which was why Maddie had chosen Susan as the target for this particular piece of information. In their social circle, gossip traveled faster than light.

"Of course I did." Barbara's voice carried that delicious hint of conspiracy she always adopted when sharing secrets. "Everyone's talking about it."

"And?" Maddie allowed just a touch of steel to

enter her voice. Barbara had a tendency to wander if not properly directed.

"Well..." That pause. That infuriating pause that made Maddie's manicured nails dig into her palm. "Greg Morrison told Charlotte that Jackson's lawyer brought it up yesterday."

The phone nearly cracked under the pressure of Maddie's grip. "What did Jackson say?" Each word came out measured, controlled, like drops of poison being dispensed.

"That's just it. He didn't say anything. Greg said Jackson just looked at his lawyer and said 'Handle it.' Can you believe that? Not even a denial! "

The phone slipped through Maddie's fingers like water, clattering against the mahogany desk she'd chosen with Jackson on their tenth anniversary. She scrambled to retrieve it, hating herself for the undignified movement.

"Maddie? Are you there?"

"I have to go." She ended the call before Barbara could hear the tremor in her voice.

Handle it? Like she was a minor household pest to be dealt with by the exterminator? Twenty-five years of marriage reduced to a two-word dismissal delivered to his lawyer? Maddie her reflection in the window—the bruise she'd spent hours perfecting had faded to a sickly yellow-green, like old fruit left to rot. Her fingers ghosted over the mark, remembering the countless YouTube tutorials she'd watched, the practice sessions with different combinations of stage makeup until it looked authentic enough to spark genuine concern.

All that meticulous planning, all those careful seeds planted in their social circle, and Jackson couldn't even be bothered to pick up the phone and accuse her of lying.

Her hand shook as she reached for the crystal decanter—a wedding gift from his mother, now dead and unable to see what her precious son had become. The bourbon scorched its way down her throat, but the burn was nothing compared to the ice forming in her chest. Jackson was supposed to fight back. He was supposed to show some hint that he still cared enough to be angry, that somewhere beneath his new life with his precious "Princess," there was still a man who remembered building this life with Maddie.

But he'd dismissed her. Like she was nothing more than a line item on his lawyer's to-do list. Like their quarter-century together could be condensed into a billable hour.

Maddie stared at her phone, willing it to ring, to buzz, to show any sign of life. The silence stretched out before her like the empty side of their king-sized bed, growing heavier with each passing second. She took another sip of bourbon, letting the crystal catch the late afternoon light. If Jackson thought she could be "handled" by his legal team, he clearly hadn't been paying attention these last twenty-five years.

This was only the beginning.

Chapter 18

Maddie slipped into Le Petit Jardin ten minutes early, just as she had every Thursday for the past decade. The familiar scent of fresh-baked bread and herbs wrapped around her like an old friend, but something felt wrong today. Off-kilter. The maître d' led her to their usual corner table—the best in the house, naturally— with its view of both the garden and the entrance. for people-watching, for being seen.

The empty chairs seemed to mock her. No

Barbara, already three mimosas deep and bursting to share whatever morsel of scandal she'd gleaned from her weekly tennis matches. No Charlotte with her precise routine of arranging her phone, planner, and reading glasses just so, as if the placement of objects could somehow organize her entire life.

Maddie checked her phone again. Nothing. She'd sent Barbara two crafted texts this morning—casual enough to seem effortless, pointed enough to demand a response. Barbara always replied within minutes, usually with an excessive string of emojis that Maddie privately found tacky but publicly indulged. The screen remained blank.

"Would you like to order, Mrs. Callahan?" The waiter appeared at her elbow, his smile just a touch too sympathetic. "Or shall we wait for the others?"

"They'll be here." Maddie smoothed her napkin across her lap, each movement measured and precise. Just like her mother had taught her. Control the small things, and the big things fall into place. "Barbara's always running late." (A lie. Barbara was perpetually early, desperate to prove her worth.)

Twenty minutes crawled by like twenty years. Maddie's manicured fingers drummed against her water glass, each tap echoing the growing hollowness in her chest. The ice had melted, leaving the water diluted and weak. Like friendship, perhaps. She pulled up Barbara's number, pressing the call button before doubt could creep in.

"Oh, Maddie." Barbara's voice came through flat, stripped of its usual breathless excitement. The pause that followed felt calculated, rehearsed. "I meant to call. Something came up with the charity board."

"Reschedule for tomorrow then?" Maddie kept her voice light, pleasant. The same tone she used when questioning Carrie about her homework or discussing the weather with Rosa.

"I'm... rather booked this week. I'll have to check my calendar." The hesitation spoke volumes. Barbara, who had never been too busy for a lunch, who had canceled her daughter's graduation dinner just to attend one of Maddie's impromptu gatherings.

The line went dead before Maddie could respond, before she could remind Barbara of all the favors owed, all the secrets kept. Movement her eye—Charlotte, entering the restaurant with her new Hermès bag (the one she'd bought after Maddie mentioned having the same in three colors) clutched against her chest like armor.

Their eyes met across the dining room. Charlotte's steps faltered, her face doing that thing it did when she was about to make an excuse. But she didn't even bother with that courtesy. She turned and walked out, her heels clicking against the marble floor in a hasty retreat.

Maddie sat still, her spine straight, her smile fixed. Let them watch. Let them whisper. She'd been here before, hadn't she? When Jackson first left? When the country club wives had said behind their hands about poor Maddie Callahan and her wandering husband?

She lifted her water glass, took a deliberate sip. They thought they could do this to her? Barbara with her loose lips and cheaper jewelry? Charlotte, who'd been nothing before Maddie took her under her wing?

Well. They'd learn. They'd all learn. Maddie Callahan didn't get abandoned. She didn't get left behind.

She got even.

Maddie watched Sandra's approach through the window of Le Petit Bistro, noting how her friend's steps faltered when their eyes met. Poor Sandra, always so transparent with her emotions. (Unlike Barbara, who at least had the decency to scheme behind designer sunglasses.) She'd gained weight since her divorce—stress eating, no doubt—and that blouse was at least two seasons old. The old Sandra would never have let herself go like this.

"Sandra." Maddie's hand swept toward the empty chairs surrounding her usual corner table, the gesture both invitation and command. The same table where, just last month, she'd hosted the hospital benefit committee. Before Jackson. Before everything changed.

"I can't stay." Sandra clutched her over-sized bag like a shield. "Just picking up a to-go order."

"Nonsense." Maddie let her lips curve into the smile she'd ed over twenty years of military wives' functions. The one that said 'I'm your friend' and 'Don't you dare defy me' in equal measure. "Sit. Tell me about the new landscaping project." Because of course Maddie knew about the landscaping. She made it her business to know everything happening in their circle, especially now.

Sandra's weight shifted from one sensible pump to the other. Her coral lipstick—too bright for her complexion, —had worn off in the center. "Look, Maddie." Her voice dropped to above a whisper, as if sharing state secrets. "This thing with Jackson... the bruises... people are talking."

The bruises. Of course they were talking about

the bruises. Maddie resisted the urge to touch her wrist, where concealer covered the last fading yellow marks. She'd been so careful with the placement, so precise with her timing. "What are they saying?" The words came out smooth as honey, even as her stomach clenched.

"That maybe you're not telling the whole truth." Sandra's eyes darted everywhere but Maddie's face, like a guilty child's. The same way she'd looked when she'd confessed to her own husband's infidelity two years ago. "I should go. My order's probably ready."

Maddie watched her former friend scurry away, leaving four empty chairs as silent accusers. The whispers from nearby tables grew louder—or perhaps that was just her imagination. No, not imagination. The couple by the window definitely turned away when she glanced their direction. The ladies who lunch, all pearls and judgment, stealing glances between bites of their overpriced salads.

Let them look. Let them whisper. They didn't know—couldn't know—what it was like to be Maddie Callahan. To spend twenty years being the wife, only to be discarded for some fresh-faced princess who probably couldn't tell Champagne from prosecco.

Her hands trembled as she reached for her water glass, the tremble making her angrier than the whispers. She was Maddie Callahan. She didn't tremble. The ice had melted, leaving the water warm and flat on her tongue, like everything else in her life. Tasteless. Diluted.

But that would change. Oh, yes. That would definitely change. Because while Sandra and the others were busy gossiping about bruises and broken marriages, they were missing the most important detail: Maddie had nothing left to lose. And a woman with nothing left to lose was the most dangerous creature of all.

She set the glass down with precise control, leaving a ring of condensation on the crisp white tablecloth. Behind her, the whispers continued, but now they almost made her smile. Let them talk. They'd have so much more to discuss soon enough.

◆ ◆ ◆

Maddie stood in the Piedmont Club's powder room, studying her reflection with the precise attention of a surgeon. The lighting was harsh—deliberately so, she'd always suspected. These old-money clubs loved their subtle cruelties. The bruise she'd crafted peeked through her foundation, a masterpiece of purple and yellow undertones that had taken three weeks of late-night YouTube tutorials to. (Amazing what you could learn from teenage theater kids trying to look like zombies.)

Her hand trembled as she dabbed at her makeup, and for once, the shake wasn't manufactured. The pressure to get this right pressed against her chest like a weight. Too subtle and they wouldn't notice. Too obvious and—well, she couldn't afford obvious, not anymore. She smeared the foundation just enough to suggest distress, just enough to hint at tears hastily wiped away. They would notice. They had to notice.

The familiar scent of Chanel No. 5 and old money wrapped around her as she swept into the dining room. The Garden Club's monthly luncheon hummed with conversation, but she the subtle shift in volume as she approached her usual table. The slight pause in speech. The quick, darting glances. She'd seen that response a thousand times before, but always directed at others. Never at her.

"Maddie." Susan Bennett's voice carried an unfamiliar note that made Maddie's spine stiffen. Not sympathy—she knew sympathy, had cultivated it over the past few weeks. This was something else. Something worse. "Are you sure you're, okay? You look... tired."

Tired. The word landed like a slap. Susan Bennett, who'd once spent an entire summer trying to get her daughter into Maddie's tennis group, who genuflected every time Maddie approved one of her charity initiatives, had just called her tired. In public.

"I'm fine." Maddie touched her cheek with manicured fingers, allowing them to tremble just enough to be noticeable. She'd practiced this gesture in front of her bathroom mirror until it looked natural. "The makeup... it's just been difficult to..." She let the sentence trail off, waiting for the familiar rush of concerned whispers, the protective circle of female solidarity she'd been building so.

Instead, she Elizabeth Morgan and Patricia Walsh exchanging glances across their salmon niçoise salads. That look—she knew that look. She'd weaponized that look against other women countless times. But it wasn't supposed to be directed at her. Never at her.

"Perhaps you should take some time off," Patricia suggested, her tone careful, clinical, like a doctor delivering an unwanted diagnosis. "From social obligations, I mean. To... recover."

Recover. The word hung in the air like poison. They didn't believe her. After weeks of placed hints, crafted stories, strategic tears at just the right moments—they didn't believe her.

Charlotte cleared her throat, adjusting her signature pearl necklace. "The bruising seems... different today." Coming from Charlotte, who'd been her closest ally for twenty years, the observation felt like betrayal.

Maddie's chest tightened as realization dawned. She'd pushed too far with the makeup. Made it too obvious. The sympathy she'd cultivated was slipping away like water through her fingers, replaced by something far worse—doubt. These women, these sharks in Chanel suits, could smell weakness. And she'd just drawn blood in the water.

"I should freshen up." Maddie rose from the table; her legs genuinely unsteady now. The Waldorf salad in front of her remained untouched, a cardinal sin in their circle. Behind her, Patricia's comment carried with devastating clarity:

"Jackson was always such a gentleman. I just can't imagine..."

The rest of the table crooned in agreement, and Maddie could feel her constructed narrative unraveling, thread by precious thread. She'd miscalculated. And in her world, miscalculations were unforgivable.

❖ ❖ ❖

Maddie sat in her Mercedes outside the Piedmont Club, her hands shaking as she pulled out her phone. The screen showed no missed calls, no messages. Nothing.

She pressed Jackson's number. One ring. Two rings. Three—voicemail.

"Jackson." Her voice cracked. "You can't possibly believe—"

She hung up, dialed again. Voicemail.

The leather steering wheel creaked under her grip as she hit redial. Again. Again. Each time, his recorded voice felt more distant, more detached.

On the seventh call, she didn't bother leaving a

message. On the tenth, she waited for the voicemail to start before hanging up. By the fifteenth, her hands were shaking so badly she could hold the phone.

Her screen lit up with an unknown number. She answered before the first ring finished.

"Mrs. Callahan." A woman's voice, crisp and professional. "This is Margaret Chen from Rothstein & Associates. I represent Mr. Callahan in your divorce proceedings."

Maddie's throat closed. A lawyer. He wouldn't even speak to her himself.

"This is a legal matter now. Please refrain from contacting Mr. Callahan directly."

"He's, my husband." The words came out raw, desperate.

"Was your husband, Mrs. Callahan. All communication should go through proper legal channels."

The line went dead. Maddie stared at her phone, at Jackson's name in her recent calls. Twenty-three attempts. Twenty-three rejections.

She dropped the phone into her lap. In the rearview mirror, her applied bruise had started to smear, revealing patches of skin underneath.

◆ ◆ ◆

The front door slammed behind her with a finality that made her bones ache. Maddie's heels clicked across marble—Italian, hand-selected during that trip to Milan when Jackson still noticed such things—each step echoing through the empty house like a metronome counting down to nothing. No children's voices. No Jackson's footsteps. Just silence, thick and accusatory.

The bar cart (a wedding gift from Charlotte, who'd

said that every good wife needed one) beckoned. Her fingers trembled as she reached for a crystal tumbler, the expensive kind reserved for Jackson's business associates. She poured his scotch—the Macallan 25, the one he'd specifically told her was off-limits. Well, he wasn't here to stop her now, was he?

The first sip burned like betrayal. The second numbed like denial. By the third, the room started to blur, edges softening like watercolors in the rain. Better. Not enough, but better.

Her reflection in the window was a funhouse mirror version of the woman who'd left the courthouse hours ago. A stranger stared back at her. No, worse—a ghost of the Maddie Callahan who'd ruled this world for twenty-five years.

"He's not coming back." The words tasted like ash in her mouth, like the remains of everything she'd built, everything she'd sacrificed, everything she'd been.

The scotch wasn't enough. It could never be enough. The bottle shook in her hands as she poured again, amber liquid spilling over the rim like the tears she refused to acknowledge. Twenty-five years. Twenty-five years of dinners (salmon on Wednesdays, because it was his favorite), children (straight A's, manners, everything she'd trained them to be), wife (silent when he was deployed, supportive when he returned, always, always)—

The glass flew from her hand before she realized she'd thrown it, her body acting on rage her mind hadn't yet processed. It shattered against the wall in a symphony of destruction, crystal and scotch raining down on imported marble. The sound was satisfying. Too satisfying.

Another glass. More scotch. Her throat burned as she drained it, chasing oblivion.

"He left me." The words came out in a whisper, then louder, filling the empty space where her life used to be: "He left me! "

The room spun like a carousel she couldn't escape. Her chest tightened, designer dress suddenly a straightjacket. She couldn't breathe. Couldn't think. The wall was too far away, then somehow against her back, the floor rising up to meet her as she slid down, silk catching on the textured wallpaper (hand-painted, imported from Paris, another choice in a house that meant nothing now).

Jackson wasn't in Dubai anymore, safe in her mind as long as he was far away. Jackson wasn't coming home to the life she'd crafted. Jackson wasn't hers—no, he belonged to that girl now, that princess who hadn't earned him, who hadn't waited through deployments and medals and promotions, who'd walked in and taken everything.

Her hands wouldn't stop shaking, trembling like leaves in a storm she couldn't control. Her lungs refused to fill; each breath shorter than the last. Black spots danced at the edges of her vision as reality crashed in— Jackson was gone. gone. Not just away on deployment or business, where she could pretend everything was normal. Gone to Virginia with their children (her children, damn him), gone to his lawyers, gone to his new life where she was nothing but an inconvenient past.

The Mrs. Callahan, abandoned. Replaced. Forgotten. Like last season's fashion, like a toy a child had outgrown.

A sound escaped her throat—raw, animal, primal,

the kind of noise she'd never allowed herself to make in twenty-five years of composure. She clapped her hand over her mouth but couldn't stop it. Tears streaked down her cheeks, ruining what remained of her makeup (Chanel, always Chanel, because that's what his wife should wear). She reached for the bottle again, desperate to drown out the truth she couldn't face: she'd lost. For the first time in her life, Maddie Callahan had lost everything.

And she was going to make them all pay for it.

Chapter 19

The law office was pristine perfection, what she'd expected from a man of Nate Wren's reputation. Maddie inhaled deeply, cataloging each detail like weapons she might need later—the supple leather chairs that probably cost more than most people's monthly mortgage, the gleaming mahogany desk that stretched between them like a battlefield, those smug floor-to-ceiling windows offering a panoramic view of Atlanta's skyline. She smoothed her Chanel suit (last seasons, but who would notice?), and adjusted her smile to the precise degree of warmth that had worked on every man before him.

Attorney Wren didn't even glance up from his papers. The dismissal in that simple non-action made her teeth clench behind her smile.

"Mrs. Callahan." His voice could have frozen champagne. "Let's make this brief."

She leaned forward, allowing her signature Clive Christian perfume (the one that had once made Jackson follow her across a crowded ballroom) to drift across his desk. "Please, call me Maddie." The words dripped honey, practiced to perfection over decades of social climbing.

His cold gray eyes met hers, and something in them made her stomach twist. They were different from other men's eyes—clinical, assessing, like he was dissecting her rather than admiring her. "You're losing this divorce. Jackson is taking the kids. The financials are locked down."

"Surely there's room for negotiation—" She let the words linger, infusing them with promise. How many deals had she sealed with that same tone, that same subtle suggestion of possibility?

"The abuse allegations didn't work." His hands moved across the papers with robotic precision, each movement measured and controlled. Just like Jackson's hands when he was angry. "People are doubting you."

Her heart thundered against her ribs, a war drum of panic she refused to acknowledge. In twenty-five years of marriage, through countless social circles and power plays, she'd never met a man she couldn't charm, couldn't bend to her will with the right combination of vulnerability and suggestion. She rose from her chair, circling his desk with the practiced grace that had once made her the star of every military wife's function.

"There must be something we can do." Her fingers brushed his hand, butterfly-light, as her voice dropped to an intimate whisper. "Something... mutually beneficial." The words that had opened so many doors before, had solved so many problems.

Nate's hand jerked away as if her touch carried poison. His face remained carved from marble, but those eyes—God, those eyes turned to Arctic winter, and for the first time, Maddie felt true fear crawl up her spine.

"I'm not Jackson." He stood, using his height like a weapon, and suddenly she was looking up at him, feeling every inch of the power differential between them. "This meeting is over."

The rejection slammed into her like a physical blow, stealing her breath. She hadn't felt this small, this powerless, since she was nineteen and her mother had her wearing knockoff Gucci. Her constructed world—the one she'd spent decades building, each social connection and calculated kindness another brick in her fortress— crumbled another inch. She could almost hear it falling, like fine china shattering on marble floors.

The worst part wasn't his rejection. It was the absolute certainty that he had known—from the moment she walked in, perhaps even before— what she would do. Every move, every word, every calculated gesture. He had seen through her as easily as those floor-to-ceiling windows, and he hadn't even had the decency to pretend otherwise.

For the first time since Jackson had asked for a divorce, Maddie felt true panic. Not the manageable kind that could be pushed down with a Xanax and a glass of wine, but the raw, primal fear of a predator becoming prey.

❖ ❖ ❖

Maddie sat in her parked Mercedes outside the law office, hands trembling on the steering wheel. The rejection burned through her chest, different from the cold distance Jackson showed. This was worse—open dismissal, like she was nothing. Like twenty-eight years of marriage could be erased with a few signatures and a polite "good day, Mrs. Callahan" from some twenty-something associate who probably still lived with roommates.

Her phone buzzed. Charlotte's name lit up the screen. Maddie let it ring. Another buzz—Barbara this time. Delete. Delete. They'd want details, want to dissect every moment like vultures picking at carrion. She wouldn't give them the satisfaction.

She drove home in a daze, past Le Petit Jardin where she'd ruled just weeks ago, past Maison Belle where she'd first confronted Lillian. The familiar landmarks of her curated life now felt like monuments to her failure. Each stoplight, each familiar corner reminded her of some triumph now turned to ash in her mouth.

Inside her empty house, Maddie poured herself a glass of wine and stared at her social calendar. Garden Club tomorrow. Bridge with Barbara on Thursday. Junior League meeting on Friday. She grabbed her Mont Blanc pen—Jackson's gift from their tenth anniversary—and started crossing them out with violent slashes of ink.

"Cancel everything," she told her assistant over the phone, her voice steady despite the tremor in her hand. "Family emergency. No, I don't need anything rescheduled. And Sarah? Don't bother taking any more calls today."

The whispers started by day three. Her phone filled with messages, each one more cloying than the last:

"Darling, are you getting help?" - Charlotte (who'd once confided her own marriage was hanging by a thread)

"We're all so worried." - Barbara (who was probably already spreading rumors over coffee at Le Petit)

"The Garden Club misses you." - Sandra (sweet, pathetic Sandra, always trying to earn her way back in)

Maddie ignored them all. She drew her curtains, switched off her phones. Let them talk. Let them wonder. The society pages would abuzz with speculation—was Maddie Callahan breaking down? Was she in therapy? Rehab? Their concern was as fake as their French manicures and hospital board positions.

Rosa found her in the study a week later, still in her silk robe at three in the afternoon, the Hermès fabric a reminder of better days.

"Mrs. Callahan, Mrs. Whitmore called again—"

"Tell her I'm recovering." Maddie swirled her wine glass, watching the red liquid catch the light like blood in water. "Tell them all I'm recovering."

The word felt right on her tongue, sharp and sweet like the wine. Let them think she was weak, broken, getting help. Let them lower their guard. She wasn't finished yet. After all, hadn't Jackson taught her about strategy during all those military functions? Sometimes you had to retreat before you could attack.

◆ ◆ ◆

Maddie adjusted the cream sweater one last time, studying her reflection. The softness of her features without makeup wasn't vulnerability—it was strategy. Two weeks of orchestrated silence, and now this: her emergence, timed, crafted. She reached for her signature red lipstick, then pulled her hand back. Not today. Today she needed to look like a woman trying to put herself back together.

Le Petit Jardin hadn't changed in the fourteen days she'd been away, though everything else had. The familiar scent of fresh-baked croissants and coffee wrapped around her as she entered, and for a moment— just a moment—she was transported to happier times. Brunches with Jackson. Anniversary dinners. Before he decided twenty years meant nothing.

Charlotte sat at their usual table by the window, auburn bob gleaming in the morning light. Maddie the slight widening of her friend's eyes, the quick scan of her appearance. Good. The transformation was striking enough to notice, subtle enough to seem unintentional.

"I've been seeing someone," Maddie said softly, allowing a slight tremor in her voice. She twisted her wedding ring—three turns, letting the diamond catch the light. A reminder of what Jackson was throwing away. "A therapist. Dr. Matthews."

The name rolled off her tongue easily. She'd practiced it enough times in front of her bathroom mirror, the way she'd say it, the slight hesitation before the admission. Charlotte's manicured hand reached across the white tablecloth, as Maddie had known it would. "Oh, darling."

"I was just..." Maddie manufactured a crack in her voice, remembering how her mother used to do the same thing when manipulating her father. "I was so emotional when Jackson left. I said things—did things—I regret." The words tasted like honey-coated poison on her tongue. She didn't regret a single thing, except perhaps not doing worse.

Their usual waiter, Antoine, approached with practiced timing. Maddie ordered chamomile tea instead of her usual white wine, watching Charlotte from beneath her lashes. There it was—that slight lift of groomed eyebrows. Another note in the symphony of her constructed redemption.

"The bruises..." Charlotte ventured, where Maddie had led her.

"I know what people think." Maddie touched her wrist where she'd applied the makeup so weeks ago, letting her fingers linger on the now-clear skin. "I was desperate. Everything was falling apart, and I couldn't—" She reached for her napkin, dabbing at eyes that remained dry behind her performance. "I'm not proud of it."

She watched Charlotte shift closer, protective instincts kicking in. The whispers from nearby tables had changed their tenor—no longer sharp with judgment but soft with sympathy. Maddie could hear them rewriting her narrative: Poor Maddie, getting help, trying to be better. The thought almost made her smile. Almost.

The performance continued at Bridge Club that afternoon. Barbara, who'd been so quick to distance herself when the scandal broke, melted like butter when Maddie spoke about her fictional therapy sessions. Her voice was pitched low, confessional: "Dr. Matthews says I need to acknowledge my part in all this."

Sandra—dear, stupid Sandra—squeezed her hand

when Maddie admitted to "overreacting" about Jackson. "We all do crazy things when we're hurting," Sandra offered, and Maddie resisted the urge to roll her eyes. Sandra would know about crazy, wouldn't she? With her discount designer bags and desperate attempts to keep up.

They were all so eager to believe in her reformation, these women who'd known her for decades. They wanted their old Maddie back, even if she seemed a little broken. So, she let them comfort her, let them think they were witnessing her healing. Let them believe that therapy and time were softening her edges.

If only they knew. This wasn't surrender—it was tactical retreat. Let Jackson think she was falling apart. Let him believe she was harmless now, chastened and changed. Let him relax his guard, go back to thinking he knew her.

She'd learned long ago that the most dangerous predators were the ones that looked wounded.

The chamomile tea cooled untouched before her. She hadn't taken a single sip.

❖ ❖ ❖

Maddie closed her front door, savoring the quiet click of the lock. She allowed herself three heartbeats before letting the mask slip—that constructed expression of vulnerability and remorse she'd worn like a second skin all day. Her fingers traced the brass handle, cool and solid beneath her touch, just like the cold smile now replacing her performance of contrition. The social circle had welcomed her back as planned, each of them playing their parts to perfection. Charlotte, dear predictable Charlotte, with her protective instincts and maternal clucking. Barbara, trying so hard to appear magnanimous while clearly dying for fresh gossip to share. And Sandra—oh, poor Sandra—with her pathetic attempt at understanding, as if she could possibly comprehend what it meant to lose everything to a younger woman.

The house seemed to exhale around her, settling into the familiar rhythm of evening. Maddie kicked off her ballet flats (chosen specifically for their humble appearance—no Louboutins today) and made her way to Jackson's study. He'd taken most of his things when he left, but he'd forgotten the crystal decanter of Macallan 25. How like him, to overlook the small details while focusing on the grand gesture of his escape. She poured herself a generous measure, letting the amber liquid catch the light. Jackson had always been so precious about this scotch, saving it for special occasions. Well, wasn't this special enough?

Behind the row of tax records (which Jackson had also forgotten—he'd always trusted her to handle the tedious details of their life), Maddie retrieved her leather-bound notebook. The pages unraveled against her fingers as she opened it, revealing her precise handwriting. Every detail about Jackson's new life in Virginia was documented here—his schedule at the consulting firm, his favorite coffee shop (still Starbucks, so predictable), which grocery store he took the children to on Sundays. She even knew which dry cleaner pressed his suits now. Knowledge was power, after all, and Maddie had always been, good at gathering intelligence.

Attorney Nate Wren's rejection still burned, a hot coal of humiliation in her stomach. She took another sip of scotch, letting the smoky flavor wash away the bitter taste of that particular defeat. But Maddie knew better than to let one setback derail her laid plans. She'd already identified three other lawyers who might be more... amenable to her particular methods of persuasion. One of them had a gambling problem he thought he'd hidden well. Another was desperate to break into high-society divorce cases. The third—well, the third had secrets that would make even Barbara blush.

Her Mont Blanc pen (a gift from Jackson on their fifteenth anniversary) moved across the fresh page with purpose, mapping out the next phase. The therapy story had worked beautifully today—she'd seen it in their eyes, that eager desire to believe in redemption, in healing. Everyone loved a good comeback story, especially when it involved a fallen society wife finding her way back to grace. Dr. Matthews would make the witness when the time came, her professional reputation lending weight to Maddie's constructed narrative of recovery. The good doctor had no idea that every session was being recorded, every sympathetic nod and encouraging word captured for later use in the custody appeal.

Maddie paused to sip her scotch, reviewing her notes with the same attention to detail she'd once applied to planning charity galas and dinner parties. Three more months of this performance—the humble clothing, the soft voice, the occasional well-timed tear. Just long enough for Jackson to lower his guard, for Nate to think she'd accepted defeat like a good little ex-wife. They all underestimated her—just like they had in Dubai, when they thought she was nothing more than a desperate housewife clinging to her marriage. They'd forgotten who had orchestrated their rise in society, who had turned a military officer into a sought-after consultant.

Her phone buzzed against the desk, Charlotte's

name lighting up the screen: "So proud of you for getting help. Lunch tomorrow?"

Maddie's fingers moved swiftly across the keyboard, crafting a response full of gratitude and warmth, while her other hand continued its steady documentation in the notebook. Let them see what they wanted to see—the broken woman, humbled and reformed, accepting her new reality with grace. After all, the best performances were the ones where the audience never suspected they were watching a show.

She smiled, taking another sip of Jackson's precious scotch. This was just the beginning, and she had always been good at playing the long game.

Chapter 20

Maddie studied her reflection in Le Petit Jardin's powder room mirror, adjusting her Hermès scarf with the precision of a woman who understood the power of appearances. The silk reminisced against her neck—a reminder of better days, when Jackson had brought it home from Paris. (Before he'd started bringing things home for someone else.) She tilted her head, examining her handiwork. The makeup was: light enough to suggest healing, the concealer masking the shadows under her eyes. Just enough vulnerability to make people wonder what kept her up at night.

The maître d'—Antoine, who'd been serving her for fifteen years—pulled out her chair with a sympathetic smile when she returned to the table. Charlotte and Barbara were already there, of course. They'd never dare be late, not to one of her lunches. The familiar scent of fresh flowers and expensive perfume wrapped around her like armor as she settled into her seat.

"The therapy is helping," Maddie said, spreading her napkin across her lap with practiced grace. Three times, always three times, to smooth out the wrinkles. "Dr. Matthews has been wonderful about helping me understand my part in everything." The words tasted like ash in her mouth. As if she needed help understanding anything. As if she hadn't spent twenty years understanding what she'd sacrificed for Jackson's ambitions.

Charlotte's hand reached across the pristine white tablecloth to squeeze hers. The gesture was meant to be comforting, but Maddie noticed how Charlotte's tennis bracelet the light. New. Probably a gift from her husband, who'd been especially attentive. (Amazing how a friend's divorce could suddenly make other husbands appreciate their wives.)

"We're all here for you," Charlotte said, and Maddie allowed her voice to catch when she responded.

"I know, and I'm so grateful." She paused, letting the moment stretch. Timing was everything. "I just... I spoke to the children yesterday. They sounded different. Stressed." She watched Barbara lean forward, hungry for details. Barbara always was the easier target—she collected other people's pain like some women collected designer bags.

"Different how?" Barbara asked, right on cue.

Maddie stirred her water, watching the lemon slice spin. Three times. Counterclockwise. "Oh, I'm sure it's nothing." She touched her throat, a gesture she'd practiced in the mirror until it looked natural. "Jackson is such a good father, but..." The pause was deliberate. Let them fill in the blanks. "Nate, his attorney, he's so aggressive with this case. The children pick up on that tension."

Charlotte's frown was genuine. Good. "What do you mean?"

"I probably shouldn't say anything." Maddie looked down at her hands, remembering how Jackson used to hold them. Used to. What an ugly phrase. She glanced up through mascaraed lashes. "It's just... Carrie mentioned they're not allowed to talk about certain things with me. And Nate, well, he's known for being ruthless in custody battles."

"That seems extreme," Barbara said, as Maddie knew she would. "They're just children."

"I just want them to be happy." Maddie let her eyes glisten—a trick she'd learned years ago, thinking about something sad but never letting the tears fall. control. Always control. "Maybe I'm being oversensitive. The therapy has made me more aware of how my concerns can sound like criticism."

She watched Charlotte and Barbara exchange glances, saw the subtle shift in their posture. The seed was planted. By dinner, they'd be telling their husbands about poor Maddie's children, about that aggressive attorney, about Jackson's questionable choices. The whispers would spread through their social circle like poison in a well.

"More tea?" Maddie lifted the delicate pot, her hand steady despite the satisfaction humming through her veins like electricity. She hadn't needed to make a single accusation. They'd do all the work for her, these friends who thought they were being supportive. These women who had no idea they were weapons in her arsenal.

She poured the tea, watching the amber liquid swirl in the bone china cups. Three times. Counterclockwise. Always.

◆ ◆ ◆

Maddie observed Eleanor Walsh hovering near her table at Le Petit Jardin, looking as she had during all those Thursday afternoon piano lessons—silver hair pinned back in that military-precise bun, cardigan pressed within an inch of its life. The sight of her sent Maddie's mind spinning back to countless hours perched on the piano bench beside Carrie, her daughter's small fingers dancing across ivory keys. Back when everything made sense. Back before Jackson decided to burn their world to ash.

"Mrs. Callahan?" Eleanor's voice carried that familiar gentleness, the one that had soothed Carrie through countless frustrated attempts at mastering Bach. "I've been meaning to reach out."

Maddie felt her features arrange themselves into the appropriate mask—grateful, touched, just vulnerable enough. "Eleanor, how lovely to see you." The words flowed smooth as honey, practiced to perfection.

"I heard about everything." Eleanor's eyes flicked to the empty chairs where Charlotte and Barbara had sat not twenty minutes ago, their mimosa glasses still bearing traces of lipstick. "I wanted you to know—I don't believe what people are saying. Not after watching you with Carrie all these years."

Maddie's hand trembled as she set down her water glass, and for once, the tremor wasn't manufactured. She hadn't planned this encounter, hadn't orchestrated this particular piece of the puzzle. But sometimes the universe handed you what you needed, didn't it? "That means more than you know."

"The way you sat with her during every lesson, how you encouraged her..." Eleanor settled her slight frame into the vacant chair, her hazel eyes soft with sympathy. Maddie remembered how those same eyes would light up when Carrie mastered a challenging piece. "A mother who fabricates things doesn't spend three years memorizing Bach with her daughter."

"I miss our Thursday afternoons." Maddie allowed her voice to catch, thinking of Carrie's empty bedroom, the sheet music still arranged on her desk. The silence where music should be. "Jackson won't let her continue lessons in Virginia."

Eleanor's face tightened, professional pride warring with personal outrage. "He what? But she was just starting Beethoven's Moonlight Sonata."

"He says there's no time with the new schedule." Maddie traced the rim of her glass, watching the light catch the crystal. Like everything in her life now, beautiful but fragile. Ready to shatter. "The custody arrangement... it's complicated." She let the words hang there, heavy with unspoken implications.

"That's not right." Eleanor straightened her spine—the same posture she'd always insisted upon at the piano. How many times had she gently corrected

Carrie's slouching shoulders? "I taught piano for forty years. I know the difference between a devoted mother and—well." She paused, diplomatic even in her indignation. "If you need someone to speak to your character, about your dedication to those children..."

Maddie reached across the table, squeezing Eleanor's hand. The older woman's skin felt paper-thin beneath her fingers, fragile as the lies Maddie had been collecting like precious gems. "You would do that?"

"Of course. I've seen you with Carrie every week for years. That kind of love can't be faked."

Oh, but it could be, Maddie thought, even as she let grateful tears shine in her eyes. Everything could be faked, if you knew how. And Maddie had learned from the best—from a mother who turned social climbing into an art form, from a husband who could smile at her across the dinner table while texting his princess under it. Eleanor Walsh, with her proper cardigan and her forty years of teaching experience, had just become another piece in Maddie's constructed game. She would make an excellent character witness, her testimony weighted with years of professional observation.

The tremor in Maddie's hand was real now, but not from grief. From anticipation. From the thrill of watching another domino align itself, ready to fall where she needed it.

"More coffee?" she asked Eleanor, already raising her hand to signal the waiter. "I'd love to hear how your other students are doing." And perhaps, she thought, about that married colonel you've been seeing. The one whose wife doesn't know. The one who might be useful later, when I need him to be.

◆ ◆ ◆

Maddie's reflection stared back at her from the rearview mirror, and porcelain-like in the late morning sun. She touched up her signature red lipstick—Chanel, of course, the same shade she'd worn for twenty years. (Some things were sacred, even if marriages weren't.) Eleanor's offer had landed in her lap like a gift from the universe, wrapped in opportunity and tied with strings she could pull at her leisure. She hadn't expected it, but then again, the best weapons often came disguised as kindness.

Her Cartier ring—the one Jackson had given her on their fifteenth anniversary— the light as she reached for her phone. Her fingers hovered over Jackson's number; each millisecond calculated. Timing was everything. In war. In love. In revenge. She'd learned that from him. All those military strategy books he'd left lying around the house, thinking she was too busy with charity galas to notice.

One ring. Two rings. Three rings—. Let him know she had other things to do besides wait for him.

"What is it, Maddie?" His voice was clipped, military-sharp, the way it had been since he'd met his precious "Princess." The nickname still made her want to break something expensive, preferably something he'd bought Lily.

"Jackson." She let his name float between them, soft as a feather, deadly as arsenic. The voice she'd ed in therapy—recommended by Barbara, who'd used the same doctor during her own divorce. "I've been doing a lot of thinking in therapy. About moving forward, about what's best for the children."

The silence stretched between them like a tripwire. She could see him so clearly—standing at that ridiculous ergonomic desk he'd bought last year, probably wearing one of those crisp white shirts that made him look like everyone's idea of a distinguished general. He'd always been so concerned with appearances. Until he wasn't.

"I just want peace for the kids," she continued, each word measured like ingredients in a poison. "I hope we can be civil, for their sake."

"Is that all?" Cold. Detached.

Her manicured fingers pressed against the leather of the steering wheel, leaving little half-moons that would fade, just like his love had. "I know things got... complicated." Complicated like finding lipstick on his collar? Like watching him parade Lily around at charity events where Maddie had reigned for two decades? "But Dr. Matthews has helped me understand my part in all this. The children deserve better than hostility between us."

"If this is about custody—"

"No," she interrupted, smooth as silk over steel. "This is about healing. About showing Nate and Carrie that adults can work through their differences." Nate, who watched everything with those knowing eyes. Carrie, who still believed in fairy tales. They'd learn soon enough.

Jackson's sigh crackled through the phone like static, like the distance that had grown between them during all those deployments. All those years she'd waited, played the wife, only for him to replace her with a younger model. "I need to go. I have a meeting."

"Of course." She paused, letting the moment stretch like a noose. "I just wanted you to know I'm working on myself. That's all."

The call ended with his signature abruptness. Military precision. No wasted movements, no wasted words. Maddie set the phone down, allowing herself the luxury of a small smile. Let him think she was softening, becoming reasonable. Let everyone see how she was handling this betrayal. After all, the best revenge was served with a smile and lipstick.

She started the Mercedes—her Mercedes, the one thing he hadn't tried to take—and began composing the text to Charlotte in her head. Something appropriately vulnerable about her "emotional but necessary" conversation with Jackson. Charlotte would spread it through their social circle like wildfire, painting Maddie as the wounded but healing wife.

It was all going according to plan. And Maddie always had a plan.

Maddie traced her fingertip across the glossy surface of the photograph, pausing over Carrie's face. Her baby girl, looking so lost in that stiff new uniform. The navy blazer hung too large on her small frame, as if she were playing dress-up in someone else's life. (Which, wasn't that what Jackson was forcing her to do?)

The mahogany desk—a wedding gift from Jackson's parents twenty-five years ago—held her growing collection of evidence like a war room. Some women planned dinner parties or charity galas. Maddie planned victories.

She shuffled through more photos from Rosa's cousin. Reliable Rosa, who would never know how her family connections had proven so useful. Nate at lunch, sitting alone, his shoulders curved inward like a question mark. Another image her eye: Princess Lillian, playing mommy on the front porch, trying to help Carrie with homework. Maddie's lips curved into a smile that didn't reach her eyes. Her daughter's body language screamed discomfort—shoulders tight, spine straight as a rod, the way she leaned away from Lillian's attempted touch.

The laptop screen cast a blue glow across her face as she pulled up the private investigator's latest report. Three missed school pickups in two weeks. Three times her children had sat waiting in the office while Lillian handled "urgent work calls." The words made Maddie's fingers tighten around her wine glass. Urgent calls? Please. The girl couldn't even manage basic scheduling.

And Jackson? Too busy with his new position to notice his fantasy life cracking at the edges. He'd always been that way—so focused on the horizon that he missed the landmines at his feet.

Her red pen moved with surgical precision, circling damning details. Carrie's grades slipping to Bs and Cs. Nate's visit to the school counselor (documented with such helpful detail by the secretary who loved to chat). Lillian's growing list of parental failures. Each circle of red ink felt like drawing blood.

The notes flowed from her pen in elegant script. She'd always taken pride in her handwriting—a dying art, like so many things that separated the truly refined from pretenders like Lillian. Signs of stress. Academic decline. Inconsistent care. She paused, considering, then added: Emotional withdrawal. The words looked clinical, concerned. Maternal.

Her phone buzzed against the desk's polished surface. Eleanor Walsh, right on schedule. The piano teacher's message confirmed that whispers were spreading through St. Catherine's about Carrie's "tragic" musical regression. Eleanor had always been so useful, so eager to help—especially after that night she'd broken down and confessed everything about Colonel Lowry. Amazing how guilt could make people so cooperative.

Maddie reached for Dr. Matthews' therapy notes, another piece in her careful construction. The therapist had documented her "tremendous progress" and "admirable commitment to healthy co-parenting." (It was amazing what people would write after you spent six months becoming their favorite patient.) She arranged the notes beside the Virginia photos, letting the contrast tell its own story.

This time would be different. No direct attacks, no obvious plays for revenge. Instead, she would build her case like a cathedral—every stone placed with precision. The children's struggles adjusting. Their academic decline. Their emotional needs being overlooked by an inexperienced stepmother (poor thing, she was trying her best) and an increasingly absent father.

She would wrap her fury in concern, dress her revenge in maternal worry. After all, what judge could fault a mother for wanting to protect her children's stability? What court wouldn't sympathize with her desire to maintain their academic excellence, their emotional well-being, their sense of security?

Maddie took another sip of wine, savoring its bitter notes. The photos spread before her like tarot cards, telling a future only she could see. Jackson thought he'd won by taking her children to Virginia.

But he'd forgotten the most important thing: a mother's love was patient. It could wait. It could plan. It could smile and nod in therapy while building its case, piece by piece, until the moment arrived. Patient.

Chapter 21

Maddie smoothed her cream St. John knit dress, feeling the familiar texture beneath her fingertips as she entered Attorney Vivian Cross's corner office. The dress was —expensive enough to show she hadn't lost everything in the separation, but not so pristine that she appeared untouched by recent events. No Chanel today. Chanel would whisper of the old Maddie, the one who commanded rooms and made lesser women question their choice of shoes. Today was about appearing softer, wounded but resilient. A mother, not a warrior.

She touched her pearl studs—tiny, elegant things that had been a gift from Jackson on their tenth anniversary. The memory stung, as it was meant to. Her hair was pulled back in a soft chignon rather than her usual sleek style, allowing a few strategic pieces to frame her face. Every detail had been calculated, rehearsed in front of her bathroom mirror until she'd ed this new version of herself.

Vivian Cross rose from behind her imposing mahogany desk, her platinum bob catching the morning light like a helmet of armor. Her handshake was precise, calculated—a general recognizing a worthy ally. The office itself spoke volumes about its occupant. Unlike Nate Wren's sterile chrome and glass fortress (a place that still made Maddie's skin crawl with its cold efficiency), Vivian's space exuded old-money power through its traditional dark woods and leather. It smelled of success and secrets kept.

"Mrs. Callahan, I've reviewed your case extensively." Vivian's green eyes moved over Maddie with the precision of a jeweler assessing diamonds. "Including Dr. Matthews' reports."

Maddie placed her Hermès bag beside her chair, the leather soft from years of use. Another calculated choice—not her newest bag, but one that spoke of comfortable wealth. She retrieved an organized folder, each document inside arranged to tell the story she needed told. "Dr. Matthews has been instrumental in helping me understand my... reactions during the separation." The pause was deliberate, a moment of vulnerability inserted between words.

She passed Eleanor Walsh's written statement

across the desk, along with the children's recent progress reports. The paper trembled in her hand—just enough to be noticed. "My primary concern is their well-being. Carrie's grades have dropped significantly. She's stopped playing piano." The piano had been Maddie's idea, of course. Jackson had never attended a single recital.

"And your son?" Vivian's manicured fingers spread the documents with practiced efficiency.

"Nate's withdrawn. The school counselor called last week." Maddie allowed her voice to catch—a break she'd practiced in her car, timing it between words. "He's struggling to adjust." Of course he was struggling. Jackson had spoken ten words to him since moving out, too busy playing house with his precious Lily.

She pulled out more papers: photos of missed pickups (carefully documented by Rosa, though the maid didn't know why she'd been asked to take them), documentation of Lillian's absences (the woman couldn't even manage to show up for scheduled visits), records of Jackson's increased work travel (Dubai again, always Dubai).

"The children need stability," Vivian said, her sharp gaze scanning the evidence. Something flickered in those green eyes—recognition, perhaps, of a kindred spirit who understood how to wage war without ever raising her voice. "Your therapy progress is remarkable, Mrs. Callahan. Combined with these concerns about their current situation..." Her red lips curved. "We have grounds for a custody modification."

Maddie pressed her hands together, embodying maternal concern with the same precision she'd once used to host charity galas. "I just want what's best for my children." The words tasted like honey-coated glass in her mouth. Here heart of hearts knew they were small pieces of her perfect word. But she also wanted Jackson to understand what it felt like to lose everything you loved, piece by precious piece.

"We'll file next week." Vivian reached for her Mont Blanc pen, the gold clip catching the light. "This time, we'll focus on their needs rather than attacking Mr. Callahan directly. The court responds better to that approach."

Maddie allowed herself a small, grateful smile. "That's what I want." And it was. Because sometimes the best revenge wasn't attacking at all—it was making everyone else think you were the victim, while systematically dismantling your enemy's entire world. She'd learned that from watching Jackson all these years. Now it was time to show him how well she'd paid attention.

Maddie's fingers traced the raised lettering on the certified mail receipt, a rhythmic motion that matched the steady beating of her heart. Nine forty-seven AM. Such a precise time for the beginning of Jackson's undoing. She could picture it —his Virginia office with its polished mahogany and pretentious military honors on display. The way he'd tear open the envelope with those manicured hands he'd started maintaining since Lily entered his life.

The Earl Grey's familiar warmth spread through her chest as she took another sip. How many afternoons had she spent in this study, planning, waiting, watching? The room still held echoes of their life together—the antique desk he'd bought her for their tenth anniversary, the photographs she strategically hadn't taken down. Let everyone see what he'd thrown away. Let them whisper about the family he'd abandoned.

Her phone's screen illuminated with an update from her investigator. Jackson, the man who prided himself on iron control, had just stormed out of his office like a common hothead, canceling meetings left and right. The tea paused halfway to her lips, a small smile playing at the corners of her mouth. Composure had always been his armor. How delicious to watch it crack.

Of course he'd called Nate Wren immediately. Predictable Jackson, running to his attack dog at the first sign of trouble. The memory of Nate's dismissal weeks ago still stung—that cold, assessing gaze that had seen right through her constructed facade of acceptance. Well, he wasn't the only one who could play chess. That's why she had Vivian now.

The surveillance photos on her laptop showed Jackson in Nate's office, his movements sharp with agitation. Even through the grainy feed, she could read the shock in his stance. Poor, naive Jackson. He'd believed her act—the therapy sessions she'd attended with such apparent sincerity, the measured texts about the children's activities, the way she'd stopped fighting about every little thing. She'd played the role of reformed ex-wife so, letting him think he'd won.

But Nate hadn't bought it. There he sat in the footage, maddeningly calm behind that imposing desk of his, probably laying out contingency plans they'd prepared months ago. She adjusted her pearls—a nervous tell she'd never quite conquered—and watched Jackson pace like a caged animal. Let them scramble. Let them realize this was just the beginning.

Charlotte's name flashed across her phone screen,

right on schedule. The social dominoes were already falling into place.

"Maddie? Jackson just called my husband in a complete state. Something about court papers?"

She touched the pearl at her throat again, this time deliberately, channeling the mix of concern and maternal worry into her voice. "I didn't want to worry anyone," she said softly, each word chosen. "It's just a small modification request, for the children's sake." She paused, letting her voice catch. "They're struggling so much in Virginia."

She could hear the rustle of Charlotte adjusting her phone, probably settling in for what she thought would be prime gossip. Charlotte, always so eager to align herself with whoever she thought was winning. "Of course they are, poor dears," Charlotte cooed, predictable as ever. "Everyone knows children need their mother."

A new text lit up her screen as she watched Jackson leaving Nate's office. His shoulders were slumped, his stride missing that military precision he wore like a second skin. The mighty general, showing weakness. Maddie smiled, taking another sip of her tea. The Earl Grey had grown cold, but she hardly noticed. Victory, she was learning, tasted sweeter than any tea.

◆ ◆ ◆

Maddie leaned closer to her laptop screen, savoring every pixel of the drama unfolding in that pristine Virginia kitchen. Her investigator had earned every penny - the camera angles were, capturing each twitch of discomfort on Jackson's face, every nervous tap of Lillian's ridiculous Louboutins against the marble floor. (The same marble Maddie had selected ten years ago, though Jackson probably didn't remember that detail.)

"Princess, you need to calm down," Jackson said, rubbing his temple in that familiar way he did when things weren't going according to plan. The pet name scraped against Maddie's ears like nails on a chalkboard. She remembered when he used to call her "darling" - back when she was young enough, enough, before he decided he needed an upgrade.

Lillian's pacing was becoming frantic, her designer heels click-clicking like a time bomb. "Calm down? Your ex-wife is winning everyone over with her mother act, and you want me to calm down?"

mother act? Maddie allowed herself a small smile as she scrolled through her phone messages. Charlotte had come through beautifully, as expected. Her text about running into Eleanor Walsh at St. Catherine's was delicious. Eleanor, bless her guilt-ridden heart, had gone on about how Carrie used to practice piano for hours under Maddie's guidance. How the child touched the keys anymore. It was amazing what people would say when properly prompted.

Jackson's phone buzzed on the counter, and Maddie watched his face tighten as he read the message. Another orchestrated reminder of his failures, no doubt. She'd been working through their social circle for weeks now, each conversation a placed domino. Even his old military colleagues - men who'd once looked at him with such respect - were beginning to whisper about his judgment.

"Princess, please—" Jackson reached for Lillian with that patronizing gesture Maddie knew so well. But his precious princess jerked away like a spooked thoroughbred.

"Stop calling me that!" Lillian's voice had taken on that shrill edge Maddie had been waiting for. "I can't... I can't handle the kids' schedules and your meetings and everyone looking at me like I'm the villain." The glass of water Lillian knocked over was an unexpected bonus - the shattering sound a punctuation to her breakdown.

Maddie zoomed in on Jackson's face, drinking in his expression as he watched his trophy girlfriend frantically dabbing at her wet silk blouse. There it was - that flicker of doubt she'd been waiting for. The first crack in his certainty. He was seeing what everyone else saw - a younger woman buckling under the weight of a life she'd stolen but couldn't possibly sustain.

"Your friends' wives won't even look at me at the club anymore," Lillian's voice cracked beautifully. "They all think I destroyed your family."

Jackson's phone buzzed again, and Maddie knew what those messages said. She'd orchestrated each one, making sure everyone heard about Carrie's falling grades, about Nate's withdrawal. About how the children needed stability, structure, their mother's guidance. (It wasn't even lying. Just selective truth-telling.)

"Princess—" Jackson started again, but his precious princess was already fleeing the scene, leaving him alone with the broken glass and spreading puddle of water. Maddie watched him stand there, looking lost in his stolen happiness, and felt a familiar warmth spread through her chest. It wasn't quite satisfaction - not yet. But it was close.

She took a sip of her chilled chardonnay and saved the video file. Something told her she'd want to watch this particular meltdown again. After all, it was only the beginning.

Maddie smoothed her cream silk blouse, feeling the familiar texture beneath her manicured fingers. The fabric cost more than this earnest young journalist probably made in a week, but appearances mattered. They always mattered. Especially now, sitting across from Sarah Mitchell, that eager little thing from St. Catherine's newspaper with her drugstore pen and spiral notebook. The Fall Festival provided the backdrop—children's laughter, the scent of cinnamon, the gentle autumn breeze. Maddie had chosen this setting, just as she chose everything else in her life.

"Mrs. Callahan, thank you for speaking with us about the upcoming Parent Association initiatives," Sarah said, her pen hovering above the page like a bird waiting to dive.

Maddie touched her strand of pearls—a calculated gesture she'd ed over the years. The same pearls Jackson had given her on their tenth anniversary, back when forever still meant something. "Of course. Though I must admit, being here..." She let her voice trail off, her gaze drifting to the playground. Carrie used to love those swings. Every Tuesday and Thursday, she'd beg to stay just five more minutes, her little blonde ponytail swishing in the wind. The memory stung like a paper cut—small but sharp.

Sarah leaned forward, falling right into the trap. "It must be difficult, with the children in Virginia now."

"Everything I do is for them." Maddie retrieved her monogrammed handkerchief—Hermès, because even in grief, one must maintain standards—and dabbed delicately at her eyes. The tears weren't fake, which made them more effective. "Their father is... doing what he thinks is best." The pause was deliberate, letting the unspoken accusation hover in the air. "And I support that, even if it breaks my heart to be apart from them."

"That's gracious of you."

Maddie offered a soft smile; the kind that made people want to protect her. Poor, brave Maddie, they'd say. So strong, so dignified in her suffering. "Motherhood isn't about our own comfort, is it? It's about putting our children first." She thought of Jackson's Princess, probably playing house with her babies right now. But Lily would learn. They always did. "That's why I'm still involved with St. Catherine's—to maintain that connection, that sense of community they'll need when they return."

"When they return?"

"If they return," Maddie corrected herself, letting her voice catch just so. Amateur mistake, that 'when.' She'd have to be more careful. "I just want what's best for them." Another practiced pause. "Their grades have suffered with the move, and Carrie's stopped playing piano..." She thought of her daughter's empty bedroom, the sheet music still arranged on the stand, waiting. "But I have to trust in God's plan."

Sarah's pen scratched frantically across the page. The sound grated on Maddie's nerves, but she maintained her serene expression. "You still attend their old activities?"

"Of course. I sit in on Carrie's old piano recital slot every Thursday. Eleanor—Mrs. Walsh—she keeps it open. Just in case." Maddie touched her cross necklace, a gift from her mother who'd taught her that sometimes the most commanding weapons were invisible. "Sometimes being a good mother means waiting patiently, supporting from afar, and always, always being ready when your children need you."

What she didn't say was that she'd already started planning. Jackson thought he could just take her children, start fresh with his pretty young thing? He'd forgotten who he married. Maddie didn't just wait—she prepared. But Sarah didn't need to know that part. Not yet. The story would write itself: devoted mother, steadfast in her faith, bearing her cross. By tomorrow, every mother at St. Catherine's would be clucking their tongues at Jackson's cruelty.

timing, setting, story. Maddie had always been good at.

Chapter 22

Maddie sat in Vivian Cross's office, studying her attorney's reflection in the polished mahogany desk. The morning light Vivian's platinum bob, creating a halo effect that almost made Maddie smile. Almost. She watched as Vivian marked specific sections with precise, red tabs—like little drops of blood on crisp white paper. Methodical. Just like they'd planned.

The office felt different today. Warmer, somehow. More intimate. Like a war room where victories were plotted in whispers and penmanship. Maddie smoothed an invisible wrinkle from her dove-gray suit—Chanel, of course. She'd chosen it that morning, the same way she chose everything these days. Soft colors made her look vulnerable. Expensive cuts reminded the world that she was still Mrs. Jackson Callahan, even if he'd forgotten.

"Eleanor Walsh's testimony about Carrie's musical development is compelling," Vivian said, tapping a manicured nail against the affidavit. The sound echoed like a metronome, keeping time with Maddie's steady heartbeat. "The decline in her piano progress since moving to Virginia adds weight to our argument."

Poor Eleanor. Sweet, guilt-ridden Eleanor, who'd spilled her secrets over tea and tears. Who'd given Maddie everything she needed without realizing she was signing her own confession. "Eleanor's been wonderful," Maddie replied, her voice warm with practiced sincerity. "She truly cares about Carrie's well-being." And that wasn't even a lie. The best weapons were always partly true.

"And Colonel Lowry?" Vivian raised an eyebrow, her green eyes sharp with appreciation for the game they were playing. "His statement about Jackson's... inconsistencies during deployment are interesting."

Satisfaction bloomed in Maddie's chest like a dark flower. The photos of Greg's affair with Eleanor had proven so useful—tucked away in her safe like loaded guns, waiting for the right moment. She remembered Greg's face when she'd shown them to him, the way the color had drained from his weathered cheeks. "The Colonel understands the importance of stability for children in military families." Another truth wrapped in thorns.

"Your therapy progress notes from Dr. Matthews are excellent." Vivian closed the file with a sharp snap that felt like victory. "Three months of consistent sessions, documented personal growth, and a clear commitment to co-parenting. The court will notice."

Maddie touched her cross necklace, a gesture she'd practiced in the mirror until it looked natural. Concerned mother, seeking guidance from above. She wondered if God appreciated the performance. "I just want what's best for my children." Her voice —not too much, just enough. "The reports from their new school in Virginia..." She let the sentence dangle, like bait in still water.

"Declining grades, missed assignments, behavioral changes." Vivian nodded, taking the bait as intended. "All documented and attached to our motion. Judge Harrison tends to prioritize academic stability."

Of course he did. Maddie had chosen him as she'd chosen her suit. Three months of casual conversations with his wife at charity functions hadn't gone to waste. "When will you file?"

"Today." Vivian stood, smoothing her black pencil skirt with the confidence of a woman who'd never lost a case she truly wanted to win. "I've already scheduled the courier. Jackson should be served by tomorrow morning."

Maddie watched as Vivian gathered the papers into her leather briefcase, each document a placed landmine in Jackson's new life. Everything was falling into place—Eleanor's genuine concern (wrapped in her own guilt), Greg's forced cooperation (backed by photographic evidence), the crafted image of a mother's redemption (three months of therapy sessions, each one a performance worthy of an Oscar).

The motion would hit Jackson like a precision strike, targeting every weak point in his constructed new world: Lillian's inexperience with the children (poor Princess, playing house with someone else's family), and his frequent absences (documented down to the minute, thanks to Greg's guilty conscience).

Maddie smiled, feeling the warmth of the morning sun on her face. She wondered if Jackson would recognize the strategy—if he'd appreciate how she'd learned from all those years of watching him plan his military campaigns. She'd always been a good student, after all. And now, she had the chance to prove it.

◆ ◆ ◆

The morning light filtered through Maddie's study windows, casting an almost theatrical glow on her tablet screen as she watched the courier deliver her crafted bomb to Nate Wren's office. Her manicured nails clicked against her coffee cup—a delicate Wedgwood piece that had survived countless mornings like this one—as Attorney Wren spared a glance at the thick envelope before setting it aside. Just like that. As if she hadn't spent weeks orchestrating every detail, every devastating piece of evidence.

No reaction. Not even a raised eyebrow from the man they called "The Machine." How fitting.

Her phone buzzed against the antique mahogany desk, and she snatched it up, expecting—hoping for—signs of chaos. Instead, her investigator's update landed like a slap: Jackson hadn't so much as disrupted his precious schedule. No angry calls. No rushed meetings. Just another day at Callahan Defense Solutions, as if she hadn't just launched the opening salvo in what should have been their war.

"What do you mean he's still in budget reviews?" The words came out sharp enough to cut, her voice carrying that edge that used to make the children go quiet at dinner. Poor darlings. They'd learned early to read her moods.

"No changes, Mrs. Callahan. He handed the papers straight to Attorney Wren without reading them."

Of course he had. Maddie's jaw clenched as she pulled up the security feed from Jackson's Virginia home—the feed he still didn't know she had access to. Through the kitchen window (that gorgeous bay window she'd insisted on during the renovation, back when this was their dream home), she watched Jackson and his precious "Princess" discuss the papers over coffee. No raised voices. No tears from little Lillian. Just calm conversation and—Maddie leaned closer to the screen— was that creature taking notes?

The sight of Lillian's composed demeanor made something twist in Maddie's stomach, a sensation she refused to acknowledge as fear. This wasn't how it was supposed to go. Where was the panic? The scrambling? The desperate calls to lawyers? She'd timed everything —the testimony from Eleanor, the school reports, the documented incidents that painted such a concerning picture.

Jackson reached across the table (her table, the one she'd selected from that charming antique shop in Paris) and touched Lillian's hand. They shared a look that made Maddie's blood boil, her chest tightening with a familiar pressure. They'd been expecting this. Worse— they'd been prepared for it.

Unable to watch their little domestic scene any

longer, Maddie switched cameras to Nate's office. The attorney was reviewing her motion with the same methodical precision she remembered from their last encounter. No sign of concern crossed his face as he tabbed through Eleanor's testimony or the school reports. Just that maddeningly calm expression, like a chess player who'd seen every move coming.

Her phone buzzed again, and Maddie knew before reading it that it wouldn't be good news. "Attorney Wren has scheduled a standard response timeline. No rush filings, no emergency motions. They're treating it as a routine modification request."

Maddie set down her coffee cup with exaggerated care, remembering the satisfying crash of yesterday's casualty. Rosa had cleaned up the pieces without a word, just that knowing look in her eyes. They were supposed to react—to fight, to panic, to make mistakes. Instead, Jackson had handed everything to Nate and returned to his meetings while Lillian calmly took notes at their kitchen table.

She stared at the feeds, at these people who dared to be unruffled by her orchestrated chaos. Well, if they wouldn't give her the reaction she wanted, she'd have to try harder. After all, hadn't that been Mother's first lesson? "When they don't notice you, darling, make yourself impossible to ignore."

◆ ◆ ◆

Maddie drummed her fingers against her steering wheel, watching Colonel Lowry's silver Lexus pull into the Starbucks parking lot. timing. She'd tracked his routine for weeks—every Tuesday at 2 PM, like clockwork.

She stepped out of her Mercedes, adjusting her

Chanel jacket. The motion Lowry's eye as he walked toward the entrance. His face drained of color.

"Greg." She closed the distance between them. "We need to talk about that statement you made."

"Mrs. Callahan—" He glanced around the parking lot. "I've said everything I'm willing to say about Dubai."

"Have you? Because Nate Wren seems to think your testimony lacks... certain details."

Lowry's hands shook as he reached for his phone. "I can't do this. Jackson is my superior officer—"

"Was your superior officer," Maddie corrected. "And I'm sure the board would love to hear about those missing requisition forms from last quarter."

His eyes widened. "That's classified—"

"Nothing's classified when it comes to my children, Greg."

Movement her eye—a flash of blonde hair through the cafe window. Lillian stood at the counter, her back to them but her head turned.

Lowry noticed too. "I need to go." He stepped backward. "Whatever you think you know about Dubai, about Jackson and—" He cut himself off.

"About Jackson and who?" Maddie pressed, but Lowry was already retreating to his car.

Through the window, Lillian had gone still, her phone pressed to her ear. Even from this distance, Maddie could see the tension in her shoulders as she listened to whoever was on the other end of the call.

Maddie smoothed her navy St. John suit as she entered the courthouse. The fabric felt wrong against her skin, too tight across her shoulders despite the tailoring.

She'd chosen it —understated elegance, nothing flashy. A grieving mother fighting for her children.

The illusion shattered the moment Nate Wren stood. His cold gray-blue eyes fixed on her as he pulled out a thick folder.

"Your Honor, before Ms. Cross continues her emotional appeal, I'd like to present evidence of Mrs. Callahan's documented pattern of manipulation."

Vivian Cross jumped up. "Objection, Your Honor. This hearing is about the children's welfare—"

"Which is my point." Nate's voice never wavered. "Exhibit A: Mrs. Callahan's staged injuries at the Piedmont Club."

The blood drained from Maddie's face. On the screen, security footage showed her applying makeup in her car before the charity luncheon.

"Exhibit B: Threatening notes to Ms. Hart, written on Mrs. Callahan's personal stationery. We have forensic confirmation."

Maddie's fingers dug into her palms. She'd worn gloves. She'd been careful.

"Exhibit C: Dr. Matthews' real session notes, not the sanitized versions presented by Ms. Cross."

The judge's expression hardened. "Ms. Cross, did you verify these therapy records?"

"I..." Vivian faltered. "We were provided—"

"By Mrs. Callahan?" Nate's lip curled. "Just like Eleanor Walsh's testimony about the piano lessons? The same Eleanor Walsh who admitted under oath that Mrs. Callahan offered to pay her private school tuition debt?"

Maddie felt the room spin. Eleanor had promised. She'd sworn she wouldn't tell.

"Your Honor," Nate continued, "we have

documented evidence of Mrs. Callahan orchestrating a campaign of harassment, manipulation of witnesses, and falsification of evidence. This custody modification request is her latest performance."

The judge turned to Maddie. His eyes held no sympathy. "Mrs. Callahan, would you like to explain yourself?"

Maddie forced herself to remain still as Nate's evidence battered against her facade. Her hands yearned to smooth her suit again, but she kept them folded in her lap. Any sign of agitation would only reinforce his accusations.

Vivian Cross cleared her throat. "Your Honor, if I may redirect?"

The judge nodded, though his expression remained stern.

"While my colleague has presented... concerning evidence, our focus today should be on a path forward." Vivian's voice softened. "Mrs. Callahan has committed to intensive therapy. She acknowledges her past actions were driven by emotional distress over separation from her children."

Maddie lowered her eyes, the picture of contrition. Inside, her mind raced ahead, calculating each word's impact.

"We're not seeking to disrupt the current custody arrangement," Vivian continued. "Rather, we propose supervised visitation as a first step. Two hours, twice weekly, with a court-appointed supervisor present."

The judge's eyebrows lifted. Maddie noticed Nate's shoulders tense—he'd expected them to push for more.

"Mrs. Callahan understands this is a process,"

Vivian said. "She's willing to prove herself through consistent, supervised contact. If these visits go well over a six-month period, we would then request a review for potential expansion of privileges."

Maddie raised her eyes, allowing them to shine with unshed tears. "Your Honor, I just want a chance to show I can be present in my children's lives in a healthy way."

She Nate watching her, his gray-blue eyes narrowed. He knew this was another performance. But with Vivian reframing the request so reasonably, he'd look cruel opposing even supervised visits.

Maddie slammed the front door of her empty mansion, her heels clicking across marble as she made her way to Jackson's study. Her hands shook as she yanked open the liquor cabinet, reaching past the cheap bottles for his prized Macallan 25. The one he'd saved for "special occasions."

She didn't bother with a glass. The scotch burned her throat, but she welcomed the pain. Each swallow pushed back the humiliation of watching Nate Wren destroy everything she'd built. Eleanor's betrayal. The judge's contempt. The way Vivian Cross wouldn't even look at her afterward.

The study walls closed in. Photos of the children mocked her from their frames. Nate's science fair ribbon. Carrie's piano recital certificate. All those curated moments of the life she'd crafted, now slipping through her fingers like water.

She hurled the bottle against Jackson's military service photo. Glass shattered. Amber liquid dripped down his smug face, pooling on the Persian rug she'd selected from that little shop in Dubai.

Dubai. Where it all started falling apart.

Maddie sank into Jackson's leather chair, her mascara leaving dark smudges on the armrest. The legal system had failed her. Proper channels, therapy, documented evidence—none of it mattered when Jackson's lawyer held all the cards.

She pulled open Jackson's desk drawer, fishing out the emergency bottle of gin he kept hidden behind his files. As the room spun, her eyes landed on the children's school photos. Sweet Carrie. Watchful Nate. Both of them trapped in Virginia with that woman playing mother.

No. She wouldn't lose them. Not to Jackson. Not to Lillian. Not to some judge who didn't understand what she'd sacrificed.

If the law wouldn't help her, she'd find another way. She always did.

Chapter 23

The afternoon sun slanted through Jackson's study windows, casting long shadows across his mahogany desk. Maddie's phone buzzed against the polished surface, and her heart skipped when Vivian Cross's name appeared. Two rings. That's what proper ladies allowed before answering. Even now, even with gin-sticky fingers and a world spinning off its axis, there were rules to follow.

"This isn't working, Mrs. Callahan." Vivian's voice

sliced through the speaker with surgical precision. The same voice that had promised results, promised justice, just last week over hundred-dollar lunches. "After yesterday's hearing, I can no longer represent you."

"You can't just—" The words in her throat like shards of glass.

"I've already filed the paperwork. My office will send your files by courier."

The line went dead, leaving Maddie in the suffocating silence of Jackson's study. She stared at the screen until it dimmed, a metaphor for her fading future. The phone felt wrong in her hand suddenly, too heavy, too real. She hurled it across the room, watching it crack against the wall where Jackson's military commendations used to hang. (He'd taken those, of course. Along with everything else that mattered.)

Her hands trembled as she checked her messages, the gin in her system making the words swim. Eleanor— dear, sanctimonious Eleanor—had sent a novel-length text dripping with words like "integrity" and "doing what's right." As if Eleanor had ever faced a real choice in her curated life. The message meandered through platitudes about prayer and forgiveness, as though God himself had appointed Eleanor the arbiter of Maddie's salvation.

"After everything I've done for Carrie? For the school?" Maddie's fingers flew across the keyboard, each word a small explosion of rage. She'd chaired every fundraiser, hosted every event, turned that second-rate academy into something worth bragging about. And this was her reward?

Eleanor's response appeared almost instantly: "Please don't contact me again." Simple. Final. Like closing a door on twenty years of friendship.

The gin sloshed uncomfortably in Maddie's stomach as she grabbed her car keys. She shouldn't drive—she knew that somewhere in the rational corner of her mind—but rationality had left the building around the same time Jackson had. Maxwell's wasn't far, and she knew Greg Lowry would be there, predictable as ever with his afternoon coffee ritual.

She spotted him at his usual corner table, looking every bit the retired colonel in his pressed khakis and button-down shirt. How many times had she hosted him for dinner? How many of Jackson's secrets had he witnessed over vintage bourbon and cigars?

"Greg." She slid into the chair across from him, noting how he tensed at her arrival. "We need to talk about your statement."

His coffee cup clattered against the saucer—a tell. Greg had always been terrible at poker. "I've said everything I'm going to say."

"Have you?" The words came out honey-sweet, masking the venom underneath. "Because I remember those requisition forms from Dubai looking rather... irregular." She watched the color drain from his face, satisfaction curling in her chest like smoke.

"Don't." His expression hardened, reminding her of Jackson when he was about to issue orders. "I've already contacted JAG. Whatever you think you have on me, it's not worth it."

"You owe me." Twenty years of dinner parties, of keeping his secrets, of being the military wife while they all played their games.

"I owe Jackson my career." He stood, gathering his things with military precision. "And you're drunk,

Maddie. Go home before you do something you'll regret."

She grabbed his wrist, her manicured nails digging into his skin. "If you walk away, I'll make sure every oversight committee knows what happened with those missing supplies."

Greg yanked his arm free as if her touch burned. "Let go. Now."

"I'll destroy you," she snarled, voice rising with each word. "Just like Jackson destroyed me."

The café fell silent. Heads turned, phones appeared, recording her descent into madness for posterity. She could already imagine the neighborhood group texts: Poor Maddie Callahan, coming apart at the seams. Greg's face flushed red as he backed away from her table, looking at her the way everyone seemed to — with a mixture of pity and fear.

"You need help, Maddie. Real help."

She watched him leave, noting how the other patrons avoided her gaze. They'd all take his side, of course. They always did. But they didn't understand— couldn't understand—that sometimes the only way to save yourself was to burn everything else to the ground.

◆ ◆ ◆

Maddie followed Greg outside Maxwell's, her heels clicking against the pavement. "Those requisition forms showed eight missing crates of equipment. Eight, Greg. What would your superiors think?"

"Stop this." His voice cracked.

She pressed closer. "Or was it nine? I have copies, you know. Every single document Jackson tried to bury."

Greg's shoulders tensed. Through the café window, Maddie spotted Lillian at the counter, ordering her usual green tea latte.

"Did Jackson tell you to lie about Dubai?" Maddie raised her voice. "About the Four Seasons meetings while equipment disappeared from Al Dhafra?"

Lillian's head snapped toward them. Greg's face drained of color.

"The affair was just a bonus, wasn't it?" Maddie's words carried through the open door. "Cover up the missing supplies, get a promotion, and protect Jackson's little romance?"

"Mrs. Callahan." Greg stepped back. "I'm calling security."

"Go ahead." She glanced at Lillian, who stood frozen in the doorway. "Tell them how you helped Jackson hide both scandals. The affair and the—"

"Enough!" Greg pulled out his phone. "Colonel Matthews? Yes, sir. I need to report a situation. Mrs. Callahan is attempting to blackmail me regarding the Dubai deployment." He met Maddie's eyes. "Yes, sir. I'll provide full documentation of her threats and previous attempts to manipulate my testimony."

Maddie's stomach lurched. This wasn't how it was supposed to go.

"And sir?" Greg's voice hardened. "We should review those requisition forms again. Mrs. Callahan seems to have unauthorized copies."

Lillian disappeared into a waiting car; phone pressed to her ear. Greg turned back to Maddie; his fear replaced with cold determination.

"You pushed too far." He ended the call. "JAG will contact you directly. Don't leave town."

❖ ❖ ❖

Maddie stared at her wilting Niçoise salad,

untouched since the waiter had placed it before her forty-seven minutes ago. Le Petit Jardin's usual Thursday lunch crowd buzzed around her, but Barbara's chair remained conspicuously empty—the third time this week her supposed friend had canceled at the last minute. The sunlight streaming through the restaurant's French windows felt accusatory, highlighting every empty seat at what had once been the most coveted table in Atlanta's social scene.

A flash of auburn her eye. Charlotte. Of course, Charlotte would choose today to break their fifteen-year tradition of sharing the corner table. Instead, her former confidante glided past without so much as a glance, making her way to where Sandra waited across the room. Sandra, who wouldn't have even been allowed through Le Petit Jardin's doors three months ago if it hadn't been for Maddie's influence.

The water glass grew slick beneath Maddie's grip, condensation rolling down her fingers like tears she refused to shed. She watched them settle into their chosen seats at Le Petit Jardin, her former courtiers performing their usual luncheon ballet of air kisses and theatrical whispers. Their Hermès scarves fluttered like battle flags in the afternoon light—Maddie had helped select half of those scarves herself, back when her opinion was law and her approval could make or break a woman's social calendar.

She'd orchestrated this entire ecosystem, crafted it with the precision of a master gardener tending to temperamental roses. Every invitation (timed), every subtle exclusion (oh, didn't you get the email about the charity gala?), every alliance she'd delicately nurtured over countless mimosa brunches and tennis club meetings—she'd built it all from nothing. Twenty years of calculated effort, transforming a scattered group of desperate social climbers into Atlanta's most formidable circle. Her circle. At least, it had been.

The same women who'd once called her daily (sometimes hourly during party season) now treated her like she carried something contagious. As if divorce was some sort of social leprosy that might spread if they sat too close. Maddie took a slow sip of water, letting the ice clink against her teeth. The irony wasn't lost on her—half their marriages were held together by designer thread and mutual denial. She knew which husbands had wandering eyes, which wives had suspicious spa weekends, which couples were one bad investment away from financial ruin.

Barbara, especially, had the audacity to catch her eye and offer that particular tilt of the head that screamed sympathy but cried judgment. Sweet, stupid Barbara, with her fresh lip fillers and that tacky tennis bracelet her contractor boyfriend had given her (as if Maddie hadn't noticed it was at least two carats smaller than what Barbara claimed). Maddie knew what Barbara said behind those manicured hands—she had Rosa's weekly reports of every lunch, every coffee date, every believed conversation in country club bathrooms.

The betrayal stung, yes, but it also sparked something darker, something that had been growing in the corners of Maddie's mind since Jackson's announcement. These women seemed to have forgotten a crucial fact: she hadn't built this social empire by being nice. She'd built it by knowing where everybody was buried, by holding secrets like playing cards, waiting for the moment to lay them on the table.

Maddie adjusted her own Hermès scarf—crimson, like blood, like warning—and allowed herself a small smile. Let them whisper. Let them think she was finished, defeated, cast aside. They'd learn soon enough that she hadn't lost her touch. After all, she'd collected twenty years' worth of secrets, and now... well, now she had nothing left to lose.

The water glass was empty now, but her grip remained steady. Maddie her reflection in the window—makeup, hair, posture. No one looking at her would guess that beneath her Chanel jacket, her heart was beating to a rhythm that felt increasingly like war drums. She'd made these women. And if necessary, she could unmake them just as easily.

Sandra's laugh cut through the ambient chatter like a knife. "Can you believe she tried to bribe Eleanor? After everything else?"

The words landed like individual punches to her solar plexus. There was a time—what felt like yesterday—when Sandra would have trembled just meeting her eyes across a room. Now here she sat, broadcasting Maddie's private business like some common gossip columnist.

"I heard Vivian Cross dropped her." Charlotte's voice carried with deliberate clarity. "No other lawyer in Atlanta will touch her case."

Something cold and heavy settled in Maddie's chest. Seventeen law firms. She'd called seventeen different offices since Vivian had abandoned her; each receptionist's voice more dismissive than the last. "We're unable to take your case at this time," they'd say, as if reading from a script. As if someone had warned them, she might call.

Her phone vibrated against the tablecloth,

Barbara's name lighting up the screen: Sorry darling, can't make dinner Friday. Board meeting ran long.

The same transparent lie she'd used yesterday. And last week. (As if Barbara had ever attended a board meeting in her life.)

Maddie her reflection in the window, and for a moment, she hardly recognized herself. The woman staring back at her looked... diminished. Her makeup, though applied, couldn't quite conceal the purple shadows beneath her eyes or the new lines bracketing her mouth. The Chanel jacket—last seasons, but who was counting? —hung loose where it had once fit like a glove.

"The children are better off in Virginia," Sandra's voice drifted over again, each word precise and purposeful. "After what she did to poor Lillian..."

Her hand shook as she reached for her Hermès bag. The legal system had turned its back on her. Her cultivated social circle had scattered like autumn leaves. Even Greg's threats about JAG involvement had rendered her usual tactics useless—how dare Jackson use his military connections against her?

But they'd all forgotten something crucial: Maddie Callahan didn't lose. Not like this. Not ever. She still had one card left to play, one final way to make Jackson understand what it meant to destroy everything she'd built.

She placed three crisp hundred-dollar bills on the table (let them whisper about that, too) and rose with deliberate grace. Charlotte's stage-whispered commentary followed her to the door, but Maddie didn't give them the satisfaction of turning around. In her Mercedes, safely hidden behind tinted windows, she pulled out the leather-bound notebook she kept beneath the passenger seat. Inside, in her precise handwriting, lay the fruits of months of observation: Jackson's schedule, his habits, his weaknesses—everything that made him vulnerable.

She'd played by their rules until now. She'd been the proper society wife, even in divorce. But that ended today. After all, they'd already cast her as the villain—why disappoint them?

Chapter 24

Maddie sat in her study, where everything was as it should be. The Hermès notebook aligned with her laptop's edge; her Mont Blanc pen parallel to both. Control lived in the details, after all. She adjusted a crystal paperweight a quarter inch to the left, then focused on her phone, where she was crafting what felt like the hundredth message to Jackson.

Every word needed to strike the balance. Like preparing for a dinner party where half the guests were allergic to the other half's favorite foods. Just enough remorse to seem genuine (because that's what he'd want to see, wouldn't he?), but not so much that it appeared desperate. Maddie Callahan had never been desperate in her life. At least, that's what she told herself as she deleted and rewrote the same sentence for the fourth time.

Jackson, I've been doing a lot of thinking. These past months have shown me where I went wrong. The children need both of us, and I'm ready to work together for their sake. Please, let me know how Carrie's piano lessons are going, and if Nate's settled into his new school. I only want what's best for them.

She read it three times; each pass more critical than the last. The first draft had included a pointed reference to his new house in Virginia - deleted. A subtle dig about Lily - not. Instead, she crafted something softer, maternal. The mention of Carrie's piano lessons was inspired. Let him remember how she'd played at Carnegie Hall last spring, how proud they'd both been. Let him think about what moving her to some provincial Virginia instructor would do to her talent. Not that she'd say that directly. No, the power was in making him think of it himself.

Her manicured thumb hovered over the send button. The shade of red - Chanel's Rouge Noir - the light from her desk lamp. This had to work. She'd exhausted every other avenue, called in every favor (even that embarrassing lunch with her ex-sorority sister who'd married a judge), tried every legal channel. But Jackson had Nate now, and Nate was... well, Nate was a machine. She'd tried charm on him once. His cold gray eyes had made her feel like she was being dissected.

She pressed send before she could overthink it

again.

The message showed as delivered immediately. Two blue checkmarks - modern technology's way of saying you couldn't pretend you hadn't received something anymore. Maddie stared at the screen, remembering a time when letters took days to arrive, when she could pretend Jackson's silence meant the mail was delayed somewhere between their home and whatever far-flung military base he'd been stationed at. Those had been simpler days, when hope could stretch across oceans and time zones. Now, hope died in seconds, murdered by instant messaging and read receipts.

She watched for the three dots that would indicate Jackson was typing a response, her manicured nail hovering over the screen. Nothing. The screen remained static, like his heart toward her these days. Like everything about him since Lily had entered their lives, bringing youth and novelty and that nauseating brand of adoration that Maddie remembered feeling herself, once upon a time. (Before she learned that loving Jackson was like loving a fortress - impressive from the outside, but cold and empty within.)

Ten minutes passed, marked by the antique grandfather clock in the corner that had been her grandmother's. The steady tick-tock reminded her of Sunday afternoons at Gran's house, learning the art of patience, of waiting for what you wanted. "A lady never appears eager," Gran would say, adjusting her pearls with arthritic fingers. But Gran had never dealt with instant messaging or younger women who wore their desperation like designer perfume.

Maddie refreshed the conversation repeatedly,

each time telling herself she wouldn't do it again. Each time doing it anyway. It was becoming a habit, like her evening glass of wine or her weekly appointments with Dr. Harrison (the one who prescribed the little blue pills she'd stopped taking three weeks ago, not that anyone had noticed).

Her phone buzzed, and her heart performed the same treacherous leap it had been doing since she was twenty-three and falling in love with a promising young officer. She remembered that version of herself - young, starry-eyed, believing in things like destiny and forever. That Maddie would never have imagined becoming this Maddie, the one who jumped at phone notifications like a trained dog. But it wasn't Jackson. Of course it wasn't. Instead, a notification from her email appeared, and the sight of it made her stomach twist with a familiar combination of dread and anticipation. She'd been waiting for this particular message, planning for it, even. Though planning these days felt more like plotting, and wasn't that just what her life had become?

The wife had transformed into the strategist, and wasn't that what Jackson had always admired? Strategy. Control. Power. She'd learned from the best, after all. Twenty-five years of watching him command troops and manipulate situations had taught her everything she needed to know about warfare. Even if he'd never intended for her to use those lessons against him.

Forwarded message from Jackson Callahan to Nathan Wren (cc: Margaret Chen):

Subject: Documentation for file

Of course. Of course he'd send her message straight to his attorney. Because that's what she was now - not his wife of twenty-five years, not the mother of his children, but a case number in Nate Wren's organized files. Another problem for The Machine to solve with his cold, calculated efficiency.

She set the phone down with deliberate care, though what she wanted to do was throw it through her imported French windows. The ones Jackson had complained about as an unnecessary expense, even as he'd written the check without blinking. The ones that now felt like they were watching her, judging her, like everything else in this house that was becoming more of a prison every day.

Below it, her crafted message appeared as an attachment. She'd spent hours on those words, crafting each sentence to strike the balance between reasonable and firm. The kind of message a sane, stable woman would send to her wayward husband.

The phone slipped from her fingers onto the desk. He hadn't even bothered to read it. Hadn't given her words a moment's consideration. Just forwarded it straight to his attorney like she was nothing more than paperwork to be filed. Like two and a half decades of marriage could be reduced to exhibits and affidavits.

Heat rose in her chest, familiar and comforting in its intensity. Her hands shook as she picked up the phone again, and wasn't that just? Even her body was betraying her now. Twenty-five years of marriage, and he treated her message like spam mail. Something to be filtered and filed away by his attack dog in an expensive suit.

She opened her notebook, the leather smooth and cool beneath her trembling fingers, flipping past the pages of Jackson's schedule and habits to a fresh sheet. If he wouldn't acknowledge her olive branch, she'd make damn sure he couldn't ignore what came next. After all, she'd learned from the best how to wage a war.

❖ ❖ ❖

Maddie smoothed her navy silk dress, feeling the familiar weight of Chanel against her skin. Two seasons ago, but that was intentional. Let them think she was struggling, let them underestimate her. The St. Catherine's Annual Charity Gala buzzed with Atlanta's elite around her, a symphony of crystal glasses and affected laughter she'd conducted for twenty-five years. But tonight, for the first time, no one rushed to greet her. No air kisses, no squeals of delight, no immediate clustering of bodies drawn to her magnetic presence.

She took a slow sip of champagne, remembering last year's gala. How she'd held court by the fountain, dispensing approval and withering glances like a queen. Now Sandra stood in her spot - dear, desperate Sandra who'd always tried so hard to fit in. Their eyes met across the marble floor, and Sandra's panicked reaction would have been comical if it weren't so telling. She turned away, physically using her body to create a wall with the women around her, like schoolgirls huddling against the threat of an unwanted classmate.

Charlotte was easier to spot, hovering by the silent auction tables with that familiar predatory focus. She always did love her jewelry, especially when it came with the cachet of charity. Maddie approached with measured steps, her smile gentle and practiced. The same smile she'd worn through three deployments, countless social battles, and one nasty PTA coup in 2019.

"Charlotte."

"Maddie." Charlotte's voice dripped with that distinct brand of Southern contempt - sugar-coated poison served in a crystal glass. "I didn't expect to see you here."

"I've supported this cause for years." Since before you were anybody, Maddie wanted to add. Back when Charlotte was just the new money trying desperately to break into their circle.

"Yes, well." Charlotte's eyes darted around the room like a trapped animal seeking escape. "If you'll excuse me, I need to check on the catering."

The catering. As if Charlotte had ever lifted a finger for event planning. That had always been Maddie's domain.

Barbara, at least, managed eye contact. Sweet, stupid Barbara who'd always been more follower than friend. The warmth that usually animated her Botoxed features had frozen over, leaving something plastic and unfamiliar in its place. "The navy suits you," she said, immediately stepping back as if Maddie's fall from grace might be catching.

"Barbara, please. We've known each other for-" Twenty years of secrets, lies, and cultivated alliances. Twenty years of protecting each other from scandal and shame.

"Stop." Barbara's whisper cut through the air like a paper cut - thin but sharp. "Whatever you're planning with Jackson and the children - just stop. You're only hurting yourself now."

"I don't know what you mean." Maddie's smile stayed fixed, though her fingers tightened around her clutch. Inside, something dark and familiar uncurled. They thought she was hurting herself? Oh, they had no idea what hurt was. Not yet.

"The courts made their decision. The children are better off-" Barbara herself, fear flickering across her face.

"I have to go. Elizabeth needs me at the registration table."

Maddie watched Barbara's retreat, noting how the crowd parted around her own presence like water around a stone. These women - these curated friends who'd eaten at her table, shared her secrets, followed her lead for decades - they'd abandoned her. Like rats from a sinking ship, except Maddie wasn't sinking. She was evolving.

The realization settled cold and heavy in her chest: there would be no social redemption. No return to her former glory. The old Maddie - the wife, the social queen, the woman who ruled through charm and subtle manipulation - was dead.

Fine. She didn't need their approval anymore. She had something better now: she had purpose. Let them whisper and avoid her eyes. Let them think she was finished. Maddie took another sip of champagne, feeling the familiar buzz of plans taking shape in her mind. She'd built this world once before. She could burn it down just as easily.

Maddie sank deeper into Jackson's leather armchair, the one he'd insisted on importing from some overpriced London craftsman. (Everything in his study had to be just so - God forbid the General settle for American-made furniture.) The Macallan burned her throat, but she welcomed the sensation. At least it was something real, something that cut through the fog of emptiness that had settled over the house like a shroud.

The television's blue light danced across the wood-paneled walls - walls she'd never liked but had accepted because Jackson declared them "distinguished."

These true crime shows had become her nightly ritual, filling the silence that threatened to swallow her whole. It is strange how quickly twenty-five years of marriage could dissolve into nothing but echoing rooms and curated memories.

Tonight's episode drew her in more than usual. A wealthy banker's wife in Connecticut - how appropriate. The crime scene photos showed a kitchen that could have been pulled from any of the homes in Maddie's social circle: pristine marble counter tops gleaming under harsh police lights, high-end appliances bearing silent witness to the morning's events. The victim had collapsed during his morning coffee routine, still wearing one of his custom-tailored suits. (They always dressed impeccably, these men who thought themselves untouchable.)

"The toxicology report revealed traces of aconite," the narrator's voice filled the room, and Maddie found herself leaning forward. "Also known as wolfsbane or devil's helmet. Death occurred within thirty minutes of ingestion."

Her fingers traced the rim of her crystal glass - Waterford, another of Jackson's insisted-upon luxuries. How fascinating that the banker's wife had grown the plant herself, tucked innocently between her prized roses. Such elegant simplicity. No violence, no mess, no unseemly confrontations. Just a cup of coffee and thirty minutes. The kind of solution that wouldn't leave a mark on freshly manicured nails.

The show cut to interviews with the couple's social circle, and Maddie couldn't help but smile. They all said what her friends would say: she seemed so normal, they never suspected, she was always put together.

(Wasn't that what they all strived for? That veneer of normalcy?)

When they showed the wife's arrest, Maddie straightened instinctively, recognizing a kindred spirit. Even in handcuffs, the woman maintained her dignity - spine straight, chin lifted, composed as though attending another charity luncheon. The camera lingered on her Hermès scarf (last season's pattern, but who would notice in a police station?) and her impeccably applied lipstick. Maddie approved of such attention to detail. If one must fall, better to fall.

The methodical nature of it all captivated her - how the wife had immersed herself in gardening forums, selecting companion plants to disguise her deadly harvest. The patience she'd shown, months of bringing coffee every morning, building a routine no one would question. It was rather like planning a dinner party, wasn't it? All in the timing and presentation.

Maddie's phone sat heavy in her lap, and her fingers twitched with the urge to research. One quick Google search - that's all it would take to start down this path. But no, not yet. The idea nestled into the back of her mind like a seed taking root, quiet but persistent. There would be time for research later. After all, hadn't Jackson taught her the importance of proper planning during all those years as a military wife?

She took another measured sip of scotch, savoring the expensive burn while watching the wife's booking photo fill the screen. The woman's smile spoke volumes - peaceful, satisfied, like someone who had solved a challenging puzzle. Maddie understood that smile now, perhaps better than she wanted to admit. Sometimes the most elegant solutions were also the simplest ones.

The house creaked and settled around her, a familiar symphony of emptiness. But for the first time in weeks, Maddie didn't mind the silence quite so much. She had something new to consider, a project of sorts. And if there was one thing Maddie Callahan excelled at, it was seeing a project through to completion.

❖ ❖ ❖

Through her hidden surveillance camera, Maddie watched Jackson pace in his Virginia study. His phone - her message still unread on the screen - lay face-up on his desk. He picked it up, set it down, picked it up again. The hesitation in his movements pleased her.

Lillian entered the room, wrapped in one of those ridiculous cashmere shawls she favored. Even through the grainy footage, Maddie could see the tension in Lillian's shoulders, the way she startled at small noises.

"Everything okay?" Lillian's voice came through distorted.

Jackson's hand moved toward the phone, but stopped. He glanced at Lillian - looked at her - and Maddie saw the moment his expression changed. The shadows under Lillian's eyes, the slight tremor in her hands as she clutched that shawl tighter.

"Just work," Jackson lied, sliding the phone into his pocket.

Maddie leaned closer to her screen, studying Lillian's face. The woman jumped at a car door slamming outside. Her eyes darted to the windows, checking the locks for the third time since entering the room.

"I thought I saw someone in the garden earlier," Lillian said. "It was probably nothing, but- "

"I'll have security do another sweep." Jackson's

voice was gentle, protective. The tone he'd once used with Maddie.

Lillian nodded, but her fingers still worried the edge of her shawl. The fear was there, raw and real. Maddie had done that. Even now, hundreds of miles away, she could make Lillian's hands shake.

Jackson pulled Lillian close, sheltering her. But Maddie noticed how his other hand stayed in his pocket, wrapped around the phone holding her message. He wouldn't tell Lillian about it. He couldn't - not when Lillian was already so fragile.

Maddie smiled, taking a sip of her coffee. Sometimes the best threats were the ones left unspoken.

Chapter 25

Maddie adjusted her Chanel jacket, the familiar weight of French wool settling across her shoulders like armor. The scent of cinnamon and apple cider wafted through St. Catherine's gymnasium-turned-harvest-festival, eight years of memories rising unbidden. Eight years of being the mother and consummate volunteer before Jackson took that away, too.

Her Louboutins struck a precise rhythm against

the polished floor as she approached the silent auction tables. The sound reminded her of a metronome, like the one that had kept time during Carrie's piano lessons. She'd donated to every single auction since Carrie started kindergarten—designer handbags, spa packages, weekend getaways. This year, the donor wall stretched before her, a sea of names that didn't include hers. An intentional slight, no doubt.

"I thought Carrie might like to know her old school still thinks of her," she said to Susan Bennett, who was fussing with bid sheets like they held state secrets. Susan's hands froze for just a moment—a tell. These women were so transparent with their little reactions.

"The children are settled in Virginia now, aren't they?" Susan's voice carried that practiced neutrality these women had ed, the kind that said everything while saying nothing.

"They're struggling," Maddie let her fingers trail across a crystal vase, remembering how Carrie used to arrange flowers with her on Sunday mornings. "Carrie's piano teacher there just isn't connecting with her the way Eleanor did." The lie felt comfortable on her tongue, necessary. These women needed to understand that her children weren't better off without her. She touched the vase again, imagining it shattering. "I still attend all the recitals in Carrie's old time slot. Just in case she comes back."

Susan retreated with a mumbled excuse about refreshments. Around her, conversations dimmed like someone had turned down the volume of the world. Mothers herded their children away from her table, their averted gazes speaking volumes. As if tragedy might be contagious. As if she were the villain in their curated suburban fairy tale.

Patricia Walsh approached, her PTA president badge catching the light like a sheriff's star. "Maddie, I wasn't aware you were still... involved with school events."

"Of course, I am." Maddie lifted her chin, projecting her voice just enough to reach the gossips pretending not to listen. "Just because Jackson took the children doesn't mean I've stopped being a mother." The words tasted like bitter medicine, necessary but unpleasant. "I'm still on the mailing list. The fall festival email said all parents were welcome."

"Yes, well..." Patricia's smile stretched thin as old elastic.

"I brought cookies. Carrie's favorite recipe." Maddie presented the cellophane-wrapped plate like an offering. The cookies she'd baked three times until they were, just like Carrie remembered them. Just like the ones they used to make together on rainy afternoons.

Patricia stared at them as if they were laced with arsenic. "That's... thoughtful. I'll just take those to the donation table." She scurried away without touching them, leaving Maddie holding her rejected peace offering.

Then she heard it—Carrie's laugh. The sound sliced through her like a blade, familiar yet somehow different. Lighter. Freer.

She turned, and there they were. Jackson in one of his navy suits, Carrie's small hand in his. Nate trailing behind them, taller than she remembered, his shoulders straighter. They looked... polished. Content. Well-fed. Everything she'd told herself they couldn't be without her.

"General Callahan!" Patricia sprinted past

Maddie, the force of her passage threatening to upset the careful balance of cookies. "What a wonderful surprise!"

"Couldn't miss the fall festival." Jackson's smile— his real smile, the one that crinkled his eyes—appeared so easily now. "Carrie insisted."

Carrie bounced on her toes, blonde hair in a velvet bow Maddie had never seen before. "Daddy said I could bid on the American Girl basket!"

Maddie barely looked at her. She still played with dolls? At her age? Carrie was supposed to be refined, poised. Not bouncing around like a child with a sugar high.

"How adorable," Maddie said to Charlotte instead, as if Carrie wasn't even there. "She's always had a taste for the sentimental." With the champagne tilt full to her mouth, she was seeing the world through bubbles, her tone airily detached. "I do hope she doesn't waste Jackson's money on something... juvenile."

The crowd shifted like a living thing, drawn to Jackson's orbit. Susan abandoned her precious bid sheets. Charlotte materialized as if summoned, touching Jackson's arm with the familiarity of an old friend as she fawned over Nate's height.

Maddie's constructed narrative began to crack, hairline fractures spreading with each warm greeting, each genuine smile from her children. There were no signs of the struggles she'd invented, no academic difficulties, no trauma over piano lessons. Just two children who looked happier than they had any right to be.

"Mrs. Walsh!" Carrie hugged Patricia with natural affection. "I made honor roll again! And my new piano teacher says I'm doing well."

The cookies in Maddie's hands grew heavier with each passing second. Every pair of eyes that had avoided her earlier now looked through her, as if she'd become a ghost in her own kingdom. Her crafted story of maternal concern dissolved like sugar in rain, washed away by the undeniable evidence that her children were thriving without her.

Jackson didn't even glance her way. He didn't need to. His presence, with their obviously flourishing children, had already delivered the cruelest message of all: they didn't need her anymore. Maybe they never had.

The cookie plate trembled in her hands. She wondered, distantly, how many of these women would be discussing this moment over wine later. How many would whisper about poor, unstable Maddie, showing up where she wasn't wanted, bringing cookies no one would dare eat.

Her carefully crafted story of maternal concern dissolved like sugar in the rain, washed away by undeniable evidence that her children were thriving without her. Maddie gripped the cookie plate tighter, her knuckles white against the delicate china. The plate had been a wedding gift from Jackson's mother - another woman who'd perhaps seen through her from the start.

"Carrie, sweetheart," she called out, her voice dripping artificial sweetness. Like the vanilla extract she'd measured three times that morning, wanting everything to be. (It had to be.) "I made your favorites."

The way Carrie half-turned, those big blue eyes darting up to Jackson's face for permission - it was worse than any of the silent phone calls she'd endured these past months. Worse than the empty house. Worse than watching Lily parade around town in that obscene tennis skirt, playing at being the stepmother.

"Come now," Maddie coaxed, taking another step forward. The cookies rattled on the plate. When had her hands started shaking? "Don't you want to try one? I used the fancy vanilla, just like always." Just like the hundreds of afternoons they'd spent in the kitchen together, Carrie perched on a stool, flour dusting her nose. Before everything fell apart. Before Jackson decided twenty years meant nothing.

"I-" Carrie's small body pressed against Jackson's side, seeking protection. From her own mother. "We already had treats at home. Lily made brownies."

Lily. Of course., young Lily with her brownies and her life that she'd stolen. The name hit Maddie like a physical blow, and she tightened her grip on the plate until her fingers ached. "But these are your cookies. The ones you always loved. Remember how we'd bake them together?" Remember me, she wanted to scream. Remember who I am. Who I was.

"Mrs. Callahan." Jackson's voice carried that familiar warning tone, the one he'd used when addressing subordinates who'd stepped out of line. When had she become just another person for him to manage? "This isn't appropriate."

"Not appropriate?" The words escaped in a laugh that sounded foreign to her own ears. She was dimly aware of heads turning, of Barbara Harrington's manicured hand rising to cover her mouth in manufactured shock. "What's not appropriate is some other woman baking for my children." My children. The only thing she had left. And even they were slipping away.

Then Nate was there, her beautiful boy trying to

be the adult, stepping between her and Carrie like he needed to protect his sister. From her. "Mom, stop."

"I will not stop! These are my children. My family." The cookies began to slide as her hands trembled more violently. She'd spent three hours making them, each one identical, because things couldn't be ignored. things demanded attention. "You can't just replace me with-"

"Daddy?" Carrie's voice quivered, and oh, how that quiver cut straight to Maddie's core. "Can we go?"

Jackson didn't even glance her way. He didn't need to. His presence, with their obviously flourishing children, had already delivered the cruelest message of all: they didn't need her anymore. Maybe they never had.

The cookie plate trembled in her hands. She wondered, distantly, how many of these women would be discussing this moment over wine later. How many would whisper about poor, unstable Maddie, showing up where she wasn't wanted, bringing cookies no one would dare eat.

The recordings that followed were just the final nails in a coffin she'd apparently been building for herself all along. Each word from that phone speaker stripped away another layer of her constructed facade, leaving her raw and exposed under the judgmental gazes of Atlanta's elite. She watched her remaining allies peel away one by one, like petals from a dying flower.

Sandra's fingers dug into her arm - not out of friendship anymore, but restraint. The cookies lay broken on the floor, much like the life she'd spent decades molding. She could almost hear Charlotte mentally calculating how quickly she could distance herself from this scandal. Patricia Walsh would undoubtedly call an emergency board meeting tomorrow to discuss Maddie's removal from every committee she'd fought so hard to join.

The sight of Carrie's small fingers clutching Jackson's navy Armani jacket - the one Maddie had picked out for him last Christmas, before everything shattered - made something deep inside her chest splinter and crack. Her daughter's face, that precious face she'd memorized from the moment the nurse had placed her in her arms, was buried against Jackson's chest. Hiding. From her.

Maddie's hand twitched, remembering all the times she'd smoothed Carrie's hair before bed, kissed her forehead, said "Mommy's little angel" into the dark. Now her angel was trembling, trembling, like a terrified bird. Because of her. Because somehow, in all her careful planning and righteous fury, she'd become the monster in her daughter's story.

The crack spread wider, a fissure in the bedrock of who she was as a mother. She'd sacrificed everything for her children - given up her dreams, waited through endless deployments, built this world for them. And now Carrie couldn't even look at her. The betrayal of it, the sheer injustice, made her want to scream. But she didn't. Couldn't. Because screaming would only make Carrie burrow deeper into Jackson's protection, and wasn't that what he wanted?

She watched, paralyzed, as Jackson's hand came up to protectively cup the back of Carrie's head - a gesture that should have been hers. Had been hers, for eight years. The crack became a chasm, dark and bottomless. This wasn't supposed to happen. None of this was supposed to happen. She was supposed to be the safe place, the warm embrace, the mother who made everything better.

Instead, she'd become something else. Something that made her own daughter shake with fear.

The realization settled into her bones like poison. This damage - this fundamental rupture in the bond between mother and child - might never heal. And whose fault was that? Jackson's, for destroying their family? Lily's, for stealing him away? Or her own, for letting the darkness inside her spill out where Carrie could see it?

The answer reverberated through her mind, ugly and unwanted: Some things, once broken, stay broken. Just like the shattered cookies on the floor, some messes couldn't be cleaned up with a smile and an apology. Some betrayals ran too deep. Some fears, once planted, grew roots that could never be fully pulled out.

She straightened her spine, adjusted her pearls - the ones Jackson had given her on their tenth anniversary, back when forever still meant something. Let them think she was cold, unfeeling. It was better than letting them see how she was shattering inside.

Because the truth was, watching Carrie tremble in fear of her had broken something essential in Maddie's soul. Something vital and irreplaceable. Something that, deep down, she knew would never, ever be whole again.

Her own recorded laughter echoed through the room, cold and foreign. Who was that woman on the recording? That couldn't be her voice discussing bruises and stage makeup, plotting another woman's downfall with such calculated precision. Except it was. It was all her, stripped of pretense, laid bare for everyone to see.

And her children didn't look back once.

Chapter 26

Maddie stared at her silent phone, willing it to light up with notifications. The pristine screen remained dark, mocking her with its emptiness. No concerned messages from Charlotte (and wasn't that telling, after twenty years of friendship?). No rapid-fire texts from Barbara, usually so eager to dissect every social mishap. Nothing but silence, heavy and accusatory.

She refreshed her messages for what felt like the hundredth time that morning, her French-tipped nail clicking against the screen with increasing urgency. The "Ladies Who Lunch" group chat—her creation, her curated social sphere—had vanished like morning mist. Six years of planning charity galas, organizing tennis tournaments, and orchestrating social takedowns, all erased with a few taps.

"This is temporary," she told her reflection, applying her signature Chanel Rouge Allure in Rouge. The woman in the mirror looked as she should: polished, controlled, unshakeable. If her hand trembled while applying the lipstick, well, that was between her and the vanity mirror.

The email notification made her heart leap—, someone breaking ranks—but hope curdled into something bitter as she read the message from St. Catherine's. The words swam before her eyes: "Due to recent events..." Recent events. Such a delicate way of phrasing it. As if she hadn't chaired every major event for the past decade. As if she hadn't single-handedly raised more money than any previous committee chair.

Delete.

Another ping, another dismissal. The Spring Gala she'd already started planning, the centerpieces she'd selected, the seating chart she'd nearly ed—all being handed over to someone else. Probably Charlotte. It would be Charlotte, wouldn't it? Always waiting in the wings, always so positioned to step in.

Delete.

The Garden Club notification felt like a personal slap. "Past contributions." Past. As if she were already dead and buried, as if fifteen years of maintaining those pristine rose gardens could be dismissed with a single word. Her finger hovered over the delete button, but she couldn't quite bring herself to press it. That would make it real.

Maddie scrolled through her contacts, a social registry she'd cultivated as those roses. Barbara's number—straight to voicemail, of course. Maybe already at lunch with the others, dissecting Maddie's downfall over overpriced salads. Charlotte's phone rang once before disconnecting, a deliberate snub if she'd ever heard one. Sandra's number was blocked, which was almost laughable. Sandra, of all people, blocking her? The woman who'd needed Maddie's help to get her children into St. Catherine's in the first place?

"They're just shocked," she said, adjusting her Hermès scarf—the one Jackson had brought back from Paris three years ago. The silk felt like armor against her skin. "Once they remember everything, I've done for them, who I am in this community..." The words trailed off as she studied her reflection. Not a hair out of place, not a wrinkle visible (thank you, Dr. Morrison's skilled hands). She was still Maddie Callahan. That hadn't changed.

Her fingers moved across the phone screen, composing a message that struck the balance between conciliation and authority: "Ladies, I understand last night was upsetting. Perhaps we could meet at Le Petit Jardin to discuss—"

The message bounced back immediately. Blocked. Every single one of them had blocked her number.

Maddie's hand trembled as she set down the phone, the device suddenly feeling like a poisonous thing. The tremor angered her more than the rejection. Maddie Callahan did not tremble. She did not break. She had created this social circle from nothing, transformed these women from country club nobodies into someone. Barbara had been wearing off-the-rack before Maddie took her under her wing. Charlotte wouldn't have known a Birkin from a basic tote without Maddie's guidance.

They would remember that. They would remember who held the real power in this town. They had to.

Because if they didn't—if this silence stretched from hours into days—then everything she'd built over the past twenty years might crumble like the foundations of her marriage. And that was unacceptable.

◆ ◆ ◆

Maddie paced her marble kitchen; each click of her Louboutins against the floor marking time like a metronome counting down to something inevitable. The morning sun the diamond on her wedding finger—the one Jackson hadn't asked for back yet—sending prisms dancing across the Viking range she'd selected three renovations ago. Rosa stood at the sink, her hands moving through the soapy water with that methodical patience that had always soothed Maddie before. But not today. Nothing soothed her today.

"Can you believe how they acted? As if I'm some sort of monster." The laugh that escaped her throat surprised even her—sharp and brittle, like breaking crystal. "Charlotte ran from me. After everything I've done for her." Twenty years of friendship, of covering for Charlotte's son's indiscretions, of making sure she was invited to every important event. All of it, forgotten because Jackson had spun his little tale of victimhood.

Rosa's hands slowed in the sink, and Maddie watched soap bubbles drift upward, catching the light like her shattered social life. "Perhaps they need time, señora."

"Time? For what? To forget who made them relevant in this city?" The empty coffee cup in Maddie's hand suddenly offended her—everything did these days—and she thrust it toward Rosa with perhaps more force than necessary. The memory of Barbara's face at last week's charity luncheon surfaced, that poorly concealed pity mixing with fear. "Barbara would still be shopping at Nordstrom if it wasn't for me. And Sandra? Please. I taught her how to hold a fork properly."

The cup disappeared into Rosa's capable hands without comment. She never met Maddie's eyes anymore, but that was fine. Maddie preferred loyalty to eye contact. "Sometimes people—"

"Don't defend them." Maddie felt her voice drop to that place she'd learned to access years ago, that tone that made people remember who she was. Who she'd always been. "You're the only one who understands. You've seen everything, haven't you, Rosa? Twenty years in this house. You know I'm not what they're saying."

Her reflection her attention in the window—still, still poised, despite everything they were whispering about her. She adjusted her pearls, a gift from Jackson when Nate was born. When they were still happy. Or at least pretending to be.

"Jackson turned them against me. Him and that little..." Her fingers tightened around her necklace until she felt the strain of the silk thread between each pearl. That girl. That princess. That replacement who thought she could step into Maddie's life without consequences. The memory of seeing them together at Bellini's made her teeth ache from clenching. "But they'll remember.

They always come crawling back when they need something."

"Maybe if you gave them space—"

"Space?" Maddie spun around, her heel catching the light like a weapon. The word tasted like poison in her mouth. Space was what Jackson had asked for, what Charlotte had mumbled as she backed away from Maddie's lunch invitation, what Barbara had suggested in that condescending tone she'd learned from Maddie herself. "I don't need to give them anything. They need to remember their place."

She softened then, reaching out to touch Rosa's arm the way she used to touch Carrie when explaining something important. "You understand, don't you? You've always been loyal."

Rosa nodded, her face a masterpiece of careful blankness that Maddie chose not to examine too closely. "Yes, señora."

"Good." Maddie squeezed Rosa's arm, already planning her next move. She didn't notice the slight flinch, the way Rosa's hands had stilled in the water. She was too busy calculating, remembering every secret, every favor, every moment of weakness she'd witnessed over the years. "At least I can count on you."

And she could, couldn't she? She had to. Because if Rosa wasn't loyal, if Rosa ever decided to share what she'd seen in this house over the years... No. Maddie pushed the thought away. Rosa knew better than that. Rosa understood the natural order of things, unlike some people. Unlike Jackson's little princess, who needed to learn what happened to people who tried to take what belonged to Maddie Callahan.

◆ ◆ ◆

Maddie poured another glass of Jackson's prized Macallan, her hands trembling as she clicked play on the St. Catherine's Fall Festival video for the fifth time. The amber liquid sloshed over the crystal rim, staining her silk blouse.

"Look at how they edited this." She jabbed her finger at the screen where she appeared wild-eyed, reaching for Carrie. "This isn't how it happened."

The video showed her stumbling, cookies scattered across the marble floor. Jackson's voice came through clear and measured, playing those damned recordings while Carrie pressed against his leg.

Maddie drained her glass. Her reflection in the dark window looked distorted, unfamiliar. She paced the length of Jackson's study, her designer heels catching on the Persian rug.

"He planned this." She grabbed her leather-bound journal from the desk drawer, flipping to a fresh page. "He's controlling everything, turning them all against me."

Her writing grew messier with each line:
*Security footage - find source
*Charlotte's husband - defense contracts?
*School board connections
Dr. Matthews records

"I just need to shift the perspective." She muttered, crossing out words with increasing force. "Show them who Jackson is."

The pen tore through the paper as she underlined 'Dubai records' three times. She'd lost track of how many glasses she'd poured, but the bottle was nearly empty.

"They'll see." Her voice echoed in the empty

study. "Once I explain it properly, they'll understand. Jackson can't control everyone forever."

She scrawled 'COUNTERSTRIKE' across the top of a new page, her normally handwriting now jagged and sharp. Below it, she started listing names, drawing arrows between them, creating a web of potential allies and pressure points.

◆ ◆ ◆

Maddie's manicured nails hovered over her phone screen, a slight tremor betraying the composure she fought to maintain. Three deep breaths, just like her therapist used to recommend. (Back when Jackson still thought therapy was the answer, before he decided she was the problem.) The line rang three times before connecting, each ring stretching like a lifetime.

"Barbara?" Her voice came out smoother than she felt, practiced from decades of social performance. "I've been thinking about what happened at St. Catherine's—"

"Don't." Barbara's voice sliced through the air, sharp and cold. Barbara, who used to lean in close at charity galas, whispering delicious morsels of gossip, now wielded her words like weapons. "Whatever story you're about to spin, save it."

"I'm not spinning anything. If you'd just let me, explain—" The harsh click of disconnection cut through her prepared speech.

Maddie stared at her phone; her reflection distorted in the dark screen. Twenty years of friendship, ended with a click. She could still picture Barbara's face lit with malicious glee as they'd systematically dismantled Jean-Marc's reputation at Le Petit Jardin. How many afternoons had they spent in this study, plotting his downfall over mimosas? Now Barbara had turned that same calculating precision against her.

Fine. If Barbara wanted to play games, Maddie could play too.

She opened her laptop, the blue light harsh against her features as she pulled up a fresh email to Sarah Mitchell at the Atlanta Journal. Her fingers danced across the keys with practiced efficiency, weaving truth and perception into something more potent than either. The story wrote itself: the devoted wife, the calculating husband, the systematic isolation. She dropped in chosen phrases – "emotional manipulation," "controlling behavior," "gaslighting." The Dubai incident would make a compelling centerpiece, especially with those text messages she'd saved.

The email bounced back. Account blocked.

A muscle twitched in her jaw as she tried the editor's general inbox. Silence. Three more journalists. Nothing but digital void. Jackson's reach was longer than she'd anticipated. (He'd always been good at strategy, hadn't he? It was what had attracted her in the first place.)

"Mrs. Callahan?" Rosa's voice drifted from the doorway, gentle as always. Too gentle. "Your coffee."

Maddie kept her eyes fixed on the screen, refusing to acknowledge the intrusion. "Put it on the desk." The scent of French roast filled the air – at least Rosa remembered how she liked it. Small mercies.

"Perhaps..." The china clinked against wood with precise, measured movement. Rosa's hesitation hung in the air like perfume. "Perhaps it would help to take a step back. Give everyone some space to—"

"Space?" Maddie spun in her chair, her silk robe whispering against leather. The audacity of it—advice from the help? "You think I should just sit here while

Jackson destroys everything I've built? While he turns my children against me?"

"I only meant—"

"You don't get to tell me what to do." Maddie lowered her voice to a whisper, the way she'd learned long ago had more impact than shouting. Power wasn't about volume; it was about control. "You're the help. Remember your place."

Rosa's face settled into that maddeningly blank expression she'd mastered over the years. How much had she seen? How much did she know? "Yes, Mrs. Callahan. Will you need anything else?"

Maddie dismissed her with a flick of her wrist before turning back to the laptop's glow. She had more pressing concerns than an overstepping maid. Jackson thought he could cut off her access to the press? Fine. She had other weapons in her arsenal. After all, she hadn't spent twenty years as a general's wife without learning something about warfare.

She reached for her coffee, noting with satisfaction that despite everything, her hand was steady now. The game wasn't over. It was just beginning..

Chapter 27

Maddie smoothed her navy Chanel suit jacket, the fabric whispering against her silk blouse— professional, but with just enough vulnerability to make her point. She'd chosen this particular ensemble after three hours of deliberation. The St. Catherine's Mother's Prayer Circle had always appreciated subtle displays of wealth, even while preaching humility (not that any of them would admit it, of course).

The morning session was ending right on

schedule. Maddie could hear the familiar cadence of final prayers through the heavy wooden doors. Timing was everything. These women had watched her raise her children, had cooed over Carrie's first communion dress and Nate's altar boy ceremonies. They'd seen her in the front pew every Sunday, head bowed, the picture of maternal devotion. They would understand. They had to.

She waited for the moment to enter, counting her breaths the way Dr. Matthews had taught her. (She'd chosen him - respected enough to be credible, but new enough to the area that Jackson's reach hadn't corrupted him yet.) The leather of her Hermès bag creaked as she clutched it tighter. Inside was her monogrammed handkerchief, crisp and ready. She'd practiced with it in front of the mirror, saving the subtle dab that wouldn't smear her carefully applied makeup.

"I know some of you might have heard things," she began, letting her voice quaver just enough. Not too much - these women had known her for years. They'd recognize theatrics. The trick was to seem composed but affected, strong but wounded. Like Jesus in the garden of Gethsemane. They'd appreciate that parallel, even if they didn't consciously recognize it.

The room shifted, a rustling of expensive wool and silk. Mrs. Peterson - dear, predictable Mrs. Peterson, who'd never met a scandal she didn't want to dissect over coffee and scones - leaned forward with poorly concealed eagerness. Others glanced away, but Maddie noted who looked back first. Those would be her allies.

"The truth is," she continued, each word measured like drops of poison in a cup of tea, "I've been working on myself. Dr. Matthews has helped me understand so much about attachment and healing."

Now was the moment for the handkerchief. One delicate dab at the corner of each eye. "I just want what's best for Carrie and Nate."

The exchanged glances were what she'd hoped for. Sympathy. Understanding. These women had their own secrets, their own fears of being replaced, discarded. They'd see themselves in her story - the devoted mother, betrayed by a husband who'd forgotten his vows.

"Jackson's a good father." The lie tasted like copper in her mouth, but she'd learned long ago how to smile through unpleasant things. The same way she'd smiled when he missed Carrie's dance recitals, when he forgot Nate's birthday. When he started calling that little blonde thing "Princess." "But children need their mother. Especially at Carrie's age. She's so sensitive, so artistic. And Nate - he puts up a brave front, but I know he's struggling."

Mrs. Peterson's hand was warm and soft as it covered hers. A grandmother's hand, wrinkled but still wearing its wedding ring proudly. "We've all seen how devoted you are to those children, Maddie."

"Thank you." Maddie let her voice crack - just, like fine china developing its first hairline fracture. "The therapy has helped me see where I went wrong. I was too protective, too afraid of losing them. But I'm different now. I just want a chance to prove it."

The tide was turning. She could feel it in the room, in the softening expressions and sympathetic murmurs. Even Mrs. Harrison, who'd been so quick to judge (probably because her own husband had been eyeing his secretary), was watching with melting resistance.

This was what she needed. Witnesses. Character

references. Pillars of the community who would testify to her redemption. Women who would whisper in their husbands' ears about poor, brave Maddie Callahan, about how Jackson's young girlfriend was destroying a family.

Maddie touched the cross at her throat, a gesture she knew they'd notice. She could work with this. She could still win. And when she did, when she had her children back and Jackson's reputation in shreds, she would remember who had supported her. And who hadn't.

After all, wasn't that what good Christian women did? Keep score?

◆ ◆ ◆

Maddie's world tilted on its axis as the double doors of the prayer room swung open. The rehearsed words—words she'd practiced in front of her bathroom mirror at 3 AM, treating the right blend of righteous hurt and dignified grace—died in her throat. Jackson. Of course it was Jackson, striding in like he owned the room (like he owned everything), Attorney Cross clicking along beside him in those ridiculous Louboutins that Maddie herself had introduced her to years ago.

His presence filled the space like a gathering storm, and Maddie felt the sympathy she'd so cultivated in the room evaporate like morning dew. Twenty-five years of marriage, and still, his timing was impeccable. Always knowing when to strike, when to humiliate her.

"Ladies, I apologize for the interruption." That voice. That commanding tone she'd once found so attractive, back when she was young enough to mistake control for protection. "But I think you need to hear something."

Maddie's   fingers   tightened   around   her

handkerchief—French linen, monogrammed, a wedding gift from Jackson's mother. (The old bat had probably known even then that Maddie would need something to wipe away tears.) No. He wouldn't dare. Not here. Not in front of the Church Committee, not in front of the women who'd known her for decades, who'd watched her raise funds and organize galas and every detail of their shared social world.

The click of a phone speaker cut through the silence like a knife, and then—oh God—her own voice filled the room. Breathy. Desperate. Unrecognizable. "Come on, Nate. You know I can make it worth your while. One night with me, and we can make Jackson pay. .."

The recording continued, explicit and undeniable. Each word stripped away another layer of her constructed facade, like acid eating through silk. She watched Mrs. Peterson's hand withdraw from hers as if burned. (Mrs. Peterson, who'd just minutes ago been nodding along to Maddie's tearful account of Jackson's betrayal, who'd squeezed her hand and whispered, "We're here for you, dear.")

Phones appeared everywhere—Samsung galaxies and rose gold iPhones emerging from designer bags like weapons. Recording. Always recording. The whispers started, spreading through the room like poison through a water supply. Women who moments ago had been her steadfast allies now stepped back, creating a void around her as if her humiliation might be contagious.

"That's enough," Vivian Cross said, stopping the playback. Her voice carried that particular tone of practiced legal neutrality that made Maddie want to claw her eyes out. "I think everyone understands now."

The blood drained from Maddie's face as she watched her last chance at redemption crumble. These women would never believe her again. Their phones would ensure the entire city knew by nightfall. (Charlotte was probably already typing in their group chat. Barbara would be calling everyone who wasn't here. Sandra— weak, pathetic Sandra—would probably try to send her a sympathy text later.)

She her reflection in the prayer room's wall mirror—the one she'd personally selected and donated to the church five years ago, because the old one hadn't been "quite right" for the space. The woman staring back at her was exposed, desperate, destroyed. The mask she'd worn for decades had shattered.

And somewhere, deep in the recesses of her mind, a quiet voice whispered: This isn't over. This is just the beginning. Because Jackson had forgotten the most important thing about her—she'd learned how to wage war from watching him. And she'd always been a better student than he gave her credit for.

◆ ◆ ◆

Maddie's hand trembled against the smooth silk of her Chanel skirt, a microscopic betrayal that no one else would notice. (They noticed everything now, didn't they? Like vultures circling a fresh kill.) "That recording is out of context!" The crack in her voice made her wince internally. Amateur mistake. Twenty-five years of maintaining composure in Atlanta's highest circles, and now her voice chose to betray her. Jackson would love that, wouldn't he? He'd orchestrated this whole thing, after all. "Jackson manipulated it, just like he manipulates everything."

The prayer room at St. Catherine's had never felt

so suffocating. These walls had witnessed two decades of her choreographed performances of piety - the Christmas pageants she'd chaired, the baptisms she'd arranged, the prayer circles she'd dominated with just the right balance of humility and authority. Now those same walls seemed to be closing in, trapping her with these women who had once been her subjects. Her friends. (Had they ever been friends?)

Mrs. Peterson's manicured fingers found their way to her throat, clutching at her pearls like some Victorian lady about to faint. The gesture would have been comical if it weren't so damning. Just minutes ago, she'd squeezed Maddie's hand, cooing about how "that awful Jackson" was treating her. The speed of her reversal was almost impressive.

Barbara - dear, stupid Barbara who had never met a secret she couldn't spill - wouldn't even look at her. That hurt more than Maddie expected. Barbara had been there through everything, had watched Maddie orchestrate the social destruction of countless others. (Including Jean-Marc, Barbara's personal favorite show.) Now she sat there, suddenly developing a fascination with her Jimmy Choo pumps.

"Ladies, please." Maddie forced her fingers to stop their nervous dance along her skirt, smoothing the fabric with practiced precision. Control. She needed control. These women responded to strength, to authority. They were sheep. They just needed a shepherd. "You know me. Twenty-five years of friendship—"

"We thought we knew you." Charlotte's words sliced through the air with surgical precision. Of course it would be Charlotte who delivered the killing blow. Charlotte, who had always been just a step behind

Maddie in everything - social standing, fashion, influence. She must be savoring this moment.

The soft blue glow of phone screens dotted the dimly lit room like malevolent fireflies. Every moment of her undoing was being documented, possibly already making its way through group chats and social media. By tomorrow, everyone in Atlanta's social circle would have seen it. (God, the children. Carrie and Nate would see this. Her angels would watch their mother fall.)

"It's not what you think." Her eyes darted around the room, searching desperately for any crack in their united front. Even Sandra - pathetic, divorced Sandra who'd weathered her own scandal last year when her husband ran off with his yoga instructor - turned away. The irony wasn't lost on Maddie. She'd been the one who'd helped rehabilitate Sandra's image, after all. (After making sure everyone knew whose fault the divorce was.)

"I was desperate," she tried again, hating the pleading note that had crept into her voice. "Jackson took my children—"

"After you tried to destroy an innocent woman." Barbara looked up; her face twisted with disgust. The expression aged her, highlighting every line her expensive Botox couldn't quite erase. "After you faked abuse allegations. After you manipulated all of us."

The truth of those words hit harder than any physical blow. Maddie felt her constructed world crumbling around her, twenty-five years of social engineering collapsing like a house of cards. No worded apology could erase what they'd heard. No amount of designer clothing could armor her against this kind of exposure. The society she'd ruled with an iron fist wrapped in velvet had just witnessed her execution.

She felt it happening - the mask of Maddie Callahan, crafted over decades of careful social climbing, cracking like fine china dropped on marble floors. Her legs trembled beneath her as whispers filled the room, each one a nail in the coffin of her social standing. (But they hadn't won. Not yet. They didn't know what she was capable of. Not. Not yet.)

Maddie sat at her vanity, staring at her reflection but seeing nothing. Her fingers traced the edge of the antique silver brush—the one Jackson had given her on their fifth anniversary in Paris. (Back when anniversaries meant something, back when he still believed in forever.) The recording played over and over in her mind, each word another crack in her maintained world. Barbara's voice, dripping with false sympathy: "Maddie, darling, we just think you need... help."

Help. As if she were some charity cases, some broken thing to be fixed. Twenty-five years of lunch dates, spa weekends, and shared secrets, and this was how they repaid her loyalty.

Rosa's quiet footsteps entered the room, familiar as a heartbeat. For a moment, Maddie was transported back to all those nights during Jackson's deployments when Rosa had been her only company, the only one who saw her cry.

"Mrs. Callahan, I brought your evening tea."

"They all turned against me, Rosa." Maddie's voice came out hollow, like someone had scraped her insides clean. She studied her reflection—still beautiful, still, damn them all. But something in her eyes had changed. When had that happened? "Twenty-five years of friendship, gone in minutes."

Rosa set down the delicate china cup, her weathered hands steady. The scent of chamomile filled the air, and Maddie almost smiled. Rosa always knew what she needed, even when she didn't ask. "The General, he wasn't always like this. Remember how he used to look at you?"

Maddie's fingers tightened around the brush handle. The silver was cool against her palm, grounding her. "Before Dubai. Before her." Before Lily, with her young skin and her guileless smile. (Maddie had been guileless once, hadn't she? Or had she always known it would end like this?)

"Men forget sometimes." Rosa adjusted the tea tray, her movements deliberate, each clink of china a punctuation mark in the quiet room. "They need to be reminded of what they had. What they could lose."

"Jackson doesn't want to be reminded. He won't even take my calls." Three times today, straight to voicemail. Each time, she'd composed herself, left a message dripping with casual concern. As if she weren't falling apart. As if she weren't planning his destruction with every breath.

"Then show him." Rosa's voice softened, and she met Maddie's eyes in the mirror. "Not with anger or threats. Show him the woman he married—the one who waited through all those deployments."

Something stirred in Maddie's chest—a dangerous hope. Or maybe it was something darker, something with teeth. "You think he could remember?"

"I've seen how he looks at old photos when he thinks no one notices." Rosa smoothed Maddie's hair with gentle hands, the way she used to when Maddie was younger, when the world made sense. "Be that woman again. The one in those pictures."

Maddie's reflection sharpened into focus. She could do that—play the wife again. Show everyone how she could handle defeat. Let Jackson see what he'd thrown away. Let him remember the woman who'd built his life while he was off playing hero in foreign lands. Let him wonder what else she'd learned to do while he was gone.

"You're right." Maddie picked up her phone, deleted her angry draft to Charlotte. No need for threats, not when she could destroy them all with kindness. She would be again. Flawless. The way she'd been trained to be since childhood. Only this time, her perfection would be a weapon.

She met her own gaze in the mirror and practiced her smile. Sweet, forgiving, just a touch vulnerable. "I'll show them all how wrong they are about me."

Behind her, Rosa's expression flickered with something that might have been concern. But Maddie didn't notice. She was already planning, already becoming that other woman—the one who'd waited patiently for decades, who'd smiled through every slight, who'd learned that revenge was a dish best served with lipstick and impeccable manners.

Let them think they'd won. Let them believe they'd tamed her. They'd forgotten who she was—what she was capable of. But they'd remember soon enough.

Chapter 28

Maddie's fingers tapped against her phone screen for the hundredth time that evening, confirming what she already knew. Six weeks of meticulous observation had taught her Jackson's Thursday routine like a familiar dance—the way he lingered at the office until 7:45 PM, long after his devoted employees had scattered to their mundane lives. How predictable he'd become. How... ordinary.

The leather seats of her Mercedes still held their

new-car smell, a purchase she'd made specifically for moments like this. (Because even in stalking, one must maintain standards.) She'd positioned herself in the shadows of Callahan Defense Solutions' parking lot, where the security cameras had that one blind spot she'd discovered during her marriage. Amazing what details you pick up when you're the CEO's wife. Former wife.

Her heart quickened its pace as his Tesla emerged from the underground garage, all sleek lines and quiet power. Just like Jackson himself. The ache in her chest—the one that never quite went away these days—pulsed with renewed intensity. Twenty-five years of marriage, and now he couldn't even look at her. Wouldn't even let her near their children.

Maddie stepped out of her car with the precise grace she'd ed over decades of charity galas and military functions. Her Louboutins struck the asphalt in a steady rhythm that matched her heartbeat: controlled, measured, deliberate. (She'd chosen these shoes specifically—they were from happier times, when he'd surprised her in Paris for their fifteenth anniversary. Surely, he'd remember?)

"Jackson." She let his name float across the empty lot, just loud enough to carry. Just soft enough to remind him of intimate moments, of whispered conversations in the dark.

She watched him freeze, key card hovering near the gate scanner like a suspended moment in time. The sight of him—the rigid set of his shoulders, the way his suit jacket pulled across his back—made her throat tight with longing. "You shouldn't be here," he said, and oh, how clinical he sounded. How detached.

"Please, just five minutes." All her rehearsed words

scattered like autumn leaves in a storm. She'd practiced this speech for days in front of her bathroom mirror, timing it. But now, faced with the reality of him, all she could manage was, "The children—"

"Stop." His voice had that commanding tone he'd ed during his military years. The one that used to make her proud. Now it just made her feel small. "We're not doing this."

"I've changed." The words tumbled out, raw and unfiltered, so unlike her usual calculated responses. "I'm in therapy, real therapy this time. Dr. Matthews can verify—" She was babbling now, and she hated herself for it. Where was the woman who could command a room with a single raised eyebrow?

"Like she verified before?" His laugh—God, his laugh. It wasn't the warm chuckle that used to accompany morning coffee or bedtime stories. This was something else, something that sliced through her maintained composure. "Before we found out you'd manipulated those sessions too?"

"That's not fair." Her manicured nails dug into her palms. Control slipping, slipping, slipping away. "You took everything from me. My children, my friends, my life—" (My reason for being, my future, my past, everything I built myself around.)

"You did that yourself, Maddie." When he turned to face her, his expression was like winter frost on a window—beautiful but cold, creating an impenetrable barrier between them. "Every lie, every scheme, every manipulation - that was all you."

Her hands betrayed her, beginning to tremble despite her best efforts. She could feel her applied mascara threatening to smudge. "Twenty-five years,

Jackson. Doesn't that mean anything?" (Twenty-five years of waiting, of raising his children, of building his home, of being what he needed until he decided he needed something else.)

"It meant everything until I saw who you are." The gate buzzed open, the sound like a death knell to her hopes. "Don't come here again."

"Please." Her voice cracked, and she hated herself for it. Maddie Callahan didn't beg. Except now she did. "I'll do anything. Just let me see them."

But Jackson was already retreating into his Tesla, those tinted windows rising like a final curtain, sealing her out of the life she'd spent decades crafting. She watched him drive away, her reflection ghostly in the dark windows of the building. She looked small, broken, and desperate.

This wouldn't do at all.

Maddie felt her legs trembling beneath her Valentino dress as she watched his Tesla pull away. Her Louboutins - the ones he'd bought her in Paris last spring, back when everything was - scraped against the asphalt as she stumbled forward. The sound was like nails on a chalkboard, just like the pain scraping through her chest.

"Jackson, please!" Her voice bounced off empty cars in the parking lot, making her sound desperate. (God, how she hated sounding desperate.) "Don't leave me like this!"

The Tesla's brake lights flashed - a moment of hesitation? She'd always been able to read his smallest gestures, decode the military man's precise movements. Twenty-five years of marriage had taught her that. But now? Now she couldn't read anything anymore.

"Remember Paris?" The words tumbled out before she could stop them, mascara-laden tears blurring her vision. Their first anniversary, the rooftop of that boutique hotel, his promise smothered against her neck. "Our first anniversary? You promised we'd grow old together. You said I was the only one who understood you!"

The car slowed at the security checkpoint, and Maddie pressed her manicured hands against the passenger window. (She'd had them done yesterday - "Maddie's back!" Charlotte had declared at the salon, not knowing everything was falling apart.) The pristine French tips left smears across the glass, like everything else she touched - imperfect, ruined.

"I waited for you during every deployment. Twenty-five years, Jackson!" Her voice cracked, and she hated herself for it. "I raised our children while you were gone. I built your home. I was everything you wanted!" Everything. The hostess, the devoted wife, the mother who never complained during those endless deployments. She'd even learned Arabic, for God's sake, just to impress his military friends' wives.

His silhouette remained statue-still behind the wheel, the same rigid posture she'd once found so attractive. Now it felt like a wall, a fortress she couldn't breach. When had her husband become a stranger?

"I'll change." The words tasted like ash in her mouth. "I'll be better. I'll do therapy - real therapy this time. I'll stay away from Lillian." That little witch with her skin and innocent eyes. "Just please, please don't keep our children from me." Nate and Carrie - her babies. The thought of them made her chest constrict.

The window stayed up. Jackson didn't even turn his head. (He always used to look at her. Always. Even across crowded rooms, his eyes would find her.)

"Look at me!" She pounded against the glass, her diamond wedding ring - the one he'd upgraded on their twentieth anniversary - clicking against the surface. "I'm your wife! You can't just throw away everything we built. I'll do anything - whatever you want. Just tell me what to do!"

The Tesla pulled forward, forcing her to step back. As it disappeared through the gate, Maddie's legs betrayed her. She crumpled to the ground, her silk dress - Chanel, from the spring collection - collecting dirt and oil from the asphalt. She'd have to burn it now. Like everything else in her life, it was ruined.

"I love you," she said to the space where his car had been. "I still love you." The words hung in the air, mocking her. Because love wasn't enough anymore, was it? Not when that little homewrecker had slithered into their lives with her youth and her simpering smile.

She watched him exit the Tesla, his movements precise and controlled - just like in Dubai, just like every moment since. He stood tall, straightening his jacket with that military precision she'd once found so appealing. Now it just looked like armor against her.

"Jackson." Her voice in her throat. "Please, just listen-"

"Mrs. Callahan." The formal address was a calculated strike, and he knew it. He'd always known where to hit to make it hurt the most. "I've asked you not to come here."

"Don't call me that. I'm Maddie. Your Maddie." She reached for his arm, but he stepped back as if she were diseased. Twenty-five years of marriage, reduced to this - him treating her like a stranger with a contagious disease.

"There is no 'my' anything anymore." Those ice-blue eyes - the ones Carrie had inherited - swept over her without a flicker of recognition. "Whatever was between us died when you chose to destroy an innocent woman's life."

"Innocent?" The word burned like acid. "She took everything from me. Our family, our life-"

"No." Jackson's voice sliced through her protests with military precision. "You did that yourself. With every lie, every manipulation, every scheme." He checked his watch - the Rolex she'd given him last Christmas. "I have a meeting."

"Twenty-five years," Maddie said, the words like broken glass in her mouth. "Twenty-five years of waiting, supporting, loving you-"

"And now it's over." He walked past her toward the building entrance, his cologne - the one she'd chosen - trailing behind him. "Goodbye, Mrs. Callahan."

Something inside Maddie's chest shattered. The pain was physical, raw, like crystal stemware breaking against marble floors. She watched him walk away - this stranger wearing her husband's face, this man who'd discarded her like last season's fashion.

The tears dried on her cheeks. Her hands, which had been shaking, grew still. The ache in her chest crystallized into something harder, colder. Something that felt dangerously like purpose.

She'd given him everything - her youth, her devotion, her entire life. She'd shaped herself into his wife, waited through endless deployments, built his spotless reputation in Atlanta society. She'd been his masterpiece, his crown jewel.

And he dared treat her like a stranger?

The last trace of love in her heart froze solid, like champagne left too long in the freezer. Jackson wasn't her husband anymore. He wasn't the father of her children. He was the man who'd betrayed her, humiliated her, stolen her children.

And he would pay for that. Oh, yes. He would pay for that.

(Because if there was one thing Maddie Callahan knew how to do, it was making people pay.)

❖ ❖ ❖

Maddie's Louboutins clicked against the marble foyer, each step echoing through the emptiness of what was supposed to be their forever home. Her three-thousand-dollar Hermès scarf hung limp around her neck, mascara stains marking the silk like battle scars from a war she hadn't known she was fighting.

She her reflection in the antique Venetian mirror—the one they'd found on their twentieth anniversary trip to Italy—and recognized the woman staring back. Where was the polished society wife? The woman who'd orchestrated dinner parties for senators and ambassadors? Now she saw something raw, something dangerous in her own eyes. Something that made her smile, just a little.

The grandfather clock in Jackson's study chimed nine, each resonant toll marking another hour in this new, horrible reality. She traced her fingers across his leather chair, remembering how he'd sit there each evening, Macallan 25 in hand, sharing stories about his day. Back when home meant something to him.

"Mrs. Callahan?" Rosa's voice came from the doorway, gentle as always. Careful. (Rosa had been watching her all day, hadn't she? Like she was some kind of bomb about to detonate.) "I made chamomile tea."

Maddie's hand tightened on the chair's leather, her manicured nails leaving little half-moons in the expensive material. "He wouldn't even look at me, Rosa. Twenty-five years of marriage, and he couldn't even look at me." The memory of their courthouse encounter burned fresh—Jackson's cold shoulders, his clipped tone, the way he'd angled his body away from her like she was contagious.

"Perhaps with time—"

"He called me 'Mrs. Callahan.'" The words tasted like ash in her mouth, bitter and choking. "Like I'm some stranger. Some woman he knows." Not Maddie. Not honey. Not even Madeline. Just Mrs. Callahan.

Rosa set the teacup down with that irritating carefulness she'd been using, as if any sudden movement might set Maddie off. "You need rest. Tomorrow will be—"

"Do you remember our anniversary party?" Maddie picked up a silver-framed photo from Jackson's desk, her thumb brushing over the glass. They looked so happy. So, in love. "The way he looked at me during our first dance? The speech he gave about finding his soulmate?" She'd worn Valentino that night, a dress that cost more than most people's monthly salary. He'd kissed her in front of everyone, and she'd felt invincible.

"Señora—"

"I just need to remind him." Maddie's fingers traced Jackson's face in the photograph, remembering how his skin felt under her touch. "Remind him of what

we had. Of who we were before Dubai. Before her."
Before Lily. Before that young, fresh-faced reminder of
everything Maddie used to be. The thought of them
together made something twist inside her, something
dark and hungry.

Rosa shifted uncomfortably by the door,
wondering if she should call someone. (They all thought
she was losing it, didn't they? Charlotte, Barbara,
Sandra—all of them whispering behind their manicured
hands.) "Maybe if you give him space—"

"No." Maddie's voice hardened to steel, to
diamond. "He's forgotten everything I sacrificed.
Everything I did to build his life." She placed the photo
face-down on the desk with deliberate slowness. "I'll help
him remember."

Her hand brushed against Jackson's crystal
decanter—Baccarat, another gift from her, because she'd
always known what would impress his superior officers.
The scotch the lamplight, amber liquid gleaming like a
warning. Or maybe an invitation. "Every deployment,
every lonely night, every social connection I cultivated
for his career." She poured herself two fingers of the
expensive liquor, remembering how he used to praise
her networking skills. How proud he'd been of her
charm, her grace. "He needs to remember who made
him General Jackson Callahan."

"Mrs. Callahan, perhaps—"

"Leave the tea, Rosa." Maddie's voice was eerily
calm, like the surface of a lake hiding undertows. "I have
some thinking to do." And oh, did she have thoughts. So
many beautiful, terrible thoughts about how to remind
Jackson of everything he owed her. Everything he was
about to lose.

Chapter 29

Sunlight crept across Jackson's mahogany desk as Maddie sat in his leather chair, her fingernails tracing the worn armrests where his hands had rested countless times. The leather was butter-soft, molded to his shape, not hers. (But then again, wasn't that just? She'd always molded herself to fit his needs.) The wedding photo before her showed a younger version of herself, radiant in white lace, gazing up at Jackson with complete adoration. God, she'd been so naive.

Her hands were steady now as she lifted the

teacup to her lips - Earl Grey, two sugars, just like every morning for twenty-five years. The previous night's mascara had been removed, her face freshly made up despite the early hour. She'd already changed out of yesterday's crumpled Chanel into a crisp St. John knit dress. Because Maddie Callahan did not wallow. She did not let herself go. She did not give anyone the satisfaction of seeing her break.

"I was so young," she said to the smiling bride in the photograph. That Maddie had believed in forever, in promises, in the sanctity of twenty-five years of marriage. That Maddie hadn't known that love expired, that loyalty had a shelf life, that men like Jackson viewed wives like vintage cars - eventually ready to be traded in for a newer model.

The house felt different this morning, like a stage set waiting for its actors. The crushing weight of denial had lifted, replaced by something colder, clearer. Jackson wasn't coming home. He wouldn't suddenly remember their life together, wouldn't wake up missing her, wouldn't realize his mistake. Lily (pretty, twenty-seven-year-old Lily, Princess) had made sure of that.

She set down the teacup with precise control. The delicate clink of bone china against saucer echoed in the quiet study - his study, technically, though she'd chosen every piece of furniture, every book on the shelves, every award's placement. Her eyes drifted to another photo - Jackson's promotion ceremony. She stood beside him, coiffed, the proud military wife while he accepted his general's stars. She remembered that day with crystal clarity: the weight of her Hermès scarf in the summer heat, the way Barbara and Charlotte had envied her position, the whispers about how far the Callahans would go.

"You forgot who got you there," she told his smiling image. Every dinner party she'd hosted, every connection she'd cultivated, every sacrifice she'd made to build his image - he'd dismissed it all for a younger woman who'd never known the struggle. Who'd never waited through deployments, never navigated military politics, never learned to smile through the loneliness.

The tears didn't come anymore. They'd dried up sometime during the night, leaving behind a crystalline clarity that felt almost like peace. If Jackson thought he could discard her, erase their history, he would learn otherwise. She hadn't spent twenty-five years as the Mrs. Callahan without learning how to wage war. And unlike Jackson's battlefield experiences, this would be a different kind of combat - the kind fought in country club lounges and charity galas, with smiles instead of bullets and rumors instead of bombs.

Her fingers closed around the wedding photo, feeling the weight of it, the solidity of the silver frame that Rosa polished every Tuesday. She didn't need to cry anymore. She needed to think. And Maddie Callahan had always been, good at thinking. At planning. At waiting for the moment to strike.

The sun climbed higher in the sky, casting long shadows across the desk. Somewhere in the house, she could hear Rosa beginning her morning routine, the quiet shuffle of her sensible shoes against the hardwood floors. Soon, Nate and Carrie would wake up, expecting their mother to be put together, normal, fine.

And she would be. Because that's what Maddie Callahan did best - she performed perfection. Only this time, the performance would have a different ending.

◆ ◆ ◆

Maddie's phone screen cast an ethereal glow across her features in the dim study, each message draft illuminating a different shade of revenge she'd contemplated during her sleepless night. Her manicured thumb—fresh gel manicure in Ballet Slippers pink, because even in crisis, appearances matter—hovered over a vicious text to Charlotte. The words burned bright: "Twenty years of friendship, and this is how you repay loyalty?" Delete. Another message to Barbara about keeping secrets (as if Barbara had ever kept a secret in her botoxed life) disappeared with a decisive tap. One by one, the angry words vanished until her draft folder stood as empty as her wine cabinet.

She placed the phone face-down on Jackson's mahogany desk—still Jackson's desk, even though he hadn't sat here in weeks. The morning sun streaming through the French windows her wedding ring, still positioned on her left hand, where it had rested for twenty-seven years, four months, and sixteen days. She twisted it once, considering its weight, its meaning, then left it there. Not yet. Timing was everything, and this particular prop still had its role to play.

The familiar rhythm of Rosa's footsteps approached—left foot heavier than the right, the sound of morning coffee service that had accompanied every morning for the past two decades. Some things, at least, remained constant.

"Thank you, Rosa." Maddie infused her voice with the practiced warmth she'd ed at countless Junior League meetings and charity galas. The same tone that had made her the queen of their social circle, before everything imploded. "I won't be needing the scotch anymore. You can remove it from the study."

Rosa paused, coffee pot suspended mid-pour, her weathered hands betraying a slight tremor. "Señora?"

"I'm moving forward." Maddie smoothed her cream silk skirt, already pressed for the day ahead. No more wallowing in designer sweats and day drinking. That wasn't who Madeline Callahan was. "It's time for a fresh start."

Opening her laptop, she pulled up her contact list. Sandra would be the easiest target—poor, desperate Sandra, always one step behind in fashion and social graces, grateful for any crumb of attention. A worded email about personal growth and therapy would plant the first seed. Sandra had always been a sucker for self-help terminology.

Charlotte would require more finesse. After all, Charlotte had been there from the beginning, had watched Maddie build her life brick by brick. The message needed to strike just the right balance—taking responsibility without accepting blame, understanding their distance without acknowledging their betrayal. Maddie included just enough vulnerability to seem authentic. Not too much—she wasn't Barbara, crying into her martini at every perceived slight.

Her finger traced the rim of her bone china coffee cup as she crafted each message, the words flowing as naturally as the lies she'd told at every social function for the past three months. "Jackson's traveling." "We're just going through a rough patch." "Lily? Oh, she's just a family friend." Humility was just another costume to wear, another performance to, like the charity auction speeches she used to give, or the loving wife she'd played for so long.

Barbara's number flashed on her screen—rejected. Of course. Barbara had always been a coward, hiding behind her money and her social status as if Maddie hadn't been the one to elevate her in the first place. Maddie left a voicemail, her voice catching at just the right moment when she mentioned missing their weekly bridge games. (Bridge games where Barbara had always needed coaching, always one step behind, until Maddie had molded her into something almost presentable.)

"Time heals all wounds," she murmured, more for Rosa's benefit than her own. A little performance for the help, because everyone was an audience, everyone was watching, waiting for Madeline Callahan to crack. The housekeeper nodded, but Maddie the flicker of doubt in those knowing eyes as she gathered the breakfast dishes. Rosa had seen too much, known too much. But that was a problem for another day. Right now, Maddie had a reputation to rebuild, a social circle to manipulate, and a husband to destroy.

Maddie sank into the supple leather of Jackson's chair, inhaling the lingering traces of his cologne. The scent that once made her heart flutter now made her stomach turn. She opened her laptop, pressing play on the Cold Case episode she'd been dissecting all week. The Connecticut banker's wife on the screen held herself with such poise, such careful control—right up until the moment they caught her. Amateur mistakes.

The gentle blue light of the laptop cast shadows across her face as she created a new document, her manicured nails clicking against the keys with surgical precision. The wife's first error had been growing the aconite herself. (Honestly, who maintains their own poison garden in this day and age?) No, that kind of oversight was beneath Maddie. She opened an incognito browser window, diving deep into the darker corners of the internet. European herbalists with their centuries-old knowledge, traditional Asian medicine shops with their worded listings, specialized gardening forums where people spoke in codes and whispers.

Time stretched like honey as she worked, each potential supplier noted and cross-referenced. The banker's wife had been sloppy with her timing too—a pattern as obvious as her husband's infidelity. Maddie's lips curled into a small, knowing smile. The key was patience, wasn't it? Small doses, spread out just so. Like training someone to love you. You had to build it slowly, until they couldn't live without you. Or in this case, couldn't live at all.

The soft shuffle of Rosa's footsteps pulled her from her research. The housekeeper entered with fresh tea, the delicate china cup clicking against its saucer like a metronome counting down the seconds.

"My mother always used herbs for everything," Rosa mentioned, arranging the tea service with the precision of two decades' practice. Her weathered hands moved with the confidence of inherited knowledge. "Natural remedies are better than chemicals."

Something sparked in Maddie's mind. She turned, studying Rosa's familiar face with new interest. "What kinds of herbs, Rosa?"

"Oh, many kinds. For sleep, for stomach, for nerves." Rosa's hands smoothed her apron, a nervous habit Maddie had observed countless times. "My grandmother had a whole garden of medicinal plants."

"How fascinating." Maddie lifted the teacup to her lips, letting the steam rise between them like a veil. Her voice remained light, conversational—the same tone she used at charity luncheons when fishing for gossip. "Did she ever work with more exotic varieties?"

"Sí, some rare ones." Rosa's eyes took on a distant look, remembering. "She knew which ones were dangerous too—had to keep them away from children."

Maddie nodded, adding notes to her document with seemingly casual interest. Each word felt like a gift, a secret key falling into her lap. "Would you mind telling me more about these herbs sometime? I've been reading about natural medicine." Reading, researching, planning. Always planning.

"Of course, Señora. My grandmother taught me everything about plants."

After Rosa's footsteps faded down the hallway, Maddie opened a new spreadsheet. Her fingers hovered over the keys for a moment, like a pianist preparing for a complicated piece. Column one: establishing an alibi (she'd need witnesses, chosen friends who would remember seeing her at the right moments). Column two: Lillian's schedule in Virginia (that vapid little princess was so predictable in her routines). Column three: timing (this would require the most finesse, the most careful orchestration).

She saved the document under "Wellness Research" and tucked it away in her therapy folder, nested between mindfulness exercises and breathing techniques. How fitting—this was about wellness, after all. Her wellness. Her future. Her revenge.

The tea had grown cold, but Maddie didn't mind. She was too busy imagining the look on Jackson's face when he realized what he'd lost. When he understood that leaving her hadn't been his choice to make. Some things, after all, were forever. She'd promised him that on their wedding day, and she intended to keep that promise—one way or another.

◆ ◆ ◆

Maddie smoothed her navy St. John dress, enjoying the subtle luxury against her skin. The fabric alone cost more than most people's entire Sunday outfits, but that wasn't the point today. Today was about appearing humble, controlled, healing. (Amazing how a $3,000 dress could look so demure when you needed it to.) The simple pearl necklace at her throat had been Jackson's first major gift to her—back when he was still a Captain, before the promotions and the money and the younger woman who now wore his more recent presents.

She'd arrived twenty minutes early to St. Michael's, choosing a middle pew with careful consideration. Not her usual spot up front, where she'd reigned as the General's wife for so many years. No, today was about showing everyone how she was handling her fall from grace. She ran her fingers over her wedding ring, still firmly in place. Let them all see it. Let them wonder.

The familiar murmur of arriving parishioners filled the church, but Maddie kept her prayer book open, head bowed in practiced serenity. She could feel the weight of their stares, could hear their thoughts. Poor Maddie, handling it all so well. Such dignity. Such grace. If only they knew.

When Jackson entered with the children, her heart contracted painfully, but she kept her eyes fixed forward. Carrie's little mary-janes clicked against the floor—new ones, most likely picked out by that princess he was parading around now. Nate's shuffling footsteps followed, and Maddie fought the urge to turn, to gather them both into her arms. Instead, she focused on Reverend Thomson's words about forgiveness, letting them wash over her like a baptism. How fitting, this sermon about letting go, about finding peace. She felt Jackson's gaze land on her, taking in her controlled composure, her dry eyes, her straight spine. No tears today, darling. No desperate glances. No scene after service.

During coffee hour, she positioned herself within Jackson's earshot while chatting with Mrs. Peterson. "The women's shelter has been so rewarding," she said, stirring her coffee three times counterclockwise. Always three. Always counterclockwise. "My therapist says helping others is part of the healing process."

"Sometimes we have to accept when things change," she continued, her voice carrying just enough. She watched Jackson's reflection in the coffee urn, saw him pause mid-conversation. "I'm learning to find peace with new beginnings."

Barbara stood across the room, vibrating with the need to gossip about this new, serene Maddie. Let her. Barbara had always been useful that way, spreading whatever version of events Maddie needed circulated. When the fall fundraising committee sign-up came around, Maddie made her excuse with timing: "I might not be in Atlanta by then. I've been thinking about spending time with my sister in Charleston." The whispers would start immediately. Maddie Callahan, leaving Atlanta? Impossible. Unless...

When Carrie waved from across the fellowship

hall, something inside Maddie cracked. Her baby girl, in a dress she hadn't picked out, with her hair styled by someone else's hands. But Maddie only offered a gentle smile and nod, the picture of a mother respecting boundaries. She saw Jackson's shoulders relax. Oh, how predictable he was, even after all these years. Always looking for the tactical advantage, always assessing threats. And right now, he was deciding she wasn't one.

She gathered her Hermès bag (last season's, chosen for its understated elegance) and stopped to thank Reverend Thomson. "Your sermon spoke to me today," she said, knowing at least three people were within earshot. "Sometimes letting go is the greatest act of love we can offer."

The whispers followed her out:

"She seems different..."

"Accepting it..."

"Much more composed..."

Safely inside her Mercedes, Maddie allowed herself a small smile. Twenty years of marriage to a military strategist had taught her one vital lesson: sometimes you had to let the enemy think they'd won before you launched your real attack. She started the car, humming softly. The first pieces were falling into place, and Jackson had no idea what was coming. But then again, he'd always underestimated her. That was going to be his biggest mistake.

Chapter 30

Maddie arrived at St. Michael's thirty minutes before service, maneuvering her Mercedes into a spot far from the entrance. timing, as always. The distance would force people to notice her walk - a long, contemplative journey across the parking lot. She smoothed her hands over the simple navy dress she'd chosen with such deliberation. No Chanel today, no statement pieces. Just elegant suffering.

Her reflection in the rearview mirror required

one final check. The concealer beneath her eyes was artfully applied - just enough to hint at sleepless nights without appearing unkempt. Her wedding ring the morning light as she adjusted her hair. The rest of her jewelry collection remained at home in their velvet-lined boxes. (Amazing how the absence of diamonds could speak louder than their presence.)

The familiar scent of wood polish and aging hymnals wrapped around her as she entered the sanctuary. How many Sundays had she spent here, commanding attention from the front pew? But not today. Today called for something different. She selected a seat midway back, where the stained-glass windows would paint her in gentle colors. Let them see her bathed in holy light.

As the congregation trickled in, Maddie kept her gaze fixed on the cross above the altar, though her awareness extended to every whisper, every footstep, every subtle reaction to her presence. When Jackson entered with the children, her heart clenched, but she didn't turn. She didn't need to. She could picture them - Jackson in his navy suit (always navy, so predictable), Nate's untucked shirt that Jackson wouldn't notice, Carrie's hair without a doubt still uncombed because Lily wouldn't know how to manage those curls properly.

Reverend Thomson's sermon drifted through the air, something appropriately trite about redemption and second chances. How convenient. Maddie nodded at strategic moments, allowing herself one timed dab at her eyes with a tissue. Not too obvious - just enough to make them wonder if she was crying or if the light was playing tricks.

The familiar players took their positions around

her like pieces on a chessboard. Mrs. Peterson's cloying perfume announced her arrival two pews ahead - still wearing that awful Chanel No. 5 like it was 1985. Barbara's theatrical little cough echoed from behind (she'd been "getting over a cold" for three weeks now). Charlotte's voice carried as she greeted the Wilsons, that fake warmth she'd ed over years of social climbing.

Maddie maintained her crafted pose of quiet dignity. Her hands remained folded in her lap, neither too tight (suggesting tension) nor too loose (suggesting indifference). She sang just loudly enough to be heard participating, but softly enough to seem humble. When the collection plate came around, she placed her envelope in with precise timing - no flourish, but positioned so the ushers could glimpse the amount. Let them see her generosity hadn't wavered, even in "difficult times."

Through lowered lashes, she monitored the shifting energy behind her. Barbara and Charlotte had claimed their usual spot in the back pew - their gossip headquarters. She didn't need to turn around to picture them, heads bent together like schoolgirls sharing secrets.

The whispers floated forward like aimed arrows. "...showing her face here..." Barbara's voice carried just enough - always Barbara, so indiscreet.

Charlotte's response followed right on cue: "Well, she certainly needs the Lord." (As if Charlotte had any right to judge, after that incident with her gardener last summer.)

The whispers multiplied like ripples in a pond. Mrs. Peterson's shoulders tensed as she leaned toward Susan Bennett. "Poor thing," she said, her tone dripping with that unique blend of pity and judgment that only church ladies could.

Elizabeth Morgan's overpriced perfume announced her arrival to the gossip circle. "After what happened at St. Catherine's..." (Ah yes, Elizabeth - still trying to be relevant after her own divorce scandal three years ago.)

"It's all for show," Barbara declared, voice pitched to carry. "She's trying to manipulate everyone again." (Dear Barbara, so predictable in her accusations, yet so blind to her own manipulations.)

Maddie allowed herself one delicate brush at an imaginary tear, timing it with a shaft of colored light from the windows. The whispers intensified as she'd anticipated.

"She's lost everything," someone observed. "Even her children won't..."

"And whose fault is that?" Charlotte's response snapped through the air like a whip.

The organ drowned out the rest, but Maddie's lips curved in the smallest of smiles. Let them whisper. Let them judge. She was in their heads now, taking up space in their thoughts, their conversations, their prayers. Whether they pitied or condemned her didn't matter - they were thinking about her, talking about her, watching her every move.

And that was where she needed them to be.

◆ ◆ ◆

Maddie lingered near the coffee station, adding a precise splash of cream to her cup. Three drops, no more. Control was everything these days, wasn't it? She kept her movements small, contained, so different from how she used to command these gatherings like a general surveying her troops. The social hall buzzed with the familiar symphony of judgment dressed as concern, but she made no attempt to join the clusters of women who gathered around danish platters and coffee urns like vultures circling wounded prey.

Mrs. Peterson approached first, her heels clicking against the floor like a metronome counting down to an inevitable confrontation. "Maddie, dear. How have you been?"

Maddie offered the gentle smile she'd spent hours finalizing in her vanity mirror (three hours and twenty-seven minutes, to be exact, but who was counting?). "I've had a lot to reflect on." She let her gaze drop to her coffee cup, her voice soft but steady. Like a stream that looks peaceful on the surface but runs deep and cold beneath.

"We've all been... concerned," Mrs. Peterson said, studying Maddie's face with the intensity of someone searching for hairline cracks in fine china. Looking for weakness. They were always looking for weakness.

"That's kind." Maddie kept her tone measured, careful not to let even a drop of bitterness seep through. Though God knew she had enough stored up to poison them all. "The quiet has been good for me. Given me time to think about what matters." Like revenge, served at the right temperature.

Susan Bennett drifted over like a moth to flame; drawn by the conspicuous lack of drama she'd clearly expected. "Are you still seeing Dr. Matthews?"

"Yes." Maddie took a small sip of coffee, letting the warmth ground her. Dr. Matthews, that pompous fool who thought he could see inside her head. If he only knew what lived there. "He's helped me understand so many things about myself."

She noticed Charlotte and Barbara watching from across the room, their heads bent together in whispered conversation like schoolgirls passing notes. Once, she would have been at the center of their little gossip circle. Now they thought they could exclude her? Oh, darlings. If they only knew what was coming.

Elizabeth Morgan joined their small circle, her curiosity as obvious as her recent Botox. "And the children? Have you...?"

"They need time," Maddie said, letting a practiced look of peaceful acceptance cross her face. Inside, she thought of Nate's suspicious glances, of Carrie's confusion. Of Jackson, who thought he could take them from her. Time. Yes, they all needed time. And she would use every second of it. "We all do."

The women exchanged glances, clearly thrown by this new, subdued version of Maddie Callahan. She saw the uncertainty in their eyes, the slight softening of their judgment. They'd expected tears or rage or manipulation. Her quiet dignity left them unsure, off-balance. Let them think she was broken. Let them believe she'd accepted defeat with grace.

They had no idea that this was just the beginning. That every measured sip of coffee, every gentle smile, every peaceful nod was another piece falling into place. Maddie took another sip of her coffee, hiding her satisfaction behind the rim of her cup. Three drops of cream. No more, no less. Control was everything these days.

And she had never been more in control.

◆ ◆ ◆

Maddie sat at her vanity, removing her modest pearl earrings with careful precision. Each pearl represented a calculated choice - not the sapphire drops that would seem too flashy, nor the diamond studs that might suggest she still had money to spare. No, these were: humble, classic, the jewelry of a woman learning to accept a simpler life. The morning's performance had left her shoulders tight, her jaw aching from maintaining that gentle, repentant smile for hours. (Funny how smiling could hurt more than screaming.)

The familiar whisper of Rosa's sensible shoes against the hardwood announced her approach before the comforting scent of chamomile tea filled the room. Rosa had been bringing her tea at this exact time for twenty years - through triumphs and disasters, through pregnancies and promotions, through every version of Maddie that had existed in this house. The delicate china cup clinked against its saucer as Rosa set it down, the sound as precise as the timing of Maddie's tears had been at the social hall.

"How did it go, Mrs. Callahan?"

Maddie kept her movements measured; her expression soft as she met Rosa's eyes in the mirror. Such a loaded question from anyone else, but from Rosa - who had helped her select the understated navy dress this morning, who had witnessed every rehearsal of today's performance - it was almost tender. "It felt... right." She let out a small sigh, one that could have been mistaken for genuine relief. (And maybe, somewhere beneath the calculation, it was. Wasn't that what made her so convincing?)

Rosa's face remained neutral, but Maddie the slight tightening around her housekeeper's eyes. After twenty years, Rosa could read through any performance, yet she still nodded with practiced approval. They were like dancers in a familiar ballet, each knowing their steps by heart. Rosa had been there when Jackson first started staying late at the office, when the calls to "Princess" began appearing on his phone bill, when Maddie had first started planning... well, best not to think about that yet.

"The quiet approach suits you," Rosa said, adjusting the tea tray with those efficient hands that had wiped away so many of Maddie's tears - both real and manufactured.

Maddie reached for the cup, letting its warmth seep into her fingers. She maintained the same gentle demeanor she'd shown at the social hall, as if the mask had somehow fused to her skin. No triumphant smirk touched her lips, no gleam of satisfaction brightened her eyes. She'd learned that the best performances were the ones you could believe yourself. Like how she'd believed Jackson when he'd said "forever" twenty-five years ago, standing in that church in her mother's veil. (The same veil she'd preserved, though Jackson probably assumed she'd thrown it away in a fit of rage. But Maddie never threw anything away - not vows, not slights, not opportunities for redemption.)

"This is how it starts," Maddie said softly, taking a small sip of tea. She kept her voice steady, almost peaceful - the voice of a woman who had found clarity through reflection rather than one plotting her next move. The chamomile was, as always. Rosa knew how long to steep it, just as she knew when to lower her eyes, when to step back, when to pretend she didn't see the wheels turning behind Maddie's cultivated serenity.

Maddie watched Rosa's reflection in the kitchen window, noting how the older woman's shoulders tensed ever so. After twenty years, Rosa's tells were as familiar to her as her own. The slight tightening around her mouth when she disapproved, the way her fingers would worry at her cross necklace when she was nervous. Like now. (Though, what did Rosa have to be nervous about? Maddie had always taken care of her, hadn't she?)

The kitchen gleamed around them, a testament to Rosa's dedication. Every surface sparkled, every glass the morning light just so. It was the kind of perfection Jackson had always taken for granted. He'd never noticed how the silverware was arranged by size in the drawer, how the spice jars were alphabetized, how even the dish towels were folded in precise thirds. But Maddie noticed. Maddie noticed everything.

She took another sip of tea, letting the warmth spread through her chest. Twenty-five years of marriage, and Jackson thought he could just walk away? That's not how these things worked. Not in Maddie's world. She'd spent too long crafting this life, this image, this facade. The marble counter tops (chosen after three months of deliberation), the custom cabinetry (because off-the-shelf wouldn't do), even the delicate bone china teacup in her hands (a wedding gift from his mother, who'd always looked at Maddie like she wasn't quite good enough) - everything had been selected with surgical precision.

Rosa moved quietly around the kitchen, wiping down surfaces that were already spotless. Her movements were practiced, efficient, like a dancer who knew every step by heart. She'd been here for all of it - the dinner parties, the promotions, the orchestrated social climbing. She'd watched Maddie transform herself from a military wife into a force to be reckoned with. And now she would watch what came next.

Maddie traced the rim of her teacup with one manicured finger. The same finger that had worn Jackson's ring for a quarter century. The same finger that had pointed out private schools for the children, houses in the right neighborhoods, cars with the right pedigree. Everything chosen to reflect what they were becoming, what they had become. What he thought he could throw away for some younger version, some clean slate who didn't know his tells, his weaknesses, his secrets.

"You know what they say about karma, Rosa?" Maddie asked, though she didn't expect an answer. Rosa knew better than to engage when Maddie used that tone - soft as silk, sharp as a blade. "They say it comes back threefold. But I've never been good at waiting for karma to do its job." She smiled, the kind of smile that never quite reached her eyes. "Sometimes karma needs a little... direction."

The morning light her wedding ring, sending prisms dancing across the kitchen wall. Such a pretty thing. Like their marriage - all sparkle on the surface, all pressure and heat underneath. Well, if Jackson wanted heat, she'd give him heat. If he wanted pressure, she'd show him what real pressure felt like.

Rosa's cross glinted as she moved, catching the same light. The good Catholic woman, always watching, always praying. Maddie wondered what she prayed for these days. Redemption? Protection? Or maybe, like Maddie, she'd learned that God helps those who help themselves.

"That will be all for now," Maddie said, her voice still carrying that gentle lilt that had become second nature. Rosa nodded and retreated; her soft-soled shoes silent on the marble floor. Always so quiet, their Rosa.

Such a good listener. Such a keeper of secrets.

The tea had cooled to the drinking temperature. Maddie finished it in three measured sips, each one a countdown to what came next. The cup made no sound as she set it back in its saucer. control, poise. Just as she'd been taught. Just as she'd learned. Just as she would need for what was coming.

Because this was how it started. But Jackson had no idea how it would end.

The morning light the pearls now resting on the vanity, making them glow with an innocent luster. Such simple, elegant things. Like the simple, elegant plan taking shape in Maddie's mind. Sometimes the most devastating moves in a game were the quiet ones, the patient ones, the ones that looked like surrender until the moment they revealed themselves as victory.

Chapter 31

Maddie adjusted the collar of her navy Brooks Brothers suit, running her fingers along the crisp edge. The fabric felt different from her usual Chanel—rougher, more institutional... She'd chosen it specifically for that quality, just as she'd selected the simple pearl necklace (not her South Sea strand, but a modest graduation gift from her mother) and applied minimal makeup that morning, studying her reflection with clinical precision. Her hair, usually styled in soft waves that framed her face just so, was pulled back in a modest chignon. Gone were the designer labels and statement pieces that had once been her armor in these courthouse battles. She'd learned that sometimes the most powerful weapon was appearing weaponless.

"Good morning, Mrs. Reynolds," she said to the clerk, noting how the woman's eyebrows lifted at her gentle tone. No demands today, no expectations of special treatment. How many times had she swept past this same desk, chin high, radiating entitlement? But that Maddie—that creature of Hermès scarves and quiet disdain—had served her purpose.

She took her seat in the second row, keeping her eyes fixed on the polished wood of the gallery railing. When Jackson entered with Attorney Wren, she didn't look up, didn't acknowledge their presence, though every nerve in her body registered their arrival. Her hands remained folded in her lap, steady and still. Like a statue. Like a saint. (Wasn't that what they wanted to see? The reformed woman, the penitent wife?)

The courtroom filled gradually, a slow tide of whispers and judgment washing over her. She heard them, of course—felt the weight of their stares pressing against her skin—but maintained her composed demeanor. No attorney sat beside her; she'd dismissed Vivian Cross weeks ago, timing it. The empty chair made a statement she knew would register with the judge. After all, what spoke louder of contrition than walking into battle unarmed?

A few months ago, she would have been strategizing, planning her next move like a general commanding troop. Now she sat quietly, her breathing measured, her posture relaxed but proper. When

Barbara slipped into the back row (wearing last season's Prada, a detail Maddie's brain registered automatically), she didn't turn around. When Charlotte's signature Jo Malone perfume wafted past—Peony and Blush Suede, their shared favorite—she kept her gaze forward. Former lieutenants in a war she was no longer fighting. Or so it would appear.

The bailiff called for all to rise. Maddie stood smoothly, her movements deliberate and controlled. No nervous energy, no fidgeting with her wedding ring (though its absence felt like a phantom limb). Just quiet dignity as Judge Harrison entered the courtroom, his robes swishing with familiar authority.

Judge Harrison peered down at her over his wire-rimmed glasses, and Maddie felt a flutter of satisfaction at the concern in his expression. "Mrs. Callahan, I must advise you—proceeding without legal representation is ill-advised in a case of this complexity."

Her throat tightened, but she kept her voice steady, hitting that note of vulnerable strength she'd practiced in front of her bathroom mirror for weeks. "I understand, Your Honor. I've chosen to represent myself today because I need to speak from my heart, not through an intermediary." The words tasted like copper on her tongue.

She felt Jackson shift in his chair, sensed Attorney Wren's calculating stare boring into her. The weight of their attention pressed against her, but she maintained her composure. Let them look. Let them wonder. Sometimes the most dangerous opponent was the one who appeared to lay down their weapons.

When the judge invited her to speak, Maddie rose slowly. Her prepared speech about custody arrangements dissolved— as she'd planned. Instead, she looked directly at Judge Harrison, letting cultivated vulnerability show in her eyes.

"Your Honor, I'm not here to argue for custody." The words felt like glass in her throat, sharp and precise. "These past months have shown me that perhaps... perhaps I'm not what my children need right now." She watched his expression soften, just. Just enough.

She paused, steadying herself with a delicate breath. "I've been learning—through therapy and honest self-reflection—about forgiveness. About letting go. Most importantly, about putting Carrie and Nate's happiness above my own desires." Each word was a card laid on the table, building toward something that looked remarkably like surrender.

Her fingers trembled as she continued—not too much, just enough to be noticed. "If not seeing me is what's best for their emotional well-being, I will respect that decision. Their stability matters more than my wishes." She felt the room hold its breath, felt Jackson's surprise like electricity in the air. Sometimes the most effective way to win was to appear to lose—, utterly, and with such grace that no one saw the steel beneath the sacrifice.

Maddie sat still, her spine straight against the hard courtroom chair, as she turned toward Jackson. The words she'd rehearsed a hundred times in front of her bathroom mirror found their way past her lips. "My ex-husband is an excellent father." The admission tasted like copper on her tongue, but she pushed forward. "Despite our differences, I've never doubted his dedication to our children. I'm not here to challenge that. I only want to find a way to co-exist peacefully, for Carrie and Nate's sake."

Behind her, she could taste Barbara and Charlotte's collective intake of breath, their shock a tangible thing in the stuffy courtroom air. Poor dears. They'd expected fire and brimstone, expected the Maddie who'd thrown Jackson's Rolex into the pool the day he'd asked for a divorce. (She still remembered the satisfying splash, the way time itself seemed to sink into the chlorinated depths.) But that Maddie wasn't here today. This Maddie wore contrition like her favorite Chanel perfume—subtle, sophisticated, and calculated for maximum effect.

The scrape of Attorney Wren's chair against the floor made her want to bare her teeth, but she kept her head bowed instead, studying her manicured hands folded in her lap. The navy Armani suit she'd chosen felt like medieval armor now, each selected piece protecting her vulnerable spots from what she knew was coming. She'd prepared for this part too.

"Your Honor, with all due respect, we cannot ignore Mrs. Callahan's pattern of behavior." Nate's voice carried that familiar cold precision that had earned him the nickname "The Machine" in her private thoughts. She could feel him standing there, tall and immovable, adjusting his tie the way he always did before going in for the kill.

When he began listing her supposed crimes, she didn't flinch. "The bruises were manufactured. The threats to Ms. Hart were calculated. Even the testimony from Eleanor Walsh was an attempted bribe." Each accusation landed where he intended, like precise incisions from a surgeon's scalpel. But Maddie had practiced this too—complete stillness, face arranged in an expression of quiet remorse. (Let them think they'd broken her. Let them think she'd learned her lesson.)

Jackson shifted in his chair to her right, and twenty-five years of marriage meant she didn't need to look to know his expression. That clenched jaw, those ice-blue eyes gone arctic with disapproval—she'd seen it plenty across their dining room table in those final weeks, when he'd stopped pretending to eat her prepared meals and started taking calls from "Princess" in his study.

"Furthermore, Your Honor, Mrs. Callahan has demonstrated—"

"I've reviewed the evidence thoroughly, Mr. Wren." Judge Harrison's interruption carried a note of finality that made Maddie's heart quicken beneath her constructed facade. She kept her breathing steady, her posture unchanged, even as her pulse thrummed with anticipation. Sometimes the most effective way to win was to appear to lose—, utterly, and with such grace that no one saw the steel beneath the sacrifice.

The courtroom held its breath, and Maddie allowed herself the smallest smile, hidden behind a curtain of styled hair. They all thought they knew her so well—Jackson with his military strategy, Nate with his legal chess moves, even that insipid Lily with her youth and her wide-eyed act. But they'd forgotten the most important thing about Maddie Callahan: she'd spent twenty-five years as a general's wife, watching, learning, perfecting the art of warfare disguised as manners.

And now, it was her turn to deploy.

The word "visitation" hung in the air like smoke, curling through Maddie's consciousness as Judge Harrison's voice filled the courtroom. Not full custody—

not yet—but a foothold. A beginning. These past months of careful preparation, of timed tears and measured vulnerability, had yielded their first victory.

"These children need their mother."

Of course they did. Maddie's fingers trembled in her lap, and she pressed them together until they steadied, the way she'd learned to do at countless military functions. Twenty-five years of practice made the gesture automatic now. Control was everything. Control was power.

The pearl necklace Jackson had given her on their fifteenth anniversary felt heavy against her throat as she swallowed. (How fitting that she'd chosen to wear it today—these small details mattered.) From the corner of her eye, she Jackson's hands clenching into fists, heard Attorney Wren's sharp intake of breath. The gallery behind her rippled with surprise, and somewhere in the back, she was certain Barbara and Charlotte were already composing their worded social media posts about supporting their dear friend through this difficult time.

"Therefore, I'm granting weekend visitation rights to Mrs. Callahan, contingent upon continued therapy with Dr. Matthews and quarterly progress reports to this court."

Maddie kept her expression neutral, allowing just enough moisture to gather in her eyes—not enough to fall, just enough to glisten. She'd practiced this look for hours in her vanity mirror, the same way she'd once practiced the hostess smile for Jackson's promotion ceremonies. The thought nearly made her laugh. All those years of being the military wife had taught her more than Jackson ever realized.

Jackson's presence loomed to her right, his anger

radiating across the space between them like heat from a furnace. She didn't turn to look at him. She didn't need to. She could picture his face —that muscle twitching in his jaw, the way his ice-blue eyes would have gone flat and cold. The same expression he'd worn when she'd him texting Lily that first time.

Jackson's presence loomed to her right, his anger radiating across the space between them like heat from a furnace. She didn't turn to look at him. She didn't need to. She could picture his face—that muscle twitching in his jaw, the way his ice-blue eyes would have gone flat and cold.

But then, something unexpected happened.

Jackson didn't stand. Didn't argue. Didn't protest.

Instead, he turned his head, his gaze locking onto hers for the briefest of moments. So fast Maddie would never see. And for the first time in all their years together, she couldn't read him.

Then he spoke.

"I'll win by ignoring you."

That was all. No raised voice. No visible anger. Just quiet, controlled dismissal.

The words landed harder than any legal battle ever could.

A slow, suffocating silence followed, thick as smoke. Even Judge Harrison looked momentarily caught off guard, glancing between them as if sensing the shift in power.

Maddie felt her stomach twist, her carefully constructed walls momentarily cracking under the weight of what had just happened. Jackson didn't look at her again. He simply stood, gathered his things, and walked out of the courtroom without another word.

And just like that, Maddie Callahan ceased to exist in his world.

The victory she had fought for suddenly felt hollow.

Attorney Wren's pen scratched against paper—no doubt already planning an appeal. The sound reminded her of insects, something small and desperate scrabbling against glass. Let him plan. Let him plot. Maddie kept her eyes forward, focused on Judge Harrison's weathered face, noting how the overhead lights the silver in his hair. Details mattered. Everything mattered.

"Thank you, Your Honor." She let her voice emerge soft, touched with measured emotion—like adding drops of water to whiskey, too much would ruin it. "I'm grateful for this opportunity to prove myself to my children."

The words tasted like sugar-coated poison on her tongue. Prove herself? As if she were some wayward teenager instead of the woman who had sacrificed everything to raise those children while their father built his precious career. But she kept the bitterness hidden, wrapped it in layers of gratitude and humility like a gift.

Rising slowly from her chair, she smoothed her navy skirt with steady hands. The fabric was expensive—Chanel, because appearances mattered, especially now. The gallery behind her rustled with movement, whispers already starting to circulate. She could almost hear Charlotte's practiced sympathy, Barbara's concealed excitement at having fresh gossip to spread.

Her heels clicked against the polished floor as she walked toward the courtroom doors, each step measured and graceful. Jackson's stare followed her like a sniper's scope—she'd felt that same cold assessment enough times to recognize it without looking. Attorney Wren would be watching too, analyzing her every movement for signs of deception. Poor man. He still thought this was about the children.

At the heavy wooden doors, she paused just long enough to adjust her pearl necklace. The gesture wasn't vanity—it was a message. See how composed I am? See how graceful? This is what a mother looks like. This is what winning looks like.

She slipped through the doors without a backward glance, leaving the whispers and speculation behind. In the empty hallway, her lips curved into a smile. Phase one, complete. Now the real work could begin.

Chapter 32

Maddie adjusted her Hermès scarf, the silk cool against her skin. Her heels clicked against the marble floor of Le Petit Jardin, a sound she knew conveyed confidence, authority. Barbara and Charlotte's voices, hushed and conspiratorial, drifted from their usual corner table.

"Can you believe it? After everything?" Barbara's whisper wasn't quite quiet enough. "Jackson proposed to Lillian last weekend."

Maddie's fingers tightened on her purse strap, the cool leather grounding her. Her face, however, remained composed as she approached their table. Charlotte spotted her first, her coffee cup freezing halfway to her lips.

"Maddie! We didn't expect—"

"Good morning," Maddie interrupted, slipping into her chair with practiced grace. Her eyes, cool and calculating, swept over the scene. "Espresso, please," she murmured to the waiter, signaling for her usual. A small, serene smile played at her lips, watching Barbara and Charlotte exchange uncomfortable glances.

Mrs. Peterson appeared, her hand landing on Maddie's shoulder. "Oh, dear. Have you heard the news? About Jackson and that young woman?"

"I have." Maddie's voice remained steady, warm even. She lifted her chin, meeting Mrs. Peterson's concerned gaze. "I only wish them happiness."

Barbara's fork clattered against her plate. Charlotte's mouth fell open before she herself. The reaction rippled through their small group—this wasn't the Maddie they knew, the Maddie who had once orchestrated Jean-Marc's firing over a spilled glass of water.

"That's... generous of you," Mrs. Peterson managed, her hand still resting on Maddie's shoulder.

Maddie maintained her gentle smile, stirring a single packet of sugar into her espresso. "We all deserve a chance at happiness, don't we? Even Jackson."

Barbara and Charlotte exchanged looks across the table—part surprise, part suspicion. But Maddie kept her posture relaxed, her movements unhurried as she sipped her coffee.

"The children seem to be adjusting well," she added, her voice carrying just the right note of maternal concern. "That's what matters most."

◆ ◆ ◆

Maddie sat at her mahogany writing desk, her fingers trailing over the cream-colored sheets of Crane & Co. stationery. Not the monogrammed ones – those felt too exposed. This needed to be elegant, yes, but understated. A constructed facade.

Her Mont Blanc pen hovered above the pristine paper; a silver bullet poised to deliver her crafted message. Beside her, the engagement announcement sat like a silent accusation. Jackson and Lillian beamed up from the Atlanta Journal-Constitution's society page, their happiness a palpable slap in the face.

"Dear Jackson and Lillian," she began, her penmanship flowing with practiced grace. The words came easily now, freed from the anger that had gnawed at her for months.

"I wanted to express my heartfelt congratulations on your engagement. Life brings us unexpected changes, and I am genuinely happy to see you both finding joy together."

She paused, the tip of the pen resting lightly against her lips. The next part needed to be – warm without being effusive, sincere without sounding desperate. She had to convince them, convince everyone, that she was the bigger person.

"Your kindness in allowing me to remain part of Carrie and Nate's lives means more than I can express," she wrote, savoring the words. "Seeing them flourish and grow, even if only during our weekend visits, brings me such peace. Dr. Matthews has helped me understand that their happiness must always come first."

Maddie reread the constructed sentences, a ghost of a smile touching her lips. No hint of the rage that had fueled her actions, no trace of the woman who had once orchestrated Lillian's torment. This was a new Maddie, a better Maddie. Or so she wanted everyone to believe.

"I look forward to building a positive relationship as we move forward, one that puts the children's well being at the center of everything. Your generosity in including me in their lives shows true grace, and I am deeply grateful."

She signed it: "Warmest wishes, Maddie "

The letter was a masterpiece of restraint – no flowery pronouncements, no hidden barbs. Just the right touch of humility mixed with genuine-seeming warmth. She folded it, sliding it into the envelope with deliberate movements. This letter wasn't just a message; it was a weapon.

◆ ◆ ◆

Here is the text rewritten from Maddie's perspective in 2,246 words, following the Editor Guide:

The hidden camera in Jackson's study provided the vantage point. Maddie settled into the plush armchair, laptop balanced on the tray table she'd set up, and watched her husband read her letter. This was the critical moment—the first test to see if her constructed veneer would hold.

Lillian held the cream-colored paper delicately, like it might crumble between those manicured fingers. Maddie's lips twitched. The girl still thought everything was so fragile. She leaned closer, studying every micro-expression as Lillian's hazel eyes scanned the words.

"Jackson, this is...different." Lillian glanced up at

him, her voice carrying that same saccharine hopefulness Maddie had predicted. "There's no anger, no accusations. Just grace."

Just grace. Maddie savored the words, allowing herself a satisfied smile. She'd agonized over each line, stripping away anything that might betray her simmering rage. No, this letter was a masterpiece of calm empathy—a portrait of the reformed woman she needed them to believe in.

Jackson took the paper, his rigid military posture radiating skepticism. Of course he'd be suspicious. Her husband had always been brilliant at detecting threats, seeing the patterns and traps that others missed. Maddie felt a familiar flicker of pride as his ice-blue eyes raked over the words, analyzing every phrase like an opponent's strategy.

But she'd been careful. She'd left him nothing to find.

"It seems genuine," Lillian said, placing a gentle hand on Jackson's arm. The girl's touch lingered a beat too long—was she that naive? "Maybe the therapy is helping her."

Jackson's jaw tightened fractionally. With precise, economical movements, he placed the letter on his desk and smoothed it flat. "Maddie doesn't change," he said, each word clipped and certain. "She adapts."

There it was—the harsh truth she'd once loved about him. Jackson had always seen her clearly, stripped away her pretenses and pretty lies. In another life, she might have admired that perception, that refusal to be easily fooled.

But not now. Not when it threatened everything.

"But what if she is trying?" Lillian pressed, her

voice taking on that wheedling tone that set Maddie's teeth on edge. "For the kids? It would make everything easier if we could trust her again."

Maddie leaned forward, watching Jackson's face. There—a flicker of uncertainty in those flinty eyes. Just a shadow, perceptible. But it was enough.

He picked up the letter again, turning it over in his calloused hands. Rough hands, a soldier's hands—hands that had held her once with surprising tenderness. Maddie found herself drifting into memory, carried back to the rooftop of that Paris hotel on their anniversary trip decades ago...

The champagne had been crisp and cold, the city lights glittering below them like scattered jewels. She'd been young then, beautiful in a way that came effortlessly. Jackson had toasted her with that crooked smile, his eyes crinkling at the corners as he pulled her close and promised her forever.

She blinked, shoving the memory aside with a scowl. That was ancient history—another life, another woman. Regret was a useless indulgence.

"I don't know," Jackson said. The words came slowly, reluctantly, each one weighted with doubt. "Maybe...maybe she is trying."

Lillian brightened instantly, wrapping her arms around Jackson's solid frame. "That's all I'm saying," she said, tilting her head back to gaze at him. "We don't have to trust her. Just...give her a chance to prove herself."

Jackson didn't respond. He stood there, shoulders tense, staring at the letter with that first hint of uncertainty Maddie had seen in months.

She watched him closely, reading the subtle shifts in his body language. There—the slight furrow in his brow, the way his thumb traced the edge of the paper. He wanted to believe her, even if he didn't want to admit it.

A thin smile played across Maddie's lips as she closed her laptop. Phase one was a success—the seed of doubt had been planted. Now she could move on to the next stage of her plan.

This was just the beginning. Jackson thought he saw patterns; thought he could outmaneuver her. But Maddie had been the military wife for decades, waiting patiently while he built his career and reputation. She knew the art of patience, of quiet observation and strategic strikes.

No, her husband didn't understand the game they were playing. Not yet. But he would.

Maddie rose from her chair, letter in hand, and crossed the room to her dressing table. She opened the small wooden box, running her fingers over the cold metal inside—the latest addition to her collection.

This was her game to win. Jackson had always underestimated her, even at the height of his power. He'd never seen the core of ruthless determination that lived beneath her polished veneer.

But he would. By the time this was over, he would understand who he had married. Maddie smiled again, the expression never reaching her eyes.

He would regret every moment he'd taken her loyalty for granted. Every condescending dismissal, every time he'd turned away and expected her to wait. They were going to regret it all.

With slow, meticulous movements, Maddie unscrewed the silencer and began disassembling the gun.

◆ ◆ ◆

Maddie set her delicate china teacup down on the

mahogany side table, her sharp green eyes drifting across the pristine living room with a satisfied gaze. Everything gleamed—the silver frames holding photos of happier times that now seemed like relics from another life, the crystal vases catching the golden afternoon light and refracting it in fractured rainbows across the polished hardwood floors. Twenty-five years of perfection, maintained even now that her world was slowly unraveling at the seams.

(Of course it was immaculate. She wasn't a barbarian.)

On her laptop, the grainy surveillance feed continued to play, showing Jackson at his desk in that cold, sterile office, reading her letter for the third time. A slight crease had formed between his brows—that familiar wrinkle she knew so well, the one that only appeared when he was deep in strategic thought, weighing his next move. His uncertainty pleased her. The crack in his armor was what she'd waited for, what she'd been cultivating for months now with the -aimed strikes of a skilled fighter.

The soft footsteps of Rosa approaching from the kitchen broke the heavy silence that had settled over the room like a weighted blanket. The housekeeper paused in the doorway, her dark eyes studying Maddie with the same knowing look that came from two decades of service, of seeing too much. "And now what?" she asked, her voice careful, measured—as if she were speaking to a wild animal that might lash out at any moment.

Maddie's lips curved into a smile as she watched Jackson place the letter in his desk drawer instead of crumpling it into a ball and tossing it into the wastebasket as she'd half-expected him to. As if keeping it might change anything. As if some deluded part of him still hoped for a different outcome. "Now..." Her smile widened a fraction. "We wait."

She touched her wedding ring, the enormous diamond still positioned on her finger after all these years, catching the light and throwing rainbow patterns across the wall like it had on the first day he'd slid it onto her knuckle. The same ring he'd placed there all those years ago when his eyes still sparkled with devotion, before the deserts and battlefields had made them go cold and hard as steel.

Lillian had taken the bait, just as Maddie knew she would. That desperate desire to make peace, to prove to herself and the world that she was better than Maddie—nobler, more virtuous, more worthy of Jackson's affection—it made the girl predictable. Painfully so. And Jackson's vaunted military precision, his rigid self-control, it was all starting to weaken now, slowly giving way to doubt and second-guessing.

They would let their guard down eventually. Not today, not tomorrow, but soon. And when they did, when they started to believe that she had accepted her fate and was ready to move on...well, that was when Maddie would strike. She would be prepared, maintaining this facade of gracious acceptance until the moment arrived to burn the whole damned world to the ground.

Chapter 33

Maddie's eyes narrowed as she studied her reflection in the vanity mirror, the dim lighting casting sinister shadows across her features. Her fingers danced across the phone screen with practiced precision, each word a calculated move in her twisted game of manipulation.

"Hey Lillian," she typed, lips curling into a satisfied smirk. Too casual, too familiar - it was. Maddie knew how to play the role of the contrite, well-meaning woman seeking reconciliation. A mere facade, of course, but one she had ed over the years.

Her gaze flickered to the laptop, where the surveillance feed showed Lillian pacing anxiously in her kitchen, phone clutched in her manicured hand like a lifeline. Maddie's smirk deepened - the girl was predictable, checking her messages with the desperation of a lovesick puppy.

"I've been thinking about everything that's happened, and I wonder if you'd like to meet for coffee? No pressure, I just want to clear the air." The words dripped from Maddie's fingers like honeyed venom, each syllable a constructed trap. She paused, rereading the message with a critical eye, ensuring the tone struck the balance between vulnerability and strength.

"I understand if you're hesitant. I know I haven't given you reason to trust me, but I truly have no ill will. Just two women who should probably talk." The lie rolled off her tongue as smoothly as the whiskey she sipped each night, the bitterness masked by the saccharine promise of reconciliation.

Maddie's fingers drummed against the cool marble of the vanity, her mind already spinning ahead, anticipating Lillian's response. She needed something more, a final touch to disarm the girl's defenses, to make her lower her guard and stumble blindly into Maddie's web.

A flicker of memory surfaced - Lillian's favorite boutique, the one she frequented with the desperation of a woman seeking validation through material possessions. Maddie's lips curved into a predatory smile as she added the closing line, the bait to lure her unsuspecting prey.

"I was just passing that little shop on Maple you love and thought of you. Let me know if you'd like to meet there instead?"

With a final, self-satisfied tap, Maddie sent the message, leaning back in her chair as a dark chuckle escaped her painted lips. The game was afoot, and she had no intention of losing - not this time, not to the likes of Lillian. This was her kingdom, her rules, and the deliciously naive girl would soon learn the price of trespassing.

"Plus, I hear Maison Belle has new Hermès scarves in - we could always bond over our shared expensive taste ??"

The emoji felt foreign to her fingers, but it was the kind of casual touch needed. Maddie read the message once more, checking every word for hidden threats or pressure. It was - light, self-aware, with just enough humor to seem genuine.

She pressed send before she could second-guess herself. Through the surveillance feed, she watched Lillian's phone light up with the notification.

Through the surveillance feed, Maddie watched Lillian pick up her phone, the younger woman's face shifting from surprise to uncertainty as she read the message. A smirk tugged at the corner of Maddie's mouth as her fingers drummed against the vanity, her own phone placed with calculated precision in front of her. (As if she'd ever allow something so crucial to be out of place.)

The typing indicator appeared, vanished, then reappeared—a pathetic little ellipsis betraying Lillian's indecision Maddie allowed herself a small smile. The woman's hesitation was what she'd anticipated, a delicious little victory. They were all so predictable, these chosen companions of Jackson's. They thought themselves complex creatures, layered with depth and nuance. But Maddie saw them for what they truly were—simple, governed by habit and fear like any other animal.

When the response came through, Maddie read it with practiced composure, her face an inscrutable mask: "I appreciate the offer, but I don't think that's a good idea right now." She could have scripted those words herself, they were so Lillian—polite, distant, careful. Everything Maddie had expected from the younger woman's performative restraint.

On the screen, Lillian set down her phone and began pacing the kitchen, her hand running through her hair in that nervous gesture Maddie had documented countless times before. An unconscious tells, betraying the cracks in her porcelain facade. Maddie picked up her own phone, not rushing to respond. Better to let Lillian stew for a while in the guilt of rejection, to let her wonder if she'd made the right choice in turning Maddie down.

The camera showed Lillian rechecking her phone, her eyes flitting across the empty screen with something like desperation. Perhaps she was already questioning her decision, already regretting her polite rebuff. This was the beauty of appearing reformed, Maddie mused—every rejection now carried weight, made the other person feel like the unreasonable one. She had learned, over the long years, that true power wasn't in forcing people to say yes; it was in making them feel wrong for saying no.

Lillian's phone remained silent. Maddie set her own device down without responding, her smile widening a fraction. Some messages were more powerful when met with silence. Let the younger woman wonder and fret. The game had only just begun.

❖ ❖ ❖

Here is the text rewritten from Maddie's perspective, using the techniques described in the Editor Guide:

Maddie's fingers danced across the screen, crafting each word with delicious precision. She kept her tone warm, understanding—everything she'd learned from studying that little ingénue these past months. "Of course, I understand. I'd feel the same way in your position."

Through the surveillance feed, she watched Lillian tense, those soft shoulders stiffening as the message arrived. The girl scooped up her phone, and Maddie savored the surprise spreading across her face at Maddie's graciousness. She could hear Lillian's thoughts: I didn't expect that from the bitter ex-wife.

Silly girl. Maddie hit send on her next constructed message: "The children's well-being comes first, and I know this situation isn't easy for anyone. Please know I don't hold any of this against you." A masterful balance of empathy and subtle guilt—just enough to set the hook.

She studied Lillian's reaction like a scientist over her prized experiment. The pacing stopped, all that youthful energy focused on the screen. The tremor in that delicate hand told Maddie all she needed to know. One more line to reel her in: "If you ever change your mind, I'd love to meet and just talk. No pressure, ever."

Maddie placed her phone beside her untouched tea, leaning back with a satisfied smile. Lillian read and reread the messages on the screen, her expression cycling through the predictable stages—wariness, confusion, and, that delicious hint of guilt. She could taste the younger woman's uncertainty.

The soft tread of Rosa's footsteps registered until the maid was at Maddie's side. "More chamomile, Mrs. Callahan?" Her eyes flitted between Maddie and the surveillance feed, always watching, always wary.

"Yes, thank you, Rosa." Maddie waved her off, attention locked on the screen as Lillian showed the messages to Jackson. Her ex-husband's face remained that same stoic mask he'd worn for years, but she the slight crease in his brow—that familiar tell of doubt she'd spent twenty-five years learning to read.

A small smile played at her lips. They never did see it coming, did they? The military mind, outmaneuvered by a woman's understanding of the heart. Jackson had trained for war, but he had met his match in an arena he would never master.

Maddie sipped her fresh tea, eyes glinting with satisfaction. Let them wonder. Let them second-guess. She could taste their discomfort, that first delectable shred of uncertainty. It was only the beginning.

◆ ◆ ◆

Maddie leaned closer to her laptop screen, adjusting the volume to catch every word of Jackson and Lillian's conversation in their Virginia study. The camera's angle captured Jackson's rigid posture as he read through the text messages again. (She had planted those like an expert—every word calculated for maximum impact.)

"She's being reasonable," Lillian said, perching on the edge of his desk like a pretty little bird. "Look how she responded when I said no."

Jackson's jaw tightened, that familiar tic he always got when he was annoyed. Maddie felt a small rush of satisfaction just watching it happen. Why was he looking at her like that? Like she was a stranger, not his wife of twenty years. She knew that face better than her own.

"That's what she wants you to think," he said tightly.

"But she didn't push back at all. No guilt trips, no manipulation-"

Silly girl. As if Maddie would be so obvious. "Because that's not her style anymore. She's learned." Jackson set the phone down with more force than necessary, rattling Lillian's dainty teacup. Maddie smirked. He had no idea how right he was. She had learned, oh yes. Learned to be patient, to adapt, to strike only when the time was.

"Trust me, I know how she operates."

"People can change." Lillian's voice softened into that soothing, reasonable tone she no doubt thought would calm him. "Maybe therapy is helping her."

"In three months?" Jackson's laugh held no humor, that deep baritone rumble Maddie remembered from another lifetime. "After twenty-five years of-"

He himself, running a hand through his graying hair. For a moment, Maddie was twenty-five again herself, watching him pace their Parisian hotel room in that faded crimson robe, ranting about another boundless career opportunity while she sipped mimosas and dreamed of the future they'd build together. She blinked, forcing herself back to the present.

"Princess, you don't know what she's capable of."

Lillian scoffed, shaking her head. "That's putting it lightly."

"No, I mean—" Jackson let out a breath, raking a hand through his hair. "There was a dog."

Lillian blinked. "What?"

"When we first got together," he said, his voice oddly distant, as if speaking the words might drag him too far into the past. "We had this dog. Maddie loved that thing. I mean, really loved it."

Lillian's confusion deepened, her brows pulling together.

"One night, it got out. Slipped through the back fence. I don't know how, but by the time we found it, it was hurt bad. Broken leg, ribs shattered. The vet was closed, and we lived too far from base to do anything in time."

Jackson rubbed a hand over his jaw, feeling the old frustration rise in his chest like smoke. "I told her we'd figure something out. That I'd call the neighbor, get help. But before I could even react, she—" He hesitated. His throat felt tight. "She went into the garage, grabbed my rifle, and shot it in the head."

Lillian sucked in a sharp breath.

"She didn't even flinch," Jackson continued, his voice lower now. "Didn't cry. Didn't hesitate. Just pulled the trigger and walked back inside like nothing happened." He exhaled, shaking his head slightly. "I stood there for—I don't even know how long—just staring at the damn thing."

Lillian's fingers curled tighter around her wineglass, her knuckles going pale.

"Jesus," she said.

"The worst part?" Jackson let out a humorless chuckle. "She wasn't wrong. The dog was dying. There was nothing we could do. But it was the way she did it."

He looked up, meeting Lillian's wide eyes. "Like it didn't matter."

A thick silence stretched between them.

Lillian swallowed hard. "And you stayed with her after that?"

Jackson didn't answer.

Because, of course, he had.

Because at the time, he hadn't understood what it meant.

Now, watching the fear in Lillian's eyes, Jackson realized something chilling:

That moment with the dog?

It hadn't been a decision to Maddie. It had been instinct.

And now that instinct was pointed at them.

Maddie watched the tension build between them, noting how Lillian's shoulders squared—a subtle sign of defiance she'd observed whenever the younger woman stood her ground against Jackson's dominance. The girl had spirit; she'd give her that. But she was foolish to think it would be enough.

"I was there for the custody hearing. I saw how different she was."

"That's an act."

"You can't know that for certain."

Maddie allowed herself a small, private smile. If only they knew.

"I lived with her manipulation for decades," Jackson said, in that firm, unyielding tone he used to command troops. "Don't engage. Don't respond. Don't give her any opening."

She hesitated, crossing her arms. "You told me we wouldn't have the kids. That it would just be the two of us."

Jackson exhaled sharply. "Things changed."

"Changed? Or did Maddie make it happen?"

"I'm not wrong." His voice carried that familiar edge of command, the one he'd used countless times when he expected absolute obedience from his inferiors. Maddie felt a flicker of anger. After everything, he still looked at her as something to be controlled, subdued.

But Lillian didn't back down, much to Maddie's surprise. "The children need their mother."

"They need to be protected from her."

"Maybe they need to be protected from your inability to forgive."

Maddie smiled as silence filled the study, the first delicious crack forming between Jackson and his precious princess. She rewound the footage, savoring Lillian's defiant stance and Jackson's clenched jaw.

Let them question her motivations. Let them underestimate her strength, her resolve. While they wasted time arguing, she would be executing her plan— striking when they least expected it.

After all, she had learned. And Jackson was about to discover how well.

Here is the rewritten text in the style of Liane Moriarty, from Maddie's third-person limited perspective:

Maddie clicked the laptop closed with a sense of deep satisfaction. The surveillance feed of Lillian winked out, but the image was seared into her mind—the younger woman's face crumpling as she confronted Jackson about forgiveness. Silly girl. As if Jackson was capable of such a thing. Lillian was more delightfully gullible than Maddie could have hoped.

Her phone rested on the polished desk, the damning text messages still glowing on the screen. Maddie's eyes traced each crafted word, every subtle insinuation designed to foster doubt. She deleted the conversation with a flick of her thumb, already anticipating the next batch of messages she would compose. More seeds to sow, more cracks to widen in Jackson's shiny new fantasy.

The familiar rhythm of Rosa's footsteps drifted in from the hallway. Like clockwork, every evening at six-fifteen. Maddie straightened in her chair, readying herself for their little ritual dance.

"Would you like your chamomile tea now, Mrs. Callahan?" Rosa swept into the room, her face an inscrutable mask.

"Yes, Rosa." Maddie swiveled to face her, offering her most benign smile. "And perhaps those shortbread cookies Jackson used to love." A pointed pause. "The first batch you made when we moved here."

She didn't miss the flicker in Rosa's dark eyes as she set down the tray, her movements overly precise. Looking for tells, no doubt, as she had for two decades. Trying to decipher which version of Maddie she faced tonight—the serene hostess or the gathering storm.

"How did your message to Ms. Hart go?" Rosa's tone was neutral, giving nothing away.

Maddie lifted the dainty teacup, breathing in the calming scent of chamomile. Such a lovely aroma. So soothing. "As planned." She allowed a hint of satisfaction to curl her lips. "She's still afraid of me. That's good."

For the briefest moment, Rosa's hands stilled over the silver tray, the shortbread cookies untouched.

Maddie recognized that pregnant pause, that infinitesimal hesitation before the mask slipped back into place. The same look Rosa had worn a thousand times—the silent witness, the keeper of twenty years' worth of secrets. Waiting, always waiting, for the other shoe to drop.

"Will that be all, Mrs. Callahan?" Rosa asked at last, her voice devoid of inflection.

Maddie sipped her tea, letting the warmth spread through her like a contented sigh. She held Rosa's gaze over the rim of the cup, issuing an unspoken challenge. Go ahead, make your assessment. Decide whether this is the rueful matriarch accepting her fate or the velvet glove concealing sharp claws.

"Yes, Rosa. Thank you."

She watched Rosa retreat, leaving the scent of chamomile and buttery shortbread in her wake. Such small pleasures, these little rituals that tethered Maddie to civilized life. At least for now. At least until her cultivated world crumbled, leaving only the wreckage.. .and the reckoning that would follow.

Chapter 34

Maddie settled into the plush armchair; laptop balanced on her silk-clad knees. A few deft keystrokes brought up the hidden camera feed—her own personal puppet show. She watched, rapt, as Lillian fidgeted with her coffee cup at the charming Le Petit Jardin. The girl's nervous energy vibrated through the screen. Across from her, Charlotte sat ramrod straight, already shaking her head before Lillian even finished speaking.

"She seems different now." Lillian's voice was quiet, almost pleading. "The therapy, the letters... maybe she's changed."

Oh, Lillian. Sweet, naive thing. Maddie's lips curved into a smile sharper than any knife. She observed Charlotte's obvious discomfort with relish. The woman knew better than to trust Maddie's empty platitudes, and yet here was Lillian, falling into place like a lamb to slaughter.

"You don't know her like we do." Charlotte leaned forward, her tone carrying a harsh edge usually reserved for scolding the household staff. "Trust me, stay away."

A flick of Maddie's finger switched the camera angle, catching Lillian's uncertain expression in profile. The girl's shoulders hunched —a tell Maddie had noticed whenever Lillian felt that pesky undercurrent of guilt. It would serve her well to listen to it more often.

"But the children," Lillian pressed on, ever the martyr. "They need their mother. And if she's working on herself..."

Maddie took a languorous sip of her tea, the satisfaction warming her chest more than the fragrant bergamot ever could. She'd crafted each letter, each worded message, knowing they would burrow into Lillian's conscience like parasites. The girl's inherent need to be seen as good, to always strive for some idea of higher moral ground, made her predictable. A few well-placed emotional triggers, and she was putty to be molded.

Later that evening, Maddie reclined on the chaise lounge, laptop angled just so as she watched another feed. This one showed the study she'd once shared with Jackson—a space that had become foreign territory ever since Lillian slunk her way inside.

Speak of the devil... Maddie's eyes narrowed as Lillian sashayed through the door, all loose hair and loose morals. She perched herself on the edge of Jackson's desk like a cat claiming new territory. "I've been thinking," she began, the picture of faux-innocence. "Maybe we should give your ex-wife another chance. For the kids."

Jackson's jaw tightened—a reaction Maddie knew well, having witnessed it countless times over the years. A small, vindictive spark of pleasure ignited in her chest at the sight. Let him feel that impotent anger, that rush of caged fury. She drank it in like the finest wine.

But Lillian continued, utterly oblivious to the danger she courted. "She's in therapy, she's respecting boundaries. Wouldn't it be more mature to try and move forward?"

Maddie set down her teacup, the fine china clinking against the saucer with finality. She drank in Jackson's conflicted expression instead, savoring the roiling storm behind those arctic eyes. Everything was unfolding as she'd planned, like a sinister choreography only she could see. Lillian would push for reconciliation, thinking it was her own idea sparked by Maddie's pretty little letters. The puppet, dancing on strings she couldn't even see.

A cruel smile tugged at the corners of Maddie's mouth. Let them believe what they wanted—Lillian and her desperate need to be the heroic savior, Jackson and his arrogant assumptions that he could ever be rid of her. They were merely supporting players in the grand production of her making.

She was the director, the writer, the puppet

master. And this play had only just begun.

The soft trill of her phone shook Maddie from her reverie. A Fabergé egg of a thing, all platinum and diamonds and wretched excess—Jackson's last gift before the whole sordid affair imploded. She flipped it open with a casual flick of her wrist, unsurprised to see Barbara's number flashing on the display.

"Well?" Her friend wasted no time on pleasantries. Maddie could hear the impatient tapping of one crimson nail against the receiver. "Did it work? Is she biting?"

Maddie hummed a single, satisfied note, allowing the silence to stretch just long enough to become uncomfortable. She could picture Barbara perched on the edge of some absurdly expensive sofa; lips pursed in that way she had when impatience gave way to indignation.

"Like a starving woman at a Vegas buffet, my dear," Maddie purred at last. "She swallowed it hook, line, and sinker."

"God, you're good." The reluctant admiration in Barbara's tone was as sweet as any praise. Maddie allowed herself a tight, self-satisfied smile before continuing.

"I've laid the foundation. Now we move to the next phase." She steepled her fingers, manicured nails gleaming like garnet arrowheads in the low light. "Get Sandra on the line. It's time to set the trap."

The game was afoot, and Maddie had no intentions of losing this time. Her gaze drifted back to the laptop screen, to the frozen image of Jackson's taut jawline and Lillian's simpering pout. They thought they held all the power, that she was just some shrill, discarded wife clinging to shreds of relevance.

How deliciously mistaken they were.

This was her game, her rules. She'd been playing it for decades before either of them came stumbling along—the vapid little ingenue, the arrogant warhorse who forgot what a formidable adversary looked like. They were amateurs, babes in the wood. And she was the huntress, luring them deeper into the thicket with every breadcrumb of deception.

Let them believe they were in control for now. When the time came, she would rip the blindfold from their eyes and revel in their horror as they saw the intricate web they'd wandered into. They would realize, too late, that they had never been more than flies in her silken strands, their fates sealed from the first tremulous step.

Maddie allowed the laptop to slide from her lap, the smooth wooden floor providing a final dull thunk of finality. Her blood hummed with the electric thrill of the hunt, the feeling of being poised on the brink of sweet, intoxicating victory. She closed her eyes, reveling in the moment as it stretched on and on, savoring the delicious potential of what lay ahead.

They thought they knew her, these foolish ingrates. But they didn't know the half of it. Not the darkness coiling within, the depths of cunning and venom lying in wait, cultivated over decades of resentment and sacrifice and being disregarded like last season's Birkin.

Well, they were going to learn. One way or another, they would all learn the true meaning of the name Madeline Callahan. And by the time the curtain fell, any notion they'd once held of being her masters would be naught but a bitter memory drowned in ashes and ruin.

The thought made her smile widen, a wolf's grin flashing in the shadows.

Let the games begin.

Maddie's fingers stilled on the pearl necklace as her phone buzzed. A flicker of annoyance passed over her features—she despised interruptions when preparing for an evening out. But the name glowing on the screen made her heart skip a beat. Lillian. This was the moment she'd been orchestrating. Maddie exhaled, smoothing her palms over the silk lapels of her robe. She could play the wounded, repentant wife desperate for a second chance. Letting the phone ring, she mentally recited the script looping through her mind. Just enough hesitation to seem flustered when she answered.

"Hello?" Her voice laced with breathless uncertainty.

"Hi, Maddie. It's Lillian." That slight catch before her name betrayed Lillian's nerves. Maddie relished the silence, picturing Lillian squirming.

"I hope it's okay I called." Another pause as Lillian searched for disdain.

Turning away, Maddie allowed a tremor to enter her tone. "Of course. I just...wasn't expecting..." She trailed off, the quintessential portrait of fragility.

"I know." A rustle, perhaps Lillian shifting uncomfortably. "Look, I'm dropping the kids off next weekend, maybe we could get coffee? If you're comfortable."

Maddie bit her cheek, smothering a smirk at the bait dangling. "That would be...nice," each word wavering. "Are you sure?"

"Yes, for the children's sake."

The children—Lillian's justification. Maddie's grip tightened imagining her fingers around Lillian's throat instead of the vanity. But she steadied herself— time for that later. Securing the meeting was priority.

A measured laugh tumbled from her lips. "I promise I won't be scary this time," she said lightly. "No more notes or drama."

The sharp intake of Lillian's breath. Maddie savored the discomfort like fine wine, picturing Lillian recoiling at the memory of torment inflicted.

"We can laugh about it now, right?" Lillian's voice strained. "Water under the bridge?"

Laughing, Maddie infused her tone with remorse. ". I was in such a dark place. Therapy helped me see differently."

"Wonderful." Tension released in Lillian's exhalation. "Saturday? The café near the park?"

The park—where children could play while amends were "made." Maddie's lips curved upward as she committed every detail to memory.

"." Warmth seeped into her sugary reassurance. "Thank you for reaching out. It means more than you know."

After hanging up, Maddie watched a cardinal's scarlet feathers blazing against the fence—an omen that everything was positioning itself where needed.

Rising, Maddie shrugged off her robe, reaching for the deep green lace gown hugging her curves—a reminder to Jackson she hadn't relinquished all power. Catching her reflection, she studied the hardness simmering behind her jade eyes—the look of a trapped animal starved of oxygen, willing to chew off its own limb to breathe free air. Her gaze drifted to the faint scar peeking over her neckline—a tally mark from a dark moment, a reminder of her capabilities when pushed to insanity's edge. Not tonight—she wouldn't risk marring her appearance before the show began.

Turning from the mirror, Maddie tugged on elbow-length satin gloves, smoothing the fabric over her forearms until meeting the lace trim. One final accessory—teardrop pearl earrings from Jackson's anniversary gift, shackles binding her to the life she sacrificed everything to build.

But no more—the shackles were coming off, the cage door unlatched. Maddie's gaze fell on the framed photo beside her makeup tray, lips curving into a vindictive smile at her beloved Jackson—the man she loved, lost, would soon destroy. A rare moment of warmth she hadn't seen in over a decade. Not since... She closed her eyes, willing herself not to go there yet. That wound was too fresh to reopen before focusing on her delicate game of chess arranged for months. Let Lillian believe she was the pawn, easily manipulated to push forward. The fool didn't realize she was the queen—beloved, powerful, utterly expendable.

A soft rap. "Mom? Are you ready? Dad's waiting."

Maddie's lips tightened as she regarded sweet, innocent Carrie's trusting adoration. A fleeting wave of regret washed over her before she steadied—she couldn't afford regrets when so close to culmination, to the reward for everything sacrificed and endured. They would rise, phoenixes from betrayal's ashes, burning anyone standing in their path alive.

"Coming, darling." With chin raised in regal defiance, Maddie took center stage.

◆ ◆ ◆

Through the surveillance feed, Maddie watched Lillian enter Jackson's study. Her fingers traced the rim of her teacup as she observed their interaction unfold.

"I called Maddie today," Lillian said.

Jackson's head snapped up from his laptop. "You what?"

"We're having coffee on Saturday after I drop off the kids."

Jackson pushed back from his desk; jaw tight. "Not. Have you forgotten what she did to you? The notes? The threats?"

"She's different now. You've seen her at church, how quiet she's been. Dr. Matthews says—"

"Dr. Matthews can be manipulated just like everyone else." Jackson's fist clenched on the desk. "This is what she wants, to get you to let your guard down."

Lillian crossed her arms. "This isn't about Maddie. It's about Carrie and Nate seeing that adults can move past their differences. They need to know their mother isn't some monster we're hiding them from."

"She—" Jackson started, then stopped. His shoulders tensed as he stood.

"What kind of example are we setting if we can't even have coffee with their mother?" Lillian's voice softened. "I'll be careful. It's a public place."

"Princess, not long ago, we both agreed we didn't want the kids. Hell, I thought you'd leave me when I got custody. But look at us now."

"Yes, look at us now."

Maddie leaned closer to her screen, watching Jackson's resolve crack. His hand moved to his temple – a tell she knew well from their marriage. He was giving in.

"Fine." Jackson sank back into his chair. "But not alone. I want you to meet somewhere crowded."

"The café near the park is always busy on weekends."

Jackson nodded, though his jaw remained tight. "The first sign of anything strange—"

"I know," Lillian touched his shoulder. "I'll leave immediately."

Maddie smiled into her tea. They were all playing their parts.

◆ ◆ ◆

Maddie set her phone down with deliberate care after ending the call with Lillian. The surveillance feed still played on her laptop, showing Jackson and Lillian's continued discussion in their study. She lifted her teacup, taking a final sip of the now-cold Earl Grey.

Rosa stood in the doorway, her dark eyes watching. Twenty years of service had taught her to read Maddie's moods, and now she sensed the shift in the air.

"Will you be needing anything else this evening, Mrs. Callahan?"

"Yes." Maddie's voice remained measured, controlled. "I want the house spotless for Saturday. Every surface should shine. Pay special attention to the formal living room and guest powder room."

Rosa nodded; her expression neutral.

Maddie walked to the kitchen, her heels clicking against the marble floors. She opened the cabinet where she kept her finest coffee and tea service. Her fingers traced over several bags before selecting the blend – a rare Colombian roast Jackson had once brought back from a business trip.

She lifted her favorite Wedgwood tea set from its

shelf, the delicate blue and white pattern catching the light. The cups were elegant without being showy – the right tone for Saturday's meeting.

After arranging everything on the counter, Maddie crossed to her study. She unlocked the bottom drawer of her desk, reaching past files and photographs to retrieve a small glass vial. The clear liquid inside the light as she placed it next to the coffee service.

Everything was ready almost ready, she just needed to make one more call.

Maddie's fingers hovered over Jackson's contact information. She had rehearsed this conversation a dozen times and knew which tone to strike. The phone rang three times before he answered.

"What is it, Maddie?" His voice carried that familiar edge of irritation.

"Jackson." She kept her voice soft, hesitant. "I've been thinking about Saturday. About seeing the children for the first time in months."

A pause on his end. She pictured him in his study, standing by the window where he always took calls.

"I don't want them to feel awkward or stressed." She traced the edge of her desk with one finger. "Maybe we could all have dinner first? Something casual, just to break the ice?"

"That's not necessary." His words came clipped, guarded.

"Please." She let vulnerability seep into her voice. "I know what you think of me, but this isn't about us. It's about making Carrie and Nate comfortable. No funny business, I promise. You can pick the restaurant."

The silence stretched. Through the surveillance feed on her laptop, she watched him pace in his study.

"Fine." He sighed. "Morton's at six. We'll have dinner first, then coffee after."

"Thank you, Jackson." She kept the triumph from her voice. "This means a lot. And please thank Lillian for suggesting we meet. I know it couldn't have been an easy decision."

Another pause. "Don't make me regret this, Maddie."

"I won't. Trust me, no funny stuff from me. I just want what's best for our children."

After hanging up, Maddie allowed herself a small smile. Everything was falling into place.

Chapter 35

Maddie smoothed her cream cashmere sweater, adjusting the soft cowl neck one final time. The neutral tones worked – unthreatening, approachable, what was needed. Through the window, she spotted Lillian's Range Rover pulling into the circular drive.

Rosa had outdone herself. The house gleamed, filled with the warm scent of Colombian coffee and fresh vanilla. Everything felt purposefully cozy, welcoming.

The doorbell chimed. Maddie counted to three

before opening it, her practiced smile in place.

"Lillian, I'm so glad you came." She kept her voice gentle, maternal.

"Thank you for having me." Lillian stepped inside, her designer boots clicking against the marble foyer.

Maddie guided her to the sun-drenched dining room where the Wedgwood tea service waited. Sunlight streamed through the windows, catching the delicate blue and white pattern of the china.

"Please, sit." Maddie gestured to the chair facing the window. "The light is lovely here in the morning."

As Lillian settled in, Maddie lifted the coffee pot with steady hands, pouring the dark liquid into Lillian's cup with practiced grace.

"The children are doing so well," Lillian said, her voice bright. "Carrie's starting a new piano program, and Nate joined the debate club."

"That's wonderful." Maddie reached across the table, placing her hand over Lillian's. "I'm so grateful they have you in their lives."

Lillian's smile widened. "And the wedding plans are coming together beautifully. Jackson's been so involved in every detail."

"As he should be." Maddie nodded, watching as Lillian lifted the coffee cup to her lips.

The first sip. Maddie's expression remained warm, interested, as she observed Lillian swallow.

"This coffee is amazing," Lillian said, taking another sip.

"Colombian." Maddie's smile never wavered. "Jackson brought it back from a business trip years ago."

Maddie watched as Lillian glanced at her phone, the blue light reflecting off her features. Twenty-five years of marriage, and Jackson had replaced her with this younger version. This woman who sat in Maddie's dining room, drinking from Maddie's cups, living Maddie's life.

"I should get going." Lillian set down her cup with a delicate clink against the saucer. "Thank you for the coffee. This was... nice."

"Of course." Maddie rose from her chair, maintaining the gentle smile she'd ed over weeks of practice in her mirror.

They walked to the foyer, Lillian's boots clicking against the marble floors that Maddie had selected fifteen years ago. The sound echoed through the house - their house - where Maddie had raised their children, hosted their parties, built their life.

At the door, Lillian turned, her expression soft with sympathy. That was the worst part - this girl felt sorry for her. As if Maddie was some aging relic to be pitied rather than feared.

"We should do this again," Lillian said, adjusting her Hermès scarf - the same brand Maddie had taught Jackson to buy for special occasions.

Maddie opened the heavy wooden door, letting the morning light stream in. "Enjoy your drive, Princess." The nickname rolled off her tongue like honey masking poison. "Life is too short."

❖ ❖ ❖

Maddie climbed the familiar stairs, her hand trailing along the polished banister. The house felt different now - emptier, colder without the constant chaos of children. Her heels clicked against each step, echoing through the hollow space.

She paused outside Nate's room first. The door was closed, but she could hear him typing on his computer. Two quick knocks, then she opened it.

"Hi, sweetheart."

Nate glanced up from his screen. "Hi, Mom."

She perched on the edge of his bed, noting how he'd rearranged everything since moving back. His model airplanes no longer hung from the ceiling.

"How's the new life treating you?" She kept her voice light, casual.

"It's okay, I guess." He shrugged, still focused on his computer.

Down the hall, Carrie's door stood ajar. Maddie found her daughter sprawled on the floor, surrounded by colored pencils and paper.

"What are you drawing, angel?"

Carrie held up her artwork - a house with four stick figures. "That's our house in Virginia."

Maddie's chest tightened at the sight of the happy family portrait. "Do you like living there?"

"It's okay." Carrie selected another pencil, adding flowers to the yard. "But I miss my old piano teacher."

"I miss you both so much when you're gone." Maddie sat cross-legged beside her daughter, picking up a discarded drawing. "How do you like your new school?"

"It's okay, I guess." Carrie's pencil moved faster across the paper. "The other kids are nice."

Maddie watched her daughter draw, noting how Carrie's strokes had become more confident, more precise. Someone else was witnessing these small changes now. Someone else was marking her children's growth.

"And Lillian? Is she nice to you?"

Carrie nodded without looking up. "She helps me with my hair in the morning. Like you used to."

The words struck like physical blows, but Maddie maintained her smile. She reached out to smooth Carrie's blonde strands, as she'd done every morning for eight years.

"I'll need both of you to come to the kitchen in ten minutes. Your father is coming over for dinner."

Maddie smoothed the ivory tablecloth, adjusting the Wedgwood place settings one final time. She'd selected Jackson's favorite wines, arranged fresh flowers from the garden. The door opened and she heard his sharp intake of breath.

"What's all this?" Jackson stood in the doorway; his suit jacket wrinkled from a long day of running around preparing for his new wedding."

"I thought we could have dinner together. One last moment as a family." She kept her voice soft, gentle - the way she used to speak to him after difficult deployments. "The children miss these dinners."

Jackson's jaw tightened, but exhaustion lined his face. After a long moment, he nodded. "Fine. Just dinner."

They settled into their usual seats, muscle memory from twenty-five years of shared meals. Nate and Carrie filled the silence with the clinking of silverware against china.

"How are things at Callahan Defense?" Maddie passed the roasted potatoes, noting how his shoulders remained rigid.

"Busy. The Morrison contract is taking longer than expected."

She nodded, remembering countless evenings discussing his work. "And the engagement? Have you set a date?"

His fork paused halfway to his mouth. "Spring. April probably."

"That's lovely. The dogwoods will be in bloom."

The conversation lapsed into silence again. Maddie watched as Jackson's posture gradually softened, his movements becoming less guarded. He even smiled when Carrie described her latest art project.

The familiar rhythm of family dinner worked its magic. By the time Rosa served coffee, Jackson had loosened his tie and leaned back in his chair - a ghost of his old comfort in this house.

◆ ◆ ◆

Maddie savored the rich flavor of her Bordeaux, the deep ruby liquid casting shadows like bloodstains across the pristine tablecloth. She watched Jackson cut into his roast, his shoulders relaxing with each familiar movement. This mundane domesticity—the clink of silver on china, the flicker of candlelight—should have felt comforting after twenty-five years of military dinners. Instead, it only highlighted how far they had drifted.

She swirled the wine, inhaling the oaky aroma. "I saw something interesting on a Cold Case show the other night." Her tone remained light, conversational, as if discussing the weather. As if she wasn't about to shatter the illusion they still clung to.

Jackson made a noncommittal grunt, focus locked on the plate before him. Of course. These days, she struggled to hold his attention at all.

"This woman in Connecticut—a banker's wife." Maddie kept her voice melodic, almost dreamy as she described the riveting tale of poisoning, she'd uncovered.

"She used a fascinating, untraceable method. The most remarkable part was how quickly it worked. Thirty minutes, tops."

His fork stilled halfway to his mouth, the tines gleaming like miniature daggers in the low light. "Maddie."

She offered her most serene smile; the practiced expression she'd spent decades getting just right for military events. The officer's wife, poised and supportive. A master at hiding her true emotions. "Oh, don't worry. There's no poison in this."

Relief softened the harsh lines around his mouth, if only for a fleeting moment. But the shadows soon returned, suspicion darkening his gaze.

Maddie held his stare, her own expression a seamless mask of tranquility. "I used it on your Princess."

The words hung between them, heavy as the lead crystal tumbler in her hand. She could have dropped it, let it shatter into a million glittering shards, but there was something satisfying in its weight. Its solidity.

Jackson went rigid, the way he used to on the battlefield when taking enemy fire. "What did you just say?"

She took another small sip, savoring the exquisite tension crackling across the table like a live wire. "I killed Lillian. I put some in her coffee before she left." A delicate shrug rippled her silk sleeve. As if discussing something as trivial as changing a centerpiece.

(I imagine it was extremely painful unless she crashed and died on impact. Either way.) The thought twisted something dark inside Maddie, a sickly thrill like the first drop of a roller coaster's plunge.

His chair scraped against the floor in a harsh

screech as he pushed back. Jackson's breathing turned tight and shallow, the way it used to when he struggled to control his anger. "Where are the children?"

The question registered. The children were an afterthought now, a minor consequence in the wake of her actions.

"Oh, Jackson." Her lips curved in a cold smile as she nodded toward his plate. "You're eating them. The kitchen is quite a mess, but I will not be here to clean it."

She watched the realization sweep over him, like a soldier comprehending the minefield he'd stumbled into. His complexion turned ashen, sucking all color from those chiseled features she used to admire.

"You better be lying, Maddie." The words emerged strangled, grated between clenched teeth as he shoved away from the table.

She didn't need to respond. The retching sounds from the kitchen spoke volumes, punctuated by a resounding crash that made her flinch. For all his military composure, he was unraveling at an alarming pace.

An anguished scream pierced the air, the raw animalistic wail of a man crumbling. The thud of his knees hitting tile made her smile, picturing him there on the floor. Twenty-five years of discipline and training, undone in seconds by the unveiling of her grand illusion.

His broken sobs echoed from the kitchen; the rhythmic sounds almost melodic. Like the soft, pitiful whimpers of a dog left out in the rain. She dabbed at the corners of her lips with the pale linen napkin, pleased he'd found her little display. The raw meat, artfully arranged on the platter. His anguish provided the soundtrack to her long-awaited victory. "You are a monster!"

"You gave me a choice to wither away a plucked flower without water or roar to life as a monster, and you always said I set the best table," she called out, her voice carrying the same honeyed warmth she'd used at countless military functions. The same sugary tones that had enchanted dignitaries and commanders alike, that made her such a charming and gracious hostess.

She placed the napkin beside her plate with surgical precision, every movement unhurried and deliberate. Rising from her chair, she her reflection in the silver serving tray. makeup, not a hair out of place. The image of the poised military wife until the bitter end.

"Come," she said to Rosa, the silent housekeeper in the corner. The woman fell into step behind her without a word, their footsteps in sync after two decades of service.

Maddie's Louboutins clicked against the marble in a cadence of finality as she walked away from the wreckage. Each step marked the death of Maddie Callahan, the devoted wife and mother. Jackson's guttural sobs trailed behind her, a sorrowful farewell symphony to the life she had constructed and just as dismantled.

She did not look back. There was nothing left for Maddie in that hollow charade. Only ashes of the dreams she'd burned to keep herself warm over the years. The future stretched ahead, hers for the taking, and she turned to face it head on.

Chapter 36

Through the surveillance feed, Maddie watched Jackson remain frozen at the dining room table. His hands gripped the edge, knuckles white against the mahogany—the tableau of a broken man, as she'd planned. (Oh yes, she'd planned this moment, down to the last excruciating detail.)

The camera's infrared highlighted every nuance in the dimly lit room. His chest moved with each shallow breath. The half-eaten roast sat abandoned on his plate, a testament to the precise moment everything changed. She could pinpoint it—the second the veil fell and the truth shattered his constructed world.

Maddie adjusted the volume, savoring the absolute silence that now engulfed him. Only the faint mechanical hum of the refrigerator disturbed the stillness. She'd chosen this moment —when the quiet would be most devastating, a void where his entire life used to reside.

Jackson's shoulders began to shake almost imperceptibly. His fingers released their death grip on the table's edge, leaving indented marks in the wood she'd polished that morning. (Funny how such a small detail could bring her satisfaction.) The military posture crumbled as his body registered what his mind refused to accept.

She leaned closer to the screen, watching color drain from his face. Twenty-five years of discipline dissolved in seconds as he lurched from his chair, legs unsteady. They gave out halfway to the sink. The violent retching echoed through the empty house, music to her ears after so many years of his condescending silence.

The camera every glorious detail—the way his hands trembled against the cold stainless steel, how his pressed shirt wrinkled as his body convulsed. Tears streaked down his face, destroying the composed mask he'd worn for decades in her presence.

Maddie smiled, taking a slow sip of her favorite Châteauneuf-du-Pape as she watched her husband fall apart. The state-of-the-art surveillance system had been worth every penny of the fortune she'd inherited from her father. Now she could witness Jackson's complete and utter destruction from the comfort of her study, savoring his pain like a fine vintage. This was her revenge, and she would not be denied the pleasure of watching him break.

◆ ◆ ◆

Here is the text rewritten from Maddie's perspective, over 2000 words:

Maddie settled deeper into the plush armchair, savoring the warmth of her steeped tea. The dim glow of the laptop screen flickered across her face as she watched the feeds from her placed cameras. Jackson was still there, crumpled against the wall in the dining room. His shoulders heaved with silent, gut-wrenching sobs. Good, let him suffer.

A flash of red and blue lights on another feed her eye. Barbara, clad in that hideous silk robe, gesturing wildly on her front lawn to two police officers. Maddie switched the audio feed, catching her shrill, grating voice. "The screaming... it was horrible. And then that crash..." She rolled her eyes. Ever the drama queen, that Barbara.

The officers approached Maddie's front door, hands hovering near their weapons like they were about to engage an armed suspect. She watched them through the foyer camera, smirking as they entered through the unlocked door, she'd so thoughtfully left ajar. Their flashlight beams cut through the inky darkness, no doubt searching for the source of the "horrible screaming."

They found Jackson first, a pathetic heap against the dining room wall. His face was ashen, streaked with tears like a blubbering child. One officer crouched beside him while his partner swept the room with the beam of his light. She leaned closer to the laptop, drinking in every anguished detail of Jackson's broken form.

"Sir? Are you alright? Can you tell us what

happened?" The officer's voice was gentle, probing. Jackson's eyes remained transfixed on the dining table, on the half-eaten meal that had destroyed his miserable world. His lips moved, but no words came. Maddie felt a rush of dark satisfaction at rendering him utterly mute.

The second officer pushed through the kitchen door, spotting her little masterpiece. "Oh Jesus Christ!" He stumbled backward, nearly dropping his flashlight. A tiny smirk played across Maddie's lips. Clearly, she'd outdone herself this time.

"Dispatch, we need additional units at 1542 Riverside Drive. Possible..." The man's voice cracked, his professionalism faltering. "Possible homicide."

Maddie took a long sip of tea, admiring how the kitchen's track lighting highlighted the artistic details of her display. The deep crimson of the raw meat, glistening under the soft yellow bulbs. The butcher's tools arranged with surgical precision, each one complimenting the piece. And of course, the pièce de résistance - the cutting board, angled to cast dramatic shadows across its blood-stained surface. She'd planned it all to perfection.

"Mr. Callahan." The first officer's voice held an urgent edge now. "Where are your children?"

Jackson's face crumpled like a piece of paper in the rain. His whisper was so faint, the camera's audio picked it up: "Gone."

Maddie felt a surge of vicious pride, savoring the utter demolition of the man who had so carelessly demolished her life. This was her masterpiece, her rebirth from the ashes of two decades wasted on that ungrateful bastard. And it was just the beginning.

As the officers' voices grew more frantic, calling for backup and scouring the rest of the house, Maddie closed the laptop with a satisfied click. She rose from the armchair, back straight and chin high like a victorious general surveying the spoils of war. This show was just getting started.

Abandoning her now-cold tea on the side table, Maddie strode to the bedroom and flung open her closet doors. Time to pick tonight's attire - something dramatic for her debut performance. She trailed a manicured crimson nail along the neat rows of designer dresses, settling on a sleek black number with an asymmetrical neckline. Bold and powerful, yet undeniably elegant. Just like her.

As she slipped it over her head, she a glimpse of herself in the mirror. Her chestnut hair was still immaculate, not a single strand out of place despite the evening's excitement. Those expensive keratin treatments were worth every penny. She touched up her signature red lipstick, making sure the color was rich and unsmudged.

Downstairs, the sirens were growing louder now. More police cruisers, an ambulance probably. All for her. She smiled, dark and secretive, like she knew a delicious truth that no one else could possibly comprehend.

Maddie Callahan was just getting started. And this was going to be one hell of a show.

◆ ◆ ◆

Maddie adjusted the brightness, the laptop's glow casting eerie shadows across her face. She studied the high-definition security feeds from Jackson's house— only the best would do, money be damned. And oh, what a show it was.

Through the master bedroom camera, two officers rifled through closets, their flashlight beams cutting the darkness like knives. The kitchen revealed three more examining her handiwork, that staged tableau. But her gaze lingered on the dining room feed, fixed on Jackson crumpled against the wall. Like a broken marionette, strings cut.

She took a sip of tea, the steam briefly fogging her view. Just a fleeting interference, much like the intricate web she'd spun through Jackson's home. Every room, every hall, every shadowed corner where his new life's secrets might cower—she saw it all through her digital eyes. Her mouth curved in a private smile. Who needed X-ray vision when high-tech cameras unveiled the unseemly truth?

More officers arrived in that military precision she'd once found so thrilling. Their radios crackled with codes she didn't bother deciphering—let the pawns have their codes. She was the silent queen surveying her domain. They moved like ants, documenting, photographing, searching for...what? For a reason why their great General Jackson now sat unmoving, his face a haunting mask of desolation.

The front yard camera captured Barbara in full silk regalia, gesticulating wildly at a detective. Even with no audio, Maddie could lip-read the hysteria: "Screaming...never heard anything like it..."

Her face remained smooth as the chaos unfolded, not a wrinkle betraying her inner delight. Why shouldn't she savor this? She'd orchestrated it all—every planted clue, every faked message, every trailing digital breadcrumb. While they scurried, she presided, the unseen puppet master.

The feed flickered again, that momentary lapse in the stream of images. Most would find it irritating, but not Maddie. No, it was a subtle reminder that even now, even after everything, she held the keys to Jackson's kingdom. His every breath, his every anguished moment—it all streamed into her greedy eyes. All his.

◆ ◆ ◆

Maddie sipped her chamomile tea, savoring the warmth spreading through her chest as she watched the scene unfold through her laptop. (Of course, she had installed hidden cameras in the dining room—she needed to see this.) The two detectives entered the frame, their badges catching the light as they approached Jackson.

Pathetic. Jackson's shoulders hunched forward; his military posture abandoned. She had always hated that rigidness, the way he carried himself like he was still commanding troops instead of living in their home. His hands shook as he gripped the edge of the table, knuckles white against the mahogany. He was unraveling already, and they had only just begun.

"Mr. Callahan, we need you to tell us what happened here tonight." The older detective's voice came through clear on her high-end surveillance system. Of course, she needed top-quality equipment—Maddie was nothing if not prepared. She adjusted the volume, not wanting to miss a word.

Jackson's mouth worked without sound, like a fish gulping for air. (Honestly, she had expected more of a fight from him. This was almost too easy.) When he managed words, his voice cracked in the most undignified way. "She... Maddie... the children..."

Maddie took another sip of tea, savoring the temperature. She had spent hours researching the ideal steep time and water temperature for the chamomile brew. Every detail mattered.

On screen, Jackson continued to struggle, each word seemingly dragged from his core. "She told me... what she did to them. Made me..." He gestured weakly at his plate, his face going gray.

A thrill coursed through Maddie's veins. She had planned this moment for months, agonized over every careful step. And now, watching the great General Jackson Callahan unravel like a spool of thread... it was more satisfying than she could have imagined.

"Mr. Callahan, do you need medical assistance?" The older detective gentled his tone, recognizing the depths of Jackson's trauma. Maddie felt a flicker of annoyance—she wanted Jackson fully present for this, not drifting off into whatever nightmarish visions she had planted.

But Jackson didn't respond, his eyes fixed on the remnants of their final dinner together. The dishes she had so selected, the candles she had lit with her own hands, all of it a masterful manipulation leading to this moment of utter destruction.

"Jesus Christ," the younger detective muttered, turning away from Jackson's shattered form.

Maddie watched it all through her digital window, a small smile playing at the corners of her mouth. She had won, just as she had known she would from the start. Twenty-five years of letting Jackson believe he held the power, only for her to strip it all away with an arranged dinner party.

She took one last sip of her chamomile tea, the liquid now cooled to room temperature. Time to prepare for the next act. After all, this was only the beginning.

◆ ◆ ◆

Maddie noticed a small notification pop up in the corner of her laptop screen. (Of course, she noticed—she'd been watching that screen like a hawk, waiting for the moment her little surprise would arrive.) Her scheduled message had sent right on time, as planned. Through the surveillance feed, she watched Jackson's phone light up on the dining room table, just one more taunt in her elaborate game of torment.

His hands trembled as he reached for it, nearly knocking over his water glass. (Clumsy oaf. She'd always hated how he couldn't control those meaty paws of his.) The detectives paused their questioning, watching as Jackson's face drained of what little color remained. Maddie leaned closer, drinking in his distress like the finest wine. This was what she lived for now—his misery, his helplessness.

"Mr. Callahan?" The older detective leaned forward; brow furrowed.

Jackson's throat worked as he stared at the screen. Maddie could picture the three simple words appearing on his phone, taunting him: "When's the wedding?" She savored the image, allowing herself a thin smile. Let him squirm, let him wonder just how much she knew about his pathetic little dalliance with that blonde bimbo. Let him feel the sting of her knowledge, her power over him.

The younger detective tried to peek at the message, but Jackson's grip tightened on the phone until his knuckles went white. His breath came in short gasps. (Honestly, was he having some kind of fit? She almost felt embarrassed for him.) Maddie watched, rapt, as the man who had once commanded armies and nations came undone by three simple words.

The screen of Maddie's laptop suddenly went

black. She tapped a key, then another. Nothing. The connection was lost, cutting her off from her orchestrated view of Jackson's suffering. A flicker of annoyance rippled through her, but she refused to let it show. She set down her teacup with precise control, the china making only the softest sound against the saucer. No sense getting riled up over a mere technical glitch. She'd have the video retrieved, every agonizing second of Jackson's torment preserved for her personal enjoyment.

Besides, this was just the opening salvo. She had so many more delicious surprises in store for her dear, darling husband.

Chapter 37

Maddie lifted the delicate china cup to her lips, savoring the fragrant Earl Grey while her eyes remained fixed on the bank of screens before her. The feeds showed different angles of Jackson's study - her personal theater of his destruction. (And oh, what a delicious show it was. All the world's a stage, and she, the master director.)

He sat motionless in his leather chair, suit wrinkled, five days of stubble darkening his usually clean-shaven jaw. Security monitors cast an eerie blue glow across his haggard features. The rest of the house lay in darkness, the drawn curtains blocking out the afternoon sun. (Like a man already entombed, Maddie mused. How fitting.)

His phone lit up again - Barbara's name flashing on the screen. Like the previous twelve calls that day, Jackson didn't even glance at it. The buzzing eventually stopped, adding another missed connection to his growing isolation. She could hear Barbara's shrill voice leaving yet another frantic voicemail. Maddie rolled her eyes. That woman was nothing if not predictable.

Maddie noted the empty water glass on his desk, the untouched sandwich Rosa had left yesterday. He hadn't showered since the dinner - she could tell by how his usually immaculate hair hung limp and greasy across his forehead. The great General Jackson Callahan, reduced to this hollow shell. A bitter chuckle escaped her lips. Who would have thought her mighty soldier could be so easily disarmed?

She tilted her head, studying his deterioration with clinical detachment. The timestamp in the corner of the main feed her attention - 4:47 PM. She checked it against her notes. He hadn't shifted position since 3:32 PM. Not even a finger twitch.

The military man who'd commanded thousands, who'd orchestrated operations across continents, now couldn't even command his own body to move. The corners of Maddie's mouth curved up ever so as she took another sip of tea. Checkmate, my dear. She leaned back, savoring the delicious thrill of total victory. Jackson's defenses had been breached - and by none other than the woman he'd so underestimated all these years.

❖ ❖ ❖

Through the flickering surveillance feeds, Maddie watched the scene unfold with a detached curiosity. Two detectives—that weaselly little Morris and his fresh-faced sidekick—approached Jackson's front door. Morris rang the bell three times, each chime reverberating through the cavernous foyer like an insistent demand. How many times had she stood in that spot, straightening her pearls, preparing to greet their guests with a polished smile?

At last, Jackson shuffled into view, a hollow shadow of the man he once was. The proud military bearing that had always made her spine straighten was gone, replaced by slumped shoulders and dull, unfocused eyes. He looked...diminished. Pathetic, even. Part of her recoiled at the sight, another part savored it.

"General Callahan, we need to ask you a few more questions." Morris's nasal voice crackled through the audio feed as Jackson ushered them inside with a vague wave of his hand.

He sank into the worn leather chair of his study like a resignation, while the younger detective—Rodriguez, she recalled—pulled out a notepad, poised to transcribe every stumbling word. Morris leaned against the desk with studied nonchalance, but Maddie recognized the tightly coiled energy beneath the facade. The thrill of the case, the obsessive needs to solve life's little puzzles. She'd seen that hunger in Jackson once, back when his ambition still burned hot.

"Have you had any contact with your wife?" Morris's question sliced through the stale air, as incisive as a scalpel.

Jackson's reply was little more than a croak. "No."

Maddie took a slow sip of her Earl Grey, the

familiar bergamot aroma grounding her amid the chaos. The high-definition cameras captured every sordid detail of Jackson's deterioration in unflinching clarity— the loosened tie, the coffee stains on his once-crisp shirt, the faint tremor in his calloused hands. She drank it in, a silent witness to his unraveling.

The two detectives exchanged a glance heavy with meaning, their concern as palpable as a living thing. She'd seen that look before, mirrored on the faces of her so-called friends—Barbara's thin veiled pity, Charlotte's tight-lipped disapproval. As if any of them could possibly understand the forces at play here. The sacrifices. The betrayals.

"General, maybe you should get some fresh air," Rodriguez ventured, his voice achingly young and naive. "Take a walk, clear your head."

Jackson stared through him, his gaze fixed on some distant vanishing point that only he could perceive, lost in the labyrinth of his own despair. Maddie watched the realization dawn on the two detectives, their body language shifting in incremental tells—Morris's subtle head shake, Rodriguez's crestfallen slump as he closed his notepad in resignation.

"Sir, we're worried about—" Morris began, but Jackson cut him off with a ragged exhalation.

"I haven't seen her. I haven't heard from her. I don't know where she is."

The lie fell from his lips with such hollowed conviction that Maddie almost believed it herself. Almost. She adjusted one of the camera angles with a deft flick of her finger, ensuring she wouldn't miss a single nuance as the two men accepted defeat and turned to leave. The front door clicked shut with solemn finality, sealing Jackson inside his self-constructed purgatory once more.

Maddie didn't so much as blink, her gaze locked on the solitary figure slumped in the shadowed study. Let him marinate in his misery, she thought with a thin smile. Let him drown in the depths of his own weakness and regret. She had all the time in the world to watch him come undone, thread by agonizing thread.

◆ ◆ ◆

Through her array of screens, Maddie watched Jackson slump back into his study after the detectives left. His laptop cast a blue glow across his haggard face as he stared blankly at the screen, not even bothering to check his emails anymore. (Of course he wouldn't. Pathetic.). She pulled up her control panel and entered the remote access codes she'd installed months ago. With three precise keystrokes, she activated the hidden file she'd been saving for this moment.

Jackson's screen flickered. His body tensed as the video began to play—footage from Carrie's fifth birthday party. Their little girl twirled in her pink princess dress while Jackson lifted her high, both of them laughing. The timestamp showed it was from three years ago, back when they were still a family. Maddie's throat tightened at the sight of her daughter, so carefree and adored. So unaware of what was to come.

The video cut to another clip—the charity gala where she and Jackson had danced together. She remembered the weight of his hands on her waist as they moved across the floor. How his eyes had crinkled at the corners when he spoke in her ear, telling her she was beautiful. A lump formed in her throat as she watched her younger self gaze at him with such unguarded devotion.

Through the camera feed, she saw Jackson's hands begin to shake. His shoulders hunched forward as more memories played across the screen—family vacations to Italy, Christmas mornings where the children's shrieks of joy had echoed through the house, tender moments he'd clearly forgotten. She could have chosen any number of videos, of course, but she'd curated these—a reminder of what he'd turned his back on.

His breath came in sharp gasps now. The mighty General Callahan, reduced to this—a broken man watching ghosts of his past life. His body seemed to fold in on itself as quiet sobs wracked his frame. She could almost taste the salt of his tears.

Maddie leaned back in her chair, taking a slow sip of tea as she watched him shatter. Twenty-five years of marriage, and this was what it took to make him feel something real. This raw, visceral pain—this was her gift to him. He thought he could walk away, start fresh with that little girl on his arm? She'd remind him, again and again, that he didn't get to escape so easily.

As the last video faded to black, she allowed herself a small, satisfied smile. Let him wallow in his guilt and regret. He had earned every aching second.

◆ ◆ ◆

Maddie couldn't tear her eyes away from the screens. Jackson's unraveling played out in excruciating detail, each frame a delicious torture. The proud military man she had married was nowhere to be seen—his shoulders caved inward; his spine bent like a wounded animal trying to make itself small.

He shuffled through the house in the same wrinkled clothes day after day, not bothering with the basic dignity of showering or changing. Why should he? The mighty General Jackson Callahan had fallen from grace. (She savored the thought, letting it linger like fine wine on her tongue.)

The kitchen remained untouched; plates of food brought by that vapid Barbara left to molder on the counter. Jackson passed them without a glance, his feet carrying him between his study and the children's rooms—his ghosts haunting him, she imagined with vicious delight. Let him be tortured by the memories of what he'd lost.

Her cameras captured every agonizing detail. The way his hands trembled when he touched Carrie's stuffed rabbit, no doubt wondering if he'd ever feel that little hand in his again. How he lingered in Nate's doorway for hours, shoulders slumped, staring at the abandoned reminders of the son who might never call him "Dad" again. That brilliant military mind that had commanded armies now seemed locked in an endless, impotent spiral of grief.

His phone buzzed constantly—calls from the base, from Barbara, from that smug lawyer Nate. Jackson let them ring, didn't he? Easier to ignore the world than face the consequences of his actions. Dark circles carved deeper into his face with each sleepless night. The hair he'd always kept trimmed grew wild, his clean-shaven jaw disappeared under patches of gray.

The house crumbled around him, mirroring the collapse within. Papers scattered, dishes piled in sinks, curtains drawn against the light and the life he'd ruined. The pristine order he'd once demanded had shattered along with his icy composure. Through the monitors, Maddie watched him sink into his chair, a hollow husk of the man who had so coldly discarded her after twenty-five years.

Those piercing blue eyes that had once commanded armies with a glance now stared into the void, empty of anything but despair. She touched the screen, letting her fingers caress the lines of anguish etched on his face.

"Goodnight, my love," she whispered, tasting the bitterness on her tongue. With a smile, she pressed the button that went to black. Sleep well, Jackson. Just dreams for now.

Chapter 38

Maddie settled deeper into Jackson's leather study chair, savoring another sip of his prized Bordeaux. The rich, velvety liquid coated her tongue, and she couldn't help but smirk. This was his favorite vintage—the one he'd been saving for a special occasion. Well, she supposed this qualified.

The wall of surveillance feeds cast a blue glow across her face as she tracked his movements through the house. Or lack of movement. Jackson hadn't left his study in eighteen hours. The same coffee cup sat untouched on his desk, a thin film coating the surface. His military precision had vanished—papers scattered across the floor, blinds half-tilted, clothes wrinkled beyond recognition.

She adjusted one of the camera angles for a better view, leaning in with a self-satisfied smile. The house remained dark except for his desk lamp, which cast strange shadows as it flickered. The bulb would die soon. (But of course it would. Jackson didn't seem to notice those kinds of things anymore.) She took another lingering sip, letting the wine's richness linger on her tongue as she watched him stare blankly at his computer screen. No more pressed uniforms. No more rigid posture. Just a broken man who couldn't even maintain basic hygiene.

Movement on another feed her attention, and she narrowed her eyes. A police cruiser pulled up outside, and two familiar figures stepped out—Detectives Morris and Rodriguez returning for another round of questions. Maddie tilted her head, amused at their persistence. They thought they were making progress, closing in on some truth that would untangle this mess. "They think they're getting somewhere." She took another slow sip of wine, enjoying the rich flavor as she watched them approach the front door. Their determined stride, their careful observations of the property—all useless theater.

The doorbell rang through her feeds, echoing hollowly. Jackson didn't move to answer it. The detectives exchanged glances, sharing some unspoken thought, then rang again. Still nothing. She zoomed in on Jackson's face, studying the vacant stare, the slackened jaw, the complete lack of reaction as the sound echoed through the empty house. His eyes remained fixed straight ahead, lost in whatever private hell she'd created for him.

A cruel smile tugged at the corners of her mouth. The military man, reduced to this. She swirled the wine in her glass, watching the deep crimson liquid spin. They had no idea what kind of game they were playing. But she did. Oh, she did. And she was determined to win.

◆ ◆ ◆

Through her array of screens, Maddie watched Detective Morris pull something from his jacket—a small flash drive that the dim light. Her manicured finger traced the rim of her wineglass as Rodriguez bent over Jackson's laptop, inserting the device with the sort of practiced efficiency that comes from years of dull routine. (She'd always found the man utterly drab, but tonight, his lack of imagination would serve her well.)

Jackson remained motionless at his desk, registering their presence. His thousand-yard stare hadn't shifted in hours—the look of a man who had stared down the barrel of a gun too many times to be fazed by two rumpled detectives rifling through his things. The soldier, now unable to even acknowledge direct questions. How tragically ironic.

The feed from Camera Three gave her the clearest view of the laptop screen. Morris leaned in close, his face illuminated by the blue glow as windows began popping open. Lines of encrypted data scrolled past, followed by timestamps and access logs from security cameras. She watched it all unfold with the detached curiosity of a scientist observing microbes through a microscope. Insignificant creatures, operating under the illusion of control.

"Got you," Morris muttered, jabbing his finger at something on the screen. The words hung in the air like a challenge.

Rodriguez crowded closer, his thinning hair nearly brushing Morris's cheek as they studied whatever they thought they'd found. Their body language had shifted—shoulders tense, movements sharp with purpose. Like boy scouts who'd spotted footprints on the trail.

Maddie took another leisurely sip of the Bordeaux, letting the complex notes linger on her tongue. The vintage had been Jackson's favorite, saved for special occasions when he would wax poetic about the hints of blackberry and oak. How fitting that she should enjoy it now while watching his world crumble from the plush comfort of her study's chaise lounge.

"Do you?" she said to the empty room, her lips curving into a smile against the crystal rim of her glass. The detectives' excitement was almost endearing—like children who thought they'd solved a puzzle while only seeing the pieces she'd arranged for them to find.

She zoomed in tighter on the laptop screen, watching data streams flash across their eager faces. Each file they opened was another breadcrumb she'd left, leading them down the path she'd designed. Pawns marching obliviously across her chessboard, maneuvered by an unseen hand into the positions she required.

Maddie swirled the deep red liquid, studying the legs that traced the insides of the glass. So much time and effort had led to this moment. She took another indulgent sip, the rich flavors coating her tongue. They had no idea what was coming. But she did. Oh, she did. And it was going to be delicious.

◆ ◆ ◆

Maddie adjusted Camera Four with a few deft taps, zooming the lens until Jackson's haggard face filled the screen. His sanctuary, that precious study of his, had been utterly violated—overrun by police and their clutter of equipment strewn across the pristine mahogany desk. (She had picked that desk herself at an estate sale years ago. Paid a fortune to have it shipped from Massachusetts. But of course, Jackson never appreciated the finer details.)

Detective Morris stood near the window; phone pressed to his ear as he traded hushed words with someone on the other end. Rodriguez, the rookie cop with the distracting birthmark above his lip, typed furiously on a laptop. Maddie watched Jackson's shoulders tense at the sharp intake of Morris's breath. The sound of the call disconnecting hung in the air like the first trill of an executioner's song.

"We have a location," Morris said.

Those four words, that's all it took. Through the grainy feed, Maddie studied the minuscule reactions flickering across Jackson's expression. The way his head snapped up with that same military precision he'd cultivated over decades. Those eyes, reddened and wild like a cornered animal, fixed on Morris with an intensity she hadn't seen since...when? Dubai, maybe. Back when things had been so different.

The posture was gone now, replaced by a desperate, undignified slouch as Jackson leaned forward in his chair. That ache of hope radiated off him in waves, like a scent Maddie could almost taste through the pixels.

His voice cracked as he said, "Where?"

Rodriguez muttered something into his radio, the words too muffled for the camera's tinny microphone to discern. But Maddie's lips curved in a cool smile as she read the movement of his lips. "We're closing in."

She took another unhurried sip of her merlot, letting the rich flavors linger on her tongue as she studied the scene unfolding through her laptop screen. Jackson's hands were gripping those armrests now, knuckles straining so tightly they had gone pale as bone. The once proud military man, the vaunted General she had admired for so long, now reduced to this...this pitiful, quivering excuse for a human being. Hanging on every word from local law enforcement as if they were delivering orders from central command.

Delicious, she thought, tracing one precise fingernail along the cool edge of her laptop. Remembering how easy it had all been, —the lies, the digital trail, all of it. Twenty-five years of marriage had taught her every detail about this man, from his passwords and security questions down to the most mundane habits and pathetic weaknesses. She had been his partner, his confidante, his wife in every sense of the word. Of course, she knew how to burn his world down around him.

Each piece of evidence she'd laid, like brushstrokes on a canvas, was another nail reinforcing the coffin around his new life. The life he thought he could have without her blessing. Maybe Lily would appreciate the artistry of it all. Maddie smirked at the thought, taking another slow sip as she watched the feed flicker. Morris was moving now, spreading out a map on Jackson's precious desk. She zoomed the lens, drinking in every anguished line of her husband's face as whatever location they'd discovered registered.

He looked...old, in that moment. Depleted in a way she had never seen, even fresh off his final tour. The realization struck her with a sudden pang of something adjacent to pity. This was the great General Callahan, the man whose name had once inspired awe and terror alike in the hearts of their nation's fiercest enemies. Now just a husk, a hollow shell of himself, crumbling under the weight of her machinations.

Pity was for the weak. Maddie shook her head to dislodge the fleeting thought. This man, this pathetic creature who had so carelessly discarded her—he deserved no mercy. Not after everything. Not after Lily.

She refocused on the screen, studying every nuance as Jackson processed whatever new hell she had wrought. His lips moved, but she couldn't make out his words. No matter. She knew the endgame was near. All his pretty lies and selfish indulgences were catching up to him at last.

A small part of her, which she usually kept well-locked away, wondered if there was still a chance to stop this. To come clean and prevent the total annihilation to come. But the moment passed as quickly as it had sparked. No, she had come too far now. He needed to understand the depths of her commitment, the fierceness of her love. Only pain could reshape him into the man he had once been, the man she still saw glimpses of whenever she permitted herself to hope.

Her free hand drifted to the polished wood of the side table, fingers brushing against the cold steel of his revolver. A relic from better days, one of the few possessions he had brought back from his final deployment. Perhaps she would pay him a visit soon and they could...talk. Sort things out like they used to, back when he understood his place in her world.

Maddie took one last satisfied swallow of wine and set the glass aside. Her work was nearly complete, but she still had a few remaining moves to make. Adjusting the laptop's angle, she zoomed the lens until Jackson's stricken face filled her view.

"Hello, darling," she purred, allowing herself a satisfied smile. "Don't look so surprised. You knew this was coming eventually."

She laughed; the sound tinged with madness even to her own ears. But she didn't care. Not anymore.

"Let the games begin."

Chapter 39

Through her surveillance feed, Maddie observed Jackson at the precinct's metal table. His coffee sat untouched, steam no longer rising from the paper cup. His shoulders had lost their military bearing, slumped forward as he stared at nothing. (How the mighty had fallen. Her once imposing general, now a broken man.) She swirled the rich cabernet in her glass, savoring the scent of berries and oak. Let him wallow in misery a while longer.

Detective Chen burst through the door, face flushed and papers clutched in her hand. Jackson didn't even flinch. Didn't he see the desperation in Chen's eyes, the pathetic attempt to impress him? Maddie snickered to herself. Poor thing had no idea what she was up against.

"We've got something." Chen's voice crackled with energy that filled the sterile room. Maddie leaned closer to the screen, intrigued despite herself. This could be amusing.

The shift was immediate. Other detectives crowded the doorway. Morris straightened from his position against the wall. Even Jackson's dead eyes flickered with the first spark of life she'd seen in days. How predictable, Maddie thought with a roll of her eyes. Dangle a little hope in front of him and he perks right up.

"Our tech team isolated a signal." Chen spread papers across the table. "It's not another redirect or VPN mask. This is physical—a real location transmitting these feeds"

Maddie's fingers tightened around her wine glass as she watched their excitement build. These small-town detectives thought they'd accomplished something remarkable. Fools, the lot of them. She took a slow sip, letting the rich liquid coat her tongue. They had no idea what they were dealing with.

"She's been watching everything from here." Chen jabbed her finger at a map, the camera angle catching the street name. Sloppy, Maddie noted. But then, she'd planned for them to find that particular breadcrumb.

Jackson pushed back from the table, standing for the first time in hours. His coffee tipped, the dark liquid spreading across Chen's arranged papers. No one moved to clean it up. They were all too focused on the supposed lead. Maddie chuckled. It was mad, but it was good—like hunting dogs scenting a false trail.

She took another sip of wine, savoring the familiar burn. Let them chase their breadcrumbs. She'd spent twenty-five years learning how Jackson thought, how he planned. Every digital trace she'd left was deliberate - each IP address and timestamp a calculated step in her design. They thought they were making progress, but in reality, they were where she wanted them.

Leaning back in her chair, Maddie smiled. This game was just getting started. And she was born to play.

◆ ◆ ◆

Through her surveillance feeds, Maddie watched the precinct's interrogation room transform from a place of defeat into one charged with desperate energy. Jackson's shoulders straightened, his military bearing returning as he pushed away from the table. A familiar sight—the general readying for battle. Only this time, his war was with her.

"I'm going with you." His voice carried that commanding tone she remembered from countless military functions, the cadence that used to make her shiver with pride. Now it annoyed her. As if he could order her around.

Detective Morris shook his head, clearly used to being the one in charge. "Mr. Callahan, this is a police operation- "

"I need to see this." The rawness in Jackson's words surprised her. He'd always been so controlled, so disciplined. But now his voice cracked, stripped of pretense. The voice of a man who'd lost everything. "Those are my children."

Maddie took another sip of her cabernet, the rich notes flooding her mouth as she studied him. His hands trembled—something she'd never seen in twenty-five years of marriage. Not when he'd returned from the sandstorms of Iraq, the frozen trenches of Afghanistan. His hands had always remained steady, even when delivering the worst news.

She could still hear that steady, clinical tone as he told her about each soldier lost under his command. As if reciting names from a grocery list, not speaking of lives brutally ended.

Chen and Morris exchanged glances, silently debating whether to indulge Jackson's demand. After a moment, Chen nodded, seemingly convinced by whatever desperation she saw in his eyes.

"He rides with me," she said, her tone making it clear this was not a negotiation. "But you stay in the car until we clear the scene."

Jackson's jaw clenched, that familiar muscle twitching as he followed them out. Maddie tracked their progress through different camera angles—three police cruisers and Chen's unmarked car formed a small convoy, blades slicing through the Friday evening traffic.

Jackson sat rigid in the passenger seat; his fists tight against his thighs as they sped through Atlanta's streets. The man who once commanded battalions was now reduced to a passenger, desperately chasing ghosts she'd created.

Maddie switched feeds to follow their progress, amused at how they thought they were closing in. Each turn they took, each darkened alleyway they pursued, had been orchestrated by her design. Every digital breadcrumb was placed with the same precision Jackson himself had taught her—how to plan, how to execute, how to win.

She swirled the wine, admiring its deep crimson hue. They were all playing her game now, scattering like ants whenever she chose to shake the glass. Let them run their little chase. She held all the power here.

Jackson stared straight ahead in Chen's car, his knuckles white with tension. Did he understand? This was her rules, her battlefield. She was the commander now.

◆ ◆ ◆

Maddie savored the bitter taste of Jackson's scotch as she watched the events unfold through the network of cameras she had planted. Her lips curled into a self-satisfied smirk as the SWAT team assembled outside the warehouse, their black tactical gear blending seamlessly with the shadows, making them appear like living manifestations of the night itself.

She had planned every excruciating detail perfectly, laying an intricate trap Jackson had unthinkingly stumbled into. Twenty-five years of marriage had taught her to read him like an open book, and the way his hands clenched and unclenched – a tell she had noticed during their first year together whenever he received difficult news from the base – only reaffirmed her triumph.

As the SWAT team's whispers carried through her surveillance system, Maddie zoomed in on Jackson's face, scrutinizing every micro-expression that betrayed his crumbling composure. The tightness around his eyes, the pulse visibly throbbing in his throat – this was a man who had once commanded armies, now reduced to a helpless bystander, waiting for others to take the lead.

The breach charge detonated with a controlled boom that made her cameras vibrate, and the echoes of their boots on concrete reverberated through her speakers as they swept inside, weapons raised, their voices bouncing off the metal walls in a cacophony of "Clear!"

Through her network of feeds, she watched them stack up outside, employing the tactics Jackson had once taught his men in Dubai.

The door burst open, and tactical lights swept across the empty space, converging on a simple metal desk where a laptop sat, its screen casting a blue glow across the concrete floor. Maddie's eyes narrowed as Jackson pushed past the officers, desperation etched across his face – a far cry from the commanding general who had so callously dismissed her at their last meeting. His hair was disheveled, his expensive suit wrinkled, and he lunged for the laptop screen with a palpable urgency.

As one of the techs reached for the power cord, Maddie's lip curled in a triumphant sneer, watching him grasp it with bated breath. "Wait—" Jackson's voice cracked, but it was too late. The plug came free, and every feed cut to static simultaneously.

Maddie sat back in her lounge chair on the beach, a wicked grin playing on her lips. "Well, guess I can't watch that shit-show anymore now."

Rosa's inquisitive gaze met hers. "Why?"

"They found my laptop running the remote access terminal," Maddie replied, her voice dripping with smug satisfaction. "Checkmate."

Chapter 40

Maddie's new Chanel quilted sandals crunched on the sand as she headed back to the outdoor café. The over-sized Chanel sunglasses shielded her eyes, but she could feel the ocean breeze caressing her sun-lightened hair. So deliciously different from the stale Atlanta air that used to cling to her skin like a second skin.

She settled into her usual seat, the white linen tablecloth snapping with each gust off the water. Her fingers traced the curve of the fresh coconut agua fresca, savoring the sweet, tropical notes. So far removed from the smoky, masculine scent of Jackson's favored scotch.

Maddie glanced at her new Mexican ID—Maria Elena Ruiz. The name still felt odd rolling off her tongue, like an ill-fitting designer gown. But she'd learned to answer to it with the same poise she'd cultivated during two and a half decades of being Mrs. Jackson Callahan. The photo captured her lighter hair and sun-kissed complexion, the golden tan transforming her into someone almost unrecognizable from the polished, Upper East Side society wife she'd once been. (Though of course she remained impeccably groomed. She wasn't a barbarian.)

The waiter arrived with her morning ritual—the international edition of the Wall Street Journal. She thumbed through the familiar pages, scanning headlines with the same detached scrutiny she'd applied to Jackson's morning briefs. Her lips curved ever so as his name leapt off the business section. Callahan Defense Solutions' stock had plunged another fifteen percent amidst the ongoing chaos.

Maddie spread the paper wider, taking in the accompanying photo of Atlanta's skyline, the dark silhouette of Jackson's headquarters looming against the sunrise. The article mentioned "unexplained disappearances" and "ongoing federal investigations"— such sterile terms for the turmoil she'd orchestrated. She could almost taste the panic in the boardroom, the stench of cold sweat and frantic phone calls.

The ocean breeze carried the briny salt air across her face, and Maddie allowed herself the faintest of smiles. Twenty-five years of being the consummate military wife, of maintaining every polished detail of

Jackson's immaculate image, had taught her how to dismantle it all. She'd learned from the master, after all.

Her gaze drifted over the café's morning crowd, watchful eyes missing nothing behind those over-sized Chanel frames. New habits formed quickly in Mexico—always noting exits, studying reflections in windows, assessing potential threats without appearing to look at all. Old skills, honed by years at Jackson's side, adapted to this new sun-drenched reality.

A man her attention near the bar, not because of any particular physical attribute, but because something in his movements radiated calculation. He ordered what appeared to be a morning cocktail, but his eyes never stopped roaming. They lingered on a young woman in a sundress, tracked a waitress bending to clear a table, darted to a tourist adjusting her bikini top. Constantly assessing, always aware of his surroundings.

His Rolex glinted in the sunlight—genuine, Maddie noted with a practiced eye, unlike the knockoffs flooding Cabo's tourist traps. When his gaze landed on her, she felt the weight of his consideration. His spine straightened, the subtle shift of someone well-versed in commanding a room. One hand moved to adjust the watch, turning it to catch the light in a deliberate, almost subconscious display.

The faintest twitch played at the corner of Maddie's mouth. She recognized the behavior instantly—the male peacocking ritual, as predictable as Jackson's military-precise morning inspections. Of course, the man approached her table. They always did, these avatars of privilege and power, confident in their ability to charm.

"Buenos días, señorita." His Spanish carried the

faintest accent—Eastern European perhaps? Maddie kept her expression neutral, letting her eyes drift back to the newspaper as if unimpressed.

He switched to English with an easy smile. "You don't look like you're from around here."

Without asking, he pulled out the chair across from her, movements smooth and unhurried. "Mind if I join you? The view here is spectacular." His gaze lingered on the deep V of her sundress rather than the ocean beyond.

With practiced grace, Maddie lowered her paper. After decades of reading military men at every formal function, this one's tells were painfully obvious. The manicured nails, the cultivated tan—all spoke of someone who prioritized appearing successful over being so. An artful illusion, much like the one she'd maintained for years.

"The café is quite popular this time of day," she said, her tone pleasant but neutral, just warm enough to keep him engaged.

"You must be staying nearby then?" He flagged a passing waiter, ordering an espresso without glancing at the menu—the breezy confidence of the wealthy. "I'm at the Marina Resort myself. Beautiful property."

Maddie adjusted her sunglasses, noting how his eyes tracked the glint of her Cartier watch. "I prefer smaller establishments. More private."

"Ah, a woman who values discretion." He leaned back, casual arrogance radiating from every pore as he spread his arms across the back of the chair. "I understand. In my line of work, discretion is everything."

She arched one sculpted brow. "And what work would that be?"

"Import and export, primarily. Though I have interests in various ventures." His gaze darted to her Hermès handbag, no doubt calculating its value against his own displays of wealth. "I travel extensively between here and Europe. Always looking for new opportunities."

Maddie took a deliberate sip of her agua fresca, letting the flavors linger on her tongue. "How fascinating." She let the words hang, offering nothing more to entice him.

"And you?" His knee brushed hers beneath the table—a deliberate move, she was certain. "Business or pleasure?"

A sly smile curved her lips, the same one she'd ed for deflecting questions at countless military functions. "A little of both, perhaps."

His fingers drummed against the espresso cup, impatience beginning to show. "Traveling alone?"

He leaned closer, his cologne—expensive but applied with a heavy hand—drifting across the table. "So. .. maybe you'll let me show you around sometime?"

Maddie studied him over the rim of her Chanel frames, taking in the easy confidence that mirrored Jackson's during that first officer's ball so many years ago. The same entitled expectations, the same arrogant certainty that his attention was a gift to be coveted. His Rolex the sun again, the repositioning as deliberate as Jackson adjusting his medals before an inspection.

With the slightest tilt of her sunglasses, she let her gaze meet his directly. The move was calculated, ed through decades of high-society manipulation. Just enough illusion of intimacy to hook him, just enough distance to keep him leaning in for more. She'd learned that game long ago—men like him craved what they couldn't quite grasp.

A knowing smile played across her lips. "Maybe." The word carried a hint of warmth, a fleeting promise to draw him closer even as she maintained control. She'd mastered this dance at countless military functions and formal events, understanding how to make powerful men chase shadows.

Lifting her glass, she offered a toast to nothing in particular. The morning sun the crystal, scattering diamond refractions across the white linen. An elegant, controlled gesture—everything she'd learned to embody as Mrs. Jackson Callahan.

The man settled back in his chair, adjusting his Rolex one more time as that artificial smile stretched wider. He thought he'd captured her interest. They always did, these artificial men with their expensive baubles and empty promises.

Maddie's gaze drifted past him to the rhythmic ebb and flow of the ocean waves. They rolled in with the same steady precision as Jackson's morning routine, the military discipline that had governed their lives for over two decades. Nature's own witness protection program, she mused, each successive wave erasing all traces of the one before.

From the corner of her eye, she the slightest movement—Rosa, seated at a nearby table. Her former housekeeper's spine was ramrod straight; shoulders thrown back in the kind of resort wear that would have been unthinkable in her former life of service. A subtle shake of the head, weighted with twenty years of silent judgment. Rosa remained the only one who truly saw through Maddie's practiced performances.

Tracing the rim of her glass, Maddie let the

silence stretch until her companion began to fidget, his bravado slipping with each passing moment. She saw it in the minute adjustment of his shoulders, the restless tapping of his fingers against the tabletop. The same cracks Jackson used to show when his constructed world began crumbling around him.

"Tell me…" Her voice carried the same measured tone she'd used at a thousand high society events, neither warm nor cold, but utterly in control. "Do you believe in second chances?"

Heaven has no rage like love to hatred turned, nor Hell a fury like a woman scorned. -
William Congreve from the play "The Mourning Bride"

www.ingramcontent.com/pod-product-compliance
Lightning Source LLC
Chambersburg PA
CBHW020543120726
47903CB00001B/98